"I don't ₁₎ ₐ₎y do this," he said.

He didn't usually kidnap women or unbutton their wedding gowns?

Crista knew she should ask. No, she shouldn't ask. She should move now, back away, lock herself in the bathroom until her emotions were under control.

But he slowly lifted his hand. His fingertips grazed her shoulder. Then his palm cradled her neck, slipping up to her hairline. The touch was smooth and warm, his obvious strength couched by tenderness.

She couldn't bring herself to pull away. In fact, it was a fight to keep from leaning into his caress.

Jackson dipped his head.

She knew what came next. Anybody would know what came next.

His lips touched hers, kissing her gently, testing her texture and then her taste. Arousal instantly flooded her body. He stepped forward, his free arm going around her waist, settling at the small of her back, strong and hot against her exposed skin.

She didn't move away.

* * *

His Stolen Bride ᵤᵥ.uk/librarys
Chica

HIS STOLEN BRIDE

BY
BARBARA DUNLOP

First Published in Great Britain 2016
By Mills & Boon, an imprint of HarperCollins*Publishers*
1 London Bridge Street, London, SE1 9GF

© 2016 Barbara Dunlop

ISBN: 978-0-263-91869-4

51-0716

Barbara Dunlop writes romantic stories while curled up in a log cabin in Canada's far north, where bears outnumber people and it snows six months of the year. Fortunately she has a brawny husband and two teenage children to haul firewood and clear the driveway while she sips cocoa and muses about her upcoming chapters. Barbara loves to hear from readers. You can contact her through her website, www.barbaradunlop.com.

To Mom with love

One

A heavy metal door clanged shut behind Jackson Rush, echoing down the hallway of the Riverway State Correctional Institute in northeast Illinois. He paused to mentally brace himself as he took in the unfamiliar surroundings. Then he walked forward, his boot heels clacking against the worn linoleum. He couldn't help thinking the prison would make a perfect movie set, with its cell bars, scarred gray cinder blocks, flickering fluorescent lights and the scattered shouts from connecting rooms and hallways.

His father, Colin Rush, had been locked up here for nearly seventeen years, ever since he was caught stealing thirty-five million dollars from the unsuspecting investors in his personal Ponzi scheme.

His dramatic arrest had taken place on Jackson's thirteenth birthday. The police rushed the backyard pool party, sending guests shrieking and scattering. Jackson could still see the two-tiered blue-and-white layer cake sliding from the table, splattering on the grass, obliterating his name as it oozed into a pile of goo.

At first, his father had stridently proclaimed his innocence. Jackson's mother had taken Jackson to the courtroom every day of the trial, where they'd sat stoically and supportively behind the defense. But it soon became clear that Colin was guilty. Far from being a brilliant investor, he was a common thief.

When one of his former clients committed suicide, he lost all public sympathy and was sentenced to twenty years in jail. Jackson hadn't seen his father since.

Now he rounded the corner to the visiting area, prepared for stark wooden benches, Plexiglas partitions and hardwired black telephone receivers. Instead, he was surprised to find himself in a bright, open room that looked like a high school cafeteria. A dozen round red tables were positioned throughout, each with four stools connected by thick metal braces directly to the table base. The hall had high rectangular windows and checkerboard tile floors. A few guards milled around while the other visitors seemed to be mostly families.

A man stood up at one of the tables and made eye contact. It took Jackson a moment to recognize his father. Colin had aged considerably, showing deep wrinkles around his eyes and along his pale, hollow cheeks. His posture was stooped, and his hairline had receded. But there was no mistaking it was him, and he smiled.

Jackson didn't smile back. He was here under protest. He didn't know why his father had insisted he come, only that the emails and voice messages had become increasingly frequent and sounded more and more urgent. He'd eventually relented in order to make them stop.

Now he marched toward the table, determined to get the visit over and done with.

"Dad," he greeted flatly, sticking out his hand, preempting what would surely be the most awkward hug in history.

"Hello, son," said Colin, emotion shimmering in his eyes as he shook Jackson's hand.

His grip was firmer than Jackson had expected.

Jackson's attention shifted to a second man seated at the round table, half annoyed by his presence, but half curious as well.

"It's good to see you," said Colin.

Jackson didn't respond, instead raising his brow inquiringly at the stranger.

Colin cleared his throat and released Jackson's hand. "Jackson, this is Trent Corday. Trent and I have been cell mates for the past year."

It seemed more than strange that Colin would bring a

friend to this meeting. But Jackson wasn't about to waste time dwelling on the question.

He looked back to his father. "What is it you want?"

He could only guess there must be a parole hearing coming up. If there was, Colin was on his own. Jackson wouldn't help him get out of prison early. Colin had three years left on his sentence, and as far as Jackson was concerned, he deserved every minute.

His selfish actions had harmed dozens of victims, not the least of which was Jackson's mother. She'd been inconsolable after the trial, drinking too much, abusing prescription painkillers, succumbing to cancer five years later just as Jackson graduated from high school.

Colin gestured to one of the stools. "Please, sit."

Jackson perched himself on the small metal seat.

"Trent has a problem," said Colin, sitting down himself.

What Trent's problem could possibly have to do with Jackson was the first question that came to mind. But he didn't ask—instead, he waited.

Trent filled the silence. "It's my daughter. I've only been inside for three years. A misunderstanding, really, I—"

"Save it," said Jackson.

Seventeen years ago, he'd listened to Colin protest endlessly about how he'd been framed, then railroaded, then misunderstood. Jackson wasn't here to listen to the lies of a stranger.

"Yes, well…" Trent glanced away.

Jackson looked at his watch.

"She's fallen victim," said Trent. He fished into the pocket of his blue cotton shirt. "It's the Gerhard family. I don't know if you've heard of them."

Jackson gave a curt nod.

Trent put a photograph on the table in front of Jackson. "Isn't she beautiful?"

Jackson's gaze flicked down.

The woman in the picture was indeed beautiful, likely

in her midtwenties, with rich auburn hair, a bright, open smile, shining green eyes. But her looks were a moot point.

"She's getting married," said Trent. "To Vern Gerhard. They hide it well. But that family's known to a lot of the guys in here. Vern is a con artist and a crook. So is his father, and his father before that."

The woman obviously had questionable taste in men. Jackson found that less than noteworthy. In his line of work, he'd come across plenty of women who'd married the wrong guy, even more whose husbands didn't meet with the approval of their fathers. Again, this had nothing to do with him.

He looked back to Colin. "What is it *you* want from me?"

"We want you to stop the wedding," said Colin.

It took a second for the words to compute inside Jackson's head. "Why would I do anything like that?"

"He's after her money," said Trent.

"She's a grown woman." Jackson's glance strayed to the photo again.

She looked to be twenty-six or twenty-seven. He doubted she was thirty. With a face like that and any kind of money in the mix, she had to know she was going to attract a few losers. If she didn't recognize them herself, there wasn't anything Jackson could do about it.

Colin spoke up again. "She can't possibly know she's being conned. The girl places a huge value on honesty and integrity, has done her entire life. If she knew the truth, she wouldn't have anything to do with him."

"So tell her."

"She won't speak to me," said Trent. "She sure won't listen to me. She doesn't trust me as far as she can throw me."

"I'm sure you can relate to that particular viewpoint," said Colin, an edge to his voice.

"*That's* what you want to say to me?" Jackson rose to his feet. No way, no how was he buying into a guilt trip from his old man.

"Sit down," said Colin.

"Please," said Trent. "Year ago, I put something in her name, shares in a diamond mine."

"Lucky for her."

The woman might well be picking the wrong husband, but at least she'd have a comfortable lifestyle.

"She doesn't know about it," said Trent.

For the first time since he'd walked in, Jackson's curiosity was piqued. "She doesn't know she owns a diamond mine?"

Both men shook their heads.

Jackson looked at the picture again, picking it up from the table. She didn't appear naive. In fact, if he had to guess, he'd say she looked intelligent. But she was drop-dead gorgeous. In his eight years as a private detective, he'd discovered features like that made women targets.

"Hear us out," said Colin. "Please, son."

"Don't call me that."

"Okay. Fine. Whatever you want." Colin was nodding again.

"You hear things in here. And the Gerhards are dangerous," said Trent.

"More dangerous than you two felons?" Jackson didn't like that he'd become intrigued by the circumstances, but he had.

"Yes," said Trent.

Jackson hesitated for a beat, but then he sat back down. Another ten minutes wouldn't kill him.

"They found out about the mine," said Trent, his tone earnest.

"You know this for sure?" asked Jackson.

"I do."

"How?"

"A friend of a friend. The Borezone Mine made a promising new discovery a year ago. Only days later, Vern Gerhard made contact with my daughter. Final assaying is about to be announced, and the value will go through the roof."

"Is it publicly traded?" asked Jackson.

"Privately held."

"Then how did Gerhard know about the discovery?"

"Friends, industry contacts, rumors. It's not that hard if you know where to ask."

"It could be a coincidence."

"It's not." There was cold anger in Trent's voice. "The Gerhards are bottom-feeders. They heard about the discovery. They targeted her. And as soon as the ink is dry on the marriage certificate, they'll rob her blind and dump her like last week's trash."

Jackson traced his index finger around the woman's face. "You have proof of that? You have evidence that he's not in love with her?"

With that fresh-faced smile and those intelligent eyes, Jackson could imagine any number of men could simply fall in love, money or no money.

"That's what we need you for," said Colin.

"Expose their con," said Trent. "Look into their secret, slimy business dealings and tell my Crista what you find. Convince her she's being played and stop that wedding."

Crista. Her name was Crista. It suited her.

Despite himself, Jackson was beginning to think his way through the problem, calculate the time he'd need for a cursory look into the Gerhard family's business. At the moment, things weren't too busy in the Chicago office of Rush Investigations. He'd planned to use the lull to visit the Boston office and discuss a possible expansion. But if push came to shove, he could make some time for this.

She was pretty. He'd give her that. Nobody in the Boston office was anywhere near this pretty.

"Will you do it?" asked Colin.

"I'll scratch the surface," said Jackson, pocketing the photo.

Trent opened his mouth, looking like he might protest

Jackson taking the picture. But he obviously thought better of it and closed his mouth again.

"Keep us posted?" asked Colin.

For a split second, Jackson wondered if this was all a ruse to keep him in contact with his father. Did Colin plan to string him along for a while for some hidden reason of his own? He was, after all, a gifted con artist.

"The wedding's Saturday," said Trent.

That diverted Jackson's attention. "*This* Saturday?"

"Yes."

That was three days away.

"Why didn't you start this sooner?" Jackson demanded. What did they expect him to accomplish in only three days?

"We did," Colin said quietly.

Jackson clamped his jaw. Yeah, his father had been trying to get hold of him for a month. He'd been studiously ignoring the requests, just like he'd been doing for years. He owed Colin nothing.

He stood. "It's not much time, but I'll see what I can find."

"She *cannot* marry him." Trent's undertone was rock hard with vehemence.

"She's a grown woman," Jackson repeated.

He'd look into the Gerhards. But if Crista Corday had fallen for a bad boy, there might be nothing her daddy or anyone else could do to change her mind.

Crista Corday swayed back and forth in front of the full-length mirror, her strapless lace and tulle wedding gown rustling softly against her legs. Her hair was swept up in a profusion of curls and braids. Her makeup had been meticulously applied. Even her underwear was white silk perfection.

She stifled a laugh at the absurdity of it all. She was a struggling jewelry designer, living in a basement suite off Winter Street. She didn't wear antique diamonds. She didn't get married in the magnificent Saint Luke's Cathedral with a reception at the Brookbend Country Club. And she didn't get swept off her feet by the most eligible prince charming in all of greater Chicago.

Except for the part where she did, and she had.

Cinderella had nothing on her.

There was a knock on the Gerhard mansion's bedroom door.

"Crista?" the male voice called out. It was Vern's cousin Hadley, one of the groomsmen.

"Come in," she called in return.

She liked Hadley. He was a few years younger than Vern, laid-back by Gerhard standards, fun-loving and friendly. Taller than most of the men in the family, he was athletic and good-looking, with a jaunty swath of dark blond hair that swooped across his forehead.

He lived in Boston rather than Chicago, but he visited often, sometimes staying at the mansion, sometimes using a hotel. Crista assumed he preferred a hotel when he had a date. Vern's mother, Delores, was staunchly religious and would not have allowed Hadley to have an overnight guest.

The door opened, and he stepped into the spacious, sumptuously decorated guest room. Crista had spent the night here, while Vern had stayed in his apartment downtown. Maybe it was Dolores's influence, but Crista had been feeling old-fashioned the past few weeks, insisting she and Vern sleep apart until the honeymoon. Vern had reluctantly agreed.

Hadley halted. Then he pushed the door shut behind him and seemed to take in her ensemble.

"What?" she asked, checking herself out, wondering if she'd missed some glaring flaw.

"You look amazing," he said.

Crista scoffed. "I sure hope I do." She spread her arms. "Do you have any idea how much this all cost?"

Hadley grinned. "Aunt Delores wouldn't have it any other way."

"I feel like an impostor." Crista's stomach fluttered with a resurgence of apprehension.

"Why?" he asked. His tone was gentle, and he moved closer.

"Because I grew up on the lower west side."

"You don't think we're your people?"

She turned back to the mirror and gazed at her reflection. The woman staring back was her, but not her. It was a surreal sensation.

"Do you think you're my people?" she asked him.

"If you want us to be," he said.

Their gazes met in the mirror.

"But it's not too late," he added.

"Too late for what?"

"To back out." He looked serious, but he had to be joking.

"You're wrong about that." Not that she wanted to back out. Not that she'd even consider backing out. In fact, she couldn't imagine how their conversation had come to this.

"You look scared," he said.

"Of the wedding, sure. I'm probably going to trip on my way down the aisle. But I'm not afraid of the marriage."

It was Vern. She was marrying smart, respectful, polite Vern. The man who'd stepped up to invest in her jewelry design company, who'd introduced her to the finer things, who'd swept her away for a fantasy weekend in New York City and another in Paris. There wasn't much about Vern that wasn't fantastic.

"The future in-laws?" Hadley asked.

Crista quirked a smile. "Intimidated, not afraid."

The intensity left his expression, and he smiled in return. "Who wouldn't be intimidated by them?"

"Nobody I know, that's for sure."

Manfred Gerhard was a humorless workaholic. He was exacting and demanding, with a cutting voice and an abrupt manner. His wife, Delores, was prim and uptight, excruciatingly conscious of the social hierarchy, but skittish whenever Manfred was in the room, constantly catering to his whims.

If Vern ever acted like his father, Crista would kick him to the curb. No way, no how would she put up with that. Then the thought brought her up short. Vern wasn't at all like his father. She'd never seen anything to even suggest he might behave like Manfred.

"He's very close to them," said Hadley.

He was watching her intently again, and for a split second Crista wondered if he could read her thoughts.

"He's talking about buying an apartment in New York City." She liked the idea of putting some distance between Vern and his family. He loved them dearly, but she couldn't see spending every Sunday evening at the mansion the way Vern seemed to like.

"I'll believe that when it happens," said Hadley.

But Crista knew it was already decided. "It's so I can expand the business," she elaborated.

"Are you having second thoughts?" asked Hadley.

"No." She turned to face him. She wasn't. "What makes you say that? What makes you ask that?"

"Maybe I want you for myself."

"Very funny."

He hesitated for a moment then gave an unconcerned shrug. "I'm not sure I'd marry into this family."

"Too bad you're already in this family."

He looked her straight in the eyes. "So, you're sure?"

"I'm sure. I love him, Hadley. And he loves me. Everything else will work itself out around that."

He gave a nod of acquiescence. "Okay. If I can't get you to call off the wedding, then I'm here to tell you the limos have arrived."

"It's time?" The flutter in her stomach turned into a spasm.

It was perfectly normal, she told herself. She was about to walk down the aisle in front of hundreds of people, including her future in-laws and a who's who list of notable Chicago-ans. She'd be a fool to be calm under these circumstances.

"You just turned pale," said Hadley.

"I told you, I'm afraid of tripping halfway down the aisle."

"You want me to walk you?"

"That's not how we rehearsed it."

Crista's father was in prison, and she didn't have a close male relative to escort her down the aisle. And in this day and age, it seemed ridiculous to scramble for a figurehead to "give her away" to Vern. She was walking down the aisle alone, and she was perfectly fine with that.

"I could still do it," said Hadley.

"No, you can't. You need to stand up front with Vern. Otherwise the numbers will be off, more bridesmaids than groomsmen. Dolores would faint dead away."

Hadley straightened the sleeves of his tux. "You got that right."

Crista pictured her six bridesmaids at the front of the cathedral in their one-shoulder crisscross aqua dresses. Their bouquets would be plum and white, smaller versions of the dramatic rose-and-peony creation Delores had ordered for Crista. It was going to be heavy, but Delores had said with a congregation that large, people needed to see it from a distance. They could probably see it from Mars.

"The flowers are here?" asked Crista, half hoping they hadn't arrived so she wouldn't have to lug the monstrosity around.

"Yes. They're looking for you downstairs to get some pictures before you leave."

"It's time," said Crista, bracing herself.

"It's not too late," said Hadley. "We can make a break for it through the rose garden."

"You need to shut up."

He grinned. "Shutting up now."

Crista was getting married today. It might have happened fast. The ceremony might be huge. And her new family might be overwhelming. But all she had to do was put one foot in front of the other, say, "I do," and smile in all the right places.

By tonight, she'd be Mrs. Vern Gerhard. By this time tomorrow, she'd be off on a Mediterranean honeymoon. A posh private jet would take them to a sleek private yacht for a vacation in keeping with the stature of the Gerhard family.

Hadley offered her his arm, and she took it, feeling a sudden need to hang on tight.

"I'll see you at the church," he said.

She could do this. She would do this. There was no downside. Any woman would be thrilled by such a complete and total change in her lifestyle.

Dressed in a crisp tuxedo, freshly shaved, his short hair neatly trimmed, Jackson stood outside Saint Luke's Cathedral north of Chicago in the Saturday afternoon sunshine pretending he belonged. It was a picture-perfect June wedding day. The last of the well-heeled guests had just been escorted inside, and the groomsmen now stood in a cluster on the outside stairs. Vern Gerhard was nowhere to be seen, likely locked up in an anteroom with the best man waiting for Crista Corday to arrive.

Jackson had learned a lot about Crista over the past three days. He'd learned she was beautiful, creative and reputedly hardworking.

As a girl, she'd grown up in a modest neighborhood, living with her single mother, her father, Trent, having visitation rights and apparently providing some small amount of financial support. She'd attended community college, taking a diploma in fine arts. It was during that time that she'd lost her mother in a car accident.

After graduation she'd found a job in women's clothing in a local department store. He assumed she must have worked on her jewelry designs in her off hours.

So far, she seemed exactly as she appeared, an ordinary,

working-class Chicago native who'd been living a perfectly ordinary life until she'd met her fiancé. The most remarkable thing about her seemed to be her father's conviction on fraud charges. Then again, maybe it wasn't so remarkable. This was Chicago, and Jackson was definitely familiar with having a convicted criminal in the family.

Vern and the Gerhards had proven harder for him to gauge. Their public and social media presence was slick and heavily controlled. Their family company, Gerhard Incorporated, was privately held, having been started as a hardware store by Vern's great-grandfather during the Depression. It now centered on commercial real estate ownership and development.

Their estimated net worth was high, but Jackson hadn't found anything illegal or shady in their business dealings. They did seem to have incredible timing, often buying up properties at fire sale prices in the months before corporate mergers, gentrification or zoning changes boosted their value. It was enough to make Jackson curious, but the individual instances weren't overly suspicious, and what he had so far didn't come close to proving they were conning Crista.

Despite Trent's suspicions, Vern Gerhard and Crista's romance seemed to be just that, a romance.

"I say more power to him." One of the groomsmen's voices carried from the cathedral staircase, catching Jackson's attention.

"I almost told her at the house," said another groomsman. This one looked younger. He had the trademark Gerhard brown eyes, but he was taller than most, younger than Vern. His flashy hairstyle made him look like he belonged in a boy band.

"Why would you do that?" asked a third. This man was shorter, balding, and his bow tie was already askew. Jackson recognized him as a brother-in-law to Vern.

"You don't think she deserves to know?" asked the younger one.

"Who cares? She's hot," said the bald one. "That body, hoo boy."

"Such a sweet ass," said the first groomsman, grinning.

"Nice," Jackson muttered under his breath. The Gerhards might be rich, but they didn't seem to have much in the way of class.

"So, why does he need Gracie?" asked the younger groomsman, glancing around the circle for support. "He should break it off already."

"You want to stick to just one ice cream flavor?" asked the balding man.

"For the rest of your life?" asked the first groomsman.

"Some days I feel like praline pecan. Some days I feel like rocky road," said the heavyset one with a chortle.

"And *that's* why you're sleeping with Lacey Hanniberry."

"Lumpy Lacey."

The other men laughed.

"Vern hit the jackpot." The first groomsman made a rude gesture with his hips.

"On both fronts," said the bald one. "Crista's the lady, Gracie's the tramp."

"She's going to find out," said the younger man with the flashy hair.

"Not if you don't tell her she won't," said the first man, a warning in his tone.

Jackson had half a mind to tell her himself. Vern sounded like a pig. And most of his friends didn't seem any better.

"Gracie won't last, anyway," said the heavyset man.

"Vern will trade up," said the balding one.

"Uncle Manfred's girlfriends have been twenty-five for the past thirty years."

"Wives age, girlfriends don't."

They all laughed, except for the young guy. He frowned instead. "Crista's different."

"No, she's not." The first groomsman slapped him on the

back. "You're young, naive. All your girlfriends are twenty-five."

"I don't cheat on them."

"Then you're not trying hard enough."

"Get with the program."

Out of the corner of his eye, Jackson saw two white limos pull up to the curb. The groomsmen spotted them, too, and they turned to head up the wide staircase to the cathedral entrance, their voices and laughter fading with the distance.

So, Vern was cheating on Crista. It was a coldhearted and idiotic move, but it was none of Jackson's business. Maybe she knew and accepted it. Or maybe she wasn't as smart as everyone seemed to think, and she was oblivious. Or maybe—and this was a real possibility—she was only marrying the guy for his money and didn't care about his fidelity one way or the other.

The limo doors opened and a group of pretty bridesmaids spilled out of one. The driver of the other vehicle quickly hopped to the back door, helping the bride step onto the sidewalk.

Crista straightened and rose in the bright sunshine, looking absolutely stunning. Her auburn hair was swept up in braids, thick at the nape of her neck, wispy and delicate around her beautiful face. Her shoulders were bare and looked creamy smooth. The white dress was tight across her breasts and her waist, showing off an amazing figure. The lace and beading on the full skirt glittered with every little movement.

Jackson didn't normally fantasize about brides. But if he had, they'd look exactly like her. His annoyance at Vern redoubled. What was the man's problem? If Jackson had someone like Crista in his bed, he'd never so much as look at another woman.

The bridesmaids giggled and clustered around her while the drivers returned to their cars to move them from the busy street.

"This is it," said one bridesmaid, fussing with Crista's bouquet and taking a critical look at her face and hairdo.

"I'm okay?" Crista asked.

"You're perfect."

Crista drew in a deep breath.

The women started for the staircase that led to the cathedral's big front doors. Jackson's first instinct was to step forward and offer his arm, but he held back.

Crista spotted him. She looked puzzled at first, as if she was struggling to recognize him. Their gazes locked, and he felt a shot to his solar plexus.

Her eyes were green as a South Pacific sea and just as deep, flickering in the sunshine. She looked honest. She looked honorable. In that split second, he knew her father's words had been true. She wouldn't put up with a cheating husband, which meant she didn't know about Vern and Gracie.

Jackson wanted to shout at her to stop, to get out of here. She might not know it, but she was making a mistake. Deep down in his gut, he knew she was making a terrible mistake.

Maybe he should tell her the truth about Vern, just call out, right here, right now. Then at least she'd know what she was getting herself into. He told himself to do it. He owed Vern absolutely nothing. He formed the words inside his head, opened his mouth and was ready to blurt it out.

But then a bridesmaid whispered to Crista. She laughed, and her gaze broke from Jackson's, releasing him from the spell.

The women moved up the staircase, and the moment was lost.

He shook himself. It was time for him to leave. There was nothing more he could do here, nothing he could do for Trent except hope the man was wrong. The Gerhards seemed like a singularly distasteful family, and if they really were after her diamond mine, she had herself some trouble. But it wasn't Jackson's trouble to borrow. He'd done as he'd promised, and he'd found nothing concrete, nothing that said the Gerhards were nefarious criminals.

The bridesmaids filed in through the doorway, chattering among themselves. Crista hung back, touching each of her earrings, fingering her necklace then grasping her large bouquet in both hands and tipping up her chin.

Then, unexpectedly, she twisted her head to look back again. He felt that same rush of emotion tighten his chest cavity. He knew with an instant certainty that she deserved better than Vern. It might be none of his business, but surely she wouldn't tolerate a husband who'd sneak off and sleep with a string of mistresses.

The heavy door swung shut behind the bridesmaids.

Just he and Crista were left outside.

Jackson glanced around and confirmed that for these short seconds, they were alone.

Before his brain could form a thought, his feet were moving. He was striding toward her.

Her green eyes went wide, and she drew her head back in obvious surprise.

"Crista Corday?" he asked.

"Are you a friend of Vern's?" Her sexy voice seemed to strum along his nervous system.

"Not for long," he said. He scooped her into his arms and began walking.

"What?" she squeaked, one of her hands pushing on his shoulder, the other gripping the big bouquet.

"I'm not going to hurt you." He lengthened his stride to the sidewalk.

"You're not...*what* are you doing?"

"There are things you don't know about Vern."

"*Put me down!*" She started to squirm, glancing frantically around.

"I will," he promised, speeding up his pace. "In a moment."

He reached out and opened the driver's door of his SUV.

He shoved her across to the passenger side. Before she had a chance to react, he jumped in behind her, cranked the engine and gunned the accelerator, peeling away from the curb, narrowly missing a taxi, which responded with a long blast from its horn.

"You can't do this," Crista cried, twisting her neck to look back at the church.

"I only want to talk."

"I'm *getting married*."

"After you hear me out if you still want to get married, I'll take you back to him."

And, he would. Trent was a criminal. He could easily be lying about the Gerhards for reasons of his own. So, if Crista was okay with infidelity, Jackson would return her to Vern. It would go against every instinct inside him, but he'd do it.

Two

"Take me back *now*," Crista shouted at the stranger who seemed to be abducting her. Her mind raced to make some sense out of the situation.

"As soon as you hear me out." His jaw was tight, his eyes straight ahead, his hands firm on the wheel as they gathered speed.

"Who *are* you?" She struggled not to panic.

She'd always considered herself a smart, sensible, capable woman. But in this scenario she had no idea what to do.

"Jackson Rush. I'm an investigator."

"Investigating what?" She struggled to stay calm. What was he doing? Why had he taken her?

Then she saw a red light coming up. He'd have to stop for it. When he did, she'd jump from the vehicle. She quickly glanced at the passenger door to locate the handle.

She'd open the door, jump out and run to… She scanned the businesses along the section of the street. The Greek restaurant might be closed. The apartment building doors would be locked. But the drug store. That would be open, and it would be crowded. Surely one of the clerks would lend a bride a phone.

She realized she was still holding onto her bouquet, and she let it slip from her hand to the floor. She didn't need it slowing her down. Vern's mother would flip. Then again, Vern's mother, along with everyone else, was probably flipping already. Had anyone seen this man, Jackson, take her?

She surreptitiously slanted a glance his way. He was maybe thirty. He looked tough and determined, maybe a little world-weary. But there was no denying he was attractive. He was obviously fit under the tux, and very well-groomed.

The vehicle was slowing. She lifted her hand, ready to grab the handle.

But suddenly he hit the accelerator, throwing her back in her seat and sideways as he made a hard right. Another car honked as their tires squealed against the pavement.

"What are you *doing*?" she demanded.

"How well do you know Vern Gerhard?"

What a ridiculous question. "He's my fiancé."

"Would it surprise you to know he was cheating on you?"

Crista's jaw dropped. "Where did that come from?"

"Would it surprise you?" Jackson repeated.

"Vern's not cheating on me." The idea was preposterous.

Vern was sweet and kind and loyal. He made no secret of the fact that he adored Crista. They were about to be married. And his family was extremely old-fashioned. Vern would never risk disappointing his mother by cheating.

No, scratch that. Vern wouldn't cheat because Vern wouldn't cheat. It had nothing to do with Delores.

"Okay," said Jackson, the skepticism clear in his tone.

"Take me back," she said.

"I can't do that. Not yet."

"There are three hundred people in that church. They're all waiting for me to walk down the aisle."

She could only imagine the scene as the guests grew more restless and Vern grew more confused. She wasn't wearing a watch, and she didn't have her cell phone. But what time was it? Exactly how late was she to her own wedding?

She scanned the dashboard for a clock. Traffic was light, and Jackson seemed able to gauge the stoplights and adjust his speed, making sure he didn't have to come to a halt.

"Would you care if he was cheating?" asked Jackson, eyeing her quickly. "Would that be a deal breaker for you?"

"He's not cheating." It didn't look like she'd have a chance to bail out anytime soon. "Do you want money? Will you call in a ransom demand? They'll probably pay. They'll probably pay more if you take me back there right away."

"This isn't about money."

"Then what's it about?" She struggled to keep her tone even but panic was creeping in.

He seemed to hesitate over his answer. "You deserve to be sure. About Vern."

"You don't even know me." She stared at him more closely. "Do you? Have we met?"

Could he be some long-lost person from her past?

"We haven't met," he said.

She racked her brain for an explanation. "Then do you know Vern? Did he do something bad to you?"

She realized she ought to be frightened. She'd been kidnapped—*kidnapped*. This stranger was holding her hostage and wouldn't let her go.

"I've never met Vern," he said.

"Then are you crazy? Though I suppose that's a stupid question. Crazy people never question their own sanity." She realized she was babbling, but she couldn't seem to help herself.

"I'm beginning to think I am," he said.

"A sure sign that you're not."

He gave a chopped laugh and seemed to drop his guard.

She tried to take advantage. "Will you let me go? Please, just pull over and drop me off. I'll find my own way back to the church."

It had to be at least fifteen minutes now. Vern would be frantic. Delores would be incensed. Unless someone saw Jackson grab her, they probably thought she ran away.

Now she wondered what Hadley was thinking. He might guess she'd taken his advice, changed her mind, that she didn't want to marry Vern after all. She scrunched her eyes shut and shook her head. How had things gotten so mixed up?

"He's cheating on you, Crista. Why would you want to marry a man who's cheating on you?"

"First of all, he's not. And…" She paused, experienced

a moment of clarity. "Wait a minute. If I say I don't care if he's cheating, will you let me go?"

"If you honestly don't care and you want to marry him anyway, yeah, I'll let you go."

"Then I don't care." Why hadn't she thought of this sooner? "It's fine. No problem." She waved a dismissive hand. "He can cheat away. I still want to marry him."

"You're lying."

"I'm not." She was.

"I don't believe you."

"You've never met me. You don't know a thing about me."

He shook his head. "I can tell you have pride."

"I have no pride. Maybe I like to share. Maybe I'm into polygamy. After this wedding, Vern might find another wife. We'll all live happily ever after."

"As if."

"Let me go!"

"I'm here because somebody out there cares about you, Crista."

"I know somebody cares about me. His name is Vern Gerhard. Do you have any idea how upset he is right now?"

Jackson's tone went dry. "Maybe Gracie could console him."

The name set a shiver through Crista's chest. "*What* did you say?"

"Gracie," Jackson repeated, doing a double take at Crista's face. "You okay?"

"I'm fine. No, I'm not. I've been kidnapped!"

"Do you know someone named Gracie?"

Crista did know Gracie Stolt. Or at least she knew *of* a Gracie Stolt. Vern had once used that name during a phone call. He'd said it was business. It *had* been business, making the name irrelevant to this conversation.

"I don't know any Gracie," she said to Jackson, her tone tart.

"He's sleeping with Gracie."

"Stop saying that."

The vehicle bounced, and she grabbed the armrest to steady herself. She realized they'd turned off the main roads and onto a tree-lined lane.

A new and horrible thought crossed her mind, and her throat went dry. Was Jackson some sicko with a thing for brides?

"Are you going to hurt me?" she rasped.

"What?" He did another double take. "No. I told you. I'm not going to harm you at all."

"I bet every psychopathic murderer says that."

The corner of his mouth tipped up, but then quickly disappeared. "We have a mutual acquaintance. The person who sent me is someone who cares about you."

"Who?"

"I can't reveal my client."

"I bet every psychopathic murderer says that, too."

She was vacillating between genuine fear and disbelief that any of this could be real.

"I'm sorry you're frightened right now, but I'm not going to hurt you. You'll figure that out soon enough, I promise."

They rounded a corner, and a lake fanned out before them, the gravel beach dotted with weathered docks. He pulled to the side of a small, deserted parking lot.

"Are we there?" she asked.

"Almost." He nodded toward one of the docks.

A tall white cabin cruiser bobbed against its moor lines.

Crista shrank back against the seat, her voice going up an octave. "You're going to dump my body in the lake?"

He extracted a cell phone from his inside jacket pocket. "I'm going to call my staff."

"You have a phone?"

"Of course I have a phone."

"You should make a ransom call. My fiancé is from a rich family. They'll pay you."

At least she hoped the Gerhards would pay to get her back. She was certain Vern would be willing. His father, maybe not so much.

Jackson hated that he was frightening Crista. But he was operating on the fly here. Taking her a quarter mile offshore on Lake Michigan was the best he could come up with to keep her safe but under wraps. He wasn't about to tie her up in a basement while Mac and some of his other guys looked into Vern Gerhard's love life.

"You're going to jail, you know," she said for about the twenty-fifth time.

She stood on the deck of the boat, gazing back at the mansions along the coastline, their lights coming up as the sun sank away. Her extravagant white wedding gown rustled in the breeze. The intricate lace-and bead-covered skirt was bell shaped, billowing out from a tight waist, while the strapless top accentuated her gorgeous figure.

She was right. He was taking a very stupid risk. But the alternative had been to let the wedding go ahead. Which he could have done. In fact, he should have done. He owed nothing to her father and nothing to his own father. And Crista was all but a stranger to him. She was an intelligent adult, and she'd made her choice in Vern. He should have walked away.

"I'm hoping you won't press charges," he said, moving to stand beside her.

"In what universe would I not press charges?"

Though he knew she was frightened, her expression was defiant. He couldn't help but be impressed with her spirit.

"In the universe where I did you a favor."

"You destroyed my wedding. Do you have any idea how important this was to my mother-in-law? How much she planned and spent?"

"To your mother-in-law?"

"Yes."

"Not to you?"

Her expression faltered. "Well, me, too, of course. It was my wedding."

"It was an odd way to put it, worrying about your mother-in-law first."

"What I meant was, from my own perspective, I can get married any old time, in the courthouse, in Vegas, whatever. But she has certain expectations, a certain standing in the community. She wants to impress her friends and the rest of the family."

"She sounds charming."

"It comes with the Gerhard territory." There was a resignation to her tone.

"What about Vern? How did he feel about the opulent wedding?"

"He was all for it. He's close to his family. He wants them to be happy."

"Does he want you to be happy?"

Crista glanced sharply up at Jackson. "Yes, he wants me to be happy. But he knows I don't sweat the small stuff."

Jackson lifted a brow. "The small stuff being your own wedding?"

She shrugged her bare shoulders, and he was suddenly seized by an urge to run his palms over them, to test the smoothness of her skin. Was she cold out here on the lake?

"It'll work just as well with three hundred people in the room as it would with two witnesses and a judge."

Jackson stifled a chuckle. "You sure don't sound like the average bride."

Her tone turned dry. "The average bride doesn't have a five-hundred-dollar wedding bouquet."

"Seriously?"

"I don't know for sure, but I think that's in the ballpark."

Jackson drew back to take in the length of her. "And the dress?"

She spread her arms. "Custom-made in Paris."

"You flew to Paris for a wedding dress."

"Don't be ridiculous. The designer flew to Chicago."

This time Jackson did laugh. "You have got to be kidding."

"And that was only the start. I'm wearing antique diamonds." She tilted her head to show him her ears.

He wanted to kiss her neck. It was ridiculous, given the circumstances, but there was something incredibly sensual about the curve of her neck, the line of her jaw, the lush red of her lips.

"And you should see my underwear," she said.

Their gazes met. She took in his stare and obviously saw a flare of desire. Those gorgeous green eyes widened in surprise, and she took a step back.

He wanted to tell her he'd give pretty much anything to see her underwear. But he kept his mouth firmly shut.

"You wouldn't," she said, worry in her tone.

"I wouldn't," he affirmed. "I won't. I'm not going to try anything out of line." He turned his attention to the shoreline.

"Will you take me back?" she asked.

"I doubt there's anybody left at the church."

"They'll be crazy with worry," she said. "They'll have called the police by now."

"The police won't take a missing-person report for twenty-four hours."

"You don't know my future in-laws."

"I know the Chicago Police Department."

"Why are you doing this?"

"I was hired to look into Vern Gerhard's integrity."

"By who?"

Jackson shook his head. "I have a strict policy of client confidentiality."

Given their understandably fractured relationship, bringing Trent's name into it would be the fastest way to completely lose her trust. Not that he'd blame her. He felt the same about anything his own father touched.

"But you don't have a strict policy against kidnapping innocent people?" she asked.

"To be honest, this is the first time it's come up."

"I *am* going to press charges." It was clear she was serious.

There was no denying that the situation had spiraled out of control. But there was also nothing to do but keep moving forward. If he took her back now, the Gerhards would definitely have him arrested. His only hope was to find proof of Vern's infidelity and turn Crista against her fiancé.

His phone rang. He kept eye contact with her as he reached for it.

It was Mac, his right-hand man.

"Hey," Jackson answered.

"Everything okay so far?" asked Mac.

"Yeah." Jackson turned away from Crista and moved along the deck toward the bridge. "You come up with anything?"

"Rumors, yes. But nothing that gives us proof. Norway's looking into Gracie."

"Pictures would be good."

"Videotape better."

"I'd take videotape," said Jackson. "Is somebody on the family?"

"I am."

"And?"

"They've contacted the police, but they're being waved off until morning. I guess runaway brides aren't that unusual."

"If Vern Gerhard is a typical example of our gender, I don't blame them."

Mac coughed out a laugh.

"I guess we've got till morning," said Jackson.

It was less time than he would have liked. But that's what happened when you threw a plan together at the last minute.

"And then?" asked Mac. "Have you thought through what happens in the morning?"

He had, and most of the options were not good. "We better have something concrete by then."

"Otherwise she's a liability," said Mac.

Jackson had to agree. "At that point, she's going to be a huge liability."

Crista was predictably angry at having her posh wedding ruined. If they didn't find something to incriminate Vern, Jackson's career if not his freedom would be at stake.

He heard a sudden splash behind him.

He spun to find the deck empty, Crista gone. His gaze moved frantically from corner to corner as he rushed to the stern and spotted her in the water. "You gotta be kidding me!"

"What?" asked Mac.

"Call you back." Jackson dropped his phone.

She was flailing in the choppy waves, obviously hampered by the voluminous white dress. She gasped and went under.

He immediately tossed two life jackets overboard, as close to her as he could.

"Grab one!" he shouted. Then he stripped off his jacket, kicked off his shoes and dived in.

The water closed icy cold around him. He surfaced and gasped in a big breath. She was twenty feet away, and he kicked hard. He dug in with his arms, propelling himself toward her.

When he looked up again, she was gone. He twisted his head, peering in all directions, spotting a wisp of white below the surface. He dived under, groping in the dark until he caught hold of her arm. He clamped his hand tight and hauled her upward, breaking the surface and wrapping his arm firmly around her chest.

She coughed and sputtered.

"Relax," he told her. "Just relax and let me do the work."

She coughed again.

He grabbed one of the life jackets and tucked it beneath her. The boat was close, but the water was frigid. He wasn't going to be able to swim for long. Her teeth were already chattering.

He found another life jacket and looped it around the arm that supported her. He used his legs and free arm to move them through the water.

"You okay?" he asked her. "You breathing?"

She nodded against his chest.

"Don't fight me," he cautioned.

"I won't," she rasped.

The side of the boat loomed closer. He aimed for the stern where there was a small swimming platform. It was a relief to grasp on to something solid. His muscles throbbed from the effects of the cold water, and his limbs were starting to shake.

He unceremoniously cupped her rear end and shoved her onto the platform. She scrambled up, her dress catching and tearing. He kept her braced until she was stable. Then he looped both forearms over the platform and hoisted himself up, sitting on the edge, dragging in deep breaths.

"What the heck?" he demanded.

She was breathing hard. "I thought I could make it."

"To the beach?"

"It's not that far."

"It's a quarter mile. And you're dressed in an anchor."

"The fabric is light."

"Maybe when it's bone-dry." He reached up and pulled himself to his feet. His legs trembled, and his knees felt weak, but he put an arm around her waist and lifted her up beside him.

With near-numb fingers, he released the catch on the deck gate and swung it open.

"Careful," he cautioned as he propelled her back onto the deck.

She held on and stepped shakily forward. "It tangled around my legs."

"You could have killed us both." He followed her.

"It'd serve you right."

"To be *dead*? You'd be dead, too."

"I'm going to be dead anyway."

"What?" He was baffled now.

She was shivering. "I heard you on the phone. You said tomorrow morning I'd be a liability. We both know what that means."

"One of us obviously doesn't."

"Don't bother to deny it."

"Nobody's killing anyone." He gazed out at the dark water. "Despite your best attempt."

"You can't let me live. I'll turn you in. You'll go to jail."

"You might not turn me in."

"Would you actually believe me if I said I wouldn't?"

"At the moment, no."

Right now, she was having a perfectly normal reaction to the circumstances. Proof of the truth might mitigate her anger eventually, but they didn't have that yet.

"Then that was a really stupid statement," she said.

"What I am going to prove is that I mean you no harm."

It was the best he could come up with for the moment. The breeze was chilling, and he ushered her past the bridge, opening the door to the cabin.

"How are you going to do that?"

"For starters by not harming you. Let's find you something dry."

She glared at him. "I'm not taking off my dress."

He pointed inside. "You can change in the head—the bathroom. I've got some T-shirts on board and maybe some sweatpants, though they'd probably drop right off you."

"This is your boat?"

"Of course it's my boat. Whose boat did you think it was?"

She passed through the door and stopped between the sofa and the kitchenette. "I thought maybe you stole it."

"I'm not a thief."

"You're a kidnapper."

He realized she'd made a fair point. "Yeah, well, that's the sum total of my criminal activity to date." He started working on his soggy tie. "If you let me get past you, I'll see what I can find."

She shrank out of his way against the counter.

He turned sideways to pass her, and their thighs brushed together. She arched her back to keep her breasts from touching his chest. It made things worse, because her wet cleavage swelled above the snug, stiff fabric.

Reaction slammed through his body, and he faltered, unable to stop himself from staring. She was soaked to the skin, her auburn hair plastered to her head, her makeup smeared. And yet she was still the most beautiful woman he'd ever seen.

"Jackson," she said, her voice coming out a whisper.

He lifted his gaze to meet hers. It was all he could do to keep his hands by his sides. He wanted to smooth her hair, brush the droplets from her cheeks and run his thumb across her lips.

"Thank you," she said.

The words took him by surprise. "You're welcome," he automatically answered.

For a minute, it seemed that neither of them could break eye contact. Longing roiled inside him. He wanted to kiss her. He wanted to do so much more. And he wanted it very, very badly.

Finally, she looked away. "You better, uh…"

"Yeah," he said. "I'd better." He moved, but the touch of her thighs made him feel like he'd been branded.

Crista reached and twisted. She stretched her arms in every direction, but no matter how she contorted, she couldn't push the tiny buttons through the loops on the back of her dress.

"Come on," she muttered. Then she whacked her elbow against a small cabinet. "Ouch!"

"You okay?" came Jackson's deep voice.

He was obviously only inches from the other side of the small door, and the sound made her jerk back. Her hip caught the corner of the vanity, and she sucked in a sharp breath.

"Fine," she called back.

"I'm getting changed out here."

"Thanks for the warning." An unwelcome picture bloomed in her mind of Jackson peeling off his dress shirt, revealing what had to be washboard abs and muscular shoulders. She'd clung to him in the ocean and again climbing onto the boat. She'd felt what was under his dress shirt, and her brain easily filled in the picture.

She shook away the vision and redoubled her efforts with the buttons. But it wasn't going to happen. She couldn't get out of the dress alone. She had two choices—stay in the soaking-wet garment or ask him for help. Both were equally disagreeable.

She caught a glimpse of herself in the small mirror. The wedding gown was stained and torn. She crouched a little, cringing at the mess of her hair. It was stringy and lopsided. If she didn't undo the braids and rinse out the mess from the lake water she'd probably have to shave it off in the morning.

"Are you decent?" she called through the door.

"Sure," he answered.

She opened the small door, stepped over the sill, and Jackson filled her vision. The cabin was softly lit around him. His hair was damp, and his chest was bare. A pair of worn gray sweatpants hung on his hips. As she'd expected, his abs were washboard hard.

"What happened?" he asked, taking in her dress.

"I can't reach the buttons."

He gave an eye roll and pulled a faded green T-shirt over his head. "I'll give you a hand."

She turned her back and steeled herself for his touch. The only reason she was letting him near her was that it was foolish to stay cold and uncomfortable in a ruined dress. She told herself that if he was going to kill her, he would have just let her go under. Instead, he'd saved her life.

His footfalls were muffled against the teak floor as he came up behind her. The sound stopped, and he drew in an audible breath. Then his fingertips grazed her skin above the top button, sending streaks of sensation up her spine. Her muscles contracted in reaction.

What was the matter with her? She wasn't attracted to him. She was appalled by him. She wanted to get away from him, to never see him again.

But as his deft fingers released each button, there was no denying her growing arousal. It had to be some pathetic version of Stockholm syndrome. If she'd paid more attention in her psychology elective, she might know how to combat it.

The dress came loose, and she clasped her forearms against her chest to keep it in place.

"That should do it," he said.

There was a husky timbre to his voice—a sexy rasp that played havoc with her emotions.

"Thanks," she said before she could stop herself. "I mean…" She turned to take the sentiment back, and her gaze caught with his. "That is…"

They stared at each other.

"I don't usually do this," he said.

She didn't know what he meant. He didn't usually kidnap women, or he didn't unbutton their wedding gowns?

She knew she should ask. No, she shouldn't ask. She should move now, lock herself in the bathroom until her emotions came under control.

But he slowly lifted his hand. His fingertips grazed her shoulder. Then his palm cradled her neck, slipping up to her hairline. The touch was smooth and warm, his obvious strength couched by tenderness.

She couldn't bring herself to pull away. In fact, it was a fight to keep from leaning into his caress.

He dipped his head.

She knew what came next. Anybody would know what came next.

His lips touched hers, kissing her gently, testing her texture and then her taste. Arousal instantly flooded her body. He stepped forward, his free arm going around her waist, settling at the small of her back, strong and hot against her exposed skin.

He pressed harder, kissed her deeper. She met his tongue, opening, drowning in the sweet sensations that enveloped her.

Good thing she didn't marry Vern today.

The thought brought her up short.

She let out a small cry and jerked away.

What was the matter with her?

"What are you doing?" she demanded, tearing from his hold.

Her dress slipped, and she struggled to catch the bodice. She was a second too late, and she flashed him her bare breasts.

His eyes glowed, and his nostrils flared.

"Back off," she ordered, quickly covering up.

"You kissed me too," he pointed out.

"You took me by surprise."

"We both know that's a lie."

"We do not," she snapped, taking a step away.

"Whatever you say."

"I'm *engaged*."

"So I've heard," he drawled. "Are you sure that's what you want?"

She couldn't seem to frame an answer.

If not for Jackson, she'd already be married to Vern.

They'd be at the reception, cutting the enormous cake and dancing to Strauss's *Snowdrops*, Delores's favorite waltz. Crista's knees suddenly felt weak, and she sat down on the padded bench beside her.

"The thought of being married makes you feel faint?" Jackson asked.

"I'm worried about my mother-in-law. I can't even imagine how she reacted. All those guests. All that planning. What did they do when I didn't show up? Did they all just go home?"

"You're not worried about Vern?"

"Yes, I'm worried about Vern. Quit putting words in my mouth."

"You never said his name."

"Vern, Vern, Vern. I'm worried sick about Vern. He's going through hell." Then a thought struck her. "You should call him. *I* should call him. I can at least let him know I'm all right."

"I can't let you use my phone."

"Because then they'd discover it was you. And they'd arrest you. And you'd go to jail. You know, sooner than you're already going to jail after I tell the police everything you did." Crista paused. Maybe she wouldn't tell them *everything*. Better to keep certain missteps off the public record.

"I've got five guys working on this." Jackson lowered himself to the bench opposite, the compact table between them.

"Five guys working on what?" Her curiosity was piqued.

"Vern's infidelity."

"Vern wasn't unfaithful."

Jackson smirked. "Right. And you never kissed me too."

Crista wasn't about to lie again. "Just tell me what you want. Whatever is going on here, let's please get this over with so I can go home."

"I want you to wait here with me while I find out exactly what your husband-to-be has been up to with Gracie."

"Gracie's a business acquaintance." Crista immediately realized her slipup.

Jackson caught it, too. "So, you do know her."

Crista wasn't about to renew the debate. She knew what she knew, and she trusted Vern.

"Why are you doing this?" she asked Jackson again.

"So you can decide whether or not you want to marry him."

"I *do* want to marry him."

His gaze slipped downward, and she realized her grip on her dress had relaxed. She was showing cleavage—a lot of cleavage. She quickly adjusted.

"Maybe," he said softly.

"There's no maybe about it."

"What's the harm in waiting?" he asked, sounding sincere. "The wedding's already ruined."

"Thanks to you."

"My point is there's no harm in waiting a few more hours."

"Except for my frantic fiancé."

Jackson seemed to think for a moment. "I can have someone call him, tell him you're okay."

"From a pay phone?" she mocked.

"Who uses pay phones? We've got plenty of burner phones."

"Of course you do."

"You want me to call?"

"Yes!" But then she thought about it. "No. Hang on. What are you going to tell him?"

"What do you want me to tell him?"

"The truth."

"Yeah, that's not going to happen."

"Then tell him I'm okay. Tell him something unexpected came up. I'm…uh…" She bit down on her lower lip. "I don't know. Other than the truth, what can I possibly say that doesn't sound terrible?"

"You got me."

"He'll think I got cold feet."

"He might."

"No, he won't." She shook her head firmly. Vern knew her better than that. He knew she was committed to their marriage.

But Jackson would never send a message that incriminated himself. And anything else could make it sound like it had been her decision to run off. Maybe it was better to keep silent.

"How long do you think this will take?" she asked. "To clear Vern's name?"

Jackson gave a shrug. "It could go pretty fast. My guys are good."

Crista rose to her feet. "Then don't call him. I'm going to change."

"Good idea."

"It doesn't mean I've capitulated."

"I took it to mean you wanted to be dry."

"That's exactly what it means."

"Okay," he agreed easily.

She turned away from his smug expression, gripping the front of her ruined wedding dress, struggling to hold on to some dignity as she made her way into the bathroom. She could feel his gaze on her back, taking in the expanse of bare skin. He knew she wasn't wearing a bra, and he could probably see the white lace at the top of her panties.

A rush of heat coursed through her. She told herself it was anger. She didn't care where he looked, or what he thought. It was the last he'd see of her that was remotely intimate.

Three

Jackson recognized Mac's number and put his phone to his ear. "Find something?"

"Norway talked to the girl," said Mac.

"Did she admit to the affair?"

"She says there's nothing between them. But she's lying. And she's doing it badly. Norway got thirty seconds alone with her phone and grabbed some photos."

That was encouraging. "Anything incriminating?"

"No nudity, but they do look intimate. Gerhard's got an arm around her shoulders, and his expression says he slept with her. We're combing through social media now."

"Good. Keep me posted."

"How are things at your end?"

Crista emerged from the bathroom. Her hair was still wet but combed straight. She'd washed her face, and she was dressed in Jackson's white and maroon U of Chicago soccer jersey. It hung nearly to her knees, which were bare, as were her calves.

"Pants didn't fit?" he asked.

"Huh?" asked Mac.

"Fell off," she said.

"Stay safe," Jackson said to Mac, setting down his phone.

"Who's that?" asked Crista, moving to the sofa. She took the end opposite to Jackson and tucked the hem of the jersey over her knees.

"Mac."

"He works for your agency?"

"He does."

She nodded. She looked curious but stayed silent.

"Are you afraid to ask?" he guessed.

She flicked back her damp hair. "I'm not afraid to ask anything."

"They found some pictures of Vern and Gracie."

"You're bluffing."

"They're not specifically incriminating—"

"I know they're not."

"But they are suggestive of more than a business relationship."

"If suggestive is all you've got, then let me go."

"It's all we've got *so far*." He glanced at his watch. "We've only been chasing this lead for five hours."

She heaved an exaggerated sigh.

"You hungry?" he asked.

He was, and he doubted brides were inclined to eat heartily before their weddings.

"No," she said.

"You really need to stop lying."

"*You're* criticizing *my* behavior?"

"You're not going to help anything by starving."

He rose, taking the few steps to the small kitchen and popping open a high cupboard.

"You're not going to make me like you," she said from behind him.

"Why would I want to make you like me?"

He wanted to convince her not to marry Vern. No, scratch that. He couldn't care less if she married Vern. No, scratch that, too. Vern didn't deserve her. If Jackson was sure of one thing in all this, it was that Vern didn't deserve a woman like Crista.

"To make me more docile and easy to manipulate."

Jackson located a stray bag of tortilla chips. "Docile? You? Are you kidding me?"

Her tone turned defensive. "I'm really quite easy to get along with. I mean, under normal circumstances."

He also found a jar of salsa. It wasn't much, but it would

keep them from starving. If they were lucky, they'd find a few cans of beer in the mini fridge.

He turned back.

She froze, her expression a study in guilt, his phone pressed to her ear.

He swore, dropping the food, taking two swift steps to grab it from her. How could he have made such an idiotic mistake?

"Nine-one-one operator," came a female voice through the phone. "What is your emergency?"

He hit the end button. "What did you do?"

"Tried to get help." Her words were bold, but she shrank back against the sofa.

Jackson hit the speed dial for Mac.

"Yeah?" Mac answered immediately.

"I have to move. This phone is compromised. Tuck's dock, zero eight hundred."

"Roger that," said Mac.

Jackson pushed open a window and tossed the phone overboard.

"That was stupid," he said to Crista.

"I was trying to escape. How was that stupid?"

"*You* were reckless. *I* was stupid."

He grasped her arm and pulled her to her feet.

"Hey," she cried.

"Listen, I'm still not going to hurt you, but you had no way of knowing that for sure. I could have been a vengeful jerk." He tugged her to the bridge, holding fast to her upper arm while he started the engine and engaged the anchor winch.

Her tone turned mulish. "I had to try."

"I shouldn't have given you the chance."

"You let your guard down."

"I did. And that was stupid."

Not to mention completely unprofessional. He wasn't sure

what had distracted him. Their kiss? Her legs? The sight of her in his jersey?

He'd have to worry about it later. Right now, he couldn't take a chance on an overzealous 911 operator tracing their location. Anchor up, he opened the throttle, and they surged forward.

She swayed, but he held her steady.

"You were trying to be nice," she said.

He struggled not to laugh at that. "You're trying to make me feel better about being stupid?"

"I'm saying… I'm not unappreciative of you offering me something to eat."

"Well, I'm definitely unappreciative of you compromising our location."

He set a course north along the coastline. His friend Tuck Tucker owned a beach house north of the city. Tuck wouldn't mind Jackson using his dock. He might mind the kidnapping part, but Jackson didn't plan to mention that. And if Mac and the others didn't come through with proof positive by morning, Tuck's reaction would be the least of Jackson's worries.

"Where are we going?" Crista asked.

Jackson did chuckle at that. "Yeah, sure. I'm going to tell you."

"It's not like we still have a phone." As she spoke, her gaze flicked to the radio.

"I'll be disconnecting the battery to that long before I take my eyes off you," he told her.

"What are you talking about?"

"You just looked at the radio. You might as well be wearing a neon sign that says it's your next move."

She drew an exasperated sigh and shifted her feet.

"You probably don't want to consider a life of crime," he said.

She lifted her chin and gave her damp hair a little toss. "I'm surprised you did."

"It's been a surprising day."

"Not exactly what I expected, either."

He'd have to hand her the win on that one.

He switched screens on the GPS, orienting himself to the shoreline.

"I'm hoping you'll thank me later," he said.

"Hoping? You don't seem as confident as before."

"The stakes just keep getting higher and higher. Now we're headed for the state line."

Her attention swung from the windshield to him. "You're taking me to *Wisconsin*?"

"What's wrong with Wisconsin?"

"It's a long way from Chicago. Why are you taking me there? What's happening?" She struggled to get away from him.

He regretted frightening her again. They weren't really going all the way to Wisconsin.

"I didn't plan to grab you today," he told her. "I was only there to get a look at Gerhard."

"Why?"

"To take his measure."

"I mean why do you care about us at all?"

"It's a job."

"Who hired you?"

"It doesn't matter. What matters to you is that your fiancé is already having an affair. You can't marry a man like that." Jackson wasn't ready to tell her more. Mention of her father would likely alienate her further. He didn't yet have proof of Trent's accusations. And if she was having trouble accepting that Vern would cheat, she'd never believe he was conning her.

"He's not like that. I don't know where you even came up with that idea."

She'd stopped struggling against his grip, and that was good. Her fear seemed to have been replaced by anger. Jackson's guilt eased off.

"Wedding guests," he said, opening the throttle to increase their speed. It was a clear, relatively calm night, thank goodness. They needed to put distance between them and the position where Crista had made the call.

"*My* wedding guests?"

"Technically, I would say they were Vern's wedding guests. They seemed to know him, and they were joking about his relationship with Gracie. I realized I couldn't in good conscience let you marry him, so I took the opportunity and grabbed you."

She was silent for a moment. "So this isn't so much crime as altruism."

"Yes. The easiest thing for me would have been to walk away."

"You can still walk away."

"We're on a boat."

"Swim away, then. Or drop me off onshore and drive away—motor away? Float away? What do you call it?"

"Navigate away. And no, I'm not dropping you off onshore." He made a show of looking her up and down, enjoying the view far too much. "You're not dressed, for one thing."

"I'll put my wedding dress back on. It might be uncomfortable, but it's better than staying here."

"I'd get thrown in jail," he said.

"Darn right. But that's going to happen anyway."

"Not for a few hours." And hopefully not ever, although Jackson's worry factor was steadily rising.

"How long until we get there?" she asked.

"Get where?"

"To the secret location, wherever it is you're taking me. How long until we stop navigating?"

"Why?"

"Because I'm hungry."

"Oh, now you're hungry. Well, you're going to have to wait."

"I can eat while you navigate."

"I'm not letting go of you."

"I'm not going to jump."

"That's what I thought last time."

"We're way too far from shore."

"Yeah, but I'm sure you've got another brilliant plan in mind already. Sabotage the engine, harpoon me from behind."

"You have harpoons on board?"

"Give me strength," he muttered.

She leaned close to him. "Am I annoying you? Frustrating you?"

"Yes on both counts."

Her argumentative nature was annoying, but his frustration came from a whole other place. She was stimulating and exciting. She was a beautiful, feisty, apparently complex and intelligent woman, and he was battling hard against his sexual attraction to her. He didn't want to be rushing from a crime scene with her as his captive, contemplating the best way to stay out of jail. He wanted to be on a date with her, somewhere great in the city, contemplating how best to get her into his bed.

"There's a simple solution," she told him.

It took a second for him to get his brain back on track. "Let you go?" he guessed.

"Bingo."

"Not until we meet up with Mac tomorrow."

"You'll let me go then?"

He knew he was being cornered, but there really was no choice. He could only hope Mac could come up with definitive proof by morning.

"Yes," said Jackson.

Crista's mouth curved into a dazzling smile. They hit a swell, and she pressed against him. Her curves were soft, and her scent was fresh. For a moment the risk of jail seemed almost worth it.

* * *

When Crista awoke, she was disoriented. It took a few seconds to realize the warm body beside her wasn't Vern. She was in bed with someone bigger, harder, with a deeper breathing pattern and an earthier scent. And the bed was moving beneath them.

Then reality came back in a rush. Long after midnight, she'd given in and laid down on the bed in the bow of Jackson's boat. He was still up, and she'd hugged one edge of the massive, triangular shape in case he decided to join her. At some point he obviously had, and in her sleep she must have moved to the middle.

Now she was cradled by his strong arm, hers thrown across his chest. And her leg…uh-oh. Her leg was draped across his thighs. The jersey had ridden up to her waist. Luckily, he was wearing sweatpants. Otherwise, there'd be nothing between them but the lacy silk of her white panties.

She knew she should move. She had to move. And she needed to do it before he woke up and caught her in such a revealing position. Now that she thought about it, she should have recoiled from him the second she was conscious.

Staying put like this was bad. The fact that she liked it was even worse. She was an engaged woman. She was all but married. She had absolutely no business enjoying the intimate embrace of another man, no matter how fit his body, no matter how handsome his face and no matter how sexy his warm palm felt against her hip.

It was all she could do not to groan out loud.

Jackson moved and she drew a sharp breath.

"Hey, there," he whispered lazily in her ear, obviously only half-awake himself, obviously believing she was someone else.

Then he kissed her hairline.

"I—" she began. But he kissed her mouth. And his arms closed around her.

Before she could gather her wits enough to struggle, the

kiss deepened. A fog of desire invaded her brain, blocking out the real world.

He was one fantastic kisser.

His hand slipped down to cradle her rear. Pulling her to him, his thigh wedged between her legs. Arousal fanned through her, hot, heavy and demanding.

She had to make this stop. She so had to shut this down.

"Jackson," she gasped. "I'm not your date. Wake up. It's me. It's Crista."

"I know." He drew back, gazing at her with dark eyes. "I know who you are."

"But—"

"And you know I'm not Gerhard."

She wanted to deny it. She desperately wanted to lie and say that, of course, she'd thought he was her fiancé. What kind of a woman would behave like this with another man? But she couldn't bring herself to lie, not with his sharp stare only inches away, and their hearts beating together.

"I was confused," she replied instead.

He answered with a knowing smile. "Confused about what?"

"Who you were."

He shook his head. "Crista, Crista. There's no real harm in not being truthful with me. But I hope you're being honest with yourself."

"I am being honest with myself."

"You claim you love Gerhard, yet you're in bed with a stranger."

"I'm not in bed with you." She immediately realized how ridiculous the protest sounded. "I mean, not like that. We didn't… We aren't…"

He glanced down between them, noting without words that they were in each other's arms.

She quickly pulled back, wriggling to get away from him.

A pained expression came over his face. "Uh, Crista, don't—"

"What?" Had she hurt him?

"The way you're moving."

And then she realized what he meant. They might be mostly dressed, but she could feel every nuance of his body. Raw arousal coursed through her all over again. She felt her face heat in embarrassment.

"However you have to move. Whatever you have to do. Just do it," she demanded hoarsely.

He cupped a palm under her knee, lifting her leg from his body and lowering it to the mattress. But his hand lingered on her thigh.

She closed her eyes, steeling herself. What was the matter with her? "Please," she whispered.

"You're going to have to be more specific." His husky voice amped up her arousal.

"We can't." But she wanted to. She couldn't remember ever wanting a man so intensely.

"We won't," he said and gathered her into his arms all over again.

She didn't protest. Instead, she reveled in the security of his strength. Yesterday had been a nightmare of fear, disappointment and confusion. It had all been Jackson's fault. But for some reason that didn't seem to matter. He was still a comfort.

"Mac will be here in a few minutes," said Jackson.

"Is he going to swim?" she asked.

"I docked the boat last night after you fell asleep."

"You mean I could have escaped?"

"You'd have had to get out of my bed without waking me. But, yeah, you could have escaped."

Crista heaved a sigh. "This isn't normal. My reaction to these circumstances," she said.

"It doesn't feel normal to me, either." He scooted to the end of the bed and stood.

"Jackson?" A man's voice came from beyond the small hatch door.

She jerked back, quickly adjusting her jersey over her thighs.

"We'll be right out," Jackson called. To Crista he said, "You didn't do anything wrong."

"Yes, I did."

He was right about one thing—she should stop lying to herself. She might love Vern, but she'd just kissed the heck out of another man. Maybe fear and stress had combined to mess with her hormones, but what she'd done was absolutely, fundamentally wrong.

Jackson slipped a T-shirt over his head. "Forget about it."

"Are you really going to let me go?" She forced herself to think ahead.

If she could make a phone call, Vern would pick her up. She didn't have her purse, no cash or credit cards or her phone. She'd have to change back into her ruined wedding dress before he got here. Man, was he going to be ticked off about that.

"After you look at what Mac found, yes, I'll let you go."

"Good." She struggled to summon her pride as she rose from the bed.

She followed Jackson up a couple of steps and ducked through the hatch to the main cabin. There she found Mac, a tall, bulky man with broad shoulders, who had a heavy brow and a military hairstyle. Jackson looked almost urbane by comparison. The contrast to Vern would be startling.

"Mac," said Jackson with a nod. "This is Crista Corday."

"Miss Corday," said Mac. His voice was as rugged as his appearance.

"I think we can skip the formality of *Miss* Corday, since you participated in my kidnapping."

"Mac had nothing to do with it," said Jackson.

"He does now," said Crista. She was telling Vern and the police everything. Jackson and his gang of men should not be allowed to roam free.

"I've got the photos," said Mac, stepping forward.

He held out his phone so she could see the screen. The first one was taken on a busy street. It was Vern, all right. Despite herself, she leaned in for a closer look.

He walking side by side with a woman, presumably Gracie. They seemed to be exiting a restaurant. The woman was tall, with a bouncy mane of wavy blond hair. Her makeup was dark—thick, sparkly liner and a coating of mascara emphasizing her bright blue eyes. Her lips were full, her bust fuller, and her waist was tiny beneath a white tank top. The next photo showed that she wore blue leather pants and black, spike–heeled ankle boots.

"They're just walking," said Crista.

She'd allow that Gracie didn't look like your average commercial real estate client, but looks could be deceiving. One thing was for certain, she was a polar opposite of Crista.

"Wait for it," said Mac. He scrolled to another picture.

Here they were holding hands, then cuddling, then Vern was kissing her on the cheek. It was persuasive, but Crista had played with Photoshop software. She knew that pictures could be manipulated. There were also other logical problems.

"Why would he marry me?" she asked.

Gracie was drop-dead, glamour-magazine, movie star–material stunning.

"What do you mean?" asked Jackson, looking genuinely puzzled.

Crista gestured to the photo. "If there's really something romantic between them, why not marry her? She's a knock-out. And he seems to like her well enough." The two were smiling and laughing in most of the pictures.

Both Mac and Jackson were frowning at her.

"What?" she asked, looking from one to the other.

"He wants you," said Jackson.

"Which means he isn't involved with her," Crista said slowly, making sure he could understand each of her words.

"Look at this," said Mac.

He produced a picture where the two were embracing. It was nighttime, and they were dressed differently. It had been taken in front of a hotel.

"April of this year," said Mac. "It's date stamped."

Crista would admit it looked damning. *If* she believed it hadn't been altered, and *if* she believed the date stamp was valid. She was about to mount another argument in Vern's defense when she realized this was her ticket home. If Jackson thought he'd won, he'd let her go.

She gave herself a moment. She had to deliver this just right.

She took the phone from Mac's hand. She stared at the photo for a long time, pretending she was having an emotional reaction. Then she gripped the back of the bench seat that curved around the table. She lowered herself down.

"It looks bad," she said in a hushed voice.

"It is what it seems," said Mac. "I also have some emails."

Crista gave what she hoped was a shaky nod, still play-acting. As if emails weren't even easier to fake than photos.

She made a show of swallowing, then she set the phone down on the table. She tried to put a catch into her voice. "I guess you were right."

"I wish I could say I was sorry."

"Don't you start lying."

To her surprise, Jackson put a comforting hand on her shoulder. "He doesn't deserve you, Crista."

"I never would have believed it," she said. "He cheated on me. He's been cheating on me the entire time. I'm such an idiot." For good measure, she pulled off her engagement ring and squeezed it in her palm.

"It's not your fault," said Jackson.

She didn't answer. If she had Jackson convinced that she'd bought his story, it was time to shut up and let it lay. It was also time to get herself out of here and back to Vern. He had to be frantic. She'd reassure him she was safe, and then she'd tell him everything. Jackson and Mac deserved whatever they got.

"Will you let me go now?" she asked.

She could feel their hesitation, but she was afraid to look up and gauge their expressions. Had she seemed too easy to convince? She hoped she hadn't overplayed her hand.

It was Jackson who spoke. "I'll drive you home."

Four

Crista had asked to be taken directly to the Gerhard mansion. Fine by Jackson. He looked forward to seeing the expression on Gerhard's face when she dumped him.

Once she'd broken it off, he'd report the success to Colin and Trent and go back to his regular life. At least, he ought to go directly back to his regular life. But he wasn't sure how quickly he wanted to walk away from her.

He found himself strongly attracted to her. But more than that, he was intrigued by her. She couldn't have had an easy life. Her father was a criminal like Jackson's. Yet, here she was, running a business, hobnobbing with Chicago's elite, almost marrying into one of the city's wealthy families.

She was obviously a survivor, and from what he'd seen of her, she was tough. She'd jumped into the bay, for goodness' sake, planning to swim for it to save herself. Okay, so maybe she was more reckless than clever. But the same could be said of him.

"Their driveway is the next right," she said.

She'd redressed in her damp wedding gown, which was now stark against the black leather seat of the Rush Investigations SUV. Jackson appreciated the drama of the visual—breaking your engagement in a ruined wedding gown—but he doubted she was thinking about that. She likely just wanted to get it over with. He couldn't say he blamed her.

He swung the vehicle into the driveway, passing a pair of brick pillars. They had lions on them. Who did that? Then he steered around the curves of a smooth, oak-lined driveway.

A quarter mile in, the mansion came into view. It was a rambling stone building, three stories high, sprawling in the center of manicured lawns and colorful flower beds. The driveway circled around a cherub fountain. Water spurted from three statues, foaming into a concrete pond.

"I should tell you," said Crista, her tone flat as he pulled to the curb and stopped in front of the grand staircase. "Just so you understand what's coming next." She angled her body to look at him. "I didn't buy it, not for a second."

He shifted to Park, his brain sorting through her words for some kind of logic. "Buy what?"

"The fake pictures of Vern. I'm sure the fake emails were just as creative."

Jackson saw where she was going, and it was nowhere good.

"I'm turning you in," she continued. Then she made a show of shoving her engagement ring back on her finger. "I'm telling them everything, and I'm not sorry." She swung open the door.

He lunged for her, but the shoulder belt brought him up short.

"Don't do that." He tore off his seat belt and leaped out of the car.

She moved fast considering her spiky shoes and the awkward dress. He rushed to catch up with her.

"They weren't fake," he said, kicking himself for having been taken in like a chump. He'd let his mind get ahead of events instead of properly focusing on the moment. He'd let himself project forward, debating whether to offer her comfort right away or wait a decent period of time before asking her out on a date. Distracted by his attraction to her, he'd missed the signs that she was lying.

At the top of the stairs, she rounded on him. "You think I don't know my own fiancé."

"Crista—"

"No."

"Crista?" A man spoke from the doorway behind her.

"Vern," she gasped in obvious relief, a smile coming over her face.

Her steps quickened, and her arms went out, obviously expecting to rush into his embrace.

But Gerhard was frowning.

"Wait until I tell—" she began.

"What were you *thinking*?" he demanded on a roar. "And who is this guy?"

She stopped short. Jackson's instincts told him to leave. His duty was done. He was risking arrest and imprisonment by staying.

"Your dress is absolutely ruined." Gerhard gestured to the soiled and torn gown.

And your fiancée is safe, Jackson wanted to shout out.

Crista drew back, obviously shocked by the reaction. "I—"

"Do you have any idea what Mother has been through?" asked Gerhard.

Jackson waited for Crista to say that she'd been through something, too. He took a reflexive step away, telling himself to make good his escape before she could tell the story of how she'd been kidnapped and held against her will.

"Mother was *mortified*," said Vern. "She nearly collapsed right there in the church. She hasn't come out of her room all morning. The doctor's with her now."

"It wasn't my—"

"Three hundred people," Gerhard interjected. "The mayor was there, for God's sake. And who is this?" Vern's beady black eyes peered in Jackson's direction.

Jackson stepped forward, his sense of justice winning over his instinct for self-preservation. "Do you even want to know what happened?"

"It doesn't take a rocket scientist to figure out what *happened*." Gerhard's attention turned back to Crista. "She got scared. Well, sweetheart, we all get scared. But you don't get scared two minutes before the wedding. You do it the day before, and we talk about it. Or do you do it the day after, and we get a divorce."

Crista's posture sagged. "A divorce?"

Jackson took her elbow, afraid she might go down.

"You'd want a divorce?" she asked Gerhard in a tone of amazement.

"There are ways to do this," he answered. "And this wasn't one of them."

"That's not what happened," said Jackson.

She grasped the hand on her elbow. "Don't."

"Crista didn't get scared," he said. "I'm the one who stopped your wedding."

"Let it go," she whispered. "Don't do it."

He glanced down at her expression. It looked like she'd changed her mind and didn't want him to confess. Well, that worked fine for him.

"Just who are you?" Gerhard demanded again.

"I'm an old boyfriend," he said, crafting a story on the fly. "I showed up at the church. I begged her for another chance. I told her she couldn't marry you until we'd talked."

Vern's jaw went tight. There was anger in his expression, but it didn't exactly look like jealousy. "You ran off with another man?"

"I insisted," said Jackson, bracing for Vern to come at him. If the tables had been turned and Crista had been his bride, Jackson would have taken the man's head off.

Gerhard didn't move. His attention swung back to Crista. "What do you expect me to do?"

"I don't care what you do," she said, determination returning to her tone.

Gerhard took a step forward, and Jackson stepped between them. "Don't touch her."

"Crista, get in the house."

Jackson countered. "Crista, get in the car."

"Mother and Father are owed an explanation," said Gerhard.

"You weren't even interested in her explanation," said Jackson.

"Get out of my way."

"No." Jackson had no intention of leaving Crista behind.

"This is none of your business."

"I'm making it my business."

Gerhard took another step.

Jackson braced his feet apart, willing the guy to take a swing. All he needed was an excuse, and he'd wipe the cocky confidence right off Gerhard's face.

"Please don't hurt him," said Crista.

"Okay," said Jackson.

"She's talking to me," said Gerhard.

Jackson couldn't help but smile at that.

"Please," Crista repeated.

"Get in the car," said Jackson.

"You won't?" she asked.

"I won't," he promised.

"We are not done talking," Gerhard called to Crista.

"Oh, yes, you are." Jackson listened to her footfalls until she slammed the passenger door.

"Make any move, and I'll defend myself," he told Gerhard.

Gerhard didn't look like he was going to try.

Still, Jackson kept an eye over his shoulder as he returned to the vehicle. Half of him hoped Gerhard would come at him. But the smarter half just wanted to get Crista away from this family.

He planted himself behind the wheel.

"Just take me home," she said, yanking her dress into place around her legs.

He started the engine and put the vehicle into gear. "You got it."

They drove away in silence.

It was five minutes before she spoke up. "You know where you're going?"

"I know where you live." He checked his rearview mirror again, making a mental note of vehicles in the block behind them.

"How do you know that?"

"Mac gave me the address."

"Mac, who was investigating Vern."

"Yes."

Both a blue sedan and a silver sports car stayed with them at the left turn.

"This is creepy, you know that?"

"I don't imagine it's any fun," said Jackson.

"You've destroyed my life."

He gave her a quick glance. "You're blaming me?"

"Of course I'm blaming you."

"Because your fiancé's a jerk?"

"Because you ruined my wedding." She paused for a moment. "It's not your fault my fiancé's a jerk."

Jackson almost smiled as he checked the side mirror.

"I don't know what that was all about," she said.

"Maybe he's not the man you thought he was."

"He's never done that before. He's very even tempered, patient, trusting."

"Is this the first time you've seen him under stress?" Jackson was no expert, but he couldn't help but think it was a bad idea to marry someone before you'd had a few knock-down, drag-out fights. A person needed to know who fought dirty and who fought clean.

"Vern's family is important to him," she said.

"You're defending that behavior?"

"He didn't cheat on me."

"He did. But that's not the point. He didn't trust you. He didn't ask you what happened to you. All he cared about was Mommy and Daddy."

Crista didn't seem to have an answer for that.

"We're being tailed," said Jackson.

"What?"

"Tailed. There's a car following us. What does Gerhard drive?"

She twisted her head to look behind them.

"Three back," said Jackson. "The blue Lexus."

"It could be."

"You're not sure?" Who didn't recognize her own boyfriend's car?

"The Gerhards own a lot of cars. I think they have one like that."

"The tribulations of the rich and famous," Jackson drawled.

"Ha-ha."

"What do you want me to do?"

"I sure don't want to talk to him again."

"Good." Jackson was even more concerned than before. Trent had claimed Gerhard's real interest was a diamond mine. And Gerhard sure hadn't acted like a man afraid for his fiancée's safety. He'd acted like a man with something to lose—maybe money to lose. And now, instead of stewing in his own self-righteousness or giving her a chance to cool down, he was having her followed. This did not strike Jackson as a typical lovers' quarrel.

"Want me to lose the tail?" he asked Crista.

"Can you?"

He smiled to himself. "I can."

"Yes. Do it."

"Seat belt tight?"

"Yes."

"Hang on."

Seeing an intersection coming up, Jackson barged his way across two lanes, moving hard to the left, cutting the yellow way too close and turning onto Crestlake. From there, he took a quick right, drove until they were behind a high-rise and pulled into an underground parking lot.

Crista held on as they bounced over the speed bumps.

He knew the lot had six exits. He took Ray Street, covered

three blocks to the park and pulled onto the scenic drive. It would take them over the bridge to the interstate. After that, they could get as far away as she wanted.

"Did we lose him?" she asked, stretching to look out the rear window.

"We lost him."

They'd probably lost him at the underground, but Jackson had wanted to be certain.

She tugged at the stiff neckline of her dress in obvious frustration, pulling it away from her cleavage. "I need some time to think."

She looked tired and uncomfortable.

"Is there somewhere you want to go?"

"Not to my place, that's for sure."

"You could probably use a change of clothes."

She tugged at the fabric again. "I'm getting a rash."

"We'll take the next exit, find someplace to buy you a pair of blue jeans."

"That would be a relief. I'd also like to throw this thing in a Dumpster."

Jackson liked that idea very much. "I can make that happen."

"Thanks."

"No problem."

"I mean, really. Thanks, Jackson. You didn't have to do any of this."

He shrugged. "I fix problems. You have a problem."

"You don't even know me."

He felt like he did know her, at least a little bit. And what he knew he admired. "I don't have to know you to help you."

"Most people don't think like that."

"Lucky for you, you ran into me."

Her brows rose in skepticism. "Ran into you?"

"I see an exit." He didn't want to get into any of the details of his investigation. He sure didn't want her asking again about who'd sent him.

She watched out the side window. "Looks like a shopping mall down there."

"That'll do. You want to go in and try things on or just tell me your size?"

She looked down at the billow of her skirt. "I'll wait in the car, if you don't mind."

"Worried you might attract attention?"

"The last thing I need is for someone to snap a picture and post it to social media."

He nodded in approval. He was relieved she understood she was being chased by the Gerhards. "Good call. I can see you going viral in that outfit."

She heaved a deep sigh, her cleavage catching his attention so that he nearly swerved off the exit ramp.

"I was supposed to be on a yacht today," she said. "Bobbing around the Mediterranean, sipping chardonnay, reading a celebrity magazine and working on my tan."

Mentally, Jackson added that she would have been under Gerhard's control, at the mercy of his family. His suspicions were pinging in earnest. Gerhard wasn't a worried groom. He was a thwarted con artist.

If everything Trent said was true, the Gerhards were organized and ruthless, and they sure wouldn't want to lose track of Crista. She'd been gone for twenty-four hours. There was every chance Daddy Gerhard had people on her apartment by now. They might even be watching her credit cards and bank account.

Jackson was definitely looking into the diamond mine, its size and location, its ownership, and how it could possibly have made it onto Gerhard's radar.

Crista was going to pay Jackson back for everything just as soon as she had access to her bank account.

For now, explaining that he was invoking his regular precautions, he'd put her up at the Fountain Lake Family Hotel, leaving his own credit card information with the front desk to cover her expenses. The place was full of boisterous vacationers, and it seemed like an easy place for her to blend in with the crowd. Her room was spacious, with a king-size bed, comfy sitting area, a small kitchenette and a furnished balcony overlooking the pool and a minigolf course.

She'd tried right away to call Ellie, her best friend and maid of honor, but she only got through to voice mail. It seemed far too complicated to leave a message, so she'd decided to try again later. Instead, she liberated a soft drink from the minibar and wandered onto the balcony.

The temperature was in the high eighties, but a breeze was blowing across the lake, cooling the air. She was on the third floor, so it was easy to make out the activity below, kids splashing in the pool, teenagers lounging on striped towels. There was a young couple in one of the gazebos. He was slathering suntan lotion on her bare back, playfully untying her bathing suit top.

The woman batted awkwardly at his hand to get him to stop. When he kissed the back of her neck and looped his arms around her, Crista quickly looked away. They were probably on their honeymoon.

She eased onto a rattan lounger, wishing she had a bathing suit herself. She wondered if Jackson's credit card was connected to the hotel shops as well as the restaurants. It would definitely be nice to take a swim, and since her three jewelry stores, Cristal Creations, were doing very well, it would be a simple matter to pay back every dime.

Afterward, she'd order something from the room service menu. She'd get a bottle of wine. Maybe gaze at the moon and the stars out here and get some perspective on life. She toyed with her engagement ring, twisting it around and around as she went over the confrontation with Vern.

He'd been quick to assume she'd run away. She was disappointed, of course, but she wasn't sure she could blame him completely for his reaction. It must have seemed like the most logical conclusion at the time. Though it would have been nice if he'd asked her what happened.

The worst part was that he'd suggested divorce. As if getting married and then quickly divorcing was preferable to ruining a party. He'd worried about the embarrassment to his family. He'd worried about her dress, his mother and the mayor. The only thing he didn't seem to worry about was Crista.

In the thick of the argument, it had seemed clear that it was over. But now other memories were crowding in, good memories. Did one ugly argument obliterate everything they'd shared?

On the other hand, it had been an alarming experience, seeing a side of Vern she'd never known existed. She found herself questioning the photographs, no longer completely convinced they were fake.

She took another swig of the soda. Maybe she should call him. Or maybe she should confront him in person again, flat-out ask him if he was cheating.

Maybe he'd tell her the truth. Or maybe he wouldn't. Or maybe she'd never know.

She came to her feet.

Ellie was her next phone call, not Vern. Ellie would have good advice. She always did.

Crista pulled open the glass door, entering the cool of the air-conditioned room. She was chilled for a moment, but then it felt good. She sat down on the bed and dialed nine for an outside line. Then she punched in Ellie's number.

Before the line connected, there was a knock on the door.

Crista didn't need towels or mints or anything else from a housekeeper. But she also didn't want a hotel employee barging in on her conversation. She quickly replaced the telephone receiver and went to the peephole.

It was Jackson.

Puzzled, she drew open the door. "Did you forget something?"

"Yes." He walked in without an invitation.

"Come on in," she muttered, letting the door swing shut behind him.

"I forget to tell you not to phone anyone from the room."

"Not even Ellie?"

"Who's Ellie?"

"My maid of honor."

"Not even Ellie. The Gerhards have a big security staff. They'll be covering all the angles."

"Their security staff looks after the Gerhard buildings. They don't care about Vern's love life."

"They care about what Manfred Gerhard tells them to care about."

"You're paranoid. And anyway, I thought you'd left."

"I'm not in a hurry."

"You don't have a job to get back to? A life that requires your attention?"

Instead of answering, he sat himself down on the small blue sofa. "What do you know about the Borezone Mine?"

"What's the Borezone Mine?"

"Have you ever heard of it?"

"No. Was it in the news?"

"No."

She waited for him to elaborate, but he didn't. She wondered if he was making small talk, delaying his departure for some reason. She tried to figure out why he might want to hang around.

"I won't go wild with your credit card, if that's what's got you worried," she tried.

"I'm not worried about my credit card."

"Are you worried I'll make a phone call? Because it won't matter if I do."

"Ha. Now I'm definitely worried you'll make a phone call."

"I need to talk to Ellie." What she needed was a girlfriend to listen to her fears about Vern.

"Talk to me instead."

She took the armchair cornerwise from where he sat. "Sure. I'll just sit here and bare my soul to the strange man who kidnapped me from my wedding. I can't see any downside to that."

"Good. Go ahead. Bare away."

"You're not funny."

Surely he could understand that this was traumatic for her.

"You absolutely need to call Ellie?" he asked.

"Yes."

With a shake of his head and an expression that looked like disgust, he pulled out his phone. But instead of handing it over, he dialed a number.

"What's Ellie's last name?"

"Sharpley. Why?"

"It's me," he said into the phone. "Crista needs to make a call. Ellie Sharpley." He paused, sliding an exasperated glance her way. "I know. It's a girl thing."

Crista squared her shoulders. "A girl thing?"

"Let me know when it's done."

"A *girl* thing?" she repeated.

He pocketed his phone. "What would you call it?"

"A conversation. A human thing."

"You'll be able to have one in about an hour. Are you hungry? You must be hungry."

"You must have people you talk things over with. Friends? Relationships?"

"I'm pretty independent."

"No girlfriend?" For some reason, she'd assumed he was single. But there was no reason for that assumption. Well, other than the way he'd kissed her. But he had only kissed her.

"No girlfriend," he said.

She was relieved. No, she wasn't relieved. She didn't care. His love life was nothing to her.

"Hungry?" he repeated.

She was hungry. She'd barely eaten yesterday. She'd been watching calories for weeks now, wanting a svelte silhouette in the formfitting dress. In retrospect, her waist size was the least of her worries. But now there wasn't a reason in the world not to indulge in pizza or pasta, or maybe some chocolate cake.

"I'm starving," she said. "I know it's only lunchtime, but any chance we can get a martini?"

"There's a patio café overlooking the back nine."

"Sold."

A martini wouldn't help her make a better decision, but it would relax her in the short term. Relaxed was good. She could use some relaxing.

She came to her feet. "It feels strange not to take a purse."

He rose with her, and they made their way toward the door. "You want to buy a purse?"

"I've got nothing to put in it."

"We could buy you a comb or some lipstick or something."

She couldn't help but appreciate his offer. She also couldn't help wondering about his motivation. It was strange that he was still here, stranger still that he was putting out an effort to help her.

She exited into the hallway. "Are you feeling guilty?"

He checked to see that the door had locked behind them, then fell into step beside her. "For what?"

"For destroying my life."

"Gerhard was the one trying to destroy your life."

"Jury's still out on that."

Sure, Vern had been a jerk back at the mansion. But to be fair, he'd been under stress. She could only imagine his parents' reaction to the disappearance of the bride. Poor Vern had been alone with them, bearing the brunt of their displeasure for nearly twenty-four hours.

Jackson pressed the elevator button. "The pictures are real, Crista."

"Can you prove it?"

"I'm sure we can. Let me look into the options for that."

They stepped onto the elevator, and it descended.

"We've been together for nearly a year," she said.

It wasn't a whirlwind. And it sure didn't make sense for Vern to marry her if he was involved with someone else.

"People aren't always honest, Crista."

She found herself glancing up at his expression. "Are you honest?"

He met her gaze. "I try to be."

"Well, there's a nonanswer."

"In my profession, I can't always tell everybody everything."

"So you only lie professionally."

There was a trace of amusement in his tone. "Not personally, and not recreationally."

"Interesting moral framework."

The doors slid open.

She started to move, but Jackson's hand shot out to block her, coming to rest on her stomach.

"What?"

He pulled her to one side then stabbed his finger hard on the close door button.

"What are you doing?"

The doors slid shut.

"You must have talked to someone since we've been here."

"No. Well, I tried to phone Ellie. But I got her voice mail. I didn't even leave a message."

Jackson swore as he punched twelve, the top floor.

"What?"

"Vern. He's in the lobby with a couple of guys."

"No way."

"I just saw him."

The elevator rose.

"How is that possible?"

"It's possible because your phone call connected and revealed the hotel number."

"I didn't call Vern." Wasn't Jackson listening? "I called Ellie."

"And Vern knows Ellie's number. They were monitoring her phone."

"That's ridiculous."

"You have a better explanation for him showing up here?"

She didn't. In fact, she was baffled. And she was starting to feel frightened.

"What do we do on the twelfth floor?" she asked as the numbers pinged higher.

"My room," he said.

It seemed every second threw her for another loop. "You have a room? Why would you need a room?"

"To sleep in. You can have a drink there."

"But why would you sleep here?"

"So I can drive you back to the city when you're ready."

"I thought I was going to take a bus back to the city."

"If we'd gone with that plan, Gerhard would already have you."

"Jackson, *what* is going on?"

It took him a moment to answer. He seemed to be weighing his words. "Vern Gerhard wants you back, and he has a lot of money to spend accomplishing that."

"I *was* coming back." She thought about that statement. "I mean, I might go back. I didn't break up with him. I still have his ring."

The doors opened on twelve.

"You should break up with him." Jackson gestured for her to exit first. "Take a right."

"I don't know for sure that he's done anything wrong. Well, except react badly to me wrecking a hundred-thousand-dollar wedding."

"You didn't wreck it."

"You did."

"True enough," he said.

He inserted a key card into a set of double doors at the end of the hallway.

"You don't seem to care."

"I don't care about Gerhard's money, that's for sure."

Crista stepped over the threshold, taken aback by the very well-appointed suite. She gazed around. "Used to traveling in style?"

"I thought I might need a room for a meeting."

"With me?" They needed a meeting?

"With Mac and some of the other guys. They'll be here later."

She digested that statement. "There's something you're not telling me."

"There are hundreds of things I'm not telling you."

The door swung shut behind him and he crossed to a wet bar.

"Those pictures of Vern are fake, aren't they? Is this extortion? Am I still kidnapped? Was this about money all along?"

"We have beer, wine or highballs. And I'm going to order room service. If you're set on a martini, I can have them bring one."

"That's not an answer."

It occurred to her that she might be a whole lot safer with Vern. The suite door was right behind her. She could be out of it before Jackson caught her. Could she make it to the elevator, or would he drag her back kicking and screaming?

"You're not kidnapped," he told her, exasperation clear in his tone. "I left you alone in your room for an hour."

She eased a bit closer to the double doors. "You could have been standing guard outside my door."

"I wasn't. I'm a whole lot more interested in food right now that I am in any of Gerhard's moves. You're free to leave. You've been free to leave since this morning. I took you back to their mansion. You could have stayed there."

He was right about that. She could have walked inside the mansion where the Gerhard family, not to mention a few security guards who would have been waiting. There wouldn't have been a thing Jackson could do to stop her.

She wasn't being held against her will.

"I'll take a glass of merlot," she told him. "And I'd kill for a mushroom and sausage pizza."

He smiled at that. "Coming up."

"We told Vern your name this morning," she felt compelled to point out. "He can probably find your room number."

"What makes you think I'm registered under my own name?" He uncorked a bottle of wine and gestured to a living room furniture grouping. "Probably better to stay off the patio."

"You've got me worried there's a sniper out there," she joked.

He crossed the room with two glasses of wine, setting them on opposite ends of a coffee table. "I'd say a long lens rather than a rifle. But it's healthy to be cautious."

"Of the whole family now?" She took one end of the sofa and lifted her wine.

"The whole family," said Jackson, giving her a mock toast.

She drank, anticipating the hit of alcohol and glad of it. These had been the strangest days of her life. She wished the insanity was over, but it seemed there was more to come.

Five

To Jackson's surprise, Mac wasn't alone.

There was a twentysomething woman in the hotel hallway beside him. She had short, dark hair, blue eyes, a pert nose and set of distracting, full red lips.

In five years working together, Jackson had never seen his security agent behave so unprofessionally. "You brought a *date*?"

"I'm not his date," the woman stated with a sniff of disgust.

"Ellie?" Crista called out from behind him.

"She's not my date," said Mac.

Ellie pushed past Jackson.

"She's the maid of honor," said Mac.

"And you brought her *here*?" Jackson wasn't sure if that made it better or worse.

The two women laughed and embraced.

"I've been frantic," said Ellie, her voice high. "We thought you were hurt or dead."

"She was frantic." Mac's tone was dry as he shut the door behind himself.

"Did anybody see you two come in?" asked Jackson, wondering if Mac had lost his mind. "Gerhard is definitely going to recognize the maid of honor."

"I saw him down there," said Mac. "And I saw his guys. They didn't see us."

"You're positive?"

"I'm positive."

Jackson felt a bit better.

"It's been crazy," said Crista, pulling Ellie toward the sofa. "Jackson hauled me away from the church. Then we were on a boat. I jumped off. When I finally got home, Vern was an absolute jerk about it."

"That doesn't sound like Vern."

"I *know*. He's acting weird. I'm so confused about this whole thing. But tell me what happened after I left."

As Ellie began to talk, Jackson returned his attention to Mac. "I thought you were giving her a burner phone."

"That was my plan."

"Didn't work out for you?"

Hearing Ellie's earnest tone and the pace of her speech, Jackson thought he could understand why.

"Not so much," said Mac.

"Talked you into the ground."

"Something like that."

"Drink?" asked Jackson.

"A beer if you've got it."

The two men moved to the wet bar, and Mac perched himself on one of the stools.

Jackson lowered his voice, glancing to the sofa where Crista and Ellie were engrossed in conversation. "I'm buying Trent's story now. This isn't just about a runaway bride."

Mac nodded. "Those guys in the lobby look way too serious for that."

Jackson twisted the tops off two bottles of beer. "We need to look into the diamond mine."

"Norway's already on it."

Jackson was glad to hear that. "Anything jumping out at him?"

"The Borezone Mine has been around forever. Trent Corday originally bought it twenty years ago at a bargain price. He nearly lost it for noncompliance with the claim. Then he did lose a huge chunk of it, apparently on a gambling debt."

"To who?"

"That's not exactly clear. Shell companies are hiding behind holding companies. But we've confirmed he put his remaining shares in his daughter's name."

"A moment of mental clarity?" Jackson speculated, thinking it was possible Trent recognized his own incompetence with money.

"Or a moment of making amends. It sounds like he was in and out of her life over the years, never provided much in the way of monetary or any other kind of support. He wasn't exactly father of the year. On the other hand, the mine wasn't worth much at the time."

"And now?"

Trent had said there'd been a recent discovery, but that could mean a lot of things.

"Depends on who you talk to," said Mac. "A numbered Cayman Islands company currently owns the majority. We haven't been able to trace the principals behind it, but they hired an exploration company that made the latest discovery. They're hyping it as a hundred million resource, talking about going public with a share offering."

"Could all be a scam—pump the share price and dump the stock on unsuspecting investors."

"Most likely," said Mac. "But we'll keep looking."

Jackson tipped back his beer and took a drink. For Crista's sake, he hoped it was a scam. The last thing she needed was a multimillion-dollar stake in a diamond mine and a group of shady characters out to exploit her.

"Is that how Gerhard found out?" he asked. "Through the exploration company's hype?"

Mac frowned. "That's the strange part. The timing doesn't add up. The hype started six months ago. Gerhard's been with Crista for a year."

"So he found out some other way."

"Or the wedding had nothing to do with the diamond mine."

"I don't believe that for a second," said Jackson. "Those guys in the lobby tell me there's lots of money at stake."

Mac nodded. Jackson's attention switched to Crista. Vern Gerhard had targeted her for the money. Jackson was certain of it. But nothing pointed to how Gerhard found out about the mine. Jackson was missing a piece, maybe more than one. There was definitely something he didn't know, and it seemed likely it was something that could hurt Crista.

"What's next?" asked Mac.

"Norway stays on the mine." Jackson formulated an initial plan in his mind. "You take Gerhard—especially look for any link between his family and that Cayman Islands company. I'll take another look at Trent. There might be more to this story than he's let on."

"Can do," said Mac. "One question."

"What's that?"

"Has someone actually hired us for this job? I mean, besides the two convicts making eight dollars a day?"

"I can't do a favor for my father?" Jackson acknowledged that things had gone beyond the few hours of time he'd planned to spend looking into Gerhard.

"You can, but you don't." Mac looked pointedly at Crista who was smiling at Ellie. "If she wasn't a bona fide ten, would you be dedicating so many resources for free?"

"We'll never know," said Jackson. "She's not going to stop being a ten, and my curiosity's going now."

"Lots of pretty women in the world."

Jackson saw Mac's gaze shift from Crista to Ellie.

"Not a lot of diamond mines."

Mac snorted a laugh. "You don't care about a diamond mine."

"True." But Jackson was finding that he did care about Crista.

It didn't make sense, but he did care. Sure, she was beautiful. And she was in some kind of trouble. And Gerhard didn't deserve to be within a mile of her. But something else was drawing him in.

The closest he could come was that her circumstances were similar to his. She'd lost her mother as a young adult, and her father was in prison. It might be as simple as that.

They were kindred spirits. She wasn't as tough as him. She wasn't as capable of taking care of herself, and he was offended that the Gerhards had targeted her.

Ellie suddenly twisted and spoke up. "Any danger in ordering room service?"

Jackson was reminded that he and Crista were practically starving.

"None at all," he said, straightening away from the bar.

"I was all set for pizza," said Crista, seeming rather cheerful under the circumstances.

"I'm in," said Ellie.

"And chocolate cake," said Crista. "Do you think they'd have chocolate cake?"

Jackson moved to the phone on a side table. "I'll ask."

"It's not like I have to fit into that dress anymore," Crista said to Ellie.

"You can always get something a size bigger," Ellie returned on a laugh.

"I'm not going to eat that much cake."

Jackson paused with the phone in his hand, not liking where she seemed to be going.

"What do you mean?" he asked Crista.

"I mean one piece will be enough."

"I'll take one, too," said Ellie.

"Get a round," said Mac.

"You're talking about getting another wedding dress," Jackson said. "Why would you need another wedding dress?"

Crista looked back at him. "The last one got ruined, remember?"

Both Ellie and Mac disappeared from his vision as it tunneled to Crista. "But you're not getting married anymore."

"Maybe not."

"Maybe?"

"I know he was a jerk back there. But it was a stressful

situation. He had to cope with his parents and all those dignitaries. It had to be incredibly embarrassing."

Jackson took a step toward her, hardly able to believe her words. "You're defending him?"

"It wasn't his finest moment, but—"

"He's messing around on you. He's *been* messing around on you for months."

"We don't know that."

Jackson jabbed his thumb in Mac's direction. "Mac is completely trustworthy."

"I don't know Mac. I never met Mac until today."

"I know Mac."

"Well, *I* don't know you."

"You'd actually give that jerk a second chance?" Did Jackson need to rethink his involvement in all this?

"We can validate the photos," said Mac.

"Why should we do that?" Jackson demanded, annoyance getting the better of him.

"To give Crista peace of mind."

"She doesn't want to believe us, that's her problem. In fact, she can head down to the lobby right now if she thinks Gerhard is so trustworthy."

"Hang on." Ellie came to her feet. "I'm not a Vern fan. But I'd be—"

"What do you mean, you're not a Vern fan?" Crista sat up straight, obviously shocked by the statement.

Ellie seemed to realize what she'd said. Her expression turned guilty.

"Explain," said Crista. "You said you liked him."

"I do. Well, you know, sort of."

"Sort of?"

"There are things about him that I like."

Jackson eased back, waiting to see where the conversation would lead. He was relieved by Ellie's support.

"He's always generous," said Ellie. "And he's always happy."

Jackson couldn't help thinking she hadn't seen his behavior this morning.

"Maybe too happy," she continued. "It's a bit unnatural, don't you think?"

"You're criticizing him for being happy?" Crista was clearly confused by Ellie's attitude.

"There's something about him that's too polished," said Ellie. "My radar sometimes kicks in. Like, he's saying and doing all the right things, but the sincerity's not there in his eyes."

Jackson was beginning to like Ellie.

Crista came to her feet. "Why didn't you say something before now?"

"You seemed so happy," said Ellie in an apologetic tone. "I wanted it to all be true. But now…"

"You've changed your mind because of some pictures? Pictures obtained by a stranger who is obviously willing to break the law, and who has something, some scheme, going on that we don't understand."

"A scheme?" Now Jackson was offended.

Mac stepped in. "I think I'll go ahead and order. Pizza and chocolate cake?"

"All I'm saying," Ellie said, gesturing with both hands as if she was appealing for calm, "is why not verify the photos? What could it hurt?"

Crista didn't seem to have an answer for that.

Quite frankly, neither did Jackson. He knew the photos were authentic. And once Crista knew it, too, she'd start to trust him. He realized he wanted that. He wanted it too much for comfort.

That wasn't good. It wasn't good at all. His instincts with her could lead him into all sorts of trouble.

Crista savored a final bite of the moist chocolate cake decorated with decadent swirls of buttercream icing.

"I bet this was better than the wedding cake," said Ellie, licking her fork.

The two women had moved outside onto the hotel suite balcony. Now that darkness had fallen, Jackson deemed it safe to sit there. He'd pointed out that someone with night-vision binoculars in a neighboring building might still be able to make them out. But he'd admitted the likelihood of that was low.

"I wonder what they did with the wedding cake," Crista mused.

"Not to mention the crab puffs. And what about the ice sculpture?"

"I suppose they could keep it in the freezer."

"For the next wedding with a precious gems theme?"

"It was unique." Crista thought back to the geometric base and the embedded colored stones.

"I thought Mrs. Gerhard was going to have an aneurysm," said Ellie. "She turned all kinds of mottled red. Manfred was bellowing orders. Security guards were rushing all over the building, out on the sidewalk. Man, I wish I'd had my cell phone to take some video."

"Have you checked social media?" Crista hated to think it, but it seemed likely somebody had taken pictures. Vern would be mortified at having the world believe he was left at the altar.

"It'll be all over town by now," said Ellie. "The bachelorettes of Chicago will either be laughing at him or hauling out their push-up bras."

Having been with Vern for a year, Crista knew how many women out there were vying for his attention. He'd been devoted to Crista, but it was clear his ego appreciated the attention from others. He'd hate the thought of becoming a joke.

A clanging sound suddenly blasted through the air.

Both women jumped up, clasping their hands over their ears.

"What on earth?" asked Ellie.

Jackson immediately bolted through the balcony door-way. He grasped Crista and pulled her back into the suite. Mac was there, too, ushering Ellie inside.

"It's the fire alarm," said Jackson.

"Gerhard," said Mac.

"Trying to flush us out."

"He wouldn't do that," said Crista.

Vern was restrained and circumspect, not to mention law-abiding. He'd never pull a false fire alarm.

"He did do that," Jackson said with conviction. "And we're not going anywhere."

"You can't know it was him," she protested.

Sirens sounded in the distance.

"There are at least six fire exits in the building," said Mac.

Jackson was glancing around. "He must have brought in more men to watch them all."

"This is ridiculous," said Crista.

Jackson and Mac exchanged some kind of a knowing look.

"Uh, guys," Ellie broke in as she gaped through the open balcony door. "I see smoke out there."

That got everybody's attention. Crista wrinkled her nose, realizing she could smell it, too.

Ellie pointed. "That's definitely smoke."

Mac was outside like a shot.

"Flames," he called over his shoulder. "Fifth floor." He came back inside. "And the third floor in the other wing."

"He set two fires?" Jackson asked, half to himself.

"What now?" asked Mac.

"We *leave the building*," said Crista. Like there was any question about it.

"You take Ellie," said Jackson. "Leave through the back."

"Will do," said Mac.

"Crista and I will go through the lobby. It'll be easier to hide in the crowd than anything else."

"Good luck," said Mac. He looked to Ellie. "Let's go."

She grabbed her purse from the coffee table and gave Crista a quick hug. "I'll call you."

Crista felt like she'd been swept up in someone else's life. "Vern didn't light the building on fire."

"I hope not," said Ellie, pulling away. But her expression said she thought it was possible.

"But—" Before Crista could finish the sentence, Ellie was out the suite door with Mac.

Jackson grabbed two hand towels and doused them with water. Then he handed her one.

"Hold this over your face and cough. Pretend the smoke is bothering you."

"This is crazy."

Jackson put a hand on her back and propelled her toward the door. "He's determined."

"I was going to call him tomorrow."

"I guess he didn't want to wait."

"This is a coincidence."

"It doesn't matter," said Jackson.

"Of course it matters. You've accused my fiancé of arson." She fell silent as they left the suite.

There were other people in the hall, some quiet, some speculating about the smell of smoke, all making their way toward the staircase.

"You might want to start referring to him as your ex-fiancé," Jackson said in her ear.

"I'm still wearing his ring."

"You can take it off anytime."

He reached over her head to grab the top of the door, holding it open as she walked through then handing it off to the man behind him.

"Protocol says I have to give it back to him," said Crista as they started down.

"So, you *are* giving it back."

"I don't know. I don't know what to do. I don't even know what to think. Do I have to answer this very moment?"

"No. You just have to stick with me. And quit defending him. And put the towel over your face. We're almost there."

The lobby door was held open by successive people exiting. When they cleared the stairwell, Jackson pulled her close beside him.

"See that family?" He pointed to a man, woman and three kids out front of them.

"Yes."

"Go walk with them. Talk to the wife if you can. Gerhard's looking for a couple, so you want to pretend you're with them."

Crista had to admit, it made sense. At least it made as much sense as anything else that was going on today.

"Okay," she agreed.

"Don't look for me. I'll keep you in sight. Just go where they go, and I'll meet you outside."

She nodded.

"Now cough."

She coughed, and he gave her a little shove of encouragement. She quickened her pace and came up beside the woman who was holding the hand of the young girl.

"Did you smell the smoke?" Crista asked her.

"We were on the fifth floor," said the woman, looking stricken. "The fire was right down the hall. We had to leave everything behind."

"Bunny," said the little girl, tears in her eyes.

"Bunny will be fine," the woman whispered, voice breaking.

Crista's heart went out to the frightened girl, and she gave her a squeeze on the shoulder. "The firemen are here. They'll use their hoses to put the fire out."

A dozen firefighters in helmets and gold-colored coveralls strode across the crowded lobby.

"Will Bunny get wet?" asked the girl.

"Bunny might get wet," said Crista. "But it'll be like a bath. Is Bunny a boy or a girl?"

"A girl."

"Does she like baths?"

"I dunno."

"Do you like baths?"

The girl nodded. "Uh-huh. I get bubbles and baby froggy. He hops on the water and spits out his mouth."

"Thank you," the woman whispered in Crista's ear, obviously grateful for the distraction.

They'd come to the front doors, which were wide-open, the night air blowing inside. The drive was a maze of fire trucks, ambulances and police vehicles. Lights flashed and uniformed people rushed past. Some were on radios, some hauling hoses and other gear, and some were aiding people to stretchers or ambulances.

The hotel guests had obviously come out of the building in whatever they were wearing. Few had sweaters, many were barefoot. They looked confused and disoriented.

For a moment, Crista could only stand and stare.

She suddenly felt an arm go firmly around her shoulders. She glanced up, afraid it was Vern. But it was Jackson.

"Let's go," he said, moving her forward.

"This is awful."

"It's under control."

"He didn't do this. He couldn't have done this." The fire had to be an accident.

"I'm not going to argue with you," said Jackson, increasing their pace around the end of a fire truck.

"You don't believe me."

"That's the least of our worries. We need to get out of here. We'll never get my car from the valet, but there's a rental place a couple of blocks away."

"I should just talk to him." The sooner she got it over with, the better.

"No, you shouldn't." Taking her hand, Jackson set an angled course across the front lawn.

She had to struggle to keep up to his pace. "I'll have to talk to him eventually."

"You can phone him."

"I thought I wasn't allowed to phone anyone."

"Don't twist my words."

She came to a halt, yanking her hand from his, annoyed by his high-handed attitude. This was still her life.

"I'm not twisting your words."

He stopped, let his shoulders drop and turned back. "You'll be able to call him, just not tonight, and not on a phone with a GPS."

"I really don't mind talking to him."

She wasn't excited about it. But the prospect of a conversation didn't need to get blown all out of proportion, either. She'd sit Vern down, look him in the eyes and tell him...

She realized she didn't exactly know what she'd tell him. Would she hand him back the ring and break it off completely? Would she ask for an explanation of his behavior? Would she demand to know if he'd been faithful?

"Crista?" Jackson interrupted.

She looked up.

"You need to sleep on this."

She recognized that he was right. That had been her first instinct. She should get a good night's sleep. It would all be clearer in the morning.

She nodded her agreement and started to walk.

To her surprise, he took her hand again. But this time his touch was gentle, and he slowed his pace.

She knew she shouldn't be grateful. He was her kidnapper, not her friend, and there were all kinds of reasons she shouldn't trust him. But she found she did trust him. And at the moment, there was no denying that she also felt gratitude.

"Thank you," she said.

He glanced down as they walked. "For what this time?"

"Rescuing me from a burning building, I guess."

He grinned at that. "Sure. No problem. I had to follow you down quite a few stairs, but that's the kind of guy I am."

"What kind?" she asked, her curiosity piqued.

"What kind what?"

"What kind of guy are you? Tell me. What would you be doing right now if you weren't with me?"

"Probably working another case."

"At ten o'clock on a Sunday night?"

"Mine isn't a nine-to-five job."

She supposed it wasn't. He'd already said he didn't have a girlfriend. "What about family and friends?"

"No family. Friends, sure. But there's not a lot of time in my life for anything serious."

"When was your last girlfriend?"

"It's been a while."

She waited, but he didn't elaborate.

"You know all about my love life," she said.

"That's a professional interest."

"Well, fair's fair. Spill."

"You see that sign?" He pointed down the street.

"The car rental place?" The familiar sign flashed orange and white on the next corner.

"That's where we're going."

"Don't think you can change the subject that easily."

"It was two years ago," he said, increasing their pace. "Her name was Melanie. She's an accountant."

In Crista's mind, it didn't fit. "You dated an accountant?"

"Something wrong with that?"

"Are you making that up?"

"Why would I make it up? You don't think I can get dates?"

The suggestion was preposterous. Jackson was a smart, successful, sexy guy. He could get all the dates he wanted.

"An accountant doesn't sound very exciting," she said as they hustled across a side street to the rental car parking lot.

"Maybe I wasn't looking for exciting."

"Jackson, everything about you says you're looking for exciting."

"How so?"

"Take this weekend. You kidnapped a bride, told one of Chicago's wealthiest men to stuff it, and there's a hotel on fire behind you."

"That doesn't mean I like it." He pulled open the glass door.

"You love it." She grinned over her shoulder as she walked past him and into the small lobby.

There was a single clerk at the counter who was already helping another customer. Crista entered the roped lineup area and followed the pattern to the front, where she stopped to wait.

Jackson came up behind her.

"See that sign on the wall?" he mumbled in her ear. "Behind the counter, with the purple letters."

"That says Weekly Rates?"

"That's the one. Do not turn your head. But look at the reflection in it."

She squinted, seeing a slightly distorted black SUV.

"That's Vern," said Jackson.

She started to look behind her.

"Don't turn," he reminded her sharply.

She held still. "Are you sure?"

"Absolutely. I want you to turn and look at me. Do *not* glance out the front window. Just ask me a question."

She turned. "What question."

"Any question."

"Tell me some more about Melanie the accountant."

"Maybe later. See that hallway at the end of the counter?" He pointed.

She looked. "Yes."

"There's a ladies' room down there. I want you to walk down the hall, go past the ladies' room and out the back door.

You can cut through the alley to Greenway. Hail a cab on Greenway. I'll be out in a minute."

"We're not renting a car?"

"We're not renting a car."

"If I talk to him, it'll stop all this madness."

Before she could move, Jackson blocked her way. "It's not safe."

"I'm going to tell him to back off and that we can have a proper conversation tomorrow. He didn't light any hotel on fire."

"If the fire wasn't a ruse to flush you out, why was he waiting to follow us?"

She opened her mouth. But then she realized it was a reasonable question. Vern had to have been outside in the SUV in order to find her.

"It could have been a coincidence," she ventured. It was possible he just happened to see them leaving the hotel.

"Could have been," said Jackson, surprising her with his lack of argument.

It seemed he'd finally decided to leave it up to her. He was letting her assess the situation and make up her own mind. It was heartening but somehow unsettling.

For some reason, without Jackson's pressure, she found herself looking at both sides. She thought her way through each scenario and decided to play it safe.

"Down the hallway?" she confirmed. "Hail a cab?"

"Good decision. I'll be right behind you."

She resisted the urge to look closer at the SUV. Instead, she sauntered toward the hallway, trying to look like she was visiting the ladies' room. She didn't know how to transmit that message by the way she walked, but she did her best.

As Jackson had said, there was an exit door out the back. It led to a small parking area surrounded on two sides by a cinder-block wall. There was a Dumpster in the corner, and several vehicles in various states of disrepair.

She walked cautiously across the uneven pavement,

coming to an alleyway where she could see a driveway between two buildings that presumably led to Greenway Street.
Avoiding the puddles, she hurried down the dark driveway
to the lights of the busy street.

It took a few minutes to catch a cab. By then Jackson had
appeared, sliding into the seat beside her.

"Anthony's Bar and Grill at Baffin and Pine."

"We're going for a drink?" she asked, surprised he'd suggest something so mundane, though not really knowing what
to expect.

"I'm thirsty, aren't you?" he asked.

She wasn't yet ready to brush past their cloak-and-dagger
escape. "How did you know there was a back entrance to the
rental place? And how did you know where it would lead?"

"I didn't pick the Fountain Lake Hotel by accident."

"You've been here before," she said, glancing back while
the taxi pulled away from the curb, comprehension dawn-
ing. "You've done this before."

"I've eluded a few people in the past." His easy smile
told her he knew what he was doing. He actually seemed to
be enjoying himself.

"You think this is fun." She'd meant it to sound like an
accusation, but it didn't. Truth was, she found his confidence reassuring.

"I think you're fun."

"I'm not having fun. My life is falling apart around my
ears, so I am not having any fun at all."

"You'll like Anthony's," he said.

What she'd like was her life back. And she almost said
so. But just as quickly she realized it wasn't true. She had
no life to get back, at least not a real life, not an honest life.
There was nowhere for her to go but forward.

"I'd like a strong drink," she said instead.

"Coming up," said Jackson as the taxi picked up speed.

"This is the strangest day of my life," she muttered.

"I wouldn't trade mine for the world." His tone was unmistakably intimate, bringing with it a wave of desire that heated her chest.

She wanted to look at him, meet his warm eyes, drink in his tender smile. But she didn't dare. No matter what Vern had said or done, she had no right to feel this way about Jackson.

She fixed her gaze on the traffic, bright headlights whizzing past in a rush. She didn't know Jackson. She didn't like Jackson. By this time tomorrow, he'd be nothing but a fading memory.

Six

Despite the humble name, Jackson knew Anthony's was an upscale restaurant housed in a redbrick colonial mansion. Owned by a close friend of his, its high ceilings, ornate woodwork and sweeping staircase gave an ambience of grandeur and a distinct sensation of class.

Tonight, he hadn't been interested in the restaurant, but in the historic B and B rooms on the third floor of the building. He knew he could count on Anthony not to ask questions or keep a record of their stay. It was the closest thing Jackson had to a safe house.

Their room had a four-poster king-size bed, a stone fireplace and sloped cedarwood ceilings. There was a small dining table in a bay window alcove, and a sofa that the housekeeper had already converted into a second bed.

Crista had opted to take a shower, while Jackson had stretched out on top of the sofa bed, a news station playing on the television and his laptop open to the photos of Vern and Gracie. The resolution on the pictures was high, so it was going to be easy to show they hadn't been altered.

His browsing was interrupted when the bathroom door opened and Crista appeared. She was dressed in a fluffy white robe, drying her auburn hair with a towel.

"That shouldn't be all it takes to make me feel better," she said in a cheerful voice as she padded toward him on bare feet. "But it does." She plunked down on the opposite side of the sofa. "I'm refreshed."

Just her appearance made him feel better. She was easy on the eyes and entertaining for his mind. He realized the only thing he liked better than looking at her was listening to her.

"I don't know if this will make you feel better or worse."
It certainly made him feel better.

He slid the laptop across the sofa bed toward her. "I've
zoomed way in on the pixels. Stare all you want. The pictures haven't been altered."

She shifted on the bed and moved the computer to her lap.

"The dates and times are registered in the metadata," he
said, anticipating that as an argument from Crista, or possibly a defense later from Vern.

"He's hugging her." Crista zoomed the view out.

"And here he's kissing her." Jackson reached over to scroll
to the next photo.

"It doesn't look brotherly," she said.

"It's not."

"This is hard to accept."

A female television announcer caught Jackson's attention.

"The Fountain Lake Family Hotel was the scene of a
structure fire this evening," she said. "Over three hundred
guests were evacuated, while engines and firefighters were
deployed from three stations in the area. Fire Chief Brandon
Dorsey says that arson has not been ruled out."

The view switched to a reporter at the front of the hotel.
He was interviewing a guest against a backdrop of fire engines and police cars.

"Is that code to say that it was arson?" asked Crista, her
gaze on the TV screen.

"It means it's early in the investigation," Jackson answered honestly. But it was arson. He knew it was arson.

"Tell me the truth," she said, her gaze not wavering.

"He did it to get us both out of the building. He wants you
back. But I'm guessing he also wants you far away from me."

She turned her head, looking surprised. "Why?"

"You have a mirror, right?"

She lifted her hand and self-consciously touched her
damp hair. It was tousled and incredibly sexy.

"He thinks I'm your ex-boyfriend," Jackson reminded her.

"I forgot about that."

"He doesn't want the competition. I don't blame him."

If Crista were his, Jackson couldn't honestly say he wouldn't set a building on fire.

Looking unsettled, she turned her attention back to the laptop.

"I'm going to have to end it, aren't I?" Her tone was regretful.

Yes! "That's up to you."

She looked back at Jackson. "I don't think I can marry a man who's been unfaithful."

"I wouldn't."

"Wouldn't marry him, or wouldn't be unfaithful?"

"Neither." He felt himself ease closer to her. It was impossible to keep his true thoughts at bay. "Any man who cheats on you is out of his ever-lovin' mind."

She gave a ghost of a smile. "That's very nice of you to say."

"It's the truth."

Silence descended between them.

He wanted to kiss her now. He desperately wanted to kiss her luscious red lips. The robe's lapels revealed the barest hint of cleavage. Her skin was dewy from the hot shower. And he was all but lost in her jewel-green eyes.

"I guess I'll talk to him tomorrow," she said.

And say what? The question was so loud inside his head that for a moment he was afraid he'd shouted it.

"Unless there's some miraculous explanation," she continued, "I'm handing back his ring and walking out of his life."

"There'll be no miracle."

She nodded, twisting the diamond around her finger.

He gently but firmly took her hands. Then he slipped the ring off her finger, reaching up to place it on the table behind the sofa.

"But—" She looked like she wanted to retrieve it.

"Afraid it might get lost?" He lifted his brows.

"It's valuable."

"It's worthless. You're valuable."

His face was inches from hers. A small lift of his hand, and it was on her hip. Then he slipped it to the base of her spine. He leaned in.

"Jackson." His name was a warning.

"It's a kiss," he said. "It's only a kiss. We've done it before."

He gave her a second to protest.

She didn't.

So he brought his lips to hers.

They were as sweet as he'd remembered, hot and tantalizing. Desire immediately registered in his brain. Passion lit his hormones, while every cell jumped to attention. His hand tightened at the small of her back, drawing her against him.

He stretched his legs out, stretched hers out, and delved into the depths of her mouth. She kissed him in return. Her slight body sank into the soft bed.

Her robe gaped loose, and he knew it would take nothing, nothing at all to untie the sash, spread it wide, feast his gaze on her gorgeous body. But he held back, kissing her neck.

"Jackson," she groaned.

He loved the sound of his name coming from her lips. Her tone breathless.

"We should stop," she said. There was a no-nonsense edge to her voice now and he told himself to pull away.

"I'm sorry," she whispered, sounding as if she was.

"My fault," he readily admitted.

"I keep kissing you back."

"I keep starting it."

"These are extraordinary circumstances."

He summoned the strength and put a few inches between them. His eyes focused on her. "You are so unbelievably beautiful."

That got him a smile, and he felt it resonate through his heart.

"How does he do it?" He had to ask. "How does a man have you and even look at another woman?"

Her smile grew a little wider. "I can ask him."

"You should ask him. Better yet, I'll ask him. No, I'll tell him. I'll tell him he lost you, and I got you, and I'm sure going to keep you."

"While you're still pretending to be my ex-boyfriend?" she joked.

"What?" It took a second for her meaning to register. "Yeah. Right. That's what I meant."

She sobered. "And then this will all be over."

Jackson wasn't ready to say that.

"I should be sad," she said. "I mean, I am sad. But I should be sadder. I should be devastated. This mess is my life."

"You'll be fine," he said.

What he wanted to say was that they'd fix her life. He'd help her fix her life. He was sticking around until everything was settled, until he understood exactly what was going on with the diamond mine and anything else that might hurt her. He was staying until she was completely safe from Vern and all of the Gerhards.

They slept apart. And in the morning, Jackson drove her to the shopping mall parking lot three miles from the Gerhard mansion.

"I'd rather come with you," he said as he passed under the colorful flags that marked the main entrance.

"He's not going to try anything with Ellie there." Crista was nervous, but she wasn't afraid.

Vern would have no choice but to accept her decision. He wasn't going to be happy. But surely at some level he would understand. His relationship with Gracie Stolt might not be a full-blown affair, but they were obviously intimate. Vern needed to do as much thinking about his future as Crista did about her own.

"He lit a hotel on fire." There was a hard edge to Jackson's voice.

"They haven't proven that yet."

"I have all the proof I need. There they are." Jackson angled the SUV across a block of empty parking spots toward a silver sedan.

"Whose car?" she asked, knowing Ellie drove a blue hatchback.

"It's a company car. Mac wouldn't risk taking Ellie back to her apartment for her car."

"They've been together all night."

"It's possible," said Jackson. "I didn't ask."

"So, you didn't assign him to protect her." For the hundredth time, Crista tried to figure out Jackson's motivation for sticking around.

"I didn't need to."

She tried to read his expression.

He seemed to sense her stare and glanced over. "What?"

"Why are you still here?"

He didn't miss a beat. "You've heard of pro bono?"

"That's for lawyers."

"It's for private detectives, too."

She didn't buy it, but let the issue drop for now.

He pulled into the spot close to Mac and Ellie.

"You know you don't have to break it off in person," he said.

"I want to do it in person. I want to see his expression. And it's the only way it'll feel final to me."

"I can come with you."

"Ellie's coming with me. Vern likes Ellie."

Jackson clenched his jaw. After a moment's pause he passed a phone to Crista. "I'm speed dial one. Call me if anything looks suspicious."

"Suspicious how?" She couldn't help but think he was

used to higher stakes and higher drama than this. She was breaking off an engagement, not spying on a foreign government.

"You'll know it if it happens," he said.

She doubted that.

He picked up the phone, waiting for her to take it in her hand. "If I don't hear from you fifteen minutes after you're inside, we're coming in."

"How will you know when we're inside?" She conjured up a silly picture of him on a hillside in camo and green face paint with a set of high-powered binoculars.

"That phone has a very accurate GPS."

"You can't storm the mansion, Jackson. They'll arrest you."

"They can try," he said.

"You're nuts."

"I'm cautious."

She reached for the car door handle. "We're going to be fine."

He put a hand on her shoulder, stopping her from exiting. "*Anything* suspicious."

"Yes. Sure." She would try. "I assume Ellie is getting the same instructions?"

"Mac's cautious, too."

"Okay." Crista took a deep breath and swung open the door.

The butterflies in her stomach had ramped up, and she told herself not to let Jackson rattle her. Yes, Vern was going to be angry. And if Manfred or Delores were there, the conversation would definitely get even more uncomfortable. But it would be over in a matter of minutes, and this would all be behind her.

As she rose to her feet, she wiggled the diamond ring that was back on her finger, checking to make sure it was loose. When she was nervous, her hands tended to swell.

The last thing she needed was to break things off and try to give back the ring only to have it get stuck on her finger.

Mac stepped out of the passenger seat of the silver sedan. He nodded a greeting to Crista and held the door open for her.

"Thanks," she said as she slid onto the seat.

Mac leaned down, looking in the open door, his gaze on Ellie. "Don't forget."

"I won't," said Ellie.

He gave another serious nod then pushed the door firmly shut.

"Don't forget what?" Crista couldn't help but ask.

Ellie gave a sheepish shrug. "I'm not sure. The list was pretty long."

Crista couldn't help but smile. "Do you have a secret agent phone, too?"

Ellie tapped the front pocket of her white shorts. "I'm packin'."

"They've got us hooked up to GPS."

"I heard."

"And Jackson said we have fifteen minutes before they storm the place."

Ellie shifted the car into Drive and glanced back to Jackson's car as she pulled through the parking spot. "Who *are* those guys?"

"I can't figure it out. I keep asking him why he's doing all this, and I keep getting vague answers."

"He's hot," Ellie said with a glance in her rearview mirror.

"Jackson?"

"Mac."

That got Crista's attention. "Really?"

"You didn't notice?"

"To be honest, I wasn't paying much attention to Mac."

"I was." Ellie headed for the traffic light at the parking lot exit. "But forget about me. Do you know what you're going to say?"

"I think so," said Crista. She'd gone over a dozen different versions in her mind. "Did Mac tell you about the pictures?"

"He showed them to me."

"He kept copies." Crista wasn't surprised.

"They weren't fakes," said Ellie.

"I know."

They completed a left turn. Traffic was light, so they'd be at the mansion in about five minutes.

"Vern is pond scum," said Ellie.

"I keep going back and forth between coming out guns a-blazing or calmly asking for an explanation."

"Could there be any reasonable explanation?"

"Not that I can think of."

"I say guns a-blazing."

"Either way, the result will be the same."

"But not as satisfying. He needs to know he hurt you."

"He knows that."

"I doubt he cares."

Crista hoped he cared. The Vern she'd fallen in love with would care.

"Hit him with both barrels," said Ellie. "If you don't, you'll be sorry later."

"I have to at least ask him what happened," Crista countered. As far-fetched as it seemed, Vern might have something to say in his own defense.

"We're here," Ellie stated unnecessarily as they turned in to the long driveway. "Are you sure you're ready?"

"I just want to get it over with."

"Then let's do it." Ellie stepped on the accelerator and took them briskly up the drive.

She wheeled through the turnaround and brought the car to the curb. A security guard immediately came out through the front door, obviously intent on asking their business. But when he saw Crista, he stopped short.

She got out of the car, pausing while Ellie came around the front bumper.

"I'm here to see Vern," she stated, holding her head high.

"Of course, ma'am," said the guard, his expression inscrutable.

For the first time ever, Crista found herself wondering if the guard was armed. Were all of the security staff armed? It seemed likely they would be. She couldn't even imagine what would happen if Jackson and Mac showed up.

"We need to hurry," she said to Ellie, trotting up the stairs. The phone in her purse suddenly felt heavy.

She'd been in the mansion foyer hundreds of times, and she knew it well. It was octagonal with a polished marble floor and ornate pillars. A set of double doors led to a grand hallway and the curving staircase. The hallway was a popular place for guests at the Gerhards' cocktail parties to gather and view the family art collection.

It had never struck her as intimidating before, but rather opulent and grand. It was fit for industrialists, celebrities, even royalty.

She heard footsteps descending the staircase. But she stayed put, not wanting to venture far from the exit. It was Jackson's fault she was feeling so skittish. All his talk of speed-dialing him or him and Mac storming the place had her pointlessly nervous.

Vern appeared in the doorway, coming to an abrupt halt when he spotted Ellie. He frowned, and his nostrils flared.

"I asked Ellie to come," said Crista.

"I would have come anyway," said Ellie.

"She can wait here," said Vern.

"I'm staying here, too," said Crista. "This won't take long."

His brows rose with obvious incredulity. "What do you mean, it won't take long? We have our entire future to discuss."

"I've seen the pictures, Vern."

"What pictures?"

"You and Gracie."

He paled a shade, and she knew all the accusations were true.

But then he regrouped and went on the attack. "Do you mean Gracie Stolt? I told you, she's a client."

"She's your mistress." Then Crista rethought the terminology. "I mean, she would have been your mistress. If we'd gotten married."

Vern moved closer, his tone hardening. "You don't know what you're talking about."

"I've seen—"

"I don't care what you think you've seen. It was obviously a misrepresentation of something. And what about you? Shacked up in a hotel with your ex-boyfriend."

"I wanted to be alone."

"Alone with *him*."

"He was *helping* me."

Ellie reached out to touch her arm. "Crista."

Vern stepped closer still. "You're going to deny you slept with him?"

Crista opened her mouth to say yes. But then she thought better of the impulse. She had no need to defend herself. "I'm here to give you back your ring."

Vern shook his head. "I won't accept it. We can work this out."

"You just accused me of infidelity."

"You accused me first."

Anger rose inside her, and she jabbed her index finger in his direction. "You *did it*." Then she pointed at her own chest. "I *didn't*."

She grasped her ring and pulled. But as she'd feared, her fingers had swollen, and it didn't want to come off. She pulled harder. "But I'm going to," she said defiantly as she tugged. "I'm going out there right now to sleep with Jackson."

The ring suddenly popped off. It slipped from her fingers and bounced across the floor.

They both watched it come to rest on a white tile.

"You're not going to do that," said Vern.

"You can't stop me."

He reached out to grasp her arm, holding her fast.

"Let me go!" She struggled against his grip, but he wouldn't let her go.

In her peripheral vision, she saw Ellie retrieve her phone.

"Don't," she cried out to Ellie.

Jackson and Mac would only make things worse. They could make things a whole lot worse.

"Do I need to call the police?" Ellie asked Vern in a cold voice.

Vern glared daggers at her but then released Crista's arm.

"We need to talk," he said to Crista, schooling his expression, clearing the anger from his face, entreaty coming into his eyes.

"Not today," said Crista. She just wanted to get out of here.

"Not ever," said Ellie.

"You don't understand," said Vern, his expression now projecting hurt and confusion.

He suddenly looked so familiar. Her heart remembered everything they'd had together, and it ached for the loss.

"I have to go," she said, mortified to hear a catch in her own voice. She needed to be stronger than that.

Then Ellie's arm was around her, urging her to the door, picking up the tempo until they were outside. She immediately saw Jackson's SUV pulling up the drive.

"Are fifteen minutes up?" asked Crista, her voice now shaky. It had seemed more like three.

"You're going to sleep with Jackson?" Ellie asked as they hustled down the steps.

"I was bluffing."

"He didn't tell you about the hot mike?"

"The what?"

Mac hopped out of the passenger seat and jumped in to drive the silver sedan.

"Jackson and Mac could hear every word we said. Me threatening to call the police was the secret signal."

"There was a secret signal?"

"Go," said Ellie, pushing her toward the open door of the SUV.

Afraid to look back, Crista hopped inside and slammed the door shut. Jackson peeled away.

Jackson was relieved to have her back. He was stupidly giddy with relief. When Ellie had uttered the distress phrase, his heart had lodged in his throat. A dozen dire scenarios flashed through his mind as they sped up the driveway.

"You're okay?" He felt the need to confirm as they made it to the road.

"Ticked off," she said, fastening her seat belt.

"He didn't hurt you?"

"He grabbed me, but he let me go. His ring's on the floor of the foyer."

"Good," said Jackson with clipped satisfaction.

She shifted in the seat, angling toward him. "You bugged Ellie's phone?"

"We thought it was safest."

"Why didn't you tell me?"

"It would have made you nervous."

"I was already nervous."

"Yes." That had been his point. "It was bad enough for you without knowing you had a bigger audience."

"That was underhanded."

"Maybe."

"It was a personal conversation."

"You mean the part where you announced your intention to sleep with me?"

"That was a bluff."

It was too tempting not to tease her. "I'm very disappointed to hear that."

She moaned in obvious embarrassment. "Mac heard me say it, didn't he?"

"He did."

"Call him. Tell him I was joking."

"He knows you were joking."

"No, he doesn't. He's going to think there's something going on between us."

Jackson glanced her way. "There's not?"

"No, there's not. Well, not that. Not…" She seemed to search for words. "I just broke up with my fiancé. I was minutes from getting married on Saturday." The pitch of her voice rose. "There can't be anything between us."

"Okay," said Jackson. "I'll play along."

"I'm not asking you to *play along*. I'm asking you to accept the reality of the situation."

"Consider it accepted."

She watched him with obvious suspicion. "Tell Mac."

"Are you serious?"

"Yes." She crossed her arms over her chest. "I was illegally recorded, and I want the record set straight."

Jackson struggled not to laugh. "Sure." He fished his phone out of his pocket, pressing the speed dial and putting it on hands-free. He dropped it on the seat between them.

"What's up?" came Mac's answer over the small speaker.

"Crista wants me to set the record straight."

"What record?" asked Mac.

"She's not going to sleep with me."

There was a silence. "Uh, okay." Mac paused. When he spoke again, Jackson detected a trace of laughter. "Why not?"

"Because I barely know him," said Crista.

"He's a great guy," said Mac. "And I hear he's a good lover."

"From who?" asked Crista without missing a beat.

Jackson caught her gaze and mouthed the word *really*?

"Was it Melanie?" she asked, obviously thinking she'd turned the tables on him.

"He told you about Melanie?"

Jackson scooped up the phone and switched it to his ear. "That's enough about me."

Mac chuckled.

"Chicken," said Crista.

"We're not taking her home," Jackson said to Mac.

"Her being me?" asked Crista.

"Where to?" asked Mac.

"The office, for a start."

"Your office?" asked Crista.

"You want to look at the other thing?" asked Mac.

"That's right," Jackson said to Mac. "My office," he said to Crista.

"I should go home," she said. "This is over, and I'm tired of running. I'm pretty sure he got the message."

"He tried to physically restrain you."

"That was for her, right?" asked Mac.

"So did you," Crista pointed out.

Jackson didn't have an argument for that. He could also understand why Crista would think it was perfectly safe for her to go home. As far as she was concerned, she'd just broken up with a cheating fiancé. She didn't know about the diamond mine, so she didn't realize Gerhard and his family might have millions, possibly tens of millions of reasons to drag her back.

"I'm driving," he pointed out.

The car was going wherever he steered it. She could like it or not.

She crossed her arms and gave a huff. "If I'm going to your office, then Ellie's coming, too."

It didn't seem necessary, but he had no particular objection.

"She's my chaperone," Crista continued. "I don't want there to be gossip about you and me."

"You're obsessing," he said.

"Tell them," said Crista.

"Crista wants Ellie to come with us."

Mac's voice went muffled. "You want to stick with us?" He paused. "She's in," he said to Jackson. "I've got a couple stops to make. But we'll meet you there."

It took thirty minutes to arrive at Rush Investigations. The offices were housed in a converted warehouse a few blocks off the river. It wasn't the swankiest address, but the brick building was solid, and it gave them the space they needed to store vehicles and equipment.

They drove into the fenced compound and then accessed the garage area with the automatic door opener, parking the SUV in one of a dozen marked spots along the back wall. There was a customer entrance on the main floor of the attached four-story office tower. It was nicely decorated with comfortable seating, coffee service and a receptionist. But Jackson rarely went through there.

"Wow," said Crista as she stepped out of the vehicle onto the concrete floor. She craned her neck to look up at the open twenty-foot ceiling, where steel beams crossed fluorescent lighting, and her voice echoed in the mostly empty space. "This is huge."

Work benches stretched along two of the walls, while the east end was given over to shelving and a small electronics shop. An orange corrugated-metal staircase led from the shelving area to the second floor of the office tower.

"There are times we need the room," he said. "But most of the vehicles are out right now. This way." He gestured to the staircase.

"Just how big is your company?" she asked as they walked.

"It's grown since I started it."

"Grown from what to what?"

"To somewhere around three hundred people."

"There's that much going on in Chicago that needs investigating?"

He couldn't help a grin. "They're not all investigators. But, yes, there's easily that much going on. We also have offices in Boston, New York and Philly."

She stopped walking and turned to look at him, eyes narrowing, her forehead furrowing. "I know I keep asking this, but what exactly are you doing?"

"A lot of missing-persons cases," he answered. "Security and protection. Infidelity's always a big one. And then there's the corporate—"

"I mean with me. What are you doing with me?"

He knew he had to tell her about the mine eventually. But he didn't want her to bolt. He knew she'd be gone like a shot if she had any inkling her father was involved.

"For the moment," he said, meeting her eyes and telling the truth, "I'm trying to give you some time and distance to consider your options."

"I did. And I just took an option. I broke it off."

"You have other options. Life options. Like what you do next?"

"Why do you care?"

"Because I've spent most of the last three days with you."

She was clearly growing exasperated with his talking in circles. "Which leads me right back to *why*. Who sent you? Why did you even come looking for me in the first place?"

"Somebody asked me a question about Vern. I got curious. And then, I guess, I just kept wading deeper and deeper."

"I'm not your concern."

He found himself moving closer, lowering his voice, increasing the intimacy of the conversation. "I spend quite a lot of time wading around in things that don't concern me."

She shook her head at what she clearly thought was his foolishness. "You normally get paid to do that."

He gave a shrug. "There's getting paid, and there's getting paid."

"One more time, Jackson, I'm not going to sleep with you." She couldn't quite keep a poker face.

He took one of her hands in his and stepped closer still. "You sure?"

She didn't answer.

He brushed his lips gently against hers. "You sure?"

"Not really. I'm not sure of anything anymore."

"You can be sure of this."

He kissed her.

She instantly responded, and he wrapped her tight in his arms, slanting his lips and deepening the kiss.

She molded against him, her softness perfect against the planes of his body. Desire rushed through him, and he gave it free rein.

They'd stop in a moment. Of course they would stop. But for now nothing in the world mattered except the sweetness of Crista's lips, the scent of her hair, and the feel of her hand in his.

Something banged in the reaches of the warehouse.

He silently cursed. Then he ended the kiss, drawing away and smoothing the pad of his thumb over her cheek.

"We have got to get alone at some point," he said.

"I'm so confused." Her green eyes were clouded and slightly unfocused.

"I'm not."

"This isn't simple."

He understood that it wasn't simple for her. It was perfectly simple for him. He desired her, and she definitely seemed attracted to him. It was pretty straightforward and a very nice starting point.

"We don't have to figure it out right away," he said.

She gave her head a small shake. "I'm not about to start dating anyone."

He didn't see why not, but he didn't want to pressure her. "Okay."

"I'm going to work out my life."

"Where do you want to start?" He'd be happy to help.

"Cristal Creations. I need to start with the company."

"How so?" He knew she had three locations around Chicago. From what he understood, they were doing well.

"They're my jewelry designs, and I manage the stores. But I don't actually own them."

Jackson wasn't happy to hear that. "Gerhard owns them," he guessed.

"It's what made sense at the time. The family already owned the shopping malls where we opened."

"So he got his hooks into your business." Jackson shook his head with disgust.

"It was only fair," said Crista. "He paid for it all. I wouldn't even have a business without Vern. He backed my designs when no one else would. Did you see the episode of *Investors Unlimited*?"

"*Investors Unlimited*?"

"It's a TV show. The kind where you pitch an idea and the rich people on the panel can offer to invest. I was on it a year ago."

"You pitched your jewelry designs to Vern?"

"Not to Vern. He wasn't on the show. Nobody there was interested. But after it aired, Vern watched it and contacted me."

"He made you an offer?"

"That's how we met."

The timing was right, and Jackson knew the information could be significant. The show might be a catalyst for the whole scam.

His needed to find out who knew what about Crista and when.

Seven

Crista and Ellie were alone in a big, comfortable room that Jackson had called the lounge. On the fourth floor of the Rush Investigations building, it had banks of windows on two sides, soft chairs and sofa groupings scattered around, along with a kitchen area stocked with snacks and drinks. Easy-listening music filled the background from speakers recessed in the ceiling. It was night and day from the utilitarian warehouse area.

After helping themselves to sodas, they'd settled into a quiet corner with a curved sofa and a low table. Crista had kicked off her sandals and raked her hair into a quick ponytail.

It felt like a long time since she'd been home, and she was struggling for normalcy. Bouncing from place to place with a man she barely knew, desiring him, kissing him, all the while wishing she could tear off his clothes, was not a long-term plan. She needed to get herself organized. She needed to get her life in order and back on track.

"I need to find a lawyer," she said to Ellie, zeroing in on a logical first step.

"At least you don't have to divorce Vern." Ellie fished a throw pillow from behind her back and tossed it to the end of the sofa, wriggling into the deep, soft cushions. "Is there something in your prenup about walking away? Wait, you didn't marry him. The prenup won't count."

"We didn't have a prenup."

The statement obviously took Ellie by surprise. "Seriously?"

Crista took a drink as she nodded. The cola cooled her throat, making her realize she was incredibly thirsty.

"But he's a superwealthy guy," said Ellie.

Crista was acutely aware of Vern's wealth. "I thought it was a show of faith. I was really quite honored."

"That's really quite weird."

"I know. Now, I have to wonder if he wanted to avoid the subject of infidelity."

"He knew your lawyer would advise a big settlement if he messed around on you. If he'd said no, you'd have been suspicious. But if he'd said yes, you'd have made a fortune."

"Assuming he ever got caught," said Crista.

"Maybe you should have married him without a prenup and then divorced him. You could have cleaned up."

"I'm not that devious." Crista wouldn't have even wanted that windfall.

"It would have served him right."

"The thing I'm worried about is Cristal Creations." Crista needed a lawyer to sort out the company. She wanted out from under Gerhard Incorporated as quickly as possible.

"It's yours," said Ellie. "He can't touch it since you never got married. But, hey, if he wants to split it, then he can split his business interests with you, too."

"The jewelry designs are all that I own," said Crista. "The stores are his. Well, his family's, anyway."

"The Gerhards own your stores?"

"They own the shopping malls the stores are inside. I need to get my designs out of there. I'd rather start from scratch than have to work with his family."

"You should definitely call a lawyer."

Crista gave a mock toast of agreement with her soft drink bottle. "Now that it's actually over, I realize how much of my life is wrapped up in Vern. How does that happen in only a year?"

Before Ellie could respond, Crista's mind galloped ahead. "I had six bridesmaids. Only one of them, you, was my friend. Five of them were from Vern's family."

"He does have a very big family."

"And I don't have any family at all. But five out of six? You'd think I'd have more friends."

"You do have more friends."

It was true. Crista did have other friends, some that she'd have loved to have as her bridesmaids. But Vern, and particularly his mother, Delores, had been insistent on including their family in the wedding party. Crista couldn't help but wonder if she'd made a mistake by giving in so easily.

"Good thing you had me," said Ellie.

"Good thing I still have you. All the people I socialize with now seem to be his friends, or his family—mostly his family."

Ellie frowned. "Count me out of that list."

"I know."

"I'm not his friend. I think he's a jerk."

"I wish you'd said something sooner."

"No, you don't."

Crista reconsidered her words. "You're right. I don't. I wouldn't have believed you."

"And I wasn't sure. I could have been wrong. He could have been a perfectly nice guy."

"Not so much." Crista took another drink. She was hungry, too. When was the last time she'd eaten?

She glanced at her watch.

"It's nearly three," said Ellie.

"I'm starving. Are you hungry?"

Ellie's glance went to the kitchen area. "We can probably grab a snack. This is quite the place."

"Isn't it?" Crista took another look around. The room was fresh, clean, with sleek styling and designer touches.

Ellie leaned closer and lowered her voice. "I get more and more curious about those two guys."

"Why are we whispering?"

"I think this place is probably bugged."

"Your secret agent phone?" It suddenly occurred to Crista that they might still be broadcasting.

"It's turned off now, but this is all very cloak-and-dagger."

"Very," Crista agreed, glancing around for surveillance cameras. "They seem frighteningly good at it."

"Do you think we can trust them?"

"Part of me wants to say no, but they've done nothing but help me so far."

"They came out of nowhere."

"True," said Crista. "But whatever this is, Jackson isn't in it for himself. He's been a gentleman. He didn't take advantage, even when I—" Crista stopped herself.

Ellie sat up straight. "Even when you what?"

Crista wasn't sure why she was hesitating. She was an adult, and Vern was now completely out of the picture. "When I kissed him back."

Ellie's brow rose. "Back? So he kissed you first?"

"Yes." It was silly not to have told Ellie. Keeping it a secret made it seem like more than it was. And it was nothing. "Yes, he did."

"When? Where? How?"

"On the boat. And in the hotel. And, well, in the warehouse, too." Crista didn't think she needed to add that it was on the mouth.

"It was mutual?" Ellie seemed rather energized by the news.

"It was very mutual. He's a really sexy guy."

"Good to hear," Jackson drawled from the doorway.

Ellie looked his way, her eyes crinkling with amusement. Crista felt her face heat.

"Don't let that go to your head," she warned him.

"I'll try my best." His footsteps sounded on the floor.

She forcibly shook off her embarrassment and turned to face him. "You shouldn't eavesdrop."

His mocha eyes glowed with amusement. "Occupational hazard."

"That's no excuse."

"I wasn't making an excuse." He sauntered farther into the room, followed closely by Mac.

She refused to stay embarrassed. If Jackson didn't already know she was attracted to him, well, he hadn't been paying attention. And he'd probably long since bragged to Mac about what had happened between them. Crista was going to hold her head high.

"I've got to get home," she said, coming to her feet. "Or to work. I should probably go into work and start figuring out the future."

"You'd planned to be away for three weeks on your honeymoon," said Ellie, rising herself. "Surely you can take a few days off."

"You can't go home," said Jackson.

"Come to my place," said Ellie.

"That's the second place he'll look," said Mac.

"So what if he does?" Crista had no intention of hiding from Vern any longer.

"Take a vacation," said Jackson. "Get out of the city for a few days."

"That's not practical," said Crista. Never mind that she had her business to worry about. She didn't have any extra money to spend on a vacation.

"It's better if you're not here," he said.

"It's better if I figure out what happens with Cristal Creations."

"She needs a lawyer," said Ellie.

"We have lawyers," said Mac.

"Down the hall," Jackson added with a tilt of his head.

"There are lawyers down the hall?" Crista couldn't keep the amazement from her tone.

"Rush Investigations lawyers," said Jackson. "Good ones. I'll introduce you."

She hesitated. The solution seemed too simple. Could she trust Jackson's lawyers? On the other hand, she knew she couldn't trust Vern's lawyers. And she sure didn't have any of her own. It seemed likely that anyone who worked for Jackson would be squarely opposed to Vern.

And it would be fast. Fast seemed like it would be good in this situation.

"They won't mind?" she asked, tempted.

"Why would they mind?"

"Because they have real work to do."

"This is real work."

She made her way toward him, watching his expression closely, trying to gauge what he was thinking. "Are you up to something?"

"Yes."

His easy admission surprised her.

"I knew it," she lied.

"What I'm up to is providing you with legal advice."

"Funny." She leaned closer, keeping her expression serious. "Why are you doing it?"

"Because your ex-fiancé ticked me off."

"And that's what you do when you're angry? Provide strangers with legal advice?"

"No." His jaw tightened. An edge came into his voice. "That's not even close to what I do when I'm angry."

He was intimidating, and it unnerved her. But her attraction to him was also back in full force.

He seemed to realize he'd unsettled her. "I'm not angry at you."

"Maybe not right now."

"Not ever."

But she could picture it. She could easily picture it.

He gave the barest shake of his head. "Don't even think about it. It's never going to happen."

Two days later, Jackson held his temper in check.

He stared across the prison table at Trent Corday. "So I sliced and diced and dissected everyone involved in *Investors Unlimited* looking for a connection to Gerhard."

He stopped speaking and waited, giving Trent a chance to react to the information he'd just tossed out. The more he'd uncovered, the more suspicious he'd become of Trent's involvement. He might not be certain how it had all unfolded, but he was certain Trent was somehow operating behind the scenes.

Trent returned his gaze evenly, his features perfectly neutral. "Why did you expect there to be a connection?"

Jackson mentally awarded the man points for composure. "Because the two events happened suspiciously close together."

"Vern Gerhard must have watched the show," said Trent.

"Seeing the show didn't tell Vern Gerhard about the mine."

"The show could have tweaked his interest in Crista."

"Interest alone wouldn't lead him to the mine."

"I don't see how it matters," said Trent.

"It matters," said Jackson.

For the barest of seconds, Trent's left eye twitched, and Jackson knew he'd found a crack. He could almost hear the wheels turning inside the man's head. Trent desperately wanted to know how much Jackson knew.

Jackson didn't know much. But he pretended he did, putting a smug expression on his face, hoping to draw out something more. "It wasn't somebody inside the show," he said, lacing his voice with confidence and conviction. "It was somebody who already knew about the mine."

"No telling who all knew about the mine."

"No telling," Jackson agreed. "But we both know one person who did."

"Who's that?"

"You." Jackson tossed a copy of a call list on the table in front of Trent.

Trent's gaze narrowed in wariness. "What's this?"

"It's a record of calls incoming to Manfred Gerhard's private line."

Trent didn't respond.

"It's from three days before *Investors Unlimited* aired the episode with Crista."

Jackson hoped Trent would react, but he didn't.

Instead, Trent calmly turned the list to face him. He stared at it for a long moment. Then he sat back and crossed his arms over his chest. "You seem to be making some kind of point."

Jackson indicated a line on the statement. "My point is that call, right there. It's from a prison pay phone, *this* prison's pay phone. You called Gerhard before the show."

Trent pretended to be affronted. "I most certainly did not."

"They record those calls," Jackson reminded him. "I can easily pull the recording."

"The call was made at ten forty-five on a Tuesday," said Trent. "I work in the laundry until noon. I couldn't have made the call."

"This was a year ago."

"I've been working in the laundry for two years. Ask anyone."

Jackson studied the confidence in Trent's expression. He reluctantly concluded Trent hadn't made the call. But he was definitely hiding something.

Jackson leaned forward. "What aren't you telling me?"

"Nothing."

The exchange was getting him nowhere. What Jackson needed was leverage, but he didn't have any.

"You want me to protect Crista?" He played his only card.

He gambled that Trent cared at least a little bit about his daughter. If he didn't, he wouldn't have contacted Jackson in the first place.

"Crista's fine," said Trent. "The wedding's been called off."

"The wedding might be off," said Jackson. "But Gerhard's not dead. He still wants what he wants."

"You don't know anything about it."

"But you do?"

Trent's face twitched a second time.

Jackson pressed his advantage. "I can walk right now, or I can watch her awhile longer. You screw with me, I walk."

Trent stilled, obviously weighing his options.

"Stop trying to play me," said Jackson. "The truth is your only option."

"I didn't call the Gerhards," said Trent.

"Then tell me what you did. Tell me what I need to know, or I'm out of here and Crista's on her own."

To punctuate his threat, Jackson started to rise.

"Fine," Trent snapped. "It was me. I told a guy about the mine. But I had no choice. I had to."

Jackson felt his blood pressure rise, while his tone went cold. "There's always a choice." He couldn't believe Trent would endanger his own daughter.

"They threatened to kill me."

"Why?"

Trent started talking fast. "I owed some guys some money. The deal was to offer her a discount price and pocket the difference. That's all it was. I swear."

"What guys?" Jackson demanded. "Who did you owe?"

Trent hesitated.

Jackson started to stand again.

"It was the Gerhards, okay? It was a land deal a few years back. I guaranteed their city permits. It didn't work out. They lost big-time, and they've been dogging me ever since."

The revelation surprised Jackson. He'd pegged Trent as a small-time criminal. He'd never guessed Trent was involved in this level of corruption.

He wasn't sure he believed it now. "How could you guarantee their permits?"

"I know a guy," said Trent.

"You know a corrupt guy in the permitting office who can be bribed?"

"The Gerhards have men inside the prison. And they *were* going to kill me. It was my only bargaining chip. I didn't think anyone would get hurt, least of all Crista."

"You painted a target on her back."

"And then I came to you when it looked like it would go bad. I came to you for help."

"You lied to me."

"It got the job done," Trent said defensively.

"They didn't get their hands on the mine."

Trent's gaze narrowed, obviously not getting the point.

"What now?" Jackson elaborated. "How are you going to pay them back?"

"I sold them information. About the mine. We're square."

"So, they're not going to kill you?"

"That was the deal," Trent repeated with conviction. He didn't look like a man who feared for his life.

But Jackson knew this wasn't over. If he'd learned anything from his father, it was that criminals didn't give up while there was still a prize to play for.

"It doesn't matter if they kill you or not, they've still got their radar locked on her."

Trent took a beat. "I didn't mean for it to go like this."

"Well, it went like this."

Trent swallowed.

"You're a sorry excuse for a father."

Trent didn't argue the point. He barely seemed to have heard the insult. His cockiness vanished, replaced by apprehension. "You'll look after her?"

"I shouldn't have to." This time, Jackson did come to his feet.

"But you will?"

Trent's emotional reaction had to be fake. But Jackson didn't care enough to lie. "I will."

Trent closed his eyes for a long second. "Thank you," he muttered.

If Jackson didn't know better, he might have thought the

man was grateful. But he did know better. Trent was a self-centered, pathetic loser who didn't deserve any daughter, never mind Crista.

He pivoted to walk away, letting his frustration and determination take him back down the long hallway.

The minute he cleared the prison building, he pulled out his cell phone and dialed his friend Tuck Tucker.

"Hey, Jackson," Tuck answered.

"Got a few minutes to meet?" Jackson asked as he strode toward his car.

"Now?"

"If you can. It's important."

"Sure. Where are you?"

"Riverway prison."

"That can't be good."

Jackson couldn't help but smile. "I'm outside the wall."

"Glad to hear it. The Copper Tavern?"

"Fifteen minutes?"

"Meet you there."

As he started his car, Jackson placed a call to Mac.

"Yo," Mac answered.

"You come across anything on the Gerhards bribing city officials?"

"Bribing them how?"

"Building permits."

Mac went quiet, obviously thinking through the question.

"Did you find something relevant?" Jackson asked as he turned from the parking lot onto the gravel-littered access road.

Poplar trees swayed beyond the ditches, and clouds shadowed the sun as the afternoon moved forward.

"It makes sense," said Mac. "A few committee decisions were overturned in their favor last year. That's not unheard of, but there were more than what might be expected. Let me look into it further."

"Check on Trent Corday while you're at it. He may have

had a hand in something bad at the city. Turns out he was the one who tipped Gerhard off about the mine."

"Why would he do that?" Surprise was clear in Mac's tone.

"He was in debt to the Gerhards and trying to avoid death or bodily harm."

"By using his own daughter?"

"Yeah. Getting the mine into their hands was payback for the debt."

Concern came into Mac's tone. "But they didn't get the mine."

"I know. Trent seems to think they're square anyway."

"That doesn't sound right," said Mac.

"Tell me about it. Did you get Crista and Ellie dropped off?"

"Safe and sound at the Gold Leaf Resort. Ellie's making spa reservations. Crista's arguing, but I think Ellie's going to win."

"I hope Ellie can get her to relax, take her mind off all this."

"If anyone can do it, it's Ellie."

"Good call. I'm meeting Tuck on my way back."

"See you when you get here." Mac signed off.

Jackson followed the expressway to the outskirts of the city, then swung off to cross the bridge and pick up the quieter streets that led to the Copper Tavern. It was a laid-back, comfortable sports-themed bar, with dark wood tables, padded leather chairs and good-humored staff that seemed to stick with the place for years on end.

It was easy to grab a parking spot in the midafternoon. Jackson left the bright sunshine behind and quickly spotted Tuck at a corner table. Tuck gave him a nod of greeting and signaled to the waitress for a couple of beers.

"Wings and ribs are on their way," said Tuck as Jackson sat down.

"Works for me."

"You're buying," Tuck added.

"You bet."

The waitress, Tammy, arrived with two frosty mugs of lager. She gave Jackson a brief, friendly greeting as she set the mugs down on printed cardboard coasters.

"What's going on?" Tuck asked Jackson as Tammy walked away.

"I need a favor." Jackson saw no point in beating about the bush.

"Sure."

"It's a big one."

"How big? Should I have ordered lobster?"

Jackson coughed out a laugh. "It's a whole lot bigger than lobster."

"Lay it on me."

"I need you to buy something for me."

Jackson slid a web address across the table. "Cristal Creations. They have three stores in Chicago. You buy the company now. I'll buy it from you in two years. I'll guarantee whatever return you want to name."

Tuck lifted the folded piece of paper. "Why?"

"I need my name to stay out of it."

"No kidding. I mean, why buy it at all?"

"I know the owner," said Jackson.

"You mean you're sleeping with the owner?"

"It's not about that."

"That wasn't an answer."

"No," said Jackson. "I'm not sleeping with her."

"Yet."

"The person I care about is the jewelry designer, not the company owner. Gerhard Incorporated owns the company. The woman's had a falling-out with them."

Tuck pocketed the paper. "Anything in particular I need to know about that situation?"

"She was set to marry Vern Gerhard. She backed out. He's not happy."

"But you are?"

Jackson didn't bother to hide his smile. "I'm satisfied with the outcome."

"And now you need her to sever all ties."

"I don't trust them. They're dirty, and they've got to be after revenge."

Tuck gave a nod. "We've got a Bahamian holding company that's not doing much of anything right now."

"Can it be traced back to you?"

"It can. But it would take quite a bit of time and a whole lot of lawyers. I don't know why anyone would bother, especially if the price was right."

Jackson tended to agree. It was common knowledge that the wedding had been canceled. And Crista had been on network television last year pitching Cristal Creations. An offer to buy the company from Gerhard should look opportunistic more than anything.

"I really appreciate this," said Jackson.

"Not a problem. My brother's got Tucker Transportation humming like a top. I have to keep myself entertained somehow. So, why'd she do it?"

Jackson didn't understand the question.

"Why'd she leave him?" asked Tuck.

"He was cheating on her."

Tuck's tone went hard. "Nice."

Jackson knew Tuck's brother, Dixon, had been a recent victim of infidelity.

"Anything else I can do to help her out?" Tuck asked.

"Not for the moment."

"You think of anything, you let me know. Dixon will help out, too."

"Thanks for that."

"I'm serious."

"I know."

There was a moment of silence.

"The guy cheated on her *before* the wedding?" Tuck asked.

Jackson pulled out the photo of Crista. He handed it across the table to Tuck. "That's the bride. And, yeah, it was before the wedding."

Tuck whistled low. "Are you kidding me?"

"She's bright, funny…good-hearted. Gerhard's an idiot." For that, Jackson was grateful.

"Or blind."

"His loss."

"Your gain."

"Not yet," said Jackson.

"You want some pointers?"

Jackson turned his attention to his beer. "No, I don't want some pointers."

Tammy arrived with the ribs and wings platter.

"Can I get you anything else?" she asked.

Tuck spoke up. "Jackson needs advice for the lovelorn."

Jackson rolled his eyes at the absurdity of the statement.

Tammy took a single step back and made a show of looking him up and down. She put a good-natured twinkle in her eyes. "Show up."

"Just doubled your tip," said Tuck.

Tammy laughed as she backed away. "Enjoy. Let me know if you need another round."

"I don't need any romantic advice from you," Jackson said to Tuck as he reached for a wing.

"What's your next move?"

"She's less than a week from leaving a man at the altar. I'm not going to crowd her."

Tuck looked skeptical. "You've got to be honest. You've got to be up front. Otherwise women can sometimes conjure up all kinds of wrong ideas."

"Just because you lucked out with Amber, that doesn't make you an expert."

There was a smug smile on Tuck's face at the mention

of his new fiancée. "That wasn't luck, my friend. That was skill, sophistication and—"

"Honesty?" Jackson got the point of the lecture. But the situation with Crista had more than its fair share of complications.

"I was going to say groveling. But let's stick with honesty for a minute. Trust is the hardest part to win and the easiest to lose."

"There are things I can't tell her."

"Like what?"

"Like the fact that her father sold her out to a criminal enterprise over a diamond mine."

Tuck raised his brow in obvious confusion. "You're going to have to throw a few more details into that story."

"Years ago, her father put some diamond mine shares in her name. She doesn't know she owns them, but her father told the Gerhards about them to settle a debt. Vern Gerhard is after the diamonds."

"The Gerhards need money?"

"More like they want money. If they based their behavior on needs, they'd have stopped building their empire a long time ago."

"How many shares does she own?" asked Tuck.

"Four."

"Four," Tuck repeated, obviously looking for confirmation that he'd heard right.

"Yes."

Tuck raised his palms in incredulity. "What can they do with four shares?"

"It's a privately held company. There are only ten shares in the world."

"She owns 40 percent of a diamond mine?"

"Yes."

"Are there diamonds in it?"

"I'm told there are."

"You have to tell her."

Jackson closed his eyes for a long second. "I know."

He'd spent the past few days telling himself there was a way around it. But there wasn't. Jackson wanted Crista, and he wanted her safe. Gerhard might have walked away from a runaway bride. But he wouldn't walk away from millions of dollars in diamonds and an outstanding debt.

Eight

When Jackson's lawyer Reginald Cooper had advised it would take several days to assess Cristal Creations and come up with a plan of action, Mac had suggested a spa getaway. Crista had vetoed the idea of leaving town again. She was tired of running from her problems.

But Ellie had begged her to reconsider. She reminded Crista that they'd been talking about a girls' getaway and how it would give her time to think. Then Jackson had added that the owner of the Gold Leaf Resort was a client of Rush Investigations, making the weekend practically free.

With all three ganging up on her, Crista had finally relented.

Now, lounging with Ellie in the outdoor mineral pool, she couldn't say she was sorry. The breeze was strengthening and clouds were closing up in the sky, but the rock pool was deliciously warm. Lounging on a seat, sculpted into the smooth boulders, with a tall glass of iced tea beside her, Crista closed her eyes and emptied her mind.

She felt more peaceful here than she had in days, and her brain had slowed down enough for her to picture her future. Maybe she'd find herself a new job. She probably would have to find a job, at least in the short term. Crista Creations was about to be dismantled. Without the Gerhards' backing, the company couldn't afford retail space. But without Crista, there'd be no more creations to sell.

She knew her designs were the unique element of the company. Without her, Cristal Creations was just another jewelry retailer. And it was a very competitive market.

She'd keep designing. But she'd pull back, retrench, rent booth space at a few jewelry fairs, work on her website and try to build up brand recognition. She'd make new pieces in the evenings, setting up in her kitchen like she'd done for so many months before Vern came along.

She pictured the work space on the island counter, the dining table covered with supplies, her closets overflowing.

Her eyes popped open. "Oh, no."

"Huh?" Ellie seemed to give herself a shake.

"I can't believe I forgot," said Crista.

"Forgot what?"

"I canceled the lease on my suite. The movers are putting the furniture into storage next week."

"You're homeless?" asked Ellie.

"It's almost impossible to find affordable rent."

"You can stay with me," said Ellie. "The new sofa folds out. It's really quite comfortable."

"That's nice of you. But it's not going to be that simple. I need to work from home again."

"Why not wait and see—" Ellie's eyes widened, focusing on a spot behind her.

"See what?" asked Crista, realizing she'd suddenly lost Ellie's attention. She twisted her neck to look behind.

A cloud partially blocked the sun, and she had to blink to adjust to the light.

Then she saw him. It was Vern. He was pacing along the pathway toward them, and there was a smile on his face.

"How did he find me?" She wasn't exactly afraid, but she was annoyed.

Ellie rose in a whoosh of water.

Crista pushed to her feet, striving for a greater sense of control. She crossed her arms and pinned him with a level stare. "What are you doing here, Vern?"

"I need to talk to you." His tone was smooth, his expression open and friendly.

He was wearing a business suit, but he bent down on one knee on the cobblestones at the edge of the pool. "I hate the way we left things, Crista."

She'd hated it, too, but it was entirely his fault, and there was no going back.

She held her ground. "Go home, Vern."

"Not until you hear me out."

She firmly shook her head. There was nothing he could say to undo infidelity.

"I know you're upset," he said.

"Upset? You think I'm *upset*?" *Try angry. Try incensed.* Everything about their relationship had been a lie.

"I can explain," he said.

"Explain a girlfriend?" Now that she was rolling, she couldn't seem to stop herself. "You can explain having both a girlfriend and a fiancée at the same time? How exactly are you going to do that?"

Ellie touched her arm. "Crista, don't."

Crista struggled to calm down. She knew Ellie was right. She shouldn't be challenging him. She shouldn't be engaging with him at all.

"She's not my girlfriend," he stated emphatically. "It was just a thing. One of those short-term, stupid things. I panicked. I knew I wanted to be with you for the rest of my life, but I panicked. I thought, well, I thought as long as it happened before the wedding—"

"Stop!" Crista all but shouted. "Quit rationalizing. You cheated. And I doubt you regretted it at all. I think you were going to keep doing it."

"That's not true."

"It's entirely true." She was certain of it.

"I love you, Crista. I want to share my life with you."

"You don't love me. You can't love someone and not want what's best for them. You don't want what's best for me. You want what's best for you. And you're willing to sacrifice me to get it."

"That's the thing. I *do* want what's best for you. And I've learned my lesson. I told myself it wouldn't hurt you. If I thought for one minute it would have hurt you—"

"Shut up," Ellie interjected. "Just shut up, Vern. Leave her alone and go away."

Vern's tone cooled as he looked at Ellie. "This is none of your business."

A clipped male voice interrupted. "Maybe not. But this conversation is over."

Jackson had appeared from nowhere.

"How did you…" Crista found herself gaping at him in surprise.

"Well, well, well," said Vern, slowly rising and looking Jackson up and down.

"Goodbye, Gerhard," said Jackson. "Or do I have to call security?"

"So you're here with her," said Vern.

Jackson didn't answer.

"He's not here with me," said Crista. "He wasn't here at all. Not until just now."

Vern shifted his gaze to Crista, clearly trying to decide if she was lying.

She wasn't. Then again, she didn't really care what he thought.

"You don't owe him an explanation," said Jackson. He took a menacing step toward Vern.

"You want to do this?" Vern challenged, widening his stance.

"She wants you gone," said Jackson. "You can walk out or be carried out. It's all the same to me."

Ellie grasped Crista's arm. "Come on." She tugged, urging Crista toward the glass-encased underwater staircase.

Crista realized it was good advice. She had absolutely nothing left to say to Vern, and her presence was only going escalate the situation. She left the pool and walked briskly away, scooping up the towels and robes they'd left draped over a pair of deck chairs.

Jackson caught up to them at the elevator.

"He's gone," he said.

"I'm beginning not to trust that."

The elevator arrived, its doors sliding open for them.

"I don't blame you," said Jackson as they walked inside.

"I'm going to hide in my room now." At least there, people would have to knock.

"You and I need to talk." His expression was too serious for her peace of mind.

"Can it wait?" she asked.

"It's important."

"You can drop me at the smoothie bar," said Ellie, pressing the button for the third floor.

Crista braced her hands on the rail behind her. "You know, I was happy in the mineral pool. All my cares and worries were flowing away."

"Five minutes," he said. "Ten, tops."

"I don't want any more bad news."

Before he could respond, the elevator stopped on three, and the doors slid open.

"Mac's around here somewhere," he said to Ellie.

Ellie's expression brightened. "He is?"

Jackson grinned at her telltale reaction.

"Catch you in a while," said Ellie, and she stepped briskly away.

"She likes Mac," said Crista, happy for her friend despite everything.

"Mac likes her back," said Jackson. "He'll track her down in no time."

"Because he's a skilled investigator," Crista guessed.

"Because she's still got the GPS phone."

"You guys make me paranoid."

"It's healthy to be paranoid."

Their eyes met as the elevator rose toward the presidential suite on the twentieth floor. His gaze was soft, and a rush of awareness heated her skin. She could fight it all she wanted, but he seemed more attractive every time she saw him.

Exiting the elevator, the suite was at the far end of the

hallway. A set of double oak doors led to a spacious set of rooms with a dramatic bay window overlooking the spa.

She extracted the key card from her bag and swiped it through the reader. Jackson reached for the handle and held the door open wide.

"Do you want to change?" he asked as they entered.

She dropped her bag on an armchair and tightened the sash on her robe. "You wanted to talk?"

"I did. I do." He seemed to give himself a mental shake. "I really missed you."

She'd missed him too. And her feelings for him were getting more confused by the moment.

He was an extraordinary man. He was sexy and self-assured in a rugged and dangerous way. But he was also classically handsome. In fact, he could probably be a model. She had a sudden vision of him in a pair of faded jeans, shirtless on a windswept beach. She wanted to tear off his shirt so that reality could mesh with her fantasy.

"Don't look at me like that," his voice rumbled.

"I'm not."

He eased forward. "You are such a liar."

It was true. She was lying to him, and she was lying to herself. She was looking at him exactly like that. She was completely attracted to him and completely turned on, and she couldn't figure out why she was fighting it.

"I'm sorry," she offered.

"For what?"

"For lying."

He seemed to take a breath. Then he squeezed her hands, causing her hormones to surge to life, and she swayed toward him.

He let go of her hands. Then he reached slowly up to cradle her cheek. He canted his head, easing his lips toward her.

"Do you want this?" he asked.

She was tired of lying. "Yes."

"Are you sure?" he persisted. "Because if we shut it down again, it might kill me."

It might kill her, too.

In answer, she reached for the buttons on his shirt, flicking open one, then another and another.

"I'm sure," she whispered and stretched up to meet his lips.

His reaction was immediate. He wrapped his arms around her, kissing her deeply. She molded against him, feeling the strength of his body and the thud of his heart.

He tugged at her sash, releasing the robe.

"I'm soaking wet," she warned. Her bathing suit was going to soak through his clothes.

"I don't care." He stripped the robe from her shoulders and let it fall to the floor.

Then he lifted her into his arms, her flip-flops falling beside her robe. "Which way?" he asked.

She pointed to the bedroom door.

He carried her through then closed the door firmly behind them, setting her bare feet on the thick carpet. The balcony door was partway open, a breeze billowing the sheers. Muted sounds from the pool area below rose into the room. The fan whirred, and dappled sunlight danced on the buttercream walls.

He brushed back her damp hair, raking his fingers through the strands. She tugged free the hem of his shirt. Then she finished with the buttons, removing his shirt to reveal a close-up view of his broad shoulders and tanned muscular chest.

"I was right," she muttered under her breath, then she kissed his smooth pec.

"Right about what?"

She was surprised he'd heard. "About you." She kissed him again, making a damp spot with her tongue.

He gasped in a breath. "In a good way, I hope."

"In a good way," she confirmed.

He slipped off the strap of her bathing suit, kissing the tip of her shoulder. "I was right about you, too." The vibrations of his deep voice penetrated her skin.

It was becoming a struggle for her to talk. "In a good way?"

"In a very good way."

He released the hook of her bathing suit top. It fell, and her cool, damp breasts tumbled free.

He stepped back to look, and his eyes turned the color of dark chocolate. Her nipples beaded and a bolt of arousal spiked through her.

"Gorgeous," he whispered with reverence.

"Not so bad yourself." She ran her fingers from his navel to his chest and across to his shoulders. He was satisfyingly solid over every inch.

His hand closed on her breast, and his smile faded. He caught her lips again and wrapped his free arm around her waist to draw her close, her bare chest coming up against his.

Their kisses seemed to last forever. She wanted them to last forever. The whole world could disappear for all she cared. She wanted this moment, these feelings, this bliss she'd found with Jackson to go on and on.

Her knees began to weaken, and she could feel her muscles relax. He kicked off his shoes and popped the button on his pants.

In a moment, they'd be naked. They'd be on the big bed, and their inevitable lovemaking would finally come to pass.

"Protection?" she asked.

"I have it."

She took a step, the backs of her knees pressing against the mattress. She gave him a sensual smile and hooked her thumbs into her bathing suit bottoms. Feeling sexy and powerful, and loving the molten expression in his eyes, she slowly peeled away the bottoms, stepping from them, standing naked in front of him.

He didn't move. His gaze went from the top of her head to the tips of her toes and back again.

Her confidence faltered.

But then he met her eyes. "I'm in awe."

"In a good way?" she joked.

"You're stunning. I'm afraid to touch you. If you're another dream, I'm going to be bitterly disappointed."

Her confidence came back, and she smiled. "*Another* dream?"

"I've had several dozen." He moved closer, stepping out of his pants.

"That's good," she told him.

"It was terrible," he countered. "They weren't real, and they were wholly unsatisfying."

She wound her arms around his neck, coming up on her toes to kiss his mouth. "I'll try to do better."

"This is better," he said. "So much better." And then he claimed her mouth.

Their naked bodies pressed tight together. She could feel every ripple of his chest, every shift of his thighs. His palms moved down her back, over her rear, smoothing the backs of her thighs.

She moved her feet apart, arching against him, a throbbing insistence growing at her core.

"Oh, Crista," he moaned, burrowing his face in her neck, kissing the tender skin, his hands kneading her fluid muscles.

"I can't wait," she told him.

He produced a condom.

Seconds later he cupped her rear and lifted her up. She twined her legs around his waist, reveling in the friction between them. He kissed her, his tongue teasing her mouth. Her hands tightened around him, gripping hard as he pushed inside, completing them.

She moaned at the instantaneous raw sensations. This wasn't merely pleasant. It wasn't merely nice. It was bril-

liant and intense, breathtakingly wonderful. Ripples of ec-
stasy radiated through her. He'd barely begun, and she was
flying away, flying off in a million directions. Colors exploded in her mind, and she cried out his name and cata-
pulted over the edge.

He stilled, giving her time to breathe.

"I'm sorry," she managed, embarrassed at her hair trigger.

"For what this time?" he rumbled.

"I didn't mean… I don't know what happened. I'm not…"
She wasn't usually like this.

He stopped her with a kiss. "That was amazing. I'm honored. And we can start all over now." There was a chuckle
in his voice. "Maybe you'll do better next time."

She was about to tell him next time never happened. It
never had. When she was done, she was done. But she'd be
patient with him. He didn't need to—

His thumb brushed her nipple, and her body zinged back
to life. Then he kissed her mouth, and the glow grew inside her.

Curious, she touched her tongue with his.

"Oh, my," she muttered.

He flexed his hips, moving against her.

Arousal teased her stomach, moving along her thighs.

She answered his thrusts, losing track of time all over
again. Their lovemaking went on and on, and he took her to
unimaginable heights, all but shattering her soul.

Afterward, they fell onto the bed together, him on top, her
tangled around him. She couldn't move. She wasn't even sure
she could breathe. She certainly couldn't talk, even though
she wanted to tell him he was fantastic and she'd never had
lovemaking like that.

Minutes slipped past while they both dragged in deep
breaths.

He finally broke the silence.

"That," he said, "was all of my dreams combined."

Crista's chest went tight. Warmth radiated within her.

She didn't know what happened next. She'd worry about that later. For now, all she wanted out of life was to bask in the glow of Jackson.

As Crista nestled against his shoulder, Jackson kept her held tight. All he could think about was how close he'd come to missing this moment. If he'd hesitated outside the church, if he'd let her walk through the door, if he hadn't grabbed her in that split second, she'd be married to Gerhard by now and forever out of his reach.

He'd settled a blanket around them, his instinct to cocoon them together. Faraway shouts from the pool below made their way through the window. He watched as the fan blades whirled slowly above them, dispersing the fresh outside air.

He wanted to order some champagne, maybe some strawberries. He wanted to lounge in her bed for hours, laughing with her, teasing her, asking about her childhood, her friends, her jewelry designs. But he knew he didn't have that luxury. He'd put this conversation off too long already.

She needed to know she was a multimillionaire and that Gerhard was after her money.

"The Borezone Mine," he whispered in her ear.

She tilted her head to glance at him, blinking her gorgeous eyes as her lips curved into a smile. "That wasn't what I expected you to say."

He brushed a lock of hair from her forehead. "You need to hear again that you were fantastic? Because you were fantastic."

She shook her head, her hair brushing his chest and shoulder. It felt good.

"But we have to have this conversation. Have you ever heard of the Borezone Mine?"

"No."

"I'm not surprised. A few years ago, some shares of the Borezone Mine were put into your name."

She didn't answer. Instead, she propped her head up on her elbow, looking curious. "Was it an accident?"

"I doubt it. But that doesn't really matter. The point is you own them."

"How do you know that?" she asked.

"Mac discovered it." Jackson hoped he wouldn't have to mention her father.

"Okay." Her tone was searching. "Should I give them back?"

"No."

"I don't understand your point."

Jackson pulled himself into a sitting position. "Thing is, Gerhard knows about your shares."

Her forehead wrinkled. "How does he know about them?"

"I'm not sure," Jackson answered honestly.

She sat up, tucking the blanket around her. "I think I know what must have happened."

"You do?" Jackson braced himself.

"It had to be my father."

Jackson was surprised at how quickly she'd worked it out.

But instead of angry, her tone turned worried. "Is it an illegal mine?"

"No. It's nothing illegal. The mine is in northern Canada. It's perfectly legitimate."

"If my father is involved in something, it'll be a scam."

"We need to talk about Gerhard."

She was clearly becoming impatient. "Do we have to? Really?" She spread her arms. "Right now?"

"He knows about the mine, Crista."

"So what?"

"So, he wants to get his hands on your shares. That's what this is all about."

She blinked for a moment, clearly parsing through the information. "Are you suggesting Vern was marrying me for a mine?"

"I—"

"Are you saying he felt nothing for me?" She suddenly sounded angry. She bounced from the bed, draping the blanket around herself. "Why would you say that?"

"I want you to be safe."

"It was something, Jackson. I'm not that naive. He wasn't faking our entire relationship."

Jackson realized he'd made a colossal error. He couldn't have picked a worse time to have this conversation.

"Let me start over," he said. "Or better still, forget it for now. We can talk about this later. I am starving."

"Oh, no." She vehemently shook her head. "I want you to finish telling me how my fiancé suckered me and strung me along for a year to get his hands on a few shares in some mine."

"I want you to be safe," said Jackson. "This is all about you staying safe."

"Since the wedding's off—thanks to you, by the way—I don't see how I'm not safe."

"Gerhard is not a nice man."

She lifted her chin but didn't answer.

"And neither is his father. The entire family is shady. We think they tried to bribe city councillors for building permits. Mac is checking into it now. And as long as you have shares in the Borezone diamond mine, you could be a target."

"It's a diamond mine?"

"Yes."

"It has to be a mistake."

"It's not a mistake," said Jackson. "It's easily verifiable."

Her anger seemed to switch back to confusion. "But the Gerhards don't need money. The last thing in the world that family needs is more money."

"I can't say I disagree with that."

"So why would they care about anything I have?"

"They do."

"That's your theory."

"You're right," he said. "It is a theory. But I know I'm

right. They won't go away. They'll try every trick in the book to reacquire you."

"*Reacquire* me?" Her tone was incredulous.

"You have to trust me."

She sat down on the edge of the bed. "Why did you make love to me?"

The question took him by surprise. He wasn't sure what she was driving at, so he didn't know how to answer.

He went with the truth. "Because I couldn't stop myself."

She frowned. "You tried to stop yourself?"

"Not today I didn't." He reached for her hand, but she tugged it away.

"Are you after the diamond mine, Jackson? Is that why you've stuck around all this time?"

"I am not after your mine." He hated that she had to ask. "The mine has nothing to do with you and me."

"Apparently it has everything to do with you and me."

"I'm here to keep you safe, full stop."

"You don't even know me."

"That's not true. I didn't know you. That day at the church, I didn't know you. But now I know you. And I care about you. And I am not about to stand by and let the Gerhards get their hooks into you."

"They can have the stupid mine," she snapped. "I don't want it. I don't care."

"You should. It will help you get your business back."

"How? Why is this so important?"

"They're criminals, Crista. And they have absolutely no right to that mine or—"

"I don't care," she cried.

"Crista." His tone was hard, but he needed to get her attention.

"*What?*"

"That mine is worth a hundred million dollars. And you own 40 percent."

The color drained from her face. Her shoulders dropped. Then her arms wrapped protectively around her stomach.

Silence ticked by, but he was afraid to speak. He didn't know what to say, and he didn't want to make it any worse.

"That's not possible." Her voice was small.

He wrapped a gentle hand over her shoulder. "To Gerhard, you represent forty million dollars."

The words sank in. "He didn't want a prenup." She tipped her chin to look at Jackson. "I thought that meant he trusted me."

Jackson gave in to his urge and pulled her protectively into his arms. "That's what he wanted you to think. You're a kind, trusting person."

She smacked her hand ineffectively against Jackson's chest. "Why didn't you tell me?"

"I just did."

"Why didn't you tell me before?"

"You wouldn't even believe he was cheating on you. I needed you to trust me first."

"I don't trust you now."

"I know, but I couldn't wait any longer. When I saw him out there at the pool, I knew it was time for some hard truths."

"It's been two hours since you saw him at the pool."

"I know that, too." Jackson spoke huskily, tightening his embrace. "But I figured you were safe with me."

"Plus, you wanted to get me naked before you confessed."

"Should I apologize for that?"

"Are you sorry?"

"I'm not remotely sorry for making love with you."

"The mine has to be a scam," she said with conviction. "It's my father. He wants people to believe it has a lot of value, but it will turn out to be worthless."

Jackson knew differently, but he didn't want to fight about it. He could show her copies of the share certificates, but she might think they were faked. It was better to wait and have Reginald take her to an official government office.

"Even if it is a scam," he said. "Gerhard believes it's true. That's the problem."

"He can't steal something I don't have."

"He can hurt you while he tries."

"I'll stay away from him," she said.

"Good decision. Give me the benefit of the doubt, and I'll show you final proof when we get back to Chicago."

"All right. I'll believe it when I see it," she said.

"Fair enough."

Her brow furrowed. "I think that means your job will be done."

"My job will be done," he agreed.

"Will you leave?" She tipped her chin to look up at him, obviously struggling to be brave but seeming vulnerable.

"I'm not leaving."

He was very, very far from leaving. His job might be done, but that didn't mean he was ready to walk away. Not from Crista. Not by a long shot.

Nine

"All I need to do is to find a new normal," Crista said from where she stood on the edge of the green on the resort's par-three golf course. Her life might be in chaos, but with a little effort she could sort it out.

"I'm normal," said Ellie, lining up her long putt. "And you can stay with me as long as you like."

"Concentrate," Mac told Ellie.

They were on the fifth hole. Jackson and Crista were ahead by four strokes. Their lead was thanks to Jackson. Crista could putt fairly well, but her drives were terrible. Conversely, Ellie could send the ball arcing beautifully down the fairway, but her accuracy on the green was abysmal.

"I am concentrating," she said to Mac.

"You're giving Crista life advice."

"I'm multitasking." Ellie hit the ball, sending it wide past the hole to the far side of the green.

Mac groaned.

"Don't know my own strength," said Ellie. "Not sure why you'd be in a rush to find a new place to rent," she said to Crista.

"Why rent?" asked Jackson as he placed his ball. "The market's good right now. You should buy."

"Why is he allowed to give advice and putt?" asked Ellie.

"Because he knows what he's doing," said Mac.

"And he's not your partner," said Ellie with a saucy smirk.

"That's true," said Mac.

Jackson sank the putt.

"But mostly it's because he knows what he's doing," Mac finished.

"And I don't take orders from him," Jackson joked, removing his ball from the fifth hole.

"Neither do I," said Ellie.

"That much is clear," said Mac.

Crista moved to her ball marker, replacing it with her ball. "I'd take orders," she said. "If they were good ones. It's not like I've made great decisions on my own lately."

"Buy a house," said Jackson. "A fixer-upper with good long-term property value. It won't cost much now, and you'll make a nice profit in a few years."

"I don't have a down payment," said Crista, eyeing the line to the hole and the slope of the green.

"She gets to talk while she putts," Ellie stage-whispered to Mac.

"Because Jackson doesn't care if they win."

"You're way too competitive."

"Jackson's a wuss," said Mac.

Crista couldn't help but smile at the exchange. On the golf course or anywhere else, Jackson was anything but a wuss.

She drew back and hit the ball. It bobbled through a hollow but then sank straight into the hole.

"Nice," said Mac.

Ellie elbowed him in the ribs.

He grabbed her, spun her to him and kissed her soundly on the lips. "Keep quiet while I putt."

Her cheeks were flushed, her eyes dazed. "Yes, sir."

"You're killing me." He kissed her again.

"You own a multimillion-dollar mine," Jackson said to Crista as Mac tromped onto the green. "A down payment is not going to be a problem."

"I'm not going anywhere near that mine," she said with a definitive shake of her head.

"You're being ridiculous."

"I'm being smart. Everything my father touches turns to garbage."

"It's legit," Mac called out.

"It might look legit," said Crista. "Trust me, the FBI will be at my door soon enough."

"Reginald can confirm its authenticity," said Jackson.

"Reginald is doing enough for me already. Besides, asking a bunch of questions will only alert the authorities that much sooner. I've got enough to worry about right now without getting involved in one of my father's schemes. I'm ignoring the stupid mine, and I want you to do the same." She stared hard at him, waiting for his confirmation.

His expression stayed perfectly neutral.

"Jackson," she pressed in a warning tone.

"Fine. No Reginald."

"He's in jail."

"Reginald?" asked Jackson.

"Very funny. My father is in jail for fraud and forgery."

"I know. We did our research. Nice shot, Mac."

Mac headed off the green, while Ellie returned.

"It doesn't give you pause," Crista asked Jackson, "that my father's a forger and a con artist?"

"My dad's done time, too," he said, his gaze on Ellie as she lined up.

"Seriously?" Crista had never known anyone else with a criminal parent.

"Embezzlement. He was arrested when I was thirteen. I don't visit him. I don't really like to talk about it."

"Does it bother you?"

"Not on a day-to-day basis."

"Do you worry you might be like him?" Crista worried about that for herself. She had half Trent's genetics. The other half was from her mother, who had married a con man. And now Crista had almost married a con man. That might be the most unnerving part of all.

"Do I seem like a criminal to you?" Jackson asked, an edge to his voice.

"I guess not. I mean, you're on the other side of crime.

You fight it. Then again, that's still a bit of an obsession with the criminal world."

"Your confidence is inspiring."

"I'm only trying to be honest."

"I'm not a criminal, Crista. And neither are you. Our fathers made their own choices—bad choices, obviously. But we're not them."

"My mother married him," she pointed out.

"You didn't marry Gerhard."

Ellie missed the putt but got a little closer to the hole.

"I'm not buying a house," said Crista.

"I hate to see you spend your money on rent, especially since you'll be trying to build your business."

"I'll manage."

"Every penny you spend on rent is a penny you can't plow into Cristal Creations."

"It's still the most practical solution," she said.

"It might be a solution, but it's not practical."

"It's every bit as practical as buying a house."

"Real estate is a capital asset," said Jackson.

Ellie sank her putt. She let out a whoop and hoisted her putter in the air.

Crista grinned at her joy.

"See what happens when you concentrate," Mac called to Ellie, loping toward her.

Crista started for her clubs.

Jackson suddenly grasped her hand and pulled her back. "Hang on."

"What?"

"I have a better idea."

"I don't want to hear about it."

"It's a very good idea."

She turned, letting out a sigh of exasperation. "Can't we just golf?"

"Come live with me," he said.

She blinked at him in astonishment, certain she couldn't have heard him right.

"I've got three bedrooms." His expression turned reflective. "I mean, not that I'm suggesting you'd need your own bedroom. I like sleeping with you. In fact, I love sleeping with you. I'd seriously like to continue sleeping with you, Crista."

She replayed his offer in her head, looking for the punch line.

"It's a great plan," he said, his gaze darting around her expression. "Gerhard would absolutely leave you alone if I was in the picture. And, really...you know..." His eyes lost focus. He had obviously gone deep into thought.

"Jackson?" she prompted.

When he didn't respond, she waved her hand in front of his face.

"I've got the solution," he said. "It's so simple."

"I'm not moving in with you."

They barely knew each other. Jackson had wandered ridiculously far afield in his ramblings.

"Marry me," he said, grasping both of her hands, his expression turning earnest.

She opened her mouth. Then she closed it again. "Uh, earth to Jackson?"

"It's perfect," he said in what looked like complete seriousness.

"Mac," she called out. "Something's gone terribly wrong with Jackson."

"What is it?" asked Mac, immediately starting toward them.

"Vegas," said Jackson, still looking straight into Crista's eyes. "We can take Tuck's jet to Vegas."

"Has he ever done this before?" she asked Mac.

Mac halted next to them. "Done what?"

"I'm proposing to her," said Jackson.

"Then, no," said Mac. "He's never done that before."

Ellie arrived in the circle. "What's going on?"

Mac answered, "Jackson asked Crista to marry him."

Ellie's face broke into a bright smile. "*Really?*"

Crista turned on her. "Be serious."

Ellie schooled her features, lowering her tone. "Really?"

"No, not really," Crista snapped. "He's joking. Or he's gone round the bend. At the moment, my money's on round the bend."

"Are you all done?" asked Jackson, looking normal again.

"Is it over?" asked Crista. "Your fit of insanity or whatever that was?"

"It's a perfect plan," said Jackson. "If you're married to me, then Gerhard is forced to give up and go away."

Neither Ellie nor Mac disputed the logic.

"Perfect plan," Crista drawled sarcastically. "What could possibly go wrong? Oh, wait. I'd be *married* to a man I barely know."

"For a good cause," said Mac.

Crista turned on Mac. "You're actually going to encourage him?"

"You can divorce me if it doesn't work out," said Jackson.

"It's not going to work out," she said, an edge of hysteria coming into her voice. "Because it's never going to happen."

He continued as if she hadn't spoken. "Just like they do in a regular marriage."

It occurred to her that she was being had. She glanced from one man to the other. "Is this a joke? Are you messing with me? Do you guys do this kind of thing all the time?"

They looked at each other.

"No," said Jackson. "I don't make a habit of proposing to women. I'd sure never do it as a joke."

She tugged her hands from his. "Fine. Whatever." She paced away and called back over her shoulder, "I'm going to tee off on six. Anybody coming with me?"

"I'm coming," called Ellie.

In a moment, Ellie was walking beside her.

"What was that?" Ellie asked.

"We were talking about rent and real estate. Next thing I knew, he was off the deep end. I should buy a house. No, I should live with him. No, I should marry him."

Ellie giggled.

"This isn't funny," said Crista.

"It is a little bit funny."

"No…" said Crista. "Okay, sure, it's a little bit funny." And there was some in the idea of marrying Jackson to keep Vern out of her life. "In an ironic way," she allowed.

"He must like you."

"Sure, he likes me. And he likes sleeping with me. Who wouldn't—" Crista stopped herself. She had been about to say the sex between them had been mind-blowing, both last night and again this morning.

"It was that good?" asked Ellie, a thread of laughter in her voice.

"We wouldn't get tired of the sex anytime soon," Crista admitted.

"I wouldn't get tired of Mac, either."

Crista stopped. "You had sex with Mac?"

"Why do you think he was there for breakfast?"

"I thought he came by this morning looking for Jackson."

Crista and Jackson had fallen asleep last night before Ellie had come back to the suite.

"You're not the only hot one, you know."

"I didn't mean—"

But Ellie was laughing. "Mac's pretty great. And he thinks the world of Jackson."

"Jackson seems pretty great, too," Crista said honestly.

"But you're not going to marry him?"

"What sane woman would do that?"

"Will you live with him?"

"No."

"It could be platonic."

"It wouldn't be platonic." Of that, Crista was certain.

"I've only got a sofa for you."

"Your sofa will be fine." They came to the sixth tee box, and Crista stopped. "Your sofa will be perfect. I am putting this crazy week—no, this crazy *year*—behind me. As soon as Reginald works out the details, I'll get to work on rebuilding Cristal Creations, and then I'll find myself a new apartment."

She selected the three wood, pushed a tee into the grass and proceeded to hit the longest drive of her life.

"The marriage proposal was out of left field," Mac observed the next day. They were back in Chicago at Jackson's house. Crista had moved in with Ellie, her belongings going to a storage unit in the morning.

"It wasn't the worst idea in the world," Jackson countered.

"It kind of was."

Maybe. But had Jackson pulled it off, it would have solved a whole lot of problems. And, truth was, the more time he spent with Crista, the more time he wanted to spend with Crista.

"You barely know her," said Mac.

"I know her better than she knew Gerhard."

"I'm not sure I see your point."

"My point is, she agreed to marry him, and he was lying to her from day one."

"That logic borders on the bizarre," said Mac. "You do know you're getting a little too close on this one."

"You think?" Even now as Jackson glanced around his living room, all he could think was how Crista would look good in the leather armchair, or on the sofa, or at the dining room table.

It wasn't clear what happened next between them. He was leaning toward inviting her over for dinner, a simple date. He'd break out the candles and wine, maybe order some flowers, do by stealth what he couldn't do with candor and get her to spend a night, or two or three.

"It may be time to move on," said Mac.

"It's not time to move on."

"She knows the score. She's not going to give the guy the time of day."

Jackson would agree on that front. But he still didn't trust Gerhard. And his gut said they didn't yet have all the pieces.

"It you want to date her, date her," said Mac. "But stop pretending you still need to protect her."

Jackson's phone rang.

He answered. "Hey, Tuck."

"We got it done," said Tuck.

"Cristal Creations?"

"Yes. They drove a hard bargain. Vern Gerhard would have walked, but the old man took double the estimated market value."

"Good."

"I hope she's worth it."

"She is," said Jackson. "Does she know yet?"

"Our Bahamian guy is calling Reginald right now."

"Reginald won't know Tucker Transportation's behind the purchase?"

"He won't. Do you want him to know?"

"No. And Dixon's okay with this?"

"Absolutely. I told him you were in love."

The statement took Jackson by surprise. "I'm not in love."

Across the living room, Mac grinned.

"Sure," Tuck said smoothly. "Keep telling yourself that." He paused. "Until you can't keep telling yourself anymore."

"You're nuts," said Jackson, and he frowned his displeasure at Mac.

"I know the signs," said Tuck.

"I'm hanging up now."

Tuck laughed. "Picturing her in a white dress yet?"

"Picturing her in Vegas." As soon as the words left his mouth, Jackson regretted them. He knew they left the wrong impression. But he also knew that explaining further wouldn't help.

"That'll do it," said Tuck. "I'll bring a jet if you let me be the best man."

"Goodbye, Tuck." Then Jackson remembered the magnitude of the favor. "And thanks. Thanks a lot."

The laughter remained in Tuck's voice. "No problem. This is the most fun I've had in weeks."

Jackson disconnected the call. "Tucker Transportation just secretly bought Cristal Creations."

"You know, you could do it the old-fashioned way," said Mac.

"Do what?"

"Date her. Win her over. And when she loves you back, propose."

Jackson rolled his eyes. "Give me a break."

"The barriers are out of the way. You don't need to be her bodyguard anymore. You're just two ordinary adults."

Jackson didn't know why he took offense to Mac's words. "She's not ordinary."

"And you're not in love."

"Let's talk about you and Ellie."

"I just met Ellie."

"Uh-huh." Jackson exaggerated the skepticism in his tone.

"Me and Ellie, that's me being your wingman."

"That's you falling for a beautiful woman."

"You're forgetting I didn't propose to her," said Mac.

"She's not the one in jeopardy."

Mac's expression turned thoughtful. "See, I can't picture that."

"Picture what?"

"Ellie in jeopardy. She's tough, and she's smart, and she'd take out any guy who tried to mess with her."

"Worried?" asked Jackson, glad to have the topic turned away from himself and Crista.

"Nope."

"Because you're tougher than her?"

"Because I'm not trying to mess with her." Mac's words rang true.

His situation with Ellie was dead simple. While Jackson's situation with Crista was anything but. He knew how she felt about her father. If he told her he'd been working with Trent, she'd never trust him. But if he didn't, their relationship would be built on a lie.

It wasn't a choice. To move forward, he had to come clean and take his chances that she wouldn't walk away.

Crista set down the phone, her brain reeling with the news.

"What?" asked Ellie. She was in the small kitchen of her apartment, tearing spinach into a salad bowl.

"Reginald says somebody bought Cristal Creations."

"What do you mean, bought it? How could they buy it?"

"They bought the company. From Gerhard. Reginald says I still have copyright on the designs."

Ellie frowned. "Is this good?"

"I think so. Reginald says they want me to keep running the company. He seems really excited about the sale."

"Who are they?"

"A group of wealthy anonymous investors."

"Does that strike you as a little hinky?"

"Should it? I do trust Reginald. He says holding companies do this all the time. And it's got to be better than Gerhard Incorporated."

"I suppose." Ellie seemed skeptical, but she went back to tearing the spinach.

Crista told herself to be practical rather than emotional. She fought an urge to call Jackson. She knew the sale had nothing to do with him. He probably wasn't even interested. Still, she found that she wanted to share the news and get his opinion.

"It's not like I have a choice," she said to Ellie instead. "I can't afford to buy it myself."

"How much did they pay?"

"It was confidential."

Ellie shrugged and turned to open a cupboard. "If it's more than fifty bucks, you couldn't have afforded it."

"I'm not that bad off," Crista protested.

"Oh, crap," said Ellie.

"What?"

"I forgot to buy almonds. The salad is going to be boring without them."

"No problem," said Crista, coming to her feet. "I'll pop down to the market. I could use the fresh air."

She could also use a little time to think. Her life felt like a pinball, bouncing off paddles, bonging over points, into traps, some things good and some things bad, but all of them on the edge of control.

"Can you grab a few limes as well?" Ellie called.

"Sure." Crista retrieved her shoulder bag.

The evening was warm, so she tucked her feet into her sandals and swung the purse over her T-shirt and shorts. She looped her hair into a ponytail in case of a breeze. Then she called goodbye and locked the dead bolt behind her.

The sun was setting on the street outside, lights coming on in the apartments above the shops. Ellie lived above a florist, which was next to a funky ladies' boutique and a toy store. There was a bakery on the corner with a compact grocery store opposite.

Traffic was light now that rush hour had passed. Neighbors and shoppers cruised the street, while laughing groups of people from the after-work crowd—or maybe they were tourists—sat drinking at the open-air café on the other side. The buzz of traffic, the aromas of yeast and cinnamon, and the bustle of ordinary Chicagoans on a Thursday night made her feel normal. It felt good.

She stopped at the corner, waiting for the walk signal.

The light was yellow, and a minivan with smoked windows came to a stop at the intersection. A silver sedan came up behind it. The minivan's door slid open and a man hopped out. Crista moved to one side so he could get around the light pole.

Suddenly, she felt a shove from behind. The man stared her straight in the eyes. He moved out of the way, and she was instantly propelled forward.

"Hey!" she shouted, angry at being jostled.

But the next thing she knew, she was inside the van.

The door slammed shut.

"Stop," she shrieked.

A hand clamped over her mouth, and an arm went around her like a steel band. The horn honked, and the van lurched away from the curb, cutting around the corner to a chorus of horns from outside on the street.

A hood was thrown over her head, and sheer terror rocked her.

"Keep quiet," a gravelly voice commanded in her ear. Then he pulled his hand from beneath the hood.

She had no intention of keeping quiet. "What do you think you're—"

A hand immediately came over her mouth, pressing the rough fabric against her teeth.

"Quiet," the voice repeated.

She felt the car slow to a stop, and she screamed at the top of her lungs, hoping someone outside would hear.

The hand stopped her again, and the man swore.

"She pierced my eardrum," he shouted.

"Crista, stop," came another voice.

She froze. She knew the voice. And now she was more frightened than ever.

"Vern?"

"Nobody's going to hurt you," he said.

"What are you doing?"

"We need to talk."

"You're *kidnapping* me."

"You should be used to it by now." His tone was cool.

She kicked the back of the driver's seat. It was out of sheer frustration because her legs were the only thing she could move.

"Hold her still," came a third voice.

"Let me go," she demanded. "This is illegal. You're all going to be arrested."

"Like you had Jackson Rush arrested?"

The question caught her off guard. "He had his reasons."

"And I have mine."

"You can't do this, Vern. Whatever you think you'll accomplish, it's not going to work. You have to let me go."

"Get rid of her cell phone," said Vern.

She felt a hand dip into her purse, rummaging around.

"Hey," she protested.

"Got it," said the voice beside her.

"Toss it," said Vern, his tone cold.

Her sliver of hope faded.

Jackson could have tracked her phone. When she didn't come back to the apartment, Ellie would get worried and she'd call Jackson. At least Crista hoped she'd call Jackson. And Jackson would have known how to access the GPS.

She heard the window roll down and the traffic noise increase, felt a breeze buffet across her, and she knew her phone was in the gutter.

She was at Vern's mercy.

She wished she knew what that meant. But the truth was she didn't know anything about him. The Vern she'd planned to marry never would have kidnapped her. He'd never have cheated on her. He'd never have terrified her like this.

Her throat went dry, and a chill took over her body. She was in the clutches of a stranger, and she had no idea what he might do.

Ten

"She's not picking up," Jackson said to Mac, his frustration turning to worry.

"Maybe she doesn't want to talk to you."

"Why wouldn't she want to talk to me?"

Jackson didn't expect her to call him the minute she finished talking to Reginald. Then again, he didn't see why she wouldn't call to tell him Cristal Creations had been sold and she didn't have to worry about Gerhard owning her company. Did she not think he'd be interested?

"It's only been ten hours since you saw her," said Mac.

"That's not the point. She's had some pretty big news since then."

"Maybe Reginald hasn't called her yet."

"He'd call her right away."

Jackson was sure about that. But he couldn't very well call Reginald to confirm it. As far as Reginald was concerned, the purchase was a completely random act of an arm's-length company. Jackson intended to keep him thinking just that.

"You're obsessing," said Mac.

Jackson tossed his phone onto the coffee table. Was he obsessing? He wanted to talk to her. Was that being obsessive?

"Call Ellie," he said.

"And say *what*?"

"I don't care. Anything. Find out if Crista is with her."

"I'm going to look like a stalker."

Jackson picked up his phone and redialed Crista. It went straight to voice mail.

"Maybe she's talking to someone," said Mac.

"For forty-five minutes?"

"Maybe it's turned off."

"Why would she turn it off?"

"In the shower, taking a nap, in bed with—" Mac cut himself off.

"She's not in bed with some other guy." Though the thought did make Jackson's stomach churn. "You have to call Ellie."

"Fine," Mac said in a clipped voice. He dialed with his thumb. "If I'm going to look stupid, just so you know, you'll owe me."

Jackson nodded.

"Hey, Ellie," Mac said into his phone.

Jackson couldn't help but notice Mac's voice changed when he talked to Ellie, going deeper, smoother, more intimate. He obviously liked Ellie more than he was letting on.

"Really?" Mac's tone turned to alert, causing Jackson to look up. "When?"

"What?" Jackson asked.

Mac's look was intent and focused. "Did you call her?"

Adrenaline rushed into Jackson's system, and he came to his feet.

Mac stood. "We'll come to you."

"What?" Jackson all but shouted.

"Sit tight," said Mac, signing off. "Crista went to the store and didn't come back."

"When?" Jackson asked, his feet already taking him to the door.

"Over an hour. Ellie said she was about to call us."

"What store?" asked Jackson. "Driving, walking?"

"Two blocks from Ellie's apartment. She walked."

Jackson swore as he flung open his front door.

"We don't know anything for sure," said Mac.

"He's got her," said Jackson.

"That's a pretty bold move."

"I shouldn't have left her alone."

"You can't watch her for the rest of her life."

"I could have watched her for the rest of the week." Jackson would have considered the rest of her life. He realized he'd have seriously considered sticking right by her side forever if it would keep her safe.

"You want me to drive?" asked Mac.

"No, I don't want you to drive." The last thing in the world Jackson could do right now was sit idle.

"Jackson, we have to treat this as just another case. Emotion is clouding your judgment."

"My judgment is fine." Jackson wrenched open the door of the SUV. "Call Ellie back," he told Mac as he peeled out of the driveway. "Get whatever details you can."

Jackson pressed on the accelerator, racking his brain. Where would they take her? It wouldn't be the mansion. That was too obvious. Maybe to one of their businesses, one of their construction sites. Would they threaten her? Would she defy them? He was terrified she would.

Then he had an idea. He dialed Rush Investigations, getting the night shift to ping her phone location. It took only moments to learn the phone was southeast of Ellie's.

Jackson disconnected. "Her phone is at Edwards and Ninety-Fifth. It's stationary."

"They ditched it," said Mac.

"Likely."

"They had to know you'd check."

Jackson smacked his hand down on the steering wheel. They could easily have changed directions right after they tossed her phone.

He took an abrupt right turn.

"Where to?" asked Mac.

"The office. Call ahead. I want a list of every known Gerhard vehicle. Give them Ellie's address. Get them to canvass local businesses for security footage. Cross-reference vehicles on Ellie's street at the time to the place where the phone was dumped."

"Roger that," said Mac, disconnecting from Ellie.

At least it was something. If they could find a vehicle

that had been in both places, maybe they could get make and model or even a license plate. If they could, they had a chance of tracking it farther.

"And Gerhard's buildings," said Jackson, his brain clicking along as he drove. "Locate *all* of his buildings. I want it mapped out by the time we get there."

They were going to need intelligence, and they were going to need reinforcements.

"Will do, boss," said Mac. Then he began relaying instructions to the Rush Investigations office.

Jackson sped up.

When they removed the hood, Crista found she was in a warehouse. It was cold and hard, with concrete floors, metal walls and high, open ceilings. The few fluorescent lights that buzzed suspended from the crossbeams did little to dispel the shadows. The cavernous room was full of rusting shelves and aging steel bins, with stacks of old lumber piled helter-skelter along the far wall.

They'd sat her in an old folding chair next to a battered wooden table and three other chairs. They'd tied her hands behind her back. But at least she could see now.

Vern stood in front her, along with his father, Manfred, and a craggy-faced man she didn't recognize. She could see two guards at a nearby door, their backs to her.

"What do you want?" she demanded of Vern.

Part of her was terrified, but another part found the entire situation too absurd to be taken seriously. It was as if Vern and Manfred were both playacting. And for a hysterical moment, she thought she might laugh out loud.

But then the moment passed, and she shivered from the cold and fear. Nobody was playacting. She was in genuine danger.

"I want you to marry me," said Vern in a matter-of-fact voice.

The statement struck her as beyond ridiculous.

"Right here, right now," he continued, glancing at the craggy-faced man. "If you do that, I promise to give you a divorce in a couple of months."

Manfred cleared his throat.

"Six months, tops," said Vern.

"I'm not marrying you," she said. "You cheated on me. You lied to me. You just kidnapped me, and you have me tied up in a warehouse." Her voice rose to an almost hysterical pitch. "I don't know what passes for romance in this dysfunctional family, but I assure you this isn't doing it for me."

Manfred raised his arm as if he was going to backhand her.

She braced herself.

But Vern stepped forward and grabbed Manfred's hand. It was the first time she'd ever seen him stand up to his father. She found herself astonished.

"That's not necessary," said Vern.

"Make her listen," Manfred hissed.

"You need to marry me," said Vern, his tone going earnest.

She kept silent. Tears burned in the corners of her eyes.

"You have two choices," said Manfred, both his voice and his expression more intimidating than she'd ever seen. "Marry my boy now. Sail the Mediterranean just like you planned. Work on your tan, enjoy the food, drink the wine. He'll divorce you soon enough."

"And keep my diamond mine," she dared to say.

"And keep your mine," Manfred agreed, not seeming surprised that she knew.

"You know it's bogus," she said.

Both men looked confused.

"I don't know how you know about it, but my father's a con artist. He will have set this up for some convoluted reason of his own. There is no mine. And if there is, it doesn't have any diamonds."

Manfred gave a chilling smile. "Oh, there's a mine, all right."

Crista shook her head. "This is pointless."

"If there's no mine," Vern added reasonably, "then there's nothing for you to protect."

"I'm not marrying you," she said.

Mine or no mine, she wouldn't promise to love and honor Vern. She'd dodged that bullet when Jackson grabbed her outside the church, and she wasn't about to throw herself back in front of it.

Jackson had shown her the truth about her fiancé. He'd shown her the truth about other things, too, like how amazing and trusting a relationship could be between two people. Despite how it had started, in such a short time, she felt closer to Jackson than she'd ever felt to Vern.

She could be herself with Jackson, her total candid self. He didn't mind if she was opinionated. He didn't mind if she argued. He even knew about her father, and he hadn't pitied her. He'd understood. He understood her embarrassment, her anger, even her denial in a way few other people could.

She suddenly missed him with all her heart. She realized she should have said yes to staying at his place. For a crazy moment, she even wished she'd married him. Maybe they'd be in Vegas right now having an outlandish honeymoon in a garish hotel, playing poker or watching a circus act.

"That brings us to choice number two," said Manfred, making a show of inspecting his manicure as he spoke.

Her thoughts of Jackson vanished, and her fear returned. The ropes were tight around her wrists, chafing her skin. And she was growing colder by the minute. It was clear that Manfred was perfectly willing to have her suffer.

"We sign the papers for you," he said, his expression remorseless.

"What papers?" She couldn't help but ask. She looked from Manfred to Vern.

"Hans over there is a very good forger."

"For the mine?" she asked. Did they want her to sign over ownership of the mine? She'd do it. She was positive there was nothing to lose in that.

Manfred clicked his teeth as he waggled a finger at her. "Oh, no, that would be too suspicious. Hans will sign the marriage license for you."

Crista drew back in the metal chair. Their plan was to forge a marriage license. Exactly how did they expect that to work? She'd only deny it the minute they let her go.

"Then it's off on your honeymoon," said Manfred, sounding like he was enjoying himself. "Only to perish in a very tragic drowning accident off the yacht."

She stilled. Had Manfred just threatened to kill her? Did he expect her to believe him?

She found herself looking to Vern again, searching for the man who'd held her so tenderly. They'd danced. They'd laughed. She'd commiserated with him over his unbending father. He'd proposed on one knee with candlelight and roses.

"You're not throwing me overboard," she said to him. There was no way she'd believe that.

"We don't have a prenup," said Vern, sounding frighteningly practical. "Our wills were drafted weeks ago. It would be tragic, but it would be completely believable."

A sick feeling welled up inside her. "I already told you, the mine's a fake. Take it. It's not about the mine. It's about not wanting to marry you."

"Give me a break," Vern scoffed.

"What about when—" Crista stopped herself. She'd been about to point out that Ellie would go to the authorities. She wouldn't for a second believe Crista had willingly married Vern.

But saying it out loud would only put Ellie in danger. The last thing she wanted to do was hurt Ellie.

As her fear grew to unbearable heights, suddenly a loud crash reverberated through the warehouse. Men shouted over the sound of running feet. Manfred turned, while Vern and the craggy man turned pale. Everything was in motion around her.

Vern grabbed her, pulling her to her feet.

"Let her go!" Jackson shouted.

Crista wanted to whoop and cheer. Mac was there. So were a bunch of other men. The Gerhards' security guards seemed stunned, too.

"Let her go," Jackson repeated and began pacing toward them.

"Don't come any closer," Vern growled, waving a gun.

"Jackson," she cried, both relieved and newly terrified.

"Walk away from this," Manfred commanded.

"Not going to happen," said Jackson.

Crista focused on Jackson, trying to send a message with her eyes. She was grateful he was here. She was so glad to see him. She didn't see a way out, but she hoped he had a plan.

She started to work on the knots, hoping to free her hands from the rope and be ready.

"He's here for the mine himself," said Vern. "Nothing more, nothing less."

"I'm here for Crista," said Jackson.

"You didn't think we'd find out?" asked Vern.

"I don't care what you think you know," Jackson spat.

"He wants the diamonds every bit as much as I want the diamonds," said Vern.

"There *are* no diamonds," Crista shouted. Why wouldn't anyone listen to her?

"Did you ever ask him how he knew?" asked Vern.

Jackson took a step forward.

Vern pulled her tighter, jabbing her with the gun.

"Ask who sent him. Ask him how he knows your daddy's cell mate. Ask him how many times he met with Trent Corday before he dragged you from our wedding."

Jackson's jaw hardened, and his nostrils flared. But he didn't deny the accusations.

Crista tried to make some sense out of it. "You know my father?"

"What was the deal?" Vern asked Jackson. "Were you going to split it fifty-fifty?"

"It's complicated," Jackson said to Crista.

Her heart sank. At the same time, her hands came free of the rope.

"What was the plan?" repeated Vern. "Were you going to marry her instead?"

Crista withered.

Jackson's frown deepened.

Vern laughed out loud. "Oh, that's too rich. You already asked her to marry you? You couldn't even wait, say, a month or so, to let the dust settle?"

"I was protecting her from you."

"You were conning her *yourself*." Vern's tone went lower, speaking to Crista. "His father is your father's cell mate. Colin Rush, the king of the Ponzi scheme. His daddy makes your daddy look like a carnival huckster. He's here for the diamonds. He doesn't give a damn about you."

"Shut up," Jackson shouted, striding forward.

Crista wrenched herself from Vern's arms.

"Crista—" Jackson began.

"You stay away," she warned him. She glanced around the room. "Everybody *stay far away from me*."

She refused to be taken in by anybody. She stopped in front of Mac. "Give me your car keys."

"You sure?"

"I'm sure. And your cash. Give me all of your cash." It was on the tip of her tongue to tell him she'd pay him back. But given the circumstances, it seemed silly to be polite.

Mac gave a small smile. "Smart girl."

"I've learned a few things along the way."

"Let me explain," Jackson pleaded with her.

She dared to look at him. "So you can tell me more lies?"

She was heartsick at his deception. Her father had sent

him. She'd been such an easy mark. She'd been a laughably easy mark.

"It wasn't lies," said Jackson.

"Do you know my father?"

Jackson's nostrils flared. "Yes."

"He sent you?" She already knew the answer.

"Yes."

"He told you about the diamond mine."

"Yes, but—"

"Joke's on you, Jackson. Trent conned you just like he's conned everybody his whole life. The mine doesn't exist."

"Mac confirmed it," said Jackson.

Crista barked out a laugh. "He thinks he confirmed it. That just says my father is one step ahead of Mac."

She turned her attention to Mac, who was reaching into his pockets. He handed her the keys and a wad of cash.

"What are you doing?" Jackson demanded of Mac.

"Letting her go," Mac said mildly.

"No," Jackson shouted.

Mac gave him a look.

"Right," said Jackson, clenching his jaw. "You're right. She needs to get out of here."

"Norway," he said to the man closest to him, "give her all your money."

The man called Norway didn't hesitate. He pulled a wad of cash out of his pocket and handed it over.

"Dump Mac's car at the bus station," said Jackson, coming close. "You lay low for a while until we clear this up."

"I know what I'm doing," said Crista. She was going to disappear into anonymity. And it was going to be for more than just a while. None of them would find her until she wanted to be found. "You'll keep Vern from coming after me?" she asked Jackson.

"Absolutely," he said.

"Good." Crista stuffed the money into the pocket of her shorts. "Tell Ellie not to worry."

Crista headed for the door.

She located Mac's SUV and started it up. She was doing exactly as Jackson had suggested. She'd ditch the vehicle at the bus station. But then she'd take a taxi to the train station, buy a ticket with cash, switch trains outside the city and find herself a quiet, budget hotel where she could pay cash and hide under a fake name.

She realized she couldn't trust Reginald anymore. But the Yellow Pages were full of lawyers. She'd find her own lawyer. Then she'd work her way through the changes at Cristal Creations all on her own. She was through depending on others for help.

Since calling the police would leave them all with a lot of explaining to do, Jackson assumed the Gerhards would keep the altercation to themselves. And though it chafed to let her go on her own, he'd made sure Crista had a three-hour head start on Vern.

Now, both groups cautiously crossed the parking lot, each watching their backs as the entered their respective vehicles.

Jackson wanted to search for Crista right away. He wanted the Rush Investigations team to head straight back to the office and get started. He knew Gerhard would do exactly that, and it killed him simply sit still and wait for her to come back.

"What if she's right about her father?" Jackson mused out loud as the sun broke the horizon, lighting the world outside the meeting room window.

"That the diamond mine is worthless?" asked Mac.

Jackson wished he could seriously consider that possibility, because no diamond mine meant Crista had no value to Gerhard, so Gerhard would disappear.

"No. Not that," said Jackson. "I'm convinced the diamond mine is legit. But that doesn't mean Trent's not running some other con."

Mac hesitated. "What con would he be running? What are we not seeing?"

Jackson scanned through the facts.

"Problem is you're not seeing anything beyond Crista," said Mac. "You get that you're in love with her, right?"

Jackson wasn't letting his emotions get in the way of solving this. He couldn't afford to do that. He ordered himself to slow down, detach, think harder.

And then it hit him. "Trent's lying."

Trent had initially downplayed his culpability in Crista's engagement. Not that Jackson was sorry about that part. In fact, he was glad Trent had lied to him back then.

"You think he's still lying?" asked Mac.

Jackson was certain of it. "The Gerhards aren't threatening to kill Trent. They're in league with him."

"That would be a cold-blooded move," said Mac. "Voluntarily setting up your own daughter."

Jackson whistled low. It was all coming clear. "Trent told them about the mine, and he told them how to get to Crista. Were they going to split the take?"

"Why wouldn't Trent just split it with Crista?"

"Crista won't even speak to him. She never would have trusted him."

"But why get cold feet at the last minute?" asked Mac. "Why would he call you in and mess it all up?"

"Because they double-crossed him." Jackson stood, absolutely certain he was right. "He didn't call me in to help Crista. He only wanted his leverage back."

Mac seemed to be considering what he'd said. "If that's the case, what's his next move?"

"I don't know." Jackson gripped the back of the chair, tightening his fingers, ordering himself to think carefully. "But she's his bargaining chip. He needs her back in his clutches."

"We better find her first," said Mac.

Jackson started for the door. "And Daddy dearest is going

to help us do that. That creep is going to tell me everything he knows."

"He'll only lie," Mac called.

"Let him try."

It was a two-hour drive to Riverway State. Jackson made it in ninety minutes. For the third time, he found himself sitting across a prison visiting table from Trent Corday.

"What's your new plan?" he barked without preamble.

"My new plan for what?"

"For Crista. Don't bother lying. Nobody's threatening you. You're all the way in Gerhard's pocket."

Trent's fleetingly shocked expression told Jackson he was right.

"You sold out your own daughter," Jackson spat. "It was a setup from minute one."

"If they told you that, they're lying."

Jackson had no interest in debating the past. He was certain Trent had orchestrated the whole thing. "How do you plan to get her back?"

Trent's complexion darkened. "I don't know what you're talking about."

"You think I'm going to let him kidnap her again?"

"What? Kidnap who?"

Jackson was through with the man's games. "Playing dumb gets you nothing."

"I'm not—"

"What is the new plan?" Jackson articulated each word slowly and carefully.

"The new plan to *what*?"

Jackson wanted to take a swing. "Don't you know that once they're married, Gerhard has no reason to keep her alive?"

"I thought the wedding was off." Trent looked confused.

Jackson wasn't buying it. "Your backup plan has a backup plan." He knew how these men worked. "If not a marriage to Gerhard for a kickback from the mine, then what? Who? What do I need to protect her from?"

Guilt flashed across Trent's face. "There was never any reason to hurt her."

"There was always a reason to hurt her. I know you're not burdened with a conscience, but don't lie to yourself. And stop lying to me. *What happens next?*"

"Nothing," Trent shouted. "I mean, I've thought about it. There are tens of millions of dollars at stake. And they're mine."

"They're Crista's."

Trent's tone went sullen. "She never even knew they existed."

"What's the new plan?"

It was clear Trent didn't want to answer.

Jackson waited.

"I haven't had time to come up with one," Trent finally admitted.

Now there was something Jackson could believe.

"Gerhard was my only play," said Trent. "I can't come at her directly. Crista has never trusted me."

"And thanks to you, she'll never trust me, either. Which only makes my job harder."

"What are you planning to do?"

"What you should have done in the first place."

"I don't understand."

"Protect Crista from the lowlifes you put in her path."

"How?"

"None of your business."

"How can it hurt to tell me?"

"You don't deserve to know."

Trent reached out to him. "I'm not as bad as you think. They were never supposed to hurt her."

"Are you saying they planned a divorce all along."

"Yes. There was no prenup to protect the mine, so all he had to do was divorce her."

Jackson couldn't believe Trent would be so stupid. "What about Gerhard's assets? Don't try to tell me he'd give her a settlement."

"It's all in Manfred's name. Vern owns nothing."

"Still, a divorce would mean giving her part of the mine. They wouldn't do that. You put her *life* at risk."

Trent paled a shade. "They said it would be a divorce."

"They lied, and you're a fool."

The two men stared at each other for a long moment.

"What's your plan?" Trent's voice broke. "Tell me how you're going to protect my little girl."

Jackson stepped back, releasing a long breath. "For one thing," he said, "Cristal Creations is out of Gerhard's hands."

"You did that?"

"I had someone do that for me. Tell them, don't tell them. It's too late for them to change anything. Tell them they'll never be able to get to her. She'll be protected 24/7 for a month or a year or forever, whatever it takes."

Jackson wished he didn't have to do all this in secret. He wanted to be honest with her. He wanted to be in her life. He wanted to *be* her life.

He was completely in love with her. It angered him that he was figuring that out in a prison. It angered him more that he was figuring it out while confronting her no-good father. The entire situation was thoroughly wrong and completely unfair.

"Why?" asked Trent, looking genuinely perplexed.

"Because she deserves it. She deserves everything."

Jackson rose from the seat. He was done here. He was done with Trent. He knew the truth now, but it didn't help him. He should have asked way more questions in the beginning. He should have been more suspicious. He might not have purposely conned Crista. But the result was the same. His stupidity had put her in harm's way.

Maybe he didn't deserve her any more than Trent did.

Eleven

It took Crista three days to figure out a solution. But she woke up one morning, and it was fully formed.

"Are you sure?" asked Ellie as they drove east from where they'd met up in Rockford.

Crista had set up an anonymous email account to communicate with Ellie. When she'd sent a message, Ellie had left Chicago, switching from a taxi to a train to a bus, while Crista had made her way from a boutique hotel over the border in Wisconsin.

"It's meaningless," said Crista. "And it's making me a target. Even if the mine is worth some money, I don't want it."

"But him? Are you sure you even want to talk to him?"

"He can't hurt me from behind bars."

"He hurt you by putting a diamond mine in your name."

"And I'm about to undo that. As soon as the mine is out of the picture, Vern walks away—and Jackson walks away." Crista couldn't help the little catch in her voice as she said Jackson's name.

He'd broken her heart. She hadn't realized how badly she'd fallen for him until that night in the warehouse. Anger had carried her for a few hours. But once the anger wore off, his betrayal had devastated her.

He'd seemed so clever, so funny, so compassionate and so incredibly handsome. She'd started to think of him as her soul mate. He'd comforted her. He made her think he genuinely cared about her.

She realized now that her upbringing had left her starved for male attention. It seemed she was willing to take a chance on anyone, including Vern and Jackson. It was entirely understandable, but it was also foolish. And she would never make that mistake again.

"I don't mean the money," said Ellie. "Cristal Creations is going to be wildly successful. I mean, seeing your father in person, talking to him, having him try to manipulate you into…I don't know. But whatever it is, it's going to upset you."

"I'm immune," said Crista.

She'd done nothing for the last three days but be angry with her father, detest Vern and build a wall against her feelings for Jackson. She dared any of the three of them to try to get under her skin.

"I hope so," said Ellie.

"It'll take five minutes," said Crista. "All I need is his signature on the legal papers, and the mine is all his. He can use it in a brand-new scam. He'll like that."

"Mac says it's real," said Ellie.

"Mac is in league with Jackson."

"True," said Ellie. "And I haven't told him a thing. He doesn't know you contacted me or anything."

Crista was surprised. "You've talked to Mac since I left Chicago?"

Ellie hesitated. "He calls me every day. He came by last night."

"You saw Mac last night?"

"Yeah, well…" Ellie turned her head to gaze out the passenger window.

"Please tell me you didn't spend the night with Mac."

"He didn't suspect a thing. I swear. And, anyway, if I didn't let him stay over, he would have been suspicious."

"You're getting serious with Mac?"

"Not exactly serious." Still, Ellie's tone said it was more serious than she wanted to let on.

Crista smiled at the irony.

"I couldn't help myself," Ellie said. "I kept thinking it

would blow over, that one of us would lose interest. And then when you and Jackson broke up—"

"We didn't *break up*. There was no relationship to start with. He was conning me. I was a mark."

"Mac thinks the world of Jackson."

"Mac is Jackson's partner. They were probably going to split the diamonds."

"You said there were no diamonds."

"Everyone seems to think there are. Otherwise…" Crista swallowed. She hated that every memory of being with Jackson made her heart hurt.

Ellie touched her shoulder.

"I'm going to get over it," said Crista. "I'm already over it. Reginald said—not that I can trust Reginald—but my new lawyer says the same thing. They said the Bahamian company is going to give me free rein on Cristal Creations. To them, it's just an investment. And they're very patient, looking for a long-term return. It's going to be great."

"I'm so glad," said Ellie.

"So am I." Crista had so much to be grateful for.

She was out from under Vern. She'd seen Jackson's true colors before it was too late. And she was about to sever the last of her ties with her father. After this, she was a free woman starting a whole new, independent life.

"That's it?" asked Ellie as a chain-link fence topped with razor wire came into view. An imposing dark gray stone building loomed up behind it.

"That's definitely it," Crista said in a hushed tone.

For the first time, she thought about what it must be like to be locked up inside the bleakness of Riverway State prison. She shuddered.

"There's a sign for visitor parking," said Ellie, pointing out the windshield. "Do you want me to come with you?"

"You can't. They needed to have your name in advance." Though the street was empty, Crista signaled right and turned into the parking lot.

She knew she needed to do this alone. Still, part of her wished she could bring Ellie along for moral support.

"It's not too late to back out," said Ellie.

Crista chose a spot and pulled in.

"This won't take long." Crista looped her purse over her shoulder, taking the manila envelope from the seat between them.

"Got a pen?" asked Ellie.

"I do."

"He's going to be surprised by this."

"He's going to be stunned by this."

Crista wasn't sure which would shock him more, that she showed up or that she was calling his bluff. In typical convoluted Trent Corday style, he'd convinced Vern that the mine was worth money. His real objective had obviously been the Gerhard wealth. He clearly thought he could get his hands on some of that if she was married to a Gerhard.

She didn't know how he'd planned to achieve that. But then, she'd never understood the conniving workings of her father's mind.

She reached for the handle and yawned open the driver's door.

"I'll be waiting," said Ellie, worry in her tone.

"I'll be right back," Crista said with determination.

She forced herself to make the long walk to the gate at the fence. There, she gave a guard her name and identification. She let him check her bag. Then a female guard patted her down before they let her in.

A pair of burly, unsmiling guards led her through a doorway and directed her down a long, dank hall. The place smelled of fish and disinfectant. Everything about it seemed hard and cold.

She was determined to feel no sympathy whatsoever for her father. He'd been guilty, no question. But on a human level, she pitied anyone stuck in here. With every step, she fought an increasing urge to turn and run.

Finally, she came to a doorway that led into a brighter room. It had high mesh-covered windows, a checkerboard floor and several small red tables with connected stools.

She scanned the room, easily spotting her father. He'd aged since she'd seen him last, his hair gray, his skin sallow and his shoulders stooped and narrower than she remembered.

When he saw her, his eyes went wide with surprise. His jaw dropped, and he gripped the table in front of him, coming slowly to his feet.

"Crista?" he mouthed.

She squared her shoulders and marched toward him.

"Crista," he repeated, and his lips curved in a smile.

She hoped he didn't reach for her. She inwardly cringed at the thought of giving him a hug.

"I need your signature," she stated up front.

"I can't believe you're here."

"I'm not staying."

"No, no." His head bobbed in a nod. "Of course you can't stay. I understand."

"I know about the mine."

He gestured for her to sit down.

She hesitated but then sat.

"I know about the mine," she repeated.

"Jackson told me."

Her chest tightened at the mention of Jackson's name. She had no intention of pursuing the discussion.

"We both know it's worthless," she said, folding back the envelope flap.

"It's not—"

"But you've obviously convinced people it has some value."

"It's not worthless."

She stared at him. "Right. You forget who I am."

"But—"

"This latest scam of yours has put me in actual danger. Vern threatened to kill me, and I think he was serious."

"He *what*?" Her father put on his shocked face.

"Please, save it."

"I never meant for—"

"Quit trying to fool me. I'm not your mark. I'm your daughter. I need one thing from you, and then I am out of your life for good."

He swallowed. He even teared up a little bit. His acting was impressive.

"What do you need?" he asked in a raspy voice.

She produced the papers. "I had a lawyer draw these up. It transfers my shares in the Borezone Mine to you."

Trent drew back.

"You and I know this is meaningless. But if there's any-one out there who believes there really are diamonds, or if you manage to convince someone in the future that there are diamonds, they'll come after you and not me. That's all I want."

His head was shaking. "It's not worthless."

"There's no point in telling me that."

He lunged for her hand, but she snapped it away.

"Check," he said. "Have a lawyer check. Better still, have a securities regulator check. At today's prices your shares are worth tens of millions."

"Ha," she scoffed, wondering why he kept up the facade.

She couldn't figure out what he hoped to gain. Then again, at the beginning of any of his cons, it was never ob-vious what he hoped to gain.

"Check it," he said with impressive sincerity. "Promise me you'll check it, and then you'll understand what I'm about to do."

Her suspicions rose. "What are you about to do?"

He took the papers from her hands.

"Dad?" The name was out before she could stop herself.

She saw him smile while he looked down. Was he signing?

He flipped through the three pages to the end. There, he made a stroke through his name and printed something else.

"Jackson Rush was here three days ago," he said.

"I bet he was."

Her father looked up. "He said something. Well, he said a lot of things. But he reminded me of something that I'd forgotten a long time ago."

She schooled her features, determined not to react.

"He reminded me that being your father meant something. I owe it to you to take care of you."

She wasn't buying it. "What did you just write?"

"He also showed me what he was, who he was. He's honest, principled and upstanding."

"Stop," she managed. She didn't believe a word of it, but her chest was getting tighter and tighter.

"I'm not going to accept the mine shares. But you're right. You can't keep them, either. They put you in danger. When I put them in your name, I had no idea they'd grow in value."

"They're not—"

"Stop," he said. "You're going to confirm their value beyond a shadow of a doubt. And then you're going to believe that I'll never do anything to hurt you ever again."

She didn't want to believe him. But she couldn't begin to guess his angle. If the shares weren't worth any money, she was going to find out. If they were, why wasn't he grabbing them?

"What did you write on the papers?" she asked again.

"I crossed out my own name. I replaced it with Jackson Rush's."

Her jaw dropped open, and a roar started in her ears.

"You can trust him."

She shook her head. She couldn't. She didn't dare.

"You can," her father insisted. "You know Cristal Creations is out of the Gerhard name."

How had he known that? How was it even relevant?

"Jackson did that for you," he said.

She peered at her father, trying desperately to decide if he was being honest or conning her. But she couldn't tell.

"You're smart," he said. "And you're right. Don't keep the shares. Give them to Jackson. He'll do right by you. He's the only person I'd trust."

"He'll give them back to you," she guessed. "Or he'll split them with you."

Trent smiled. "Then why don't I take them right now?"

She didn't have an answer for that.

"I conned Jackson. I used his father. I blamed the Gerhards. I told him you were in danger and counted on his principles and nothing else to get you out of it. He helped you because he's honest and trustworthy. Trust him, Crista. It's your best and only play. Don't keep these shares a minute longer than you have to."

She searched for the flaw, knowing there had to be something she didn't see. Her father would never willingly give up anything of value.

"It's exactly what it seems," he said softly. Then he tucked the papers back into the envelope. "You don't even have to believe me. You're going to verify every single thing for yourself."

Crista didn't know what to say. She didn't know what to do.

"I'll understand if you never come back," said Trent. "But I hope you will. I hope someday you'll be able to forgive me, and you'll come and see me." His eyes teared up again. "You'll come and tell me how you're doing."

Sympathy welled up inside her, and she knew she was in trouble. Despite her best efforts, he'd gotten to her all over again. She quickly scooped up the papers, jumped up and rushed for the door.

It wasn't until she was through the gate that she felt like she could take a breath. There she stopped, steadying herself.

In the distance, she saw Ellie get out of the car.

"Crista?" she called out.

"I'm coming." Crista's voice was far too dry for Ellie to hear. So she started walking. She gave a wave to show she was all right.

Ellie met her halfway. "What happened?"

"It was weird."

"Weird how? Are you okay?"

"He wouldn't sign." Crista handed Ellie the envelope.

Ellie stared down at it. "What? What do you mean he wouldn't sign?"

They came to the car.

"Take that to Jackson. Tell him to sign it and get Reginald to notarize it. I'm so done with this stupid mine."

"What do you mean, take it to Jackson?" Ellie stopped beside the passenger door, looking over the roof at Crista.

"This is going to sound crazy." It was crazy. "My father says he trusts Jackson. He doesn't want the shares for himself. He agrees I shouldn't keep them. So he wants me to give them to Jackson."

"Mac trusts Jackson," said Ellie. "And I trust Mac."

"Then we're all in agreement, aren't we?"

"Are you mad at me?"

"No."

"For saying I trust Mac?"

Crista let out a deep sigh. "I'm tired. I'm baffled, and I'm too exhausted to figure out the truth. Did you know Jackson was behind the Bahamian company that bought Cristal Creations?"

Ellie's eyes narrowed in obvious puzzlement.

"For some reason, Jackson got Cristal Creations out of Vern's hands. He's somehow set it up so that I can run my own company."

"That was an incredibly nice thing for him to do."

"I don't know why he did it."

"Why don't you ask him?"

"I can't."

"Sure you can."

But Crista knew she couldn't bring herself to face him. "If I was right about him, then I don't ever want to see him again. And if I was wrong about him, well, I doubt he ever wants to see me again."

"That's not true."

"Take him the papers. Let's get this over with."

Crista pulled open the door. By tomorrow, the next day at the latest, she'd be free of the Borezone Mine. She could finally get back to work and push Jackson out of her mind.

Jackson stared at the ownership transfer agreement for the Borezone Mine. "What's the catch?" he asked to no one in particular.

"None that I can see," said Reginald.

"Do you think her old man has really changed?" asked Mac.

"She doesn't believe they're worth anything," said Ellie.

Jackson looked up and took in the three faces. "But they are worth something. We all know they're worth millions. I can't take them." He shoved the papers across the meeting table in his Rush Investigations office.

"That's how you protect her," said Mac.

"She definitely wants you to have them," said Ellie.

"You can still use them to her benefit," said Reginald.

"It's not the same thing," said Jackson. "They belong to her. She has every right to own them, sell them—"

"Or give them away," said Mac.

"Not to me," said Jackson.

"Then who? Give her another solution. What is she supposed to do, sit at home and wait for Gerhard to come back?"

"If only you hadn't lied to her," said Ellie.

"That's not helping," said Mac.

"She's right," said Jackson. "But I didn't think I had a choice," he told Ellie. "If I'd revealed the whole truth up front, she'd have run fast and far from me. Gerhard would have convinced her to come back."

"Maybe," Ellie allowed.

"We should have gone to Vegas," said Jackson. "It was always the best plan."

"Want me to call Tuck?" asked Mac.

Jackson coughed out a laugh. "Right. Great idea. I could kidnap her all over again."

"I wouldn't kidnap her," said Ellie.

"No kidding," said Jackson. Clearly, he had to work on his sarcastic voice.

"But you can probably persuade her."

Jackson huffed. "I can't persuade her. I wouldn't try."

He loved Crista. There was no way he'd do a single thing to cause her more hurt.

"For her own good," said Ellie.

"Not a chance."

"Refuse to sign the papers."

"I already did," said Jackson.

"Offer to marry her instead."

"I already did that, too. She turned me down flat."

"Did you tell her you love her?" asked Ellie.

"I—"

"Don't bother denying it," said Mac.

"I think she knows," said Jackson.

Everyone else had figured it out. He was starting to feel like he was wearing a neon sign. Besides, what other explanation could there be for his behavior?

"She thinks you're angry with her," said Ellie.

"Why would she think that?"

"Because she refused to trust you."

"That's just good sense," said Mac.

Jackson frowned at him.

"I'm serious," said Ellie. "She's afraid you won't forgive her."

"There's nothing to forgive." His brain latched on to the word *afraid*. Why would Crista care about his forgiveness?

Ellie gave him a secretive smile.

"Are you saying…" he asked.

"I don't know anything for sure," said Ellie.

But she suspected. It was clear Ellie suspected. She thought Crista might have feelings for him.

"Where is she?"

"She's in Wisconsin by now. But I can take you to her."

"Wisconsin?"

"Far away from Vern Gerhard."

Okay, that was good.

Mac put his phone to his ear. "I'll get Tuck to warm up the jet."

Jackson was about to protest. Tuck had already done enough. But then he calculated the time savings and decided it was worth asking. Tuck could always say no.

"Good plan," he said to Mac.

"Wisconsin only?" asked Mac. "Or all the way to Vegas?"

Jackson grinned. Persuasion and even kidnapping was starting to sound like a very good idea. "All the way to Vegas."

Crista was in her motel room staring at her email, willing a message to arrive from Ellie. Surely she'd taken the papers to Jackson by now. Surely he'd signed. Crista knew he had to be angry with her, but she also believed he'd been trying to help her. Surely he'd be willing to do this one small thing.

She hit the refresh button, but there were no new messages.

"Come on," she said out loud.

A knock on her door startled her.

Fear immediately contracted her stomach. Her first thought was that it was Vern. Had he followed her from Chicago? Had he staked out the prison? Or maybe he'd threat-ened Ellie and forced her to reveal Crista's location.

The knock sounded again.

Crista carefully rose to her feet. The chain was on the door, but she had no doubt Gerhard's burly security men would break it down. She could tell them Jackson already owned the shares. But she had no proof. They probably wouldn't believe her.

She started to back away, thinking she'd lock herself in the bathroom and call the police.

"Crista?" came a man's voice.

No...

"Crista, it's me, Jackson."

Relief instantly rushed from her scalp to her toes.

"Open the door," he called.

"Jackson?" She rushed forward. "Jackson?" she called louder.

"Ellie gave me the papers."

"Good. That's good." She gulped a couple of deep breaths, staring at the door.

"Ellie and Mac are in the car."

"Ellie's here?"

"Yes."

That had to be good. It was all good. Vern hadn't found her. She wasn't afraid of Jackson. He must have signed the papers. Maybe he was here to give her a copy.

Her hands trembled as she pulled off the chain. Then she turned the dead bolt and twisted the door handle, open-ing the door.

Jackson was there, smiling. She was glad to see him. She was ridiculously glad to see him.

"Hi," she managed.

"Hi yourself."

"Ellie brought you?" That much was obvious, but she didn't really know what else to say to him.

"Can I come in?"

"Yes." She stepped back.

She glanced out at the parking lot. "Just you?"

"I need to talk to you alone."

"Okay." She shut the door behind him.

Then she turned to where he was standing, close, looking strong and sexy and not even a little bit angry.

"You signed?" she asked, so happy to have this all behind her.

She wanted to walk into his arms. She could hug him at least, couldn't she?

"I didn't sign," he said.

She stopped herself short. "What?"

"I didn't sign," he repeated.

"Why not?"

"I don't want your diamond mine, Crista."

"But…it's just a formality. You know that. Why would you refuse?"

Had everything he'd said been a lie? Did he not care about her at all? Was he so angry he was willing to let her take her chances with Vern and Manfred?

"Is transferring the shares all about the Gerhards?" he asked.

"Yes. If I don't own the mine, they go away."

"That's true."

She was starting to get annoyed. "So? What's your problem?"

"The problem is, my earlier deal stands," he said.

"You had a deal with my father?" What secret angle had she missed? She braced herself for what he was about to reveal.

"My deal was with you."

She didn't respond. He was talking in riddles.

"Vegas," he continued. "The deal was that I'd keep you safe from Gerhard by marrying you in Vegas."

"Is that a joke?"

"But I don't think I presented it right," he said.

She was growing more confused by the minute. "It was pretty straightforward."

They got married and foiled Vern's plan.

"No." Jackson shook his head, taking a step forward to bring them close together. "It wasn't straightforward at all. What I should have said back then was I love you, Crista Corday. Will you marry me and spend the rest of our lives together? Let's do it in Vegas, because I can't wait another second for you to be my wife."

His face went blurry in front of her and she blinked, realizing her eyes had teared up.

"What did you say?" she rasped. "You're not playing me?"

"I'm not playing you." He cradled her face with his palms. "I've never been more serious in my life."

"Because—" Her voice broke. "Because I couldn't take it if you were. Money I can lose."

"Trust in this, Crista. I love you with all my heart."

He kissed her, and joy sang through her chest. It was long minutes before he broke the kiss.

"I love you," she answered, breathless. "And I'll marry you in Vegas or anywhere else you want."

His arms went around her, and she hung on tight.

"You love me?" he asked.

"More than that. I trust you. I trust you with my heart, my soul and my life."

There was laughter in his voice. "And the diamonds, because the diamonds are very real."

"The diamonds aren't real." How many times did she have to say it?

"Maybe you'll believe it when you start turning them into jewelry designs."

"Maybe." If diamonds showed up in her workshop, she'd concede they were real.

"In the meantime, my friend Tuck is waiting at the airport with his jet."

"Oh, right. Your friend Tuck who has a jet."

"I told him he could be the best man."

"And you brought Ellie for maid of honor?"

"I brought Ellie. Though I don't know what you'll do for dresses and flowers."

"They have stores in Vegas."

"That they do. I'm sure we can find anything our hearts desire in Vegas."

She burrowed against his shoulder, drinking in the solid warmth of his body. "The only thing my heart desires is you."

He rocked her back and forth. "I am so monumentally glad to hear that."

The motel room door opened.

"Are we going to Vegas?" asked Ellie.

Crista grinned. "We're going to Vegas."

"Bachelorette at the Lion Lounge," Ellie sang.

"You'll have maybe an hour before the wedding," said Jackson. "I'd suggest you spend it shopping."

"You will need a dress." Ellie sounded disappointed.

"So will you," said Mac, his arm going around Ellie. "Something slinky. I've always had a thing for bridesmaids."

"Too much information," said Jackson.

Mac just grinned.

"I hope you have a thing for brides," Crista whispered to Jackson.

"I have a thing for one particular bride," he whispered back. "From the first second I saw her, I knew she had to be mine."

"But this time," she said, smiling up at him. "It'll be *my* dress. *My* wedding. But with you, Jackson. Forever."

* * * * *

"We could see each other for dinner."

Avery frowned, shifting the chart in her hands. "Maybe socializing isn't such a good idea with me being your physical therapist."

"Why not? Because you said everything outside of the office was fair game."

Her face flushed. "That's not what I meant and you know it."

His male instincts urged him to stalk closer, crowd her in and make her admit she was just as attracted as he was. Instead he forced himself to remain still, using words to reel her in. "Come on. You want an adventure. I want to help you find one. Let's talk about it over dinner."

"Well…" Her flush deepened, but she also straightened her shoulders. "I guess I could do dinner one night."

As he came to his feet, Avery's quizzical little smile distracted him. He saw nothing else. Not taupe walls, nor yellow scrubs. Just pale blue eyes and bow-shaped lips as she moved closer.

Before he could reach for his cane, his legs gave him the old heave-ho and collapsed. Avery had moved close, too close to miss out on his game of timber. Down they both went.

"Sweetheart, you're the softest landing place I've had in a while."

* * *

The Renegade Returns is part of the
Mill Town Millionaires series from Dani Wade.

THE RENEGADE
RETURNS

BY
DANI WADE

First Published in Great Britain 2016
By Mills & Boon, an imprint of HarperCollins*Publishers*
1 London Bridge Street, London, SE1 9GF

© 2016 Katherine Worsham

ISBN: 978-0-263-91869-4

51-0716

Our policy is to use papers that are natural, renewable and recyclable products and made from wood grown in sustainable forests. The logging and manufacturing processes conform to the legal environmental regulations of the country of origin.

Printed and bound in Spain
by CPI, Barcelona

Dani Wade astonished her local librarians as a teenager when she carried home ten books every week—and actually read them all. Now she writes her own characters, who clamor for attention in the midst of the chaos that is her life. Residing in the Southern United States with a husband, two kids, two dogs and one grumpy cat, she stays busy until she can closet herself away with her characters once more.

To My Mother

You instilled an early love of reading in me that has shaped who I truly am. Your encouragement throughout my life has helped me believe in myself, even when it was hard. Every day I use the dedicated work ethic and practicality you taught me to make my dreams a reality. Thank you.

I've watched up close as you've fought hard, worked steadfastly, prayed with belief and loved with everything in you. I only hope someday to be able to do the same half as well as you. All my love…

One

Ignoring stares and whispers was an art form Lucas Blackstone had perfected. The more wins he claimed as a stock car racer, the more attention he attracted. Which was normally fine by him. In fact, he thrived on it.

Used to thrive on it.

Tonight, he wished he could fade into the wainscoting on the walls so people would stop staring. Stop whispering about his arrival at the country club. Stop measuring the difficulty with which he walked to his family's chosen table. Stop speculating about whether his racing days as Renegade Blackstone were permanently over.

Just as he did during the long, dark hours of every night.

Instead, he pretended this was a normal night, a normal dinner with his family. Not his debut before his hometown after having his body broken into more pieces than any man should experience.

His back straight, he vowed to himself that he would beat this with every single step.

"You're doing so well," Christina softly encouraged him as he carefully placed each footfall on the way to their table. As their resident nurse and his brother Aiden's wife, she had been tracking Luke's progress since his accident earlier this year. "But by the end of the evening, you might be wishing for that wheelchair you refused."

"No," he said through teeth he tried not to clench. He didn't quite succeed.

He would not resort to invalid status. The marble-handled cane he leaned on was his single concession to his still-healing legs. The *plonk* every time it met the floor sounded loud in his head, even though he knew it hardly made a sound.

"All that macho stoicism will lead to one thing," she warned as they reached their destination. Then she rolled her eyes when the men all booed. "I'm serious, Luke. Pretending you don't need help will just make getting out of bed tomorrow more painful."

"You're so cute when you're concerned," he cooed back, laughing when she stuck out her tongue.

The reality couldn't always be covered by his teasing mask—but he sure tried. He'd become a close buddy with pain since his car accident. During everyday tasks, during rehabilitation. Sometimes it shot through him under the cloak of a dead sleep. He hated it, but pain could be good. The sharp sting reminded him he was alive. Not just a shell, a body that would never feel again.

Luke lived for high speeds. Recovery at a snail's pace could only be described as pure torture. Some days, he'd give anything to take his mind off his present state.

"You keep babying him, and he'll wish he'd never consented to coming home," Aiden teased his bride.

All the attention aside, Luke knew being back in Black Hills would be good for him. Helping his brothers out at the mill that supported the entire town would surely blunt the aching need to return to his race car. After a year of what they all suspected was sabotage to their business by an inside source, the family needed all hands on deck.

This is only temporary...

To his relief, he managed to seat himself after only a minor skirmish with the long tablecloth. *Damn accoutrements.* But the formal atmosphere had been the deciding factor in choosing to eat here tonight. Hope against hope it might keep nosy, small-town people in their seats—for a while.

"Stop pulling at your collar, Luke," his twin brother, Jacob, reprimanded.

But Luke couldn't help it. He was as ill at ease as his brother was comfortable in a suit. Even now his hand crept back up to tug at the tie around his neck—give him a racing suit any day. "This damn thing is almost as uncomfortable as all the people staring," he grumped. His comfort zone had always been his car—not polished silver, gold-rimmed china and fresh flower centerpieces.

"Well, most of these people are family friends, but they still love a celebrity. They can't help the need to watch," Aiden explained in his tolerant older-brother voice.

"I just enjoyed it more when they were in awe of my good looks." *Instead of speculating about my doom.*

Luke's teasing tone left his brothers and the women laughing, and gratitude added another layer to his self-defense. The maudlin martyr was not his most sought-after role. Only he knew there was a kernel of truth in his humor, and he would keep it that way. So he covered his discomfort as carefully as he draped his cloth napkin over his lap.

After ordering, Luke deemed it safe to let his gaze skim the softly lit room. A lot of faces had aged since he'd been in high school, though they were still familiar. It had been many years since he'd left town to start an incredibly successful racing career but he'd returned for a few events.

Some fund-raisers. Anything to make his visits home more bearable. He had spent time with his incapacitated mother and Christina, who was her nurse. After that, his only thought had been getting himself out of the house without running into his domineering grandfather.

Escape. If his life had a theme song, that would be the refrain. Now that the old man had kicked the bucket, Blackstone Manor had transformed into a home—thanks to the people around this table.

About halfway across the crowded space Luke's gaze snagged on a tawny, upswept head of hair. The woman's profile was sharper than it had been in high school, more refined. Gone was the softness of a young woman, now honed into a sphinxlike silhouette that immediately captured his eye.

Avery Prescott. Now that he thought about it, he hadn't seen her on any of his visits home. Which was odd—and from the looks of her, a total shame.

As if feeling his gaze, she glanced his way with pale blue eyes. Despite the distance between them, something jolted through his body. Deeper than an *I know you*, but not a lightning flash. More a wash of awareness that flooded over all his uncomfortable emotions, muting them to radio silence. When she quickly turned back to her dining companions, he had an urge to stand, to command her attention.

This was a pleasant surprise. Luke had always enjoyed women—the sight, sound and smell of them—but there'd been nothing since his accident. Not even when surrounded by a hospital floor full of pretty nurses. Oh, he'd flirt and play, but it had covered a storm of pain, worry and frustration that he didn't know how to calm now that his one mode of escape had been snatched from him.

But tonight, watching Avery as she smiled and conversed with her dinner companions sent an electric spark of attraction tingling down his spine. Her frequent glances in his direction made him wonder if she felt it, too, but their eyes never met again.

Avoiding him, huh?

Throughout dinner and conversing with a few brave visitors, his awareness remained. Finally she stood to leave, giving him his first unhindered look at her slender figure. Her sheath dress showcased curves right where he liked them, proportionate to her delicate bone structure.

She made her way through the tables with elegant grace, pausing to smile and speak to several people, but never for long. The candlelight from the centerpieces reflected off her earrings, lending sparkle to her slight glow. Her black sequined dress reminded him of her family's wealth and the undeniable fact that she belonged in this place. Still she refused to look his way.

He thought she was going to avoid their table altogether, until Christina stood to wave. "Avery, over here," she called.

Avery's hesitation was noticeable, at least to Luke. But then again, he'd barely taken his eyes off her to look at his plate. Why didn't she want to stop and say hi?

His memories were of a gawky girl, shy, always on the fringes. Under direct attention, she would stumble over her words, drop things, trip over her own feet. Tonight she moved with a type of deliberate grace. Head high. Steps secure. This new Avery fascinated him.

Her greeting included them all, when a need inside Luke wanted her to rest those pale blue eyes on him. He kept his body on lockdown, refusing to draw her attention until it was freely given.

"Having dinner with Doc Morris again, I see?" Aiden said with a grin.

"If his wife wasn't with us, some rumors might have started by now."

Luke soaked in the slight movements of her hands, the shrug of those delicate shoulders as everyone chatted around him. *This is crazy—the last thing you need is to get involved with someone here. You're recovering.* Still he couldn't look away, couldn't ignore the draw he felt growing deep inside.

"Doc says someone has to make sure I'm eating. We don't want to lose a community asset after he worked so hard to get me into good schools and internships," she added in a decent replication of the older man.

As a round of chuckles rose from the table, she finally glanced his way—and those sparks inside him multiplied. "Um, hi, Luke." With that slight stall, the first small chink in her sophisticated armor appeared.

He remembered those same words spoken to him with the enthusiasm of a young girl trying hard to hide her crush, but not quite succeeding. Now, that awkward innocence had morphed into a sophisticated woman with a restrained politeness, as if by keeping herself under tight control she could prevent a repeat of the embarrassments of her youth.

Somehow, he didn't like this as much as his memories.

"Are you a doctor now?" Luke asked. How could he have been home so often and never thought to ask what had happened to the young girl who had hung around the edges of their social circle?

Her gaze touched on his before skittering away. "Actually, I'm a physical therapist."

Ouch. His recent painful visits for therapy did not make that a happy revelation. Very unexpected. Very unwelcome.

"In fact," Aiden said with an amused tone that set Luke's nerves on edge, "she's *your* physical therapist."

In a flash, Luke relived the agony of his therapy sessions over the last three months and winced. Pain forced things to the surface, compelled a man to reveal way more emotion than he wanted other people to see. "Oh, hell no," he muttered.

Apparently his words weren't low enough, because Avery's elegant features took on a hint of frost. "I'm afraid you don't have a choice. I'm the only physical therapist in Black Hills. Or within fifty miles of it."

Damn. "I didn't mean…"

Her body straightened, gaining only a slight inch in stature. "And I'm a damn good one, too."

"Everyone around here knows that."

Luke had been so focused on Avery that he hadn't noticed the approach of anyone else. Next to her now stood Mark Zabinski, an old high school friend of Jacob's and part of the upper management at Blackstone Mills.

"So the Renegade is back," Mark went on, ignoring Luke's lack of welcome. "And causing quite the stir."

"That I am." Might as well own it.

Avery glanced around the table, surveying the reunited Blackstone family. Her voice was hushed compared to Mark's forceful tone. "It must be strange, having all of you back here, together again."

Very few people would notice the phenomenon, much less mention how each brother had left, then returned to find their place in Black Hills now that their grandfather was dead. But this was Avery. He remembered glimpses of her standing on the edge of the crowd in high school, alone but not missing an ounce of what occurred.

Aiden's dark gaze swept over them all before he smiled. "Yes, but family is good. Very good."

Luke wouldn't have gotten through the last few months without family, including both his brothers, Christina and Jacob's fiancé, KC. "Amen," he agreed.

But as the conversation continued around them, Luke didn't miss the dark shadow that clouded Avery's eyes, the

subtle shift of her expression. And he certainly didn't miss
Mark's hand casually lying against the small of her back.
A sign of ownership, possessiveness, protection. Comfort
for a friend? Or something more?

Avery didn't move away, but she also didn't relax into
the touch, either. *Interesting.*

"Mark," Jacob said, his tone firming to one of authority, "I'm glad you stopped by. The computer gurus are finally coming to install the new computer system at the
plant. Time for an upgrade like we talked about last month,"
Jacob continued. "We'll meet early tomorrow morning to
discuss it."

Mark shifted on his feet, his dress shoes squeaking
under the stress. "Great."

Mark smiled as he said it, but Luke suspected he wasn't
as thrilled as he tried to look. Something about the over-
stretch of his smile, giving his face a slightly Joker edge.

"Avery, let me escort you to the valet," Mark said, using
that damnable hand to steer her away. She nodded, her
gaze making a warm sweep of the table…while studiously
avoiding Luke.

Why did that leave him feeling cold?

Escorting a woman—something Luke couldn't do with
ease anymore. As if she knew his thoughts followed them,
Avery glanced back over her shoulder, but a cool mask still
protected her emotions.

Great. Just what he needed—a ticked-off physical therapist with the ability to visit pain on him with a simple
twitch of her wrist. His dismissal of her abilities had given
her motivation aplenty for inflicting a twinge or two on
him.

But Luke was used to using his charm to get out of
sticky situations—turning them into something positive,
something entertaining. Despite the complication, his curiosity grew. So did his unexpected need. He'd been lost

in a miasma of pain and frustration that seriously weighed him down. But this kick-start to his motor had lifted him up, exhilarated him. A relationship was nowhere on his agenda, but a little battle of wills would definitely liven up his current dull existence.

A few fireworks to dull the pain. What could be more fun than that?

How could anyone look so cute in scrubs? Not that Avery was the type to appreciate being categorized as *cute*. She probably preferred *capable*. Her sunny yellow scrubs were paired with a no-nonsense expression and friendly, but impersonal, tone. Her detachment caused him to itch after the receptionist brought him through the double doors into the heart of the therapy facility.

If Avery thought her all-business attitude would keep him at arm's length, she'd get a surprise. He'd just tease his way through whatever crack he could find in her armor. The challenge brought a surge of energy. Besides, befriending her might keep her from taking any vengeance out on his bones.

An impressive workout room occupied an open central space in the main part of the building. Top-of-the-line equipment gleamed from careful upkeep. Avery gestured him through a side door and closed them inside. The treatment room had the same look of quality, including a padded table, small desk and comfortable chairs. "This place is really nice. You've done well for yourself, Avery," he said.

The compliment garnered him his first genuine smile. No pretense. "Thank you. This building has been a blessing to me and to my patients."

And it obviously meant a lot to her. "You named the clinic after your mother."

"Yes." Her smile dimmed a little, awakening an urge

to give her a comforting hug just as he would Christina, who'd proven to be a true friend.

Avery continued. "We became exceptionally close during her illness. Besides, she provided the funding for a bigger, better clinic for the community in my inheritance. We're very lucky to have it."

Her pride in her accomplishment added a glow to her expression, awakening jealousy in Luke's gut. He remembered being proud of what he did, but the memories were fading from sharp to hazy, obscured by the turmoil of recent months.

This woman used her healing talents every day in a community that needed her. How fulfilling must that be? "You have plenty of patients?"

She nodded, sending her thick ponytail swinging. "I like to think it's because I do good work, and not just because I'm the only convenient choice."

"I bet it is. You must be good with your hands, huh?"

To his surprise, that professional demeanor slipped and she fumbled the chart from her hands. It hit the ground with a clatter. "That's really inappropriate, Luke," she warned with a frown.

He hadn't meant it to be, but now that he thought about it that way... He watched as a flush of pink swept up her neck and into her cheeks. Oh, she could be proper all she wanted, but now he knew—she might've grown up, but this chickadee was still as easily flustered as she'd been in high school.

Teasing her was gonna be entertaining. And her all-business attitude screamed for him to bring a little fun, a little laughter into her life. Since he could use some fun, too, he'd be doing them both a favor. Right?

"I'm pretty well known for saying whatever comes to mind," he said with a grin. "And being handsome. And charming." It wasn't bragging, 'cause it was true.

"And obnoxiously self-absorbed?" The contrast between her words and sickly sweet tone made him laugh. A true laugh. Man, that felt good.

He conceded with a sexy grin. "Maybe. Occasionally."

That professional mask slipped a fraction more before she smoothed her palms over already sleek hair, back to her ponytail.

He was getting somewhere now. Just a little more ribbing, and she might actually laugh like a real person instead of a robot.

She pulled out a rolling stool and sat, propping his folder on her lap. Guess it was down-to-business time, which wasn't nearly as amusing. Luke had worked hard at recovery, but this was the first time fun had appeared anywhere in his current nightmare. He didn't want to leave it behind.

"Goals?" she asked, focusing her attention on the papers.

That was easy enough. His one goal had been blazing in his brain since the accident. "To be back in my car. ASAP."

Avery glanced up, those gorgeous eyes wide, drawing him in. "That's pretty decisive."

"You say that like it's a bad thing." Her tone left him defensive, when there was no need for it. Then again, Luke's life had been spent on goals other people just didn't get. "You asked. I answered."

Her frown and longer-than-polite stare awakened an urge to squirm he hadn't encountered since third grade.

"Most of my patients are more worried about walking unaided again," she mused, as if talking to herself rather than him.

Alarm streaked along his nerves. He didn't want her thinking too hard, digging too deep. So he grinned. "Oh, I have other goals."

After a minute of silence, she made a speed-up gesture with the pen in her hand. "And…"

"Having a good time doesn't sound nearly as professional, if you know what I mean."

The pen hit the floor. Instant color stained her creamy cheeks. Wow. When was the last time he'd seen a blush like that? It must have been— A memory burst inside his brain. *High school.*

"Do you need some help with that?"

The jolt that rushed through him had to be from surprise. After all, who would have expected Little Miss Perfect to offer to help him change clothes? A blush spread over her rounded cheeks to match the heat racing over his body.

He looked from the dry shorts in his hand back to Avery in the first bikini he'd ever seen her wear. Must have been bought special for this final summer bash for seniors at the lake before everyone flew off to the colleges of their choice. Everyone except him—his destination was North Carolina and any racing track they'd let him drive on. But even the prospect of finally leaving home hadn't made him reckless enough to initiate the greenest girl in their group. No matter what her pale blue eyes were begging for. "Honey, helping me would involve a lot more than a change of clothes."

"I know." But that flush on her fair skin, bright enough to see in the dim light this far from the bonfire, told him she didn't truly know what she was offering.

To his surprise, a shot of adrenaline flashed through his veins. The same kind that came with hundred-mile-an-hour speeds and the feel of the wheel beneath his palms. Not the sexy slide into arousal he usually got with girls. Even his alcohol-soaked brain knew this was a bad idea, despite his body's approval. Better to stop this before it began, even if it meant being harsh...

"I think somebody with more experience would be a bigger help to me."

* * *

Oh, no. How could Luke have forgotten that long-ago summer night? Without thought, he said, "Holy— Avery, I can't believe you came on to me that night."

The little rolling stool shot backward, as far across the tiny exam room as she could go. The thump as she hit the opposite wall went unnoticed by her. She only stared, her flush deepening, spreading down her neck and chest to disappear under the yellow scrubs. "I—"

Why had he said that? Whatever he thought usually slid out of his mouth without any semblance of a stop sign in between, that's why. Most people found it funny. But her utter mortification was not what he'd wanted.

"I'm sorry, Avery. I should never have said that." His mama had taught him to own up to his mistakes. People might think he was all ego—and he let them keep believing it—but he'd never dishonor a woman or ignore her distress. "Seriously, I may not always play the gentleman, but I would never intentionally embarrass a friend."

Her recovery was quick. She straightened on the stool and crept forward with her heels until she'd crossed half the little room. He couldn't help but notice she still kept some distance between them. The return of the professional mask took a little longer, though. "Friends, huh?"

He grinned, hoping to put her at ease. "I'd like to think so."

She nodded, as if that settled things. But it took her a few moments to say, "So I wanted a little walk on the wild side." She shrugged those delicately built shoulders, keeping her eyes trained on his chart. "What high school senior doesn't?"

His libido urged him to ask if she'd gotten it, but for once he kept his trap shut. He sifted through his memories for any gossip he'd heard about her, but came up empty.

All Jacob had supplied last night were the directions to the therapy center. No bad behavior. No scandalous liaisons.

Was there no gossip to be had? Last night she'd been at dinner with Doctor Morris and his wife, who were seventy if they were a day. She'd had no date accompanying her, even though Mark had joined her to walk out. No wedding ring on her long, slender fingers. Her last name hadn't changed. Maybe there hadn't been any wild times…

Maybe he should change that?

Oh. Hell. No. The last thing he needed was a casual hookup with the least casual woman he knew. He tried to erase the seductive thought as she spoke again.

"We'll start each session with a warm-up, then build strength with resistance exercises—first using just your body weight, then moving up," she was saying, using her pen to check off her points. Her precision marks were a little too perfect, holding her interest a little too much. "Your therapist in North Carolina gave me your records. You've come an incredibly long way, but today I'd like to see what's happening for myself…"

Luke didn't want to think about any of it—so he distracted himself with the fall of soft yellow scrubs that skimmed her curves. If she knew what he was thinking right now, she'd probably give him an exaggerated frown and tell him that activity wasn't on his approved list.

Maybe he'd have to prove her wrong.

"Okay, Luke?"

"Yep," he automatically answered.

"You weren't listening, were you?"

"Nope."

The look on her face implied he'd been naughty, but it was her big sigh, the one that lifted her nicely rounded breasts, that drew his attention. Not the sigh, just the—

Boy, he was in *so* much trouble.

"I guess I'll explain as we go along," she said, ignoring

his distraction. She rose to her feet and turned to open the door. "Let's see what you're capable of…"

That didn't sound good, and his previous experience with physical therapy told Luke it wouldn't be. She started him on a slow walk around the room, moving alongside him. Her soothing voice washed over him, almost relaxing despite the awkward coordination of his uncooperative legs and the cane.

Except he knew what was coming.

The upper body work wasn't an issue. Moving and challenging those muscles actually felt good. His hips and legs—not so much. Avery put him through some resistance training, range-of-motion work and stretching. An hour later, drenched in sweat, he had to wonder if a sadistic grin lurked behind her ardent expression. Her encouraging words said she wanted to help, but was she secretly satisfied by his pain?

After all, he'd humiliated her in high school. That he'd done it for her own good didn't seem like adequate justification now that he was an adult. But maybe he could make it up to her somehow?

Or would spending time with Avery outside of his therapy be the equivalent of playing with fire?

Two

Avery ignored the shake of her hands as she removed electrode pads from Luke's legs and lower back. Thank goodness she didn't have to do anything complicated. Otherwise she'd surely have made an idiot of herself. The sight of his body in nothing but athletic shorts was a test to her professionalism.

She cleared her throat, trying to ease the constriction. "I'll let you get dressed and then meet you up front."

Except thoughts of Luke and clothes only reminded her of their earlier conversation, and her immature offer to help him dress. *Ah, there are those stomach-twisting nerves again.* She hurried out the door with only a small bump against the frame.

Luke was so much like she remembered—only ten times more dangerous. Obviously, he'd figured out that these joking innuendos were the way to get beneath her guard. She needed a way to counteract them.

Her current method wasn't working very well.

Teasing from any man under sixty flustered her, but her reactions to Luke were too strong—a tempest compared to a sprinkle of rain when it came to other men. The fact that she found him amazingly attractive only made her nerves worse. Her interest had nothing to do with him being a local celebrity and everything to do with him being, well, Luke.

His charm and ready smile had drawn her from the moment she'd met him. Whenever they'd seen each other as teenagers at country club dinners or various gatherings, Avery would follow him around, subtly watching him. Unlike his brother Jacob, who had surrounded himself with a businesslike wall, Luke knew how to make himself comfortable in any social situation.

A skill Avery had never developed.

Oh, she could chat with people in town, people she'd known all her life. Her genuine interest in and sympathy for her patients made interacting with them easy. And she had a few girlfriends, like Christina, whom she could turn to when she really needed to talk.

But drop her into a bunch of strangers and Avery simply froze. She reverted back to her high school speech class, with all those eyes staring at her, waiting for her to say something brilliant—and all she could do was squeak.

"So how often do I need to be here?"

As Luke approached, Avery looked up from the chart she wasn't really reading. Even with the cane, she could have sworn a sexy male model had invaded her territory. Her breath caught in her throat once more, before she released it on a sigh.

Who was she kidding? She'd tried to ride that train once, and Luke had made it plain she wasn't his type. If he never brought that night up again, it would be too soon. Besides, Luke wouldn't be sticking around for long. He'd made that perfectly plain during their discussion.

Why risk more humiliation by reading into his teasing more than he could possibly mean? She knew from countless hours of observation that, for Luke, flirting was a way of life.

She forced herself to erase any mooning, wistful tendencies from her voice. She kept it short and, okay, maybe a little stiff. "Let's get you set up for Wednesday, shall we? I won't have an exact plan until I've looked over my notes from today."

Avery's receptionist was flirtier than usual, giving Luke a run for his money. Cindy had all the outgoing personality that had passed Avery by. She chatted and giggled with Luke as she scheduled his next appointment. Normally Avery appreciated that Cindy made their patients smile, but today their laughter left her feeling like an outsider—though she'd never admit that to anyone.

"And what's this?"

Avery barely quelled the instinctive grab for what she didn't want him to see. She narrowed her eyes at Cindy. They'd been looking at the brochure earlier and Avery was pretty sure she'd asked Cindy to put it away. Yet there it was, sitting on the checkout counter, as pretty as you please.

"Cindy…" Avery warned. That innocent expression didn't fool Avery.

She tried a glare, but Cindy just laughed it off. "Rock climbing and rappelling—not far from here," the receptionist said. "Can you believe it? Avery's been on a search for 'adventure' lately." The air quotes didn't help Avery feel better.

"Really?"

Luke's drawl should not send shivers down her spine. And his slow perusal over her body should not make her mouth water. As if satisfied with what he saw, he broke out a wicked grin. "Lucky for you, adventure just walked through your door."

"I'm doing just fine on my own, thankyouverymuch," Avery said, embarrassed by the childish huff that ended her words.

Luke's glance across the counter at Cindy was answered with a sad shake of the woman's head. As Avery flushed from head to toe, she vowed to murder her receptionist—as soon as she got Luke out the door.

Those amber eyes swung back to study her. "You sure about that?" he asked.

The intensity of his gaze caught her, held her. His expression was still amused, but gone from his eyes was the teasing, smiling Luke. In the amber depths she saw darkness simmering beneath the surface.

"I keep telling you," Cindy said, "what you need is a nice man who will give you lots of fun without having to resort to stunts like this." She waved the recovered brochure in the air.

With a single lift of his brow, Luke added, "What are the men in this town thinking?"

"They sure don't know what they're missing," Cindy teased.

Had Avery's blush reached lobster levels yet? "I don't need sex to have fun." Oh dear, had she really just said that out loud?

"Nobody said you did, sugar," Luke said. His teeth bit into his full lower lip, but that didn't stop his grin. "But why don't you tell me exactly what kind of adventure you're looking for? I might be able to help."

The ring of the door chime saved her from answering. "Gotta go," she mumbled as she moved, only to stumble over her own feet.

Luke was quick to catch her arm, helping her upright

again. "Why don't we talk about it over dinner?" he asked, too soft for anyone else to hear.

Or maybe not. Cindy's happy dance in the background had Avery's face burning once more.

"Nope," she said. "I'm good."

Again his husky voice played along her nerves. "I'm sure you are, but with me it would be better."

Oh, Lordy. Avery almost choked. She wanted nothing more than to get out of here. Forget whoever had come through the door.

Twisting out of Luke's grasp, she chose the other direction and the safety of the therapy room. She threw an "I'm sure you have better things to do," over her shoulder as she escaped, praying she didn't damage her dignity by falling flat on her face.

Heaven help her, Luke Blackstone was gonna be a handful.

"Has she made you cry like a girl yet?"

Luke quelled his sudden urge to smack his twin. After all, they weren't twelve anymore. "No. There's been no crying." Though his control had been shaky sometimes, he'd held it together. Jacob was teasing, but thankfully he didn't know how close to home his statement hit.

As the oldest brother, Aiden obviously thought he had a say, too. "I thought for sure she'd pulverize you after what you said at the country club."

Of course, someone had to bring that up. "I'm too cute for her not to forgive me."

Aiden smirked, then made a quick retreat behind his desk before Luke's swing could connect. So his restraint hadn't lasted long. He'd always been a big kid.

Unlike Aiden, who looked perfectly at home behind the heavy desk in the study at Blackstone Manor—though the studious furniture and shelves full of books were slightly deceiving. Aiden had been born too big for his britches. Luke's earliest memories were of Aiden being punished in this very room by their grandfather for some teenage rebellion or another. The adult Aiden refused to back down, either. It was there in the artistic tumble of his dark hair and lack of a tie.

His brothers shared a grin that awoke suspicions in Luke's mind. "Spill it."

"Just be careful, that's all," Aiden said.

Luke looked from one to the other, settling on the familiar face of his twin. "What's he mean? What could little ol' Avery do to me?"

"Oh, it's not Avery you need to watch out for," Jacob said. "It's the town."

Huh?

Jacob went on. "Avery is notorious in Black Hills. This entire town has tried to marry her off ever since her mother died. They're relentless."

"Why?"

Aiden smirked. "You've been away from a small town for too long if you have to ask. She's young, pretty and single. Every matron in the county sees her as a princess in need of someone to take care of her."

They both eyed Luke, who quickly held up his hands in surrender. "The last thing I need is a princess." He moved over to one of the long windows, hiding his reaction from the others, because deep inside he couldn't deny his attraction. He could ignore it as long as he wanted, but it was there all the same.

"Just be careful," Jacob said. "They'll marry you off before a first date."

"Not. Me."

His twin just laughed, making him look more like Luke despite his close-cropped hair. "Yeah, right. The princess and the local celebrity—they'd eat that up."

Definitely time to change the subject. "Didn't we meet here to talk about something more important than local gossip? Like this spying job you have for me?"

Aiden choked, so Jacob answered, "Well, I wouldn't call it that."

"Why not? Don't think I can pull off the James Bond bit?" He mimed straightening a suit jacket and tie, just for kicks.

"I don't think he went in for corporate sabotage. A little too tame for him."

Luke shrugged. "Hey, I've got to start somewhere."

Jacob threw up his hands and dropped into one of the chairs, obviously knowing when he'd been verbally out-maneuvered. But Aiden didn't give up. "I'm hoping, if you come in with the stated purpose of inspecting the mill to bring you up to snuff as a full partner, then maybe you'll see something Jacob and I have missed."

The brothers, along with their new head of security, Zachary Gatlin, had been secretly investigating a sabo-teur who seemed intent on ruining Blackstone Mills. The brothers had eliminated several suspects, but still had no clue who the actual culprit was. Or if they were even still out there. Whoever it was intent on destroying Black Mills would end up destroying the whole town in the process, since they were the biggest supplier of both jobs and hous-ing in the area—heck, the whole county. Without the mill, Black Hills would cease to exist.

It had been a grueling year for his brothers, dealing with all of that on top of Luke's car accident. "Anything new?" Luke asked.

"Nothing I can prove, yet," Jacob said, his amber eyes darkening.

"That sounds promising."

His twin nodded. "Zach has one of his men following

the trail, but it looks like we also have some embezzling going on."

"That's bold," Luke said. "The orders, company equipment, our cotton supply and the Manor itself...now money. Is there anything this guy isn't afraid to put his hands on?"

"Not that we can tell," Aiden said with a slow shake of his head. He pressed his palms against the desktop. "As soon as we cut off one avenue, he finds another. All too easily."

Luke paced across the room despite some lingering muscle pain from his therapy session. His rising anxiety made the walls close in, leaving him eager to move, to escape. An all-too-familiar feeling. "That's disheartening."

"Well," Aiden said, "I hope I can cheer you up with my news."

"Yeah?" the twins said in chorus.

"The legalities of Grandfather's will are all finished. The mill is now mine," Aiden said.

"Wow. That was quicker than you thought," Luke said. "Congratulations."

"It *was* quicker than I thought," Aiden conceded. "But I'm glad, because now I can move on to plan B."

A short glance at Jake didn't provide any clues as to what that might be. He looked as expectant as Luke felt. Aiden pulled a thick envelope out of his inner jacket pocket.

"I've had my personal lawyer pull up this paperwork," he said. "I'm changing the ownership of the mill to all three of us, instead of just me."

Luke simply stared, not fully comprehending.

Jacob spoke for both of them. "But Aiden, this is *your* inheritance."

"It shouldn't be. It should be *ours*. Not just mine. Not a weapon to turn us against each other, as Grandfather intended." He took a solid breath. "A family investment.

We're all putting our lives into the mill, the town. We're sharing the responsibility. We should share the benefits."

"Whoa. Wait a minute."

Jacob's smile faded as he looked over at Luke, but Luke couldn't give in just to make his twin happy.

"I'm not staying here," he reminded them. "The only thing I plan on investing my life in is my racing career— the minute I'm cleared to get behind the wheel. I'm here only because I have to be."

Luke could almost feel Jacob's emotions fall along with his expression. Aiden remained more stoic as he said, "You never know what might happen in the future, Luke."

"Is this why you insisted I come home?" Luke asked, panic rising in his chest. "Did you think you could force me home, force me to find something of value here, and then I'd never want to leave? Like you two have?"

He didn't even realize his voice had risen until he stopped talking. The three of them stared at each other in silence. Embarrassment swept over Luke like a heated blanket. Where had that come from? "Look, I'm sorry. I know y'all would never do that to me."

"No, I wouldn't," Aiden agreed quietly. "I would never trick you into coming here. After all, I know very well how that feels."

Their grandfather had faked his own death, bringing Aiden home to care for their sick mother, but it was only a trick to force Aiden and Christina into marrying. Even though the man really was dead now, Aiden faced what James Blackstone had done to him every day. Luckily, he'd been given a happy ending.

Luke didn't want one. Not here.

Aiden wasn't finished. "I'd never force you to sign this paperwork," he said, giving the envelope a little shake. "But that doesn't mean I don't wish you would. Regardless of what your immediate future holds, you're still a part of this family. I hope one day you can willingly put your name on the mill, and reap the benefits along with the rest of your family."

All the work would be done by Aiden and Jacob. They should have the rewards—they *would* have the rewards. And Luke would have his freedom. He loved his brothers, loved the new family they'd built. But how could he stay here and still feed his love for the road?

Unbidden, an image of Avery's face as she flushed with embarrassment came to him. He shook the enticing image away. He had never let anything in Black Hills hold him back. He certainly wasn't going to start now.

He and Avery would have a little fun, something to liven up his time here, but he could still walk away on his own terms. When he was good and ready.

Three

All work and no play made Avery a dull girl—and apparently made Luke a frisky boy. Just the look on his face as he settled into one of the treatment rooms warned her he would be trouble.

Avery experienced a lot of feelings during her therapy sessions with clients: pride, sympathy, joy…but never this mixture of irritation and interest. How did he get under her skin with such little effort? A few words and she was tripping over her own feet.

His very presence seemed to inject her with pheromones that clouded her mind and drew her thoughts where they shouldn't go in a professional setting. Especially when her work required her to have her hands all over him.

Then there was the return of the awkwardness. She'd stopped dating because of it. Better to avoid it than to wonder if she had a medical condition—one that caused shaking, clumsiness and unintelligent muttering—all with a single look from any eligible, attractive man. The sight of a handsome man shot her adrenaline up, and if he spoke to her, she immediately became all thumbs. Her considerable intelligence didn't help at all. And her fellow citizens' determination to marry her off meant she'd had a wealth of humiliating experiences.

Dropping things, stumbling into door frames, bumping into all manner of furniture, and—her favorite—jerking her fork so that food ended up in all kinds of crazy places. One time, she'd actually flicked pasta onto her date's eyebrow. She couldn't remember that incident without cringing. So Mark escorted her to many functions, which gave her a reprieve from the matchmaking mamas.

The only time it didn't happen was when she put on her scrubs and became her professional self—comfortable in her knowledge and authority.

Until Luke. And he knew it, too.

Luke—with his sexy stare and flirty ways—jumpstarted the phenomenon quicker than any guy ever had. Which was why she approached him for this second session with her professional facade firmly in place. And it would stay that way. "I've worked up a comprehensive plan for you," she said, "now that I've had a chance to evaluate you firsthand—"

"Firsthand evaluation?" he asked, bending to catch her gaze. "How did I miss that? Can I have a do-over?" His wiggling brows didn't help her nerves. She gripped his chart hard before it could get loose.

"Behave," she said in her sternest voice.

"Oh, honey, I don't know how," he said with a wicked grin that sent shivers racing over her.

How could he derail her so easily, so completely? She dared not speak for a moment, afraid she'd get out no more than a croak as her throat tried to close. That would be humiliating.

Finally, she cleared the constriction. "Look, in this

clinic, I'm the boss. This is my career." She adopted a stern look, despite the amusement on his face. "Here, I'm not your friend, family, or—" She almost said *girlfriend*. Where the heck had that come from? "So stop playing and get busy."

He didn't respond right away, which surprised her. Luke always seemed quick on the draw. But she could feel him watching her. Probably preparing for battle.

Lord, have mercy. His teasing made her want to combust from the inside out. Her cheeks burned in a flash fire she couldn't control. She hadn't felt like this since, well, since Luke had jokingly teased her in high school. Good or bad, she wasn't sure. The mixture of irritation and utter fascination with someone who could dive right into the good parts of life while she was left hugging the walls in fear confused her.

"You know what I mean," she finally said, swallowing her emotions down. "We can be friends elsewhere—"

"We can?"

"—but here, business only." Maybe the less she spoke the better. He seemed intent on twisting her words for his own amusement.

"So out there you're fair game?" he asked with a quirk of his brow. Smart-ass.

"Down to work. Now," she said, holding out the folder, open to the plan she'd worked up for him.

"Can I just say one thing before the friendship blackout starts?" he asked.

Knowing anything she said would just encourage him, she simply watched him without responding.

"Look, I wasn't kidding about dinner," he said, bending a little to look her in the eyes.

Startled, she met his gaze without hesitation, getting a spark of deep connection before turning away. "Don't worry about it," she said, hoping to shoo the subject away like an unwelcome bug.

"Look, you said you wanted to have some fun, an adventure—"

"Actually, Cindy said that."

"And I can help."

She remembered his whispered words from the other day. There was no doubt in her mind that any adventure would be incredible with Luke along for the ride. "What are you talking about?"

"Hey, every day is an adventure for me. And I don't need to climb the side of a mountain for a thrill. I'd go so far as to bet that there are some pretty interesting adventures right here close to home that you haven't even thought about."

"And you plan to show them to me?"

He straightened a little. "Why not?"

She couldn't raise her voice above a whisper. "Why are you doing this?"

"In my book, I owe you. I acted like a jerk…before… but I've always seen you as a friend. Besides, this sounds a whole lot more interesting than what I had planned—jaunts over here for my therapist to torture me, and… Nope, that's about it for the next few months." His smile was hopeful. "Let me do this for you."

"I don't know…"

"Scared?"

Heck, yes. "Maybe."

His teasing smirk said he knew he would win. "That's okay. It's all part of the fun."

Suddenly it was all too much—the teasing, the attraction, the nerves. She desperately needed to shift gears. Holding up her hands, she said, "Look, today, we're talking about you. Not me."

"Um, not so far."

"Stop playing and pay attention." Her schoolmarm demands only made him smile wider, but this time he actually cooperated. Miracle of miracles.

That grin said he wasn't finished with her yet, sparking anticipation low in her core, but he finally reached his hand out for the chart.

With relief, she let him read because she didn't have any starch left for her voice.

"This plan is mapped out for ten months."

His unexpected dark tone warned her she might need starch for her backbone, too. "Yes. This is a reasonable prognosis to have you completely healed, strengthened and back on the racing circuit for the season after next."

"That's too long."

She frowned. "But your other therapist projected that from the time of his initial evaluation it could be a year or more before your body is strong enough to return without a risk of further injury. I have to agree."

Luke was shaking his head before she was even half-finished. "Not an option."

She could totally sympathize as the last of the teasing disappeared from his eyes, replaced by frustration. "Our bodies don't always agree to the timelines we want," she reminded him, her voice going soft with sympathy.

"This one damn well better." There was no room for anything but determination in Luke's voice. "I will be back on the racing circuit this next season. No later."

Avery knew when pushing would gain her ground, and this definitely wasn't the time. So she let his remark go. She'd found when men got something in their heads, especially something they were passionate about, there wasn't any argument that would do much good.

And she was frankly relieved that his determination got his focus off her. By the time they moved into the workout room, her control was firmly back in place. A return to the comfortable fit of her therapist persona.

Luke's rippling upper body muscles distracted her at times—clearly he worked out regularly. His body was slim but strong, deceptively so when hidden beneath his clothes. But it met every challenge she gave him and more. His lower body performed, though it was obviously not to his satisfaction.

He gave it his all—she couldn't fault him for not trying. About halfway through the circuit, she started thinking of him as Tough Guy. No matter the demand, he did it without question. He never asked to stop, never cried— almost 90 percent of her patients did in the early days. He just kept pushing forward.

His expression was the most serious she'd seen on him since his return, except for the stoic one she'd glimpsed as he'd made his way across the dining room floor that first night. She'd seen similar expressions on many patients—that determination to ignore the stares, ignore the pain and force yourself to move regardless of your body's protests.

As they came to the end of his session, she bent and twisted his legs, pulling them into positions that would ease the tension, improve his range of motion and hopefully lessen his pain. Time and again she forced her gaze away from glistening muscles and sexy hollows. Not to mention the scars that had her heart cramping in sympathy.

But he'd worked hard today and there was a much better way to help him recover than a simple muscle stimulation session, even though she knew she shouldn't touch him any more than necessary. But it would help. By morning, Luke would appreciate anything that would make it easier for him to get out of bed.

At least, that's the excuse she gave herself.

* * *

"Come on," Avery said, urging Luke to his feet after helping him stretch. He'd always had a love/hate relationship with stretching. He'd rather be running or pumping weights, but one of his former trainers had convinced him how good it was for his body. After that, he'd been able to relax into it.

But somehow stretching with Avery was different. It should feel good, did feel good, but not in the way he'd experienced before. Male hands, male strength—his other physical therapist had a no-nonsense touch that did the job at hand and nothing else.

Avery's hands during their sessions gave him a sense of comfort, as if he could feel her desire for him to heal within each touch. Even through the pain he caught a hint of awareness beneath his skin, an itch for more. And always, that low-level hum distracted him.

"Reward time," she said.

Too bad that couldn't mean what his body hoped it did. Nope. It would be the usual post-therapy ritual that included heat and some electrical muscle stimulation to reduce pain and atrophy. Sad when getting shocked was the highlight of his visit.

He assured his disappointed body that this was a good thing. After all, he had rules of his own. Namely, he was not staying in Black Hills—which meant no entanglements. No relationships. His body would simply have to mourn the loss of more intimate contact.

Her rules challenged and intrigued him. Professionalism was very important to her, especially when dealing with a lot of people who had watched her grow up. Still, he longed to break through her professional facade. One, because she needed some fun more than any person he'd met in forever. Someone to push her buttons, force her to loosen up.

Two, he needed a distraction from the first true attraction he'd felt in a long time. Especially since it was toward a woman he would not be able to get away from in the coming months. But they could be friends, right? Just friends.

"So how come I never saw you when I came home?" He chuckled. "It's almost like you were avoiding me."

He almost bumped into her backside as she halted. The odd look she threw over her shoulder smothered his teasing. Had she really—?

"Why would you avoid me?" he asked.

"Do you want your reward?" she countered in a cool tone.

"Um, yeah."

"Then don't ask irrelevant questions."

She just might have found the key to making him fall in line. But that didn't stop him from being curious. He'd bet his racing car that she had avoided him…and didn't want him to know it.

As she walked away, she said, "I guarantee you won't want to miss this."

Just like that, his mouth watered, hunger rising out of nowhere to overwhelm him. It was totally out of character for him, this physical need to be close to someone. If it had been anyone else, he'd have let the hunger lead him, but he couldn't. Not with Avery. Indulging in something physical with her wouldn't be fair, knowing he would never make his home here.

But now curiosity had joined the mix of anticipation and arousal, so he leaned a little heavier on his cane to gain speed. What could be better than the usual after-workout routine? At least it eased the soreness long enough for him to get home. By tomorrow morning, he'd be stiff again. Even the massive whirlpool tub Aiden had installed in his suite didn't help for long. His body resisted what he wanted.

He'd been told he pushed too hard before, but each moment without definitive recovery ramped up a panic inside. Getting back on the track was a need that called to him day and night. He couldn't rest for the jitters beneath his skin.

An itch to escape.

It only subsided when he was with Avery. With her, he felt a constant, low-level hum that drew his gaze, his attention—hell, his body—in her direction. An illusion that, if he could just get close enough, all the fears and doubts and nerves would stop. Dangerous territory. Which gave him one more reason to keep his hands to himself.

When Avery opened the door to one of the smaller rooms around the perimeter and Luke glimpsed a thickly padded massage table, he wanted to groan. Have mercy. Now he had an itch for something completely different.

"Take off your shoes. I just want to work some of the tension out of your legs and back," she said.

He wanted to joke, to throw something stupid out there to break the tension building under his skin. But nothing came to him. "Is massage an extra perk?" he tried, his voice sounding strained.

A slight choke had him glancing at her with a tight grin, but she'd turned away.

"Um, no," she finally said, though her voice was muffled. It took him a minute to realize she was off balance, uncertain. Did she not normally do this?

That settled him down, and he was able to tease her again. "So am I simply special?"

Her obvious embarrassment was so cute he wanted to kiss it away. Her flushed cheeks and shaky hands made him warm, awoke a need to hug her and share a grin. Not the reaction he was used to, but definitely safer. Shucking his shoes and socks, Luke approached the table with a breathless anticipation that was exponentially higher than the situation warranted.

To his surprise, she launched a comeback. "It's not actually on the fee schedule, but I do need to put my massage therapy license to use now and then."

With those words, every muscle in his body went taut. For someone who already had mobility issues, it was not the best state of affairs. But how could he relax knowing Avery had even more skills in her arsenal that could slay him in an instant? He lay facedown as best he could and breathed through the pain of getting his legs prone. That took his mind off the ache forming in his groin pretty quick.

"Moving a little more slowly would make changing positions easier," Avery chided.

"Can't hide anything from you, huh?"

Her voiced softened as she drew closer. "Oh, I'm a bit more observant than most."

What did she see in him? He was used to projecting the fun-loving, hard-playing athletic image. This wasn't his finest hour. Could she spot the desperation, the bone-deep need to get back behind the wheel? The fear that lingered beneath his determination? His thoughts opened up a dark cave he'd rather not explore.

The sound of a cabinet door broke the silence, then familiar heat blanketed his upper back in a thick weight. His whole body automatically melted into the cloth-covered table beneath him. Then Avery's hands found the small of his back and thinking ceased—he could only feel.

Definitely not like a dude. He'd never before had a therapeutic massage where he had to bite his lip to keep from begging his masseuse for more. Hell, her technique was flawless. Now his body wanted to take this far away from the office to a much more private setting.

Yep, he was in a heap of trouble here.

Those slender fingers traced and kneaded every inch of every muscle on his legs and lower back. Every one except the one he wanted her to touch with an ache that was inherently male. Trapped beneath him, that essential part of his body throbbed in an attempt to gain attention. Luke was grateful for the safeguard, even while he reveled in the return of his body's most basic demands. So much better than his struggle with fear and loathing.

He'd enjoyed a steady stream of sexual encounters until the accident. But why did this feel like the perfect unique blend of innocence and sensuality to spur his body into hyperdrive?

Oh, yeah, she was definitely trying to torture him.

Her fingers traced over muscles, hills, and into valleys. Smoothing out the tension, working out the knots, drawing out the moans. This girl had some hidden talents.

"You have magic fingers," he moaned.

She dug particularly deep into his thigh.

"Ouch, woman."

"Behave." The prim schoolteacher voice was back. Not the direction he was looking for.

"It was a compliment. I swear."

He lifted a little to glance over his shoulder, only to find her cheeks flushed, eyes a little heavy-lidded. But all of it disappeared when her gaze met his. Then one brow lifted and her lips pressed together.

Even as he settled back in place, the image of that aroused look on her refined features wouldn't disappear from his mind. That expression like she'd enjoyed touching him as much as he'd enjoyed being touched. It was a temptation he didn't need. Then the slide of her hands transformed from a baker kneading dough to the skilled glide of a woman savoring the skin beneath her fingers.

The very air around him grew heavy. His breath sped up to match his heartbeat. Could this torture continue forever? But certain parts of him demanded it end quickly, in a very satisfying way. Time to change the tempo.

"You never did say why I haven't seen you around…"

He left the sentence hanging, hoping to introduce some sane conversation before he went out of his ever-lovin' mind. She paused midstroke, his thigh muscle twitching before she continued again.

"I didn't really socialize much until my mother died," she said, her voice low. "There wasn't really time—or rather, when there was, I was too exhausted to care. I stuck close to home mostly. And establishing a practice takes a lot of work, even with the ready-made clientele here."

Which was no doubt true, even if he still sensed a cover-up. His heartbeat slowed as he focused on her. "I'm sure she was very grateful for all you did for her."

"I know she was. She told me every day."

Luke thought of his own mother, Lily, who had been comatose since a stroke. She'd already sustained injuries from a car accident that had left her unable to walk. There'd been more than once that Luke had wished his mother could tell them something, anything to let them know she was okay—even if it was goodbye. But she couldn't.

"You're lucky," he mumbled, then realized how callous that might sound and glanced over his shoulder.

Avery met his look, understanding in her gentle eyes. "I know."

She pressed her palms flat against his skin, sending that tingle through him once more. A confusing mix of arousal and comfort.

Some people didn't know, could never understand what it was like to lose a parent…but not really lose them. To wish so badly that you could speak to them, but realize it would never happen again. But Avery understood. Her observant ways had probably told her far more about the situation than anyone else knew.

Then she threw him into the fire. "What about you?

Did you ever think you'd be moving back here, even for a temporary hiatus?"

Luke was glad his face didn't show. Being home was still a touchy subject for him—more than he wanted anyone to know. "Nope."

"But it's better now, right?"

His body stilled even more. "How did you know?"

"Everyone knows James Blackstone was a difficult man—"

"Try demon…"

"—but the way he treated you boys was unconscionable."

He shouldn't ask. He really shouldn't. "How did you know?"

"Just from the sheer amount of time I spent watching those around me. It's amazing what people will say in front of you when they don't realize you're there."

Ouch. Despite the magic of her fingers, Luke rolled to his side. "Did we really do that to you, Avery? Ignore you? Make you feel invisible?"

"Luke, y'all weren't the only ones. I was shy, and worked very hard to fade into the woodwork. Do it often enough, and people expect it."

He remembered seeing her walk across the country club dining room and realized just how far she'd come. That walk was probably as hard for her as his own had been. "How did you become so smart?"

"Smart? No. Just…practical."

"Practical, huh? Doesn't that ever get boring?"

This conversation was way deeper than he'd planned.

She shook her head, a slight smile tilting the corners of her pink bow lips. "No," she said. "There isn't time to be bored."

He wanted to ask if she felt the same way in the dark

of night, when she was home alone with no one to laugh and cuddle with, but he didn't. He couldn't.

The deep stuff wasn't what he was here for.

"Let's get you set up for your next appointment," she said as she moved away from the table.

The fun was over.

Flipping over on the narrow table proved harder than he thought, but at least he had the coward's comfort of knowing Avery faced away from him. Easier was getting himself upright with his legs hanging off the table. Boy, her magic hands had turned his muscles to jelly.

When Avery turned back, she was studying his chart. He could have called her on avoiding him, but he let it go. For now.

She was back to being all business. "Let's shoot for three days a week."

"Sure." Not like he had much else going on. "However often it takes."

"That means we will see each other on Friday. Monday, Wednesday, Friday good for you?"

He nodded. Deep in his brain, he searched for a way to instigate himself into other parts of her life. She might have forgotten about him helping her have fun, but he hadn't. "We could see each other before then. You know, for dinner?"

"Are we back to that again?" she asked, her face completely blanking for a moment.

"Mary makes a mean prime rib up at Blackstone Manor. Why don't you join me? I could even ask her to make her famous chocolate chip cookies."

Avery frowned, shifting the chart in her hands. "I don't think that's a good idea."

"Why not?" Luke had a pretty decent puppy-dog look when he tried.

"It's just, um…"

Yep, the look was working.

She swallowed. "With me being, you know, your physical therapist, maybe socializing isn't such a good idea."

"Why not? Because you said everything outside of the office was fair game."

Her face flushed and he knew he'd gotten her. "That's not what I meant and you know it."

His male instincts urged him to stalk closer, crowd her in and make her admit she was just as attracted to him as he was to her. Instead he forced himself to remain still, using words to reel her in. "Come on. You want an adventure. I want to help you find one. Let's talk about it over dinner."

"Well…" Her flush deepened, but she also straightened her shoulders. "I guess I could do dinner one night."

Was that a slight squeak he heard in her voice? "Good. I know Christina has been dying to see you, too."

A little of the starch drained from her posture. "Oh, um, yes. That sounds nice."

Obviously she hadn't been to a dinner with all of them home. *Nice* wasn't the word he'd use. *Chaotic*, maybe. Just what she needed.

"It will be interesting, to say the least." Not like the gloom and doom his grandfather had presided over. James Blackstone had demanded the appearance of a family dinner, but they had been mostly silent events with none of the laughing, joking and talking Luke associated with that idea. Especially not since his mother's car accident.

As he came to his feet, the quizzical little smile Avery gave distracted him. He saw nothing else. Not taupe walls, nor yellow scrubs. Just pale blue eyes and bow-shaped lips moving closer as she stepped forward.

Before he could reach for his cane, his legs gave him the old heave-ho and collapsed. Avery had moved close, too close to miss out on his game of Timber. Down they both went.

He tried to twist, but his body wouldn't cooperate. They hit the floor hard. Or rather, Avery did. Luke's arms worked better than his legs, catching him before he landed on her. *Oh, that elbow was gonna bruise.* Of course, the rest of his body couldn't help but tangle all up in hers.

They came to rest hip to hip, stomach to stomach, and all of Luke's pent-up need was blatantly evident. Once more, the first thing that popped into his head came out of his mouth, even though he knew he'd pay for it later.

"Sweetheart, you're the softest landing place I've had in a while." The scary part—it was true.

Four

For once, Luke was able to walk into breakfast at Blackstone Manor like a normal person, albeit relying on his cane, instead of a hunched-over hobbit moaning in pain. He tossed Christina a grin as he approached the breakfast dishes on the mahogany sideboard.

Though she seemed a little pale and not her usual serene self this morning, she returned his smile. "Someone's looking much better than the last time I saw him," she teased.

Since neither of his brothers were there to rag him, Luke spoke freely. "I swear that woman has magic in her fingers."

"I bet."

Without thought, Luke whipped his head around, pinning her with a glare until he realized she was joking with him. *Busted.*

Christina raised her hands in surrender. "Just kidding." But that smug smile said she'd gotten all the information she needed.

The pressure to explain rose. For once, he gave in. Maybe if he talked some of his thoughts out, he could make more sense of them. Somehow, he could share with Christina things he'd normally keep to himself. He attributed it to her peaceful bedside manner. His brother Aiden was one of the few people who could shake her calm attitude.

Yet he was grateful to be filling his plate as he spoke, instead of facing her across the lace-covered table. "Avery gave me a massage after my session yesterday. My muscles haven't felt this good since *before* my accident."

"Nice," she murmured. Again she tossed him the knowing look, but thankfully she held her teasing. "She worked on my shoulder once. Definitely skilled. I'm glad she could help you out."

Why did he remember his *therapeutic* massage with less-than-clinical nuances? He shouldn't…he knew he shouldn't. Trying to shake the memory, he finished filling his plate and settled across the table from Christina.

She went on. "This is the most pain-free I've seen you since you moved back."

Luke was a little shocked himself.

Christina studied her plate for a moment. "I know it seems silly to be worried about a grown woman, but Avery has pulled away some since KC and I became involved with your brothers. Maybe hanging out with us makes her feel like a third wheel. But I think Avery needs someone to shake her out of her rut, so to speak." She gave Luke one of her patented purposeful looks.

He didn't disappoint. "Well, I do need a hostess for dinner."

Christina lowered her fork despite the bite of waffle on the end. "She agreed?"

"Yes. She tried to brush me off, so I told her how much you missed her…and how disappointed you would be if she didn't come."

He leaned back in his chair, accompanied by a creak of wood. Part of him wanted to confess how conflicted he was, how much he wanted Avery to come to dinner for himself. He didn't want to admit to the attraction that grew every time he saw her, but he was drawn to the chance to make the laughter, the spark of life in Avery's eyes grow.

"She's funny—so dedicated to her work, holding fast to this therapist-patient bit. But I think she needs someone to push her outside her safety zone." A cohort in crime, so to speak. Luke didn't want Christina to know how desperate he was for the job.

The whole time he spoke, Christina's expression grew in excitement until she practically glowed. "So you are interested! I knew it."

Uh-oh. Christina would be unbearable once she thought she was right.

"No, ma'am." He would not let anything sexual even start between him and Avery. Not when he had no plans to hang around. She was obviously rooted in this town, and the last thing he could see himself as was a small town husband. "You can put that emerging matchmaker back in her cage, because it's not gonna happen." He waved his arms around the room. "This version of happily-ever-after is not for me."

"That's what Aiden and Jacob said," she mumbled beneath a smile.

"I'm serious, Christina." Christina's astute look had him adding, "I just want to be her friend. I owe her that." And much, much more. Even though he'd brushed her off as a teenager for all the right reasons, he still felt bad about it now.

"As long as you're careful with her," Christina gave the obligatory warning, but Luke could see her concern for her friend in her darkened eyes. "Honestly, she deserves more than a little bit of fun after all she's been through."

"Has it been rough since her mother died?"

"Oh, it was rough way before that." Christina shifted the pieces of waffle on her plate as a thoughtful look softened her face.

"How come I haven't heard anything about her when I've been home?"

"Because there wasn't much to hear. She went to college and things were good until the summer after her sophomore year. Then her mother was diagnosed with cancer. She'd been dating a guy pretty steadily, but when she buckled down to finish her studies early, he lost interest."

Ouch. Just what she needed—someone who abandoned her the minute she needed support.

Christina stared into space as she spoke. "She was home as much as her studies would allow, but she finished within a year and a half. Came home and started to build her clientele while taking care of her mom full-time."

"How long was her mom sick?"

"She went into remission once, for a couple of years, I think?" Christina shook her head, sending her thick, dark hair swinging. "She died almost two years ago."

Wow. "That's a long time to be a caregiver."

"Yeah," Christina whispered, trailing off into silence that was punctuated by the clink of their silverware. Finally she said, "She's given her all for Black Hills, but she deserves more—just for herself. I'm glad to see she isn't going to settle."

Luke thought of dinner and Avery's lack of response to Mark's hand at her back. "You mean that Mark guy?"

"Don't get me started," Christina groaned.

"Please don't," Aiden added as he strolled into the room. "Her opinion is less than stellar, I assure you."

A pang stung Luke's chest as Aiden kissed Christina on the temple, but he shook his head. Absolutely no touchy-feely stuff for him. No, sir. Settling down was not in his current timeline.

"Avery and Mark have gone to a lot of functions together since her mother died. I think it started out as convenient, especially for her, since she gets comments about a single woman needing to get married all the time, but I think he's always been more interested than she realizes."

Luke tried to ignore the burn of something unpleasant building in his gut. He hadn't known they'd actually been such a "thing." Part of him did not like that thought...*at all*.

"I've never cared for him, but Aiden says there aren't any complaints at work," Christina went on.

"There aren't," Aiden agreed. He shook his head. "He's perfectly adequate at his job. Of course, adequate and not exemplary is what has kept him where he is at the moment. I can't judge the guy based on feminine intuition."

When Christina threw him a sideways glance, Aiden grinned. "Even if it's coming from one of the smartest, sexiest women I know."

She rolled her eyes as her husband kissed her cheek. "I'll accept the compliment," she said, "but I just haven't ever been able to get past it." With a glance at Luke, she said, "When Mark started pressuring for more—that's when she broke it off."

"How long ago?" Luke asked, keeping his gaze trained on Aiden while he fixed his plate so Christina wouldn't see how much the thought bothered him.

"About six weeks ago, maybe?"

Had that pressure for more than she wanted to deliver been a wake-up call, urging her to break out of her inertia?

Aiden added his two cents worth as he took his seat. "Avery is a very hard worker. When she isn't treating patients, she's helping with fund-raisers or volunteering with local charities. All kinds of community stuff."

Was that because she truly wanted to be busy…or because she just didn't want to go home alone?

"I think—" Christina began.

"—and you would know," Aiden teased, smoothing a hand over his wife's hair.

Christina raised an eyebrow in what Luke liked to call her "lady of the manor" look. "Of course I would. She's one of my best friends and a great person. She deserves some happiness after all she's lost. Someone to help her loosen up and have fun—like KC did for Jacob."

Aiden shook his head. "She may have loosened him up too much. Do you know he actually took a day off work last week? Just because?"

Luke grinned as Christina smacked Aiden's arm. A day off for a workaholic like Jacob was a freakin' miracle.

"I think I can handle that." Not the romantic part, he reminded himself. Luke felt compelled to specify so Christina wouldn't get any ideas about forever. "While I'm home, it'll be my mission to teach her all about good ol' fun."

Aiden winked at Christina. "Sounds like a worthwhile mission to have."

She nodded. "Since her mother died, her only fun has been charity events, community stuff. She needs something for *her*."

"Can. Do," Luke said. "Starting with dinner."

Christina simply stared. "I thought for sure you'd be more adventurous than that."

"You know me so well. But trust me, this is just the beginning." That rock climbing brochure might be what Avery *thought* she wanted…but Luke knew exactly what he was doing. He swallowed down a big bite of homemade waffles, licking syrup off his top lip. "Do we still have that old tire swing around here somewhere?"

Five

Why did going to dinner at a friend's house spark uncomfortable butterflies in her stomach? Avery had been to Blackstone Manor many times before, but this felt different.

Yes, Luke would be here. Yes, he had invited her. But it was a family dinner, for goodness' sake.

In all the years she'd been coming to Blackstone Manor to see Christina—and even before that for social events as a teenager—Avery had always been greeted at the door by the Blackstone butler, Nolen. Tonight the heavy door with its lion knocker swung back to reveal Luke.

As a concession to the cooling night air, he wore khakis with a smooth, deep blue polo shirt that made his amber eyes almost glow in contrast. His blond hair, longer than his twin's, was stylishly disheveled. He'd probably just dried it with a towel, applied a quick comb and been done. His casual good looks took her breath away.

Avery always felt like she was trying too hard. She'd

give anything for a set of yellow scrubs right now, instead of her casual black jeans and thin gray sweater with a bright blue argyle pattern down the center. At least then she'd feel more in control than she did right now, with him eyeing her from head to toe. Professional distance might be the only thing to save her sanity in the face of this undeniable draw to Luke Blackstone.

Heaven help her.

As jitters set in, she eyed the door frame while she approached in an effort not to catch it with her shoulder. *Careful.* Luke's grin widened just a touch, as if he knew exactly what she was thinking.

Then—*oompf.*

Avery stumbled over the doorstep, tripping as momentum propelled her forward until she landed right in Luke's outstretched arms. He mumbled something. She wasn't sure what, because her senses narrowed down to the warm, spicy scent of his skin and the heat of his hands as they rested against her back. He pressed her closer, making her feel at once safe and unbridled.

Then reality returned. She jerked upright, only to be held in place by his embrace. A sneaking glance found his amber eyes filled with laughter.

"Are you trying to throw yourself at me?" he asked.

As if she could coordinate her limbs to do that on purpose.

She searched for her strictest voice. "I was simply testing your stability. That's all." *Oh, could this floor open up and swallow me?* Her heart raced as his hands inched back until they rested on her upper arms.

He wasn't quite convinced. "Uh-huh." Then he fingered a strand of her hair. "Gorgeous."

Startled, she remembered this was one of the few occasions she'd worn it completely down. A ponytail was a necessity for work, especially with the thickness of her hair.

For most formal occasions she wore an elegant, upswept hairdo because it kept the thick mass out of her face and she could accessorize it with jeweled combs and such. But tonight, facing the mirror and seeing the same old, same old, she'd opted to leave it loose around her face.

Suddenly a masculine voice filled the foyer. "Master Luke, is that the proper way to answer the door?" Nolen asked. His voice remained completely deadpan, but Avery could swear his knowing eyes twinkled.

She stepped back, only to hear Luke's cane clatter as it fell to the floor. "Oh, no," Luke said as she bent to sweep it up. "That was most improper of me. I should be fired, Nolen. On the spot."

Turning toward the butler, Avery smiled. "Completely my fault, Nolen. I'm so clumsy sometimes." Even now her knees shook. She couldn't tell if it was from her almost-fall, or from being close enough to sniff Luke Blackstone. His clean, warm scent lingered on her clothes, though it seemed as though she hadn't been close nearly long enough for that to be possible.

"A gentleman never lays the blame with a woman," Nolen said. "Welcome, Miss Avery."

"Thank you, Nolen."

"Yes," Luke murmured. "Welcome."

How could just the tone of his voice make her every cell sit up and beg for attention? The simple words were spoken low and smooth. But his sexy, teasing tone lingered over her, becoming absorbed within the earlier sensations and fogging her brain for a moment.

With a quick shake of her head, she carefully stepped forward, following Nolen through the breezeway into the front parlor. Another fall would be too embarrassing for words. She could feel the emotions burning on her fair cheeks. Hopefully it wasn't too noticeable as she hugged Christina in greeting.

Tonight should have been like any other night that she'd joined the Blackstones for dinner. Casual conversation among friends. Mary's wonderful food and fine wine. But as they chatted, then moved into the elegant dining room and were served, a constant awareness hummed beneath Avery's skin.

It didn't help that Luke seemed to have developed a fascination with her hair. She caught him studying it more than once, with a sort of longing on his face that made her breath catch. Even when Luke wasn't paying her direct attention, the feeling remained. What would he do if she actually responded to his teasing with interest? Would he run for the hills? Laugh?

Kiss her?

She shouldn't think like that. It would never happen. Not for a girl like her. He simply liked to joke and play games. She was something to alleviate his boredom. That's all. Instead she tried to focus on the conversation flowing around her.

The Blackstone brothers began talking about the horrible incidences of sabotage that had threatened to put Blackstone Mills out of business over the last year. Avery had closely watched the drama unfold, along with the rest of the community.

She couldn't help asking, "Do you think it's over? Or is someone just waiting out there for another opportunity?" That thought sent shivers over her, though she was far from the target. How could someone in their community work so hard to tear the very people who supported it apart?

"Let's just say I'm cautiously optimistic," Aiden said, though he wore a slight frown that fit his dark good looks. "We've been without a major incident for two months now. Since the cotton crop debacle."

Avery remembered the widespread gossip and panic when Zachary Gatlin, now the Blackstones' head of security, had flown the plane that sprayed the majority of the county's cotton crop with defoliant long before it was ready. He'd maintained his innocence, stating he'd been framed by someone who had secretly switched out the chemicals in the tanks, but small towns bred distrust.

Jacob shook his head. "This lull makes me suspicious. Worried. I have a feeling whoever did this isn't done yet."

Though he and Jacob looked a lot alike, apparently Luke had his own opinion that fell somewhere in the middle. "Maybe he figured out we're gonna fix whatever he breaks, instead of abandoning the mill or the town. Might as well hit the road, Jack."

The other two didn't look convinced. Neither did Christina, but she said, "Worrying about it won't help. We have to keep living, keep working, while continuing to implement the tightest security we can for now. If we let our guard down, one of our employees could pay the price."

Or one of us. The words were unspoken, but even Avery could feel their impression. Whoever the saboteur had been, he'd struck out at each of the Blackstone brothers in turn. Almost fatally in Aiden's case, when an attempt to burn down his sculpting studio occurred with Christina trapped inside. Avery looked at Luke, and prayed he wouldn't become another target in whatever game this crazy person was playing.

"Thank goodness Zach agreed to put his military training to good use," Jacob said.

"Amen," KC said. "Now, can we talk about something more pleasant, please?" Jacob's fiancée handed their son, Carter, over to his dad so she could dig into her lasagna without baby fingers in her plate.

"What do you suggest, my dear?" he asked in a sotto voice that earned him a raised eyebrow.

But Christina quickly filled the gap. "How about the Christmas dinner and dance?" she said, a pleading look coming over her elegant features. "Avery, you must help. Taking this event from the country club to the civic ball-room and opening it up to the public has increased inter-est by leaps and bounds. Which is great for fund-raising, but not so great on its organizers..." Her voice trailed off as she and KC shared a look.

KC nodded, a crease appearing between her eyebrows. "Especially since one of those organizers has never done anything fancy before. I'm much more comfortable with county fairs and hoedowns."

"It'll be fun," Christina reassured her friend. "I prom-ise."

And it would be. Avery always had a good time coordi-nating the fund-raisers that helped sustain and build their community. A new playground. School support. A new building for the senior center. They were fun and helped her feel like she was contributing something worthwhile, like her life meant something more than her just working day in and day out. But she couldn't help wondering if—when—there would be something more.

"I'm trying to talk Lucas into helping me with a little side project," Christina said.

Oh, this sounded interesting. Luke's glare across the table told Avery how he felt about it.

"No," he said. "I'd be horrible."

Christina had her protests all lined up. "Why? You're great in front of a camera, with your hundred-watt charm. You've got experience from being interviewed many, many times. Heck, this would even be scripted—sort of."

"Sort of?" Luke's brow shot sky high. "You want me to appear on camera with a dozen or so little kids. How the heck is that gonna be scripted?"

The other brothers laughed. Avery suppressed a grin of her own. Luke always appeared one hundred percent com-fortable in front of a camera...but with a bunch of kids?

That seemed like a recipe for disaster. She didn't know a single child that was predictable.

Christina leaned forward against the edge of the table. "It's to help with the fund-raising efforts for the new pediatric ER. Imagine how much exposure we could get statewide with you on the screen."

"I realize I'm a handsome devil," Luke conceded with a smirk that quickly disappeared. "But, no."

Avery happily stepped into the fray. Having something to tease Luke about was fun, since it was usually the other way around. "Come on, Mr. Big Shot. Surely you aren't afraid of a few grimy fingers and wet diapers?"

The incredulous look he shot her sent her into giggles. She had this mental image of Luke standing tall while dozens of kids swarmed him from all sides, climbing him like he was a mountain. Talk about an adventure.

"I'm not good with kids," he insisted. "I barely know what to do with this one."

He gestured to little Carter, sitting proud in his daddy's lap. As if realizing all eyes were on him, the little boy gurgled. The sound and his golden curls were sweetness overload.

"Well, you better figure it out quick," Aiden said. "We'll have another here soon for you to practice on."

For just a moment, the light reflecting off the hundreds of crystal teardrops on the chandelier was too hot, too bright for Avery. Then the room erupted into smiles and congratulations as Christina glowed with happiness. Avery thought that was the biggest grin she'd ever seen on Aiden's face. The normally stoic businessman only softened around his wife, but he'd soon have another reason to let down that infamous guard.

As Avery watched the family rejoice, she couldn't help but compare their happiness to her own barren life. She had friends aplenty, but no one to go home to. No life events on the horizon. She looked at Luke, so full of vitality despite his accident and all the hard work he had to do just to return to normal—and wanted a taste of that experience.

Surely she deserved a little taste.

But she wouldn't get even a nibble in Black Hills. After all, Luke wasn't a wedding-and-babies kind of guy. Why should he be? A baby meant roots, staying put, not a lifetime in perpetual motion. It was a reminder Avery needed, but it still made her sad. Why? She couldn't say, but the feeling lingered.

"Luke, you'll be a great uncle…again," Christina said.

He would. Luke could charm the warts off a toad. Even when it was a tantrum-throwing toddler. Even if he didn't know it yet.

Just like he charmed her, no matter how many times she hid behind her professionalism. She'd wondered earlier if he would run screaming if she responded in kind, teased and flirted instead of trying to steer him back on a straighter road.

Maybe it was time to shuck the scrubs and embrace an overload of adventure.

Luke could almost feel the moment Avery decided it was time to leave.

KC and Jacob had excused themselves earlier to put Carter to bed. They didn't always stay at Blackstone Manor, preferring the privacy of KC's little house closer to town, but tonight they were using their suite on the third floor.

Conversation between the remaining four of them slowed. No more exciting baby news or community improvement plans, thank goodness. Seated so close to her on a couch in the front parlor, Luke felt tension creep over Avery. Her shoulders pulled up slightly and her hands rubbed against her jeans along the front of her thighs. Even though his brain said to let the evening come to its natural end, the rest of him didn't want her to walk out the door.

He stood, leaning nonchalantly on his cane as he faced her. "Walk with me."

"Oh, I should probably get going." Avery avoided his gaze, but also didn't look at Christina or Aiden. Obviously she hadn't registered that his statement wasn't a question.

Since he wasn't the type to go all caveman, he forced himself to play the hated invalid card... "I kinda figured my physical therapist would encourage me to walk, keep from stiffening up and all—"

Her delightfully creamy skin flushed from collar to cheekbones. "Oh, right."

Those funny nerves that hit her from time to time made an appearance, leaving Luke afraid she might trip again. But he could see the professional mask cover her expression as she consciously slipped behind it. She could think she was in control all she wanted—until he was ready for her to know otherwise. Would he ever get her to relax with him? For him alone?

The women did that huggy thing, then Luke preceded Avery across the breezeway back to the dining room. He led her through the swinging door to the adjacent kitchen. Mary and Nolen were cleaning up the last of dinner.

"Mary," Avery said, "dinner was absolutely delicious. And whatever that chocolate dessert was—yum!"

The older woman grinned. "Well, I had something a little simpler planned, but such big news warranted an extraspecial dessert, you know."

Luke should have known Mary would have the 411 before everyone else in the house. He wasn't sure how, but Mary and Nolen knew everything that went on in Blackstone Manor—no matter how secret it might be.

Mary wiped her hands and hurried over for a hug. "So you have to tell me—how are you, girl?"

"I'm good," Avery said with a smile.

Behind the older woman with her Kiss the Cook apron, Luke spied an entire rack of little beauties cooling down. Mary's infamous chocolate chip cookies. He drew in a deep breath. Yep, chocolate was definitely in order tonight.

"Does my favorite cook have anything left for me?" he asked.

The woman eyed him with the same suspicion she had when he was a teenager up to no good. "There's only one thing worth you nosing around my kitchen," she said. "If I let you have one chocolate chip cookie, then all the other men want one, and on it goes."

"But they've already had dessert," he argued. "It should be safe."

He wasn't pulling anything over on Mary. "So have you, Lucas Blackstone. But I guess I can make an exception for ya."

She scooped a couple of cookies off the cooling rack and set them on napkins before handing them each one. Nolen frowned. "What about me?"

Mary's brow shot up. "When you finish your work, you can have one, too."

The butler muttered as he headed back through the door to the dining room, leaving them all smiling. Mary turned back to Avery. "So everything going okay? The clinic is doing well?"

Luke saw Avery blossom beneath the older woman's attention. "It sure is. How're those hips doing?"

"Good, thanks to you." Mary glanced over at Luke with the wisdom of ages in her eyes. "This girl works wonders, you know."

He remembered that heavenly massage. "Oh, I'm getting the picture."

Mary pointed in his direction. "You see you do everything she says, and it'll all work out fine."

"Yes, ma'am."

The words were forced as Luke's mind flooded with Avery's warnings to wait another season to return to racing. He wanted to push the concern away, but it kept resurfacing—especially at night when he lay in bed, legs aching from the day's exertions.

Luke knew his body. He could return to tip-top shape by February. He had to believe that. The question was, could he prove it to everyone else? Only he understood the danger of losing his worth the longer he was away from the track. Why wait and have to rebuild his reputation when he could come back sooner and stay on top?

All of his hard work up to this point *would not* be for nothing.

Luke's thoughts distracted him as they finished their cookies, then stepped out the back door into the cooling fall air. Avery snuggled into her light leather jacket as the slight breeze ruffled the long strands of her hair. The varying shades of blond, the highlights visible even in the dark, fascinated him. All Luke's memories of her were with her hair up or back. He'd known her ponytail was thick, but never realized just how full and glossy her hair would be in its unfettered glory.

Down as it was now, it transformed into a waterfall of pure temptation. Luke's palms itched to dig in, experience that silkiness against his skin. A groan slipped out unbidden, whisked away by the night air.

"Are you okay?" Avery asked. "Should we go back inside?"

"No, I'm fine." If no one counted the throbbing ache behind his zipper.

"Do you like being back?" she asked, her voice quiet.

"It's okay," he said, leading her down the gentle slope of the lush back lawn, past heirloom iris beds that were only greenery now. "Every nomad needs a home base, right?"

"Doesn't North Carolina feel like home to you?"

Nothing really did. "I have an apartment there, but I wouldn't really call it home. A place to stay, maybe."

She gestured back toward Blackstone Manor, impressively handsome despite the dim light. "Here, neither? Even with your brothers both home?"

"No. I mean, Aiden and Jacob gutted Grandfather's suite on the second floor so I'd have a convenient space—but it isn't really mine."

"I'm sorry," she murmured.

"Why?"

After a moment's pause, she said, "I'd be lost without my house, and I hate that you don't have the same comfort." She was quiet for a few steps before she went on. "A lot of people asked why I didn't sell it after Mom died. Move closer to the clinic. After all, it's way too big for a woman all alone." Her laugh was a huff in the air. "An old maid—I'm sure they say when I'm not around."

"Honey, you're as far from a typical old maid as a woman can get." He reached out to touch that hair, rubbing a small swath between his finger and thumb.

He knew she felt him from the slight hesitation of her body and words, but then she continued walking without looking his way.

"That house has been the one constant in my life. I've been through a lot of bad times there, but also my best. I don't want to let it go. Guess that makes me overly sentimental, huh?"

"Not at all." Without thought, Luke said, "If I called anywhere home, it would be my garage. Crazy, I know, but I'd rather be there than anywhere."

"Makes perfect sense to me, Luke," Avery whispered.

She paused, looking up at the night sky. It was chilly, but clear, with stars in abundance. Luke didn't care. He was too busy soaking up Avery's shadowy profile.

When had this conversation turned so serious? He should be concentrating on fun—not home and hearth.

Finding her arm in the dark, he let his hand slip down to grasp hers. "Come here," he said, changing their direction toward the nearby oak tree. Massive in size, family lore said it had been there since they settled this land many years ago. Now other trees kept it company, including a couple of magnolias and a pretty old weeping willow, but the oak stood above them all.

Luke and Avery slipped below the bottommost branches to the sheltered circle beneath the tree.

"How pretty," she breathed, as a small amount of moonlight dappled through the leaves.

Luke led her around to the other side where Aiden had helped him hang the tire swing. Now the fun would really begin. "Ever play on one of these?"

"Hmm…no, can't say that I have."

Her dubious tone thrilled him. Even in the dark, he could feel her eyeing him as if he needed to be watched. He might be heading for craziness, after all. That was fine. The more she resisted, the sweeter the surprise when she gave in.

"Never?" he challenged. "Come on. When was the last time you sat on a swing? Any swing?"

Her sigh sounded long-suffering, as if she were indulging him. "When I was a kid, I guess."

"Then it's way past time. Hop on."

"What?" She took a few steps back. "Me? No."

"Yes," he said in a singsong voice. "I dare you."

"Luke, I'm not dressed for a tire swing."

Oh, she was reaching for excuses now. "What? They're pants, at least. Besides, getting dirty makes it a lot more fun."

He hadn't meant his words to come out quite like that,

or for desire to deepen his voice, but his fascination with her was outstripping his control.

"Come on, where's that little adventurer that's trying to break free?" he goaded.

That did the trick, because she moved in his direction. Yes, one hesitant step at a time, but she was moving toward the swing instead of away from it. *Baby steps.*

She stood next to the tire for long moments, then Luke heard a small laugh. "You're gonna find this hilarious, I'm sure," she said, "but I don't even know how to get on this thing."

He moved close, resting his free hand against the small of her back. Just that simple touch was as electric as her falling into his arms earlier. He let the forbidden thrill move through him, savoring it for just a moment.

"Well, you can climb on top and ride." He paused, clearing his throat. When had something so simple become so riddled with innuendos? "Or you can slide your legs through the middle."

And sit on that delectable rear of hers. He did not need to think about her anatomy right now or he'd end up in a world of hurt.

Avery, of course, chose the safer option of sitting in the middle. Luke held the tire steady for her, then moved into position behind her back.

"Don't you dare push me," she said, looking over her shoulder. "You'll hurt yourself."

Luke gave a playful growl but a growl nonetheless. "Don't tell me what to do, woman. My body is operational in all the places I need it to be."

Let her think about that for a while. He let his cane fall to the ground and grasped the tire on either side of her. His balance held steady as he got her moving. Avery caught her breath with the first swoop. Luke grinned. The sound lent strength to his pushes, making her soar.

For long moments, the only thing heard was the creak of the rope, the rustle of leaves in the tree and the sound of their breath. Then something new joined in—slow at first, but gathering speed. The sound of her enjoyment, laughter mixed with a sort of breathlessness that radiated in his soul.

He had a vivid memory of that same sensation, the first time he could remember feeling it. His first time behind the wheel, alone in a car. Following the road to the deserted outskirts of town, and indulging in his need for speed. He hadn't reached racing heights, or even come close, but it had been his first taste, leaving him hungry for more.

With each push her breath caught, then laughter sprung forth as she reached the apex and hung suspended a moment before rushing back down. He backed up to give her more room, just enjoying the show. Her indulgence lit him up inside, mixing with lingering passion. Almost as if he were living vicariously through her.

No. He'd always lived his own life, on his own terms. But he could still enjoy her journey, right?

So he let the sound of her flow over him, through him— letting his eyes slip closed to hold it inside. Then a small cry and *wham*!

The weight against his chest toppled his balance. Luckily he'd been trained to fall. His body instinctively rolled along one side rather than slam down, but he lay disoriented for a moment. Within seconds he heard feet running in his direction.

"Luke? Luke, are you hurt?"

Avery's breathlessness only made him want to take her breath away in a whole other manner. The warmth of palms meeting his pants-clad legs and seeking upward took his own breath away. He peeked at her. "If I say yes, can I get a massage?"

She loomed closer. "Are you kidding me?"

He ignored her exasperated tone, the dull pain in his hips, and focused on the red of her full lips in the darkness and the wealth of hair like a waterfall as she leaned over him. There was no stopping himself. No talking himself out of it. Before he thought, his hand was buried in her hair, and he was pulling her down, closer to where he wanted her.

Then their lips met, and Luke sank into a world of sensation. So soft. So smooth. The taste of sugar and chocolate. Her lips parted. Tentatively her tongue swept against his and he was lost. Need exploded through his body, draining his control. He retreated, sucking in much-needed air.

Only then did he register that sweet palm still high on his thigh, just inches from where he wanted it. Avery seemed oblivious. "Are you okay?" she asked again.

"I swear, if you ask me that one more time, I'm going to flip you over and show you just how okay I am."

Just like that, the hand was gone. Damn shame, but probably for the best right now.

He'd veered onto a dangerous road tonight—led astray by her inherent beauty and his own need for adventure—and he hadn't applied the brakes in time.

Knowing himself, he wasn't sure he could stop now. And his next crash might leave more damage than his last.

Six

If looks could kill, Luke Blackstone would be deader than a doornail.

He hadn't expected resistance to his appearance at the mill, since his brothers had already reestablished the Blackstone family presence. But with one look, Mark Zabinski had made his feelings toward Luke clear.

"I'm glad you came in, Luke," Jacob was saying. He turned back toward the employees in the office. "Everyone, I'm sure you know my brother Luke. He'll be joining us as a partner, so he wanted to take some time to learn more about operations."

The secretaries in the office smiled and welcomed him. The daytime shift manager shook his hand. The dagger look from Mark had been quickly suppressed, but a frown still lingered on a face already going soft around the edges. No one else seemed to notice.

Luckily, Aiden walked through the door just then. As he paused beside Jacob, Luke wanted to laugh. He'd never understood how those two could look so comfortable in their suits, even though Aiden still maintained a messy artistic style to his hair. Just the thought of wearing a suit jacket every day caused Luke's throat to start closing.

"Well, ladies, we don't want to keep you from your lunch," Jacob said, much to Luke's relief. He was ready to get the espionage part of his visit over, so he could see Avery.

He simply couldn't get her out of his brain. Her soft hair, silky skin and eager kiss. He had every intention of going to the therapy center this afternoon. No appointment. No reason for going…except for not being able to forget the taste of her tongue. Her sweetness flavored her, and had given Luke a contact sugar rush. He could tell himself he simply wanted to invite her out on an adventure, but deep down, he knew he was lying to himself.

"We do need to head out," Clara said softly. "I don't want to get caught in that bad weather coming in this afternoon."

"Oh, I think it will be this evening before that hits," Aiden said. "Y'all will be safely home before that."

"Most definitely," Jacob agreed. "We want everyone to be safe."

The significance of those words wasn't lost on Luke as he gave the ladies a quick goodbye, then followed his brothers out the door. What they were doing here today, and in the days to come, was about the safety of everyone involved with Blackstone Mills—both employees and family.

Still, Luke tried to keep it light. "Let's get on with this," he said, rubbing his hands together. "I've got places to be—"

"Places more important than this?"

Luke didn't care much for Mark's hard tone, so he slowly swiveled his head to stare at the man who had followed them out of the office. "As a matter of fact, yes. I have plans for Avery tonight." Only she didn't know it yet.

The flush that swept over Mark's jaw and neck was satisfying to Luke, even if it was petty of him.

"Let's head over to the manufacturing floor, then back this way," Jacob suggested.

"I'll catch up with you when you get to the accounting office," Mark said. "I need to check out a computer problem over there."

"Good deal," Jacob said on his way down the hall. "We need to go over the plans for the computer system in that department anyway."

Aiden and Jacob were gone in seconds, but Luke couldn't stop himself from looking back. He glimpsed Mark's face blazing with an inordinate amount of fury before the other man turned away, leaving Luke to wonder if he had pulled a tiger's tail with his needling remark.

He followed his brothers over to the manufacturing part of the plant, easily slipping into his public persona as he greeted acquaintances. He may not truly be joining the company as a full partner, but he cared about these people.

He'd do whatever was necessary to ensure their safety.

Dealing with people had always come easy to him. Until his accident, he'd been quite the extrovert. The dark period following his accident had birthed an extreme need for solitude. Slowly exposing himself to people again was going okay, as long as it wasn't a big crowd.

Today was working well for both purposes.

Talking with people in small groups of two or three, casually leaning on his cane and offering his TV-interview smile, allowed him to be accepted, to let down guards and to see what more familiar eyes might miss. After a couple of hours, he hadn't found anything suspicious. But at least they'd accomplished the first step: making his presence at the mill a natural occurrence.

For everyone except Mark, at least. Luke could still feel his resistance when they met up again near the accounting department. He knew things were about to get interesting when Jacob waved them on while he and Aiden talked over a problem with an employee.

The small accounting office was quiet. A lot of the employees had left early to prepare for bad weather. Being overly cautious, schools had let out early. Plus this tour had taken a bit longer than Luke had planned. He hoped to rush them through this last department so he could get over to Avery's before the thunderstorms started.

Mark made himself look busy fiddling with papers on one of the desks. Luke ignored the other man's aimless movements, his mind wandering to thoughts of what he would say to Avery.

Finally tired of the manager and all the noise he was making, Luke turned to face him. "What're you doing?"

"What do you mean?"

Mark's stiff shoulders and tight mouth gave Luke confirmation that Mark was gathering his courage for…something. Luke didn't have the patience to wait. "Why don't you just spit it out?"

His gaze slid away from Luke's, but Mark's chin jutted out in challenge. "I simply want to understand. I mean, why would you bother with Avery when before long you'll be heading back to fame and fortune? After all, it's not like she's your usual arm candy, is she?"

Luke didn't answer. He needed to get his temper under control first. Mark's words had a derogatory tone. Luke wasn't sure if it was directed toward Avery or himself. Neither would be appropriate.

His silence didn't impact Mark, who seemed to gain courage the more he talked. "It's okay. Somebody will be here to pick up the pieces after you *walk* away."

Again, Luke let the jab go, but he couldn't keep quiet.

The more information he had, the more he could warn Avery. Well, that probably wouldn't go over well, but he'd figure out something. "You mean you?" He cocked his head to the side as if he were truly interested.

Mark just shrugged, grinning.

That lit Luke's fire. He was known to say stupid stuff before checking himself, and anger weakened his already tenuous control. He didn't often lash out, but when he did—ugly stuff. "If I understand gossip correctly, you and Avery have been dating for almost a year. Or rather, *had been* dating. If you had closed the deal before I got here, picking up the pieces wouldn't be an issue—but then again, I guess coming in second might be an experience you need."

Luke knew his arrogant grin topped Mark's smirk any day. Not that Avery had ever mentioned being upset over not seeing Mark romantically, if their dates had even been that. Besides, Luke would probably be the last person she'd talk with about Mark, but Mark didn't need to know.

"Tell Jacob I had to leave," Mark snapped.

Luke didn't manage to wait for Mark's office door to slam before he murmured, "If I feel like it, a-hole...which I won't."

Luke stared at the tight seal of the door for long moments, his frustration urging him to burst through and remind that jerk whose family was in charge here. But he didn't let himself move. Getting all up in Mark's grill would make him look jealous.

Just like Mark's overt comments had done for him.

Luke had nothing to prove. But that didn't stop him from wanting to.

"Mr. Hutchens, I want you to pay close attention to how you're feeling. Call me immediately if those muscles seize up again, instead of waiting until you can barely make it here. Got it?"

Avery gave the old man a stern stare, wishing she could just follow him home and watch him 24/7 to make sure he was okay. Or as okay as he could be with terminal pancreatic cancer.

"Are you bossing me around, missy?" His stare was a challenge all its own.

But Avery wasn't backing down. "You betcha."

"Well…all right." The fact that he retreated so quickly concerned her. Mr. Hutchens had been her patient for a while, and he liked to play the crotchety old dude when she gave him orders. But always playfully. He'd rather hurt himself before he hurt her.

If he wasn't playing the game today, he definitely wasn't feeling well. Of course, having your back muscles contract and not let go didn't feel so good, no matter what your other health issues were.

"Now, come in again tomorrow—"

"I can't afford that and you know it."

The bell over the door sounded as she glared at him. "You will come and you're not going to pay for it, either, so get over that pride of yours. I want to keep you upright and mobile. That's the goal." *For as long as I can.*

He gave a sage nod before glancing over her shoulder at the newcomer. "Well, I'll be. Lucas Renegade Blackstone. I haven't seen you since you went and got all famous." He grinned. "At least, not in person."

Avery breathed deep, almost able to feel Luke's gaze on her back. Unable to think of a delay, she reluctantly turned around to face him. Heat burned her cheeks as she remembered his kiss from the night before…and her response.

"Avery here working on you, too?" Mr. Hutchens asked.

"Sure is," Luke said, flashing a grin in her direction. *But not today.* She'd have remembered if she had an appointment for him on today's schedule, especially since they'd canceled the rest of the afternoon appointments for impending bad weather. So why was he here?

"She treating you right?" Luke asked, oblivious to her inner panic.

Mr. Hutchens stood a little taller, though Avery could tell by his quick breath that it hurt to do so. "Always," the older man said. "And how're the legs? I saw the footage on television. That wasn't a pretty wreck."

The practice footage had played on newscasts in their county for weeks following the accident, then again after Luke had been released from the hospital. Since he was a homegrown celebrity, everyone around Black Hills had devoured the slightest tidbits about his accident and recovery.

Avery studied Luke from under her lashes as the men talked sports. He leaned casually against his cane, as if it were an accessory instead of a necessity. While charming, he wasn't laying it on thick. His responses to whatever Mr. Hutchens said were genuinely warm. She'd seen that same sincerity on his face during television interviews. He was honestly interested in other people, which made him so much more darn appealing.

As if he needed any help with that.

"Would you do me a favor, Mr. Hutchens? As soon as my slave driver here clears me to get back behind the wheel, how about we go for a nice, fast drive?"

"Wow. I've never ridden in a really fast car. Reliable ones, yes, but never fast." And the twinkle in the older man's eyes told them just how exciting that would be for him.

"Well, I have a beaut. She drives smooth and steady—unless there's an operator error." Luke winked at the older man. "Don't worry. I'll be careful."

"I'm pretty sure you won't."

Avery laughed. Leave it to Mr. Hutchens to peg Luke so accurately.

"You laugh, young lady," Mr. Hutchens said, "but the truth is, when a chance comes once in a lifetime, you take it. And don't rely on the brakes or you'll regret it."

"Very sound advice," Luke agreed. He tilted his head in Avery's direction. "See? I'm right."

Ah, the polite male equivalent of *I told you so.*

"Mr. Hutchens," he said. "I'll be in touch."

"I see my daughter pulling up in the parking lot," Mr. Hutchens said. "And it's almost time for my medicine. I will see you tomorrow, missy."

"Yes, sir," she said, indulging in a quick hug.

"And you," he said, pinning Luke with a look, "you take good care of her, you hear?"

"Oh, I will, sir."

Was she reading an innuendo in Luke's reply that wasn't there? A flush swept up her neck and across her cheeks.

Maybe not, because Mr. Hutchens winked. "I can see she's in good hands. Good afternoon, son. Missy."

"Let me walk you out, Mr. Hutchens," Cindy said.

"Are you leaving now, too, girlie?"

"I'm hoping to get home before it pours," she said. "You sure you'll be okay, Avery?" she asked with a quick glance at Luke.

Avery appreciated the support, since her shaky insides were making her wish that her sassy receptionist would stick around for once. "Yeah," she said instead. "I'll get everything closed up." She ushered them to the door, eager to get any conversation over and done with. "Y'all be safe."

She and Luke stood side by side as they exited the door and walked slowly to Mr. Hutchens's daughter's car. The wind from the coming storm whipped at their clothes.

"What's the matter with him?" Luke finally asked in a low tone.

Avery matched it, though there wasn't anyone left to hear. "It's not a secret. Pancreatic cancer. Not too much longer now."

"Any insurance?"

"Yes, but therapy benefits can run out pretty quickly." Something that frustrated Avery to no end. Not because she needed money, but because it kept her patients from seeing her as often as they needed to.

Luke glanced across at her. "Why wouldn't you let him pay?"

"Because then he'd use not having enough money as an excuse to not show up." She shrugged. "I'm not really helping with the cancer anyway. Just trying to keep him as mobile as possible for as long as we can. Manage the pain a little. He's got a great attitude despite a terrible prognosis."

"That's wonderful, Avery...what you're doing."

She dismissed the compliment, because tooting her own horn wasn't ladylike. "Somebody needs to take care of them." And she'd been doing it all her life, right? That was her place. And her joy.

"I see."

She couldn't tell if he was agreeing with her statement or what, so she simply nodded. But his next words caught her attention.

"So who takes care of you?"

Her gaze shot to his, clashing with those amber eyes while the implications hit her hard. Who *did* take care of her? Who ever had? No one since she was a kid. At least, not that she could remember.

Uncomfortable exploring the question any deeper, she walked back toward the checkout counter. "I know you didn't have an appointment this afternoon. What do you need, Luke?"

"I'm here," he said with a charming grin, "because I

thought it would be more fun to create mischief than be tortured."

She should have teased back, slipped into casual mode. But a flood of remembered sensations from the night before held her immobile.

Luke tried again. "I think it's time for another adventure."

Oh, Lord help her. "I don't think an adventure is a good idea."

Considering how much she wanted a repeat of yesterday's kiss—definitely not.

Would she even survive another? Between the fun and the fear of hurting him from last night, she wasn't sure her heart could take it.

Could it? "Definitely not a good idea."

Luke took her concern in stride. "It rarely is but that's what makes it fun. The danger."

Oh, it was dangerous all right. This was getting out of hand.

A taste, remember? Oh, yeah. She'd almost forgotten that little pep talk to herself—and she desperately wanted a taste like she'd had last night. But was she willing to put herself out there, to risk making herself vulnerable again to Lucas Blackstone, of all people? She tried to clear the tightness from her throat. "What did you have in mind?"

Luke didn't blink. "How about the drive-in? They always have something fun to see." He wiggled his eyebrows and grinned. "Something spooky, for good cuddling. And it won't be open too many more weekends before closing for the winter."

Before she could respond, the lights blinked out. Avery froze. Then the emergency lights clicked on, lending an eerie green glow to the room. Only then did Avery notice that the world outside had darkened to midnight and rain had started coming down in heavy drops.

"I don't think Cindy beat the rain home," she murmured.

"Nope," Luke said. "And neither will we."

Instantly alert, Avery walked to the window and searched the slope of the parking lot through the increasing sheets of rain. "Where's Nolen?"

Luke shifted beside her, his arm brushing hers. Such an innocent touch for such a sensual response deep inside.

"He didn't bring me. Aiden dropped me off and was gonna send Nolen back for me later."

Despite the gloom, she turned an incredulous eye in his direction. "Have you not listened to the weather today?"

She saw a flash of his white teeth. "Guess I didn't think this through very well. But in my defense, having your brother wait while you ask a woman out is a bit awkward, if I could even convince him not to get out of the car."

Avery didn't have siblings, but she knew from observing others that a man's brothers were his first source of friendly ridicule. Aiden would never have stayed in the car. "Well, you won't be going anywhere anytime soon."

Luke stared out the front windows. Rain lashed at the asphalt so heavily as to obscure the view. An occasional glimpse of tree limbs dancing was all that made it through. "I see that," he said.

"No." She shook her head. "I mean, for longer than you think. Remember the bridge at the bottom of the hill?" They couldn't see it from here, but it was the only access to the facility drive. Avery's heart pounded as her brain kicked into overdrive. "It floods in heavy rains like these. That's why we canceled our afternoon appointments."

Luke moved closer to the window. "That quick, huh?"

"All the water from uphill flows back down here. It flash floods, so we take extra precautions." Including having a comfortable living space that allowed her to stay here cozy and safe—and usually alone.

"So this means we're stuck here—for the night?" Luke asked, a curious tone in his voice.

Avery swallowed hard, her mind on her fear of the storm and a new fear…of being cooped up with the sexiest man she knew…for hours on end. "Probably so."

"Well, that's an adventure by itself, right?"

Seven

"I need to lock everything down," Avery said. She stepped over to secure the front doors, then walked in the other direction, leaving Luke to stand there and twiddle his thumbs—a safe distance away.

Only he'd never been a twiddle-his-thumbs kind of guy. Following along to the workout room, he watched as she made sure all of the equipment was unplugged, including the computers. She was as thorough as he'd expected her to be—just as she was with her patients.

His meeting with Mr. Hutchens still haunted him. The elder man's stalwart attitude. Avery's careful attention to the man's needs and lack of concern for his wallet. Yet through it all, she'd approached the whole situation in a way that got the job done without attacking the man's pride.

A lot like she'd done with Luke. Guess all those years of studying others had paid off.

Just then, a rumble of thunder built outside, shaking the

building until it ended in a crack. Avery's breath caught and she winced.

Luke realized something that he'd missed in all his years of knowing Avery: she definitely did not like storms.

As she finished securing the back door, she turned toward him. Her stiff back and wary look left him wondering if she thought he would pounce. Or was it just the weather?

"We can wait it out in my office, if you want," she said quietly.

He didn't really have a choice, and that made him inordinately glad.

He followed her down a short, windowless hallway by sound rather than sight, his cane plonking with every step. She disappeared to the left and he paused in the doorway. A few fumbling sounds, then a drawer closing, and an electric lantern flared to life.

Luke blinked to clear his vision, then found himself staring in surprise. This might be Avery's office, but it looked more like a plush, feminine version of the retreat Aiden had built for himself at Blackstone Manor. One corner was dominated by an antique desk with the expected accoutrements, but there the usual description of a doctor's office ended.

He couldn't tell what color the walls were, but it was warm even in the deep shadows. There was an armoire, which he suspected held a media system, and a deep upholstered couch that looked wide enough for him to sleep on—though not wide enough for them together.

Not that he should be thinking about that— Hell, who was he kidding?

Avery gestured toward the high-end furniture. "Make yourself at home. It's gonna be a while."

Seeming oblivious to him, she reached into the bottom of the armoire and pulled out a radio. She'd obviously used it before because it was tuned perfectly when she turned it on.

The announcer was moving quickly through a multitude of weather warnings and storm watches, including a flash flood warning for their county.

"No kidding," Avery muttered under her breath.

Luke could only grin. Avery often projected the image of being calm and in control—except in the face of two things: any form of sexual attention from a man and, from what he'd seen tonight, thunderstorms.

"This is really nice for an office," he said, hoping to soothe her nerves as he settled onto the couch.

She surveyed the space from behind her desk. He couldn't see clearly, but he was pretty sure she blushed.

"Well, I end up staying here overnight some due to weather, so I wanted it to be comfortable."

"Does this happen often?" he asked.

"I realize it's probably foreign to you," she said, shuffling the papers in front of her, "but some of us are afraid to drive in storms. And I can get caught here unexpectedly." She chuckled, though it sounded strained. "So it's less stressful than trying to get to my house since it's so far out of town."

"That sounds like a safe option to me," he said.

Her shoulders relaxed a bit, but she didn't look up. The papers were slowly migrated into a series of neat little piles. Then she began moving them to the nearby filing cabinet.

It couldn't be more obvious that she was uncomfortable having him here. Of course, she'd been on edge since that kiss last night—and he seemed to be making it worse rather than better.

On her next trip past him he leaned forward to reach for her. Her eyes widened, then she tried to sidestep and change direction just as his hand met her arm. A moment's push and pull, then she tumbled into his arms with a cry.

Unexpected, but oh so right.

Warm weight, softly honey scented and extra wiggly. Just like that, all the reasons he shouldn't touch her disappeared. Then a loud crash of thunder shook the building and Avery changed direction. Instead of pulling away, she dove in close, clutching at his shirt, burrowing against his chest.

The slight tremble in her hands brought his barriers down even more. His palms found the skin of her upper arms. Up and down, under her sleeves, he instinctively moved to comfort her—

Only comfort wasn't the result.

He'd wondered since meeting this adult version of Avery how she would feel against—and under—him. He had to admit it. But he couldn't have fantasized how perfect she would feel in his arms. Slowly his hand traveled up along her neck to her chin and lifted her face to his.

This kiss wasn't tentative, but Luke didn't rush. As he leaned in, he breathed deep, soaking in her honey scent. Then his lips brushed over hers, coaxing her to open.

She signaled her surrender by melting against him. Soft flesh pressed to his chest. All he could do was pull her closer. Then his focus narrowed to the play of her tongue against his.

Avery twisted more fully toward him, their bodies meeting in a collision that had Luke seeing stars. The good kind.

Her hands fisted into his shirt and Luke shot straight into overdrive. He guided her legs over his until she straddled his lap, but their mouths never parted.

All that lovely pressure right where he wanted it. And he wanted *more* of it.

He pulled her hips tight against his groin while he

sucked lightly at her bottom lip, then moved his lips back over her jawline to the sensitive column of her neck. He couldn't stop his hands from roaming, sneaking beneath her scrub shirt to finally cup the breasts he'd been fantasizing about all too often.

She moaned, arching her back to press into his palms. Only it wasn't nearly enough.

Something happened as he whisked the material over her head, because suddenly the silken mass of her hair swept down around them. Her scent flooded the air. Luke's heart raced, rivaling the speed of his favorite car.

His mouth migrated to the plump mounds now in reach. He squeezed with his hands, plumping them even more. Then he let go of his control, nibbling and sucking until she squirmed in his lap. Her nipples hardened. Her thighs tensed. Her cries filled his ears to the exclusion of all else.

She raised her arms, lifting her long hair up, then letting it sift through her fingers to cover her bare shoulders once more. Luke moaned. Avery's gaze swept down to his, her gorgeous irises now darkened in the glow of the lamp.

For a brief moment, sanity returned. Alarm bells sounded, reminding him how vulnerable she was, how caring.

But then she lowered her mouth to his once more and he could only feel. Not think.

Luke wasn't sure if it was five minutes or five hours later—all he knew was that some new sound had invaded their world of pounding rain, sighs and groans. It jangled along his nerves until he could no longer ignore its presence.

His phone.

Pulling back forced a protesting groan from deep in his throat, but his family might be worried. "Just a minute, baby," he murmured.

Digging the phone out of his pants pocket proved a

challenge—one he didn't accomplish until the ring tone had silenced. But then it was too late.

The screen lit up in the dark with a missed-call message from "Aiden's wife."

The nickname he jokingly used to poke fun at Christina when she got too bossy cut through the haze of lust quicker than a hot knife through butter.

Luke's brain sped from zero to sixty. His brother Aiden had come home…and found a wife. His twin had come home…and found a family.

Luke had come home…and found himself making out with Black Hill's most eligible bachelorette.

This was not a pattern he wanted to follow.

He found himself acting on instinct rather than logic. The first part came easily: he lifted Avery from his lap and set her next to him on the couch. The second part, not so much. Not bothering to search for his cane, he forced himself upright by sheer will and limped to the door. Before slipping through, he turned back to the silent woman behind him.

"I'm sorry, Avery."

"I thought you were taking Avery to the drive-in tonight."

Luke turned from his solemn stare out the front parlor window to face Christina's question. "I am. Maybe. At least, I hope so."

Her dark, perfectly arched brows lifted. "Well," she demanded, "are you or aren't you?"

He wanted to tease her, but his nerves wouldn't let him. "I guess I'll find out when I get there."

"So…what did you do?"

The teasing grin came more easily to his lips than a confession. "What makes you think I did anything?"

"The crack in your confident veneer was my first clue."

Hmm…he should have known she was too smart for his own good. "I screwed up and she's probably mad at me."

"Let me guess—you aren't gonna let that stand in your way?"

He probably should. Holding Avery close had been the best thing to happen to him in a long time…sweeter than he'd remembered from their first kiss. It was territory he shouldn't explore. Indulging himself wasn't fair to Avery when he wasn't sticking around for anything permanent.

So why was he going back to the therapy center just two days later? He shook his head. "I promised Avery I would help her have fun. This is just a little pothole, that's all."

"Good."

Now he raised a brow. Would she say the same thing if she knew what he'd really done? "Come again?"

"Avery needs someone who will help her get out of her own way. And you need someone who will demand a little more of you than looking pretty and driving fast."

"But—"

"Just work with what you have and see where it leads. After all, surprises are fun, too. Right?"

Christina's words rolled around in his brain as he made his way back to the kitchen. They made perfect sense. Except Luke still felt the dangerous desire to take his relationship with Avery further than friendship.

Surely they could go out on a public date without him giving in to temptation? They couldn't get in too much trouble in a parked car surrounded by people. Well, teenagers did, but they were grown adults. He could control himself…right? He ignored his misgivings by focusing on the task at hand. "Mary, you're a sweetheart for putting this together."

Luke had jumped on the chance to take a picnic snack pack on his date with Avery, instead of having to stand in line at the concessions stand. The thought of all those people made him feel like he was breaking out in hives. Besides, Mary made the best food.

He wanted a quiet night—just him and Avery watching a movie together in the back of her SUV. If she would even let him in the therapy center after his behavior night before last.

He had no idea whether she would welcome him with a forgiving smile or slam the door in his face—which was why he'd decided to spring this date on her at the end of her workday. She'd be less likely to make a scene, which would give him a chance to at least argue his side. And he'd have Cindy there to help plead his case…if Avery hadn't turned her against him yet.

He just wished he was picking her up instead of being driven there by Nolen. He hadn't been cleared to drive yet. The emasculating feeling would have come to any take-charge male, but for Luke, it was multiplied by his extreme need to be behind the wheel.

"What made you choose the drive-in for your date, Lucas?" Mary asked.

Luke grinned, letting her chatter push aside the self-doubt. Mary called all the boys by their given names. No nicknames for her. He could remember many a rainy afternoon he'd spent down here having cookies, warm right out of the oven. Sometimes alone. Sometimes with one or both of his brothers. But every time Mary used the cookies to bribe them into talking. About school, girls, their dreams, life.

She was a good woman. One who deserved all Christina had gone through to ensure she and Nolen were taken care of for the rest of their lives.

"You remember how Avery's mother was," he said after swallowing.

Mary nodded. "Rumor was, she could be pretty strict."

"Yes, ma'am. Avery didn't get to do a lot of the normal

hangout stuff the rest of us did. Formal events? Green light. Swimming in the creek or going bowling? Not so much. I thought this would be fun for her." But he hadn't thought the level of temptation through all the way.

"If anyone can show that girl how to have fun, it would be you. You always were off doing something more interesting than chores or schoolwork."

Luke grinned. "I tried."

"Y'all have fun." Mary winked. "But not too much fun. You'll be in public, after all."

"Since when has that ever stopped me?" Luke teased, flashing his trademark wicked grin. But after their night flooded in, Luke needed to be very careful. He fully intended to get them back on friendly ground. He liked Avery…a lot more than he should. But it wasn't fair to her to get sexually involved, then return to his normal life a whole state away.

They could still be friends, though, right?

So he lifted the basket, balancing it on the side opposite his cane, and walked out the back door to meet Nolen.

He distracted himself with thoughts of Avery. Too bad she was so darn cute when she got flustered. He couldn't resist teasing her. Any other woman might smile in invitation, look at him through her lashes, even lick her lips in response. Not Avery. She tripped over her own feet and dropped things. It amused him, but not in a condescending way. Almost as if he had to smile. His heart filled with happiness every time she stumbled, because that was her reaction to *him*.

The only frustrating part of this whole scenario was the fact that he would be sitting in the passenger seat, waiting to arrive. This wasn't his thing. *He* should be driving. *He* should be picking her up. When would his life return to normal? He might be able to cope with not racing, if he could just get behind the damn wheel again.

It wasn't just frustration. So much of his identity was wrapped up in racing that he felt like half a person when he couldn't do it. Half a man when he couldn't drive to a date.

No one else seemed to get that.

Luke stuffed his feelings of inadequacy down hard as he reached the car. But they popped back up to the surface over the littlest of things, like when Nolen took the basket and loaded it himself.

All these new, dark emotions were difficult for Luke to handle, a somber doppelgänger he wasn't used to facing. His biggest fear through all of this was that this new part of his personality would linger, dig deep into him, instead of letting him return to the easygoing, superficial star he'd been before.

But tonight wasn't about him. It was about helping Avery loosen up and have a good time. Though not too good a time—for either of them.

So he swallowed his pride and made his way to the passenger-side door, praying rejection wasn't waiting for him at the end of this ride.

Eight

Cindy's eyes widening was Avery's first clue that Luke had walked through the front door. Since he'd canceled his appointment for earlier today, she should have been surprised. Somehow she wasn't.

Luke didn't give up. He took things in stride and kept on truckin'. Avery wished she was capable of doing the same.

She smoothed her facial features to a careful neutral and prayed she would get through this first meeting post-humiliation as quickly as possible. After all, she was still his therapist. They needed to be able to be in the same room together for her to help him recover—though she had no idea how she would touch him again without remembering how it felt to have her hands moving on his body with passion. Or how it felt to have his hands on her.

She glanced nervously at Cindy. She hadn't told the other woman what had happened. Somehow it was too personal, too private to share even with one of her best friends. Eventually…but not today.

She cleared her throat and tried to take control of this situation. "I'm sorry, Luke. I don't have any more appointment times this afternoon. We're closing."

"But we could—" Cindy halted when Avery shot a glance full of daggers in her direction.

"Not a problem, since I'm not here for an appointment," he said.

Avery's head swam at his words.

"I thought we'd try that drive-in date."

Her mind went blank. "Why?"

"It's Friday." He grinned, charming and carefree. Her complete opposite. "It'll be fun. You deserve some downtime after this week, don't you?"

That sounded well and good, but why was he really doing this? Before he'd left the office the other morning, he'd babbled a whole speech about wanting to still be friends, but she hadn't been buying it. No sexy, charming man like Luke had ever wanted to just be her "friend."

"She's overthinking it." Cindy had to add her two cents' worth.

"I am not."

He and Cindy just stared at her in silence.

"Okay, I usually am." She simply didn't know how to stop.

Luke didn't have the same problem. "Don't think. Just do."

Easy for him to say. But she had promised herself a taste—of freedom, of passion, of Luke. *Stop hemming and hawing and do it.* She should just take what little she could get.

After all, it could be fun. The old-fashioned drive-in theater on the north side of Black Hills had never been on Avery's radar. She loved movies, actually—but in the comfort of her own home. Of course, other than the drive-in, there was only a two-screen theater in the Black Hills square. And it mostly featured kids' movies and oldies.

The drive-in usually showed current movies. The double features were pretty popular, especially in the summer, when families could go for a kid-friendly movie first, then the adults would watch the more mature movies after laying the kids down to sleep in their cars. So she'd be in public, which should keep her from giving in to all the exciting tingles Luke inspired.

Or maybe not. After all, she'd be in a parked car. In the dark. With Luke.

Stop analyzing. Just do it. "Okay. Want me to drive?"

Luke frowned, none too happy about that, but still nodded his head slowly. "Yeah, that will be easiest." Then he snapped back to happy Luke. "I've brought everything we will need."

Cindy chuckled, sparking Avery's irritation. "You planned ahead?"

"Yep."

"What if I had said no?" Avery asked.

This time, Avery's assistant didn't restrain herself to just laughing. She said, "An inexperienced girl like you is not gonna turn down a chance to make out at the drive-in."

Ouch! Avery couldn't even look at Luke. Instead she glared across the counter. She must have been at least a little frightening, because her friend grimaced and walked back into the equipment room.

Turning her attention to Luke, Avery startled when she found him up close and personal. Within-kissing-distance close. Something she couldn't stop noticing.

"I wasn't trying to insult you," he said.

"Um, okay." What was she supposed to say?

"Really, I wasn't." He tilted his head to the side. Probably to see her better, but Avery couldn't help thinking it was the perfect angle for kissing. Man, he'd tasted so good.

"I know your parents didn't let you do a lot of the same stuff the rest of us did as teenagers. Especially after your dad died," he said. "I just thought this would be one of those things you don't have any experience with…and I could give you that."

Oh Lordy, was he for real?

"That's very sweet of you, Luke."

"I'm not doing it to be sweet. I have my own ulterior motives."

Finally he leaned in, brushing his lips against her cheek. Compared to the other night, the step down in passion was almost an insult. Her skepticism must have shown on her face, so he tried again.

"Listen, you're the first thing that's gotten my heart racing in a long time. I think that's worth exploring, don't you? Yes, I let things get out of hand the other night, and that's not fair to you. I'm sorry."

At least this humiliation wasn't public. Luke could never know how far she'd wanted to go the other night. Especially since it was obvious he didn't feel the same.

"So what do you say?" he asked.

"I'm all about a new experience." Even if it wasn't the one she really wanted to have with Luke.

Apparently not being able to drive was going to be an ongoing irritation for him. Avery pulled the car around and Nolen loaded it. Standing around waiting did not come naturally to Luke.

He swallowed his pride and made his way to the passenger-side door, reminding himself he should be grateful just to be alive. Avery lowered the hatch back, the basket safely stowed inside, then grinned at him as she climbed into the driver's seat.

That smile was infectious, as was the excitement behind it. Like a kid in a candy store—and he intended to feed her all the sweets she could eat tonight.

"What's in the basket?" she asked.

"It's a surprise from Mary."

"Chocolate chip cookies?"

"Good guess, but I'm not telling. You'll have to wait and see."

Her full lips turned into a plump pout, but the excitement practically sparkled in her eyes. So she liked surprises. As much as he liked giving them.

He tried not to think of the ways he could use this to his advantage—and for her satisfaction. That could be dangerously addictive.

Trying to get his mind back on track, Luke directed Avery on where to enter the theater grounds, purchase tickets and choose one of the rows. As she started to pull into one of the slots next to an old-school microphone stand, he stopped her. "Reverse it."

She froze with her hands properly held in the ten-and two-o'clock positions on the steering wheel. "What?"

"Back in—so we can climb in the rear and watch from there." He grinned at her startled look. She really hadn't been to a drive-in theater. "Just trust me."

"Um, I don't back up very well." Her look met his under her raised brows. "Would you do it?"

The lump in his throat was hard to swallow down, embarrassingly so. "I thought I wasn't allowed to drive."

"I'm hoping you won't be driving over the speed limit here, which is, what? Five miles an hour?" She grinned. "Don't think you can do much damage going that fast, can you?"

As he rounded the car and slid behind the wheel, the slight shake in his hands left Luke disconcerted. Avery waited outside as he shifted the car into Reverse and smoothly backed it in with minute precision. He sat for a moment, savoring the feel of the wheel in his hands, the hum of the vehicle beneath him, and ached for what he couldn't have.

Yet. Not if he wanted to heal properly. Some days it didn't seem worth the wait, but he wanted his lower body to work the rest of his life.

So he forced himself to wait it out, not risk the pressure a sudden accident might put on his healing bones. Not long ago, he'd have trusted in his skills to avoid an accident. Now doubt had set in.

Avery's gentle knock on the window pulled Luke from his thoughts. He stepped out of the car. "See, easy."

"Show-off."

"I can't help that I have skills." He winked, officially leaving his melancholy behind. Then he opened the hatch. Propping his cane against the bumper, he started to arrange the back area of her car to his satisfaction. Finally he turned to her. "Climb in."

With a bemused look she did, then inched her way toward the basket.

"Oh, no you don't," Luke said with a chuckle. "No peeking until I say."

Again with the lovely pout. Those lips might just be the biggest temptation he'd ever faced.

He got the speaker box set up in the corner, then maneuvered himself into the car. The back gate was designed so he could close the hatch, but leave the pop-out window lifted to view the screen. Perfect. The warmth from Avery's body soaked into his skin as he settled next to her. Had any race ever felt this dangerous?

"And this is why we sit in the back," he said after clearing his throat. "Much more comfortable."

"I see." Avery's voice sounded breathy.

Good. His considerable ache left him needing to know that she was affected by him, too.

Opening the basket, he pulled out the softest blanket he'd been able to find at Blackstone Manor and draped it over them. The heat multiplied beneath the barrier between them and the cooling autumn air.

"Um, Luke?" That breathlessness had strengthened.

He couldn't force himself away—not even an inch. "Yes?"

"Is this, um, what you're supposed to do at the drive-in?"

"Yes." *Oh, yes.*

"No wonder my mother never let me come here."

He grinned, then pulled the basket over to him once more to unearth the goodies inside.

Around them the lot filled with cars. There was lots of chattering as their neighbors got ready for the movies to start. First an older release about a group of kids hunting for treasure, then a current thriller sequel for the adults. Luke had gotten them there early so they could settle in without being recognized.

He'd forgotten what a social event this was for most people. Big groups of teenagers would congregate down front during the first movie, then retire to their cars for necking during the second. Families spent time visiting with other families, and during the summer there would be lines of blankets on the ground with supper picnics.

He'd forgotten all about that, because frankly making out had been more interesting as a teenager.

But inside their little cocoon, snuggled beneath a blanket that thankfully disguised just how much he was enjoying this, they would avoid the crowd. Even though he knew he shouldn't—Luke wanted Avery all to himself. He pulled out the popcorn and offered her a choice of pouches. "Caramel, cinnamon sugar or ranch?"

She smiled. "Miss Mary knows I love cinnamon sugar anything."

So that's why the housekeeper had insisted on that flavor. "Try this." He opened the bag and pulled out a couple of popped kernels encased in a brown syrupy coating. She tried to reach up with her fingers, but he was having none of that. Catching her gaze, he eased the food forward until he breached her lips. Their gazes connected as she glanced up in question; she never looked away. The pleasure that spread over her face lit him up inside.

"Good?" he asked.

"Mmm-hmm," she murmured, still chewing.

Intrigued, he fed her again, and again, the last time brushing his fingertips along the seam of her lips. He barely caught the shiver that snuck over her. Then he licked his fingertips clean of the sweet coating. "Delicious."

"Wanna try some?" she whispered.

He wondered if she realized the invitation that displayed so prominently in her eyes. He'd guess not, but that was one of the things that drew him. No overt invitations, no cookie-cutter come-ons…just Avery. He bet she was the sweetest, hottest thing he was ever going to taste.

What better time than now?

Just as he leaned in, her eyes widened. That quick guilt snuck in. It was an unfamiliar emotion. Luke lived his life full throttle. Regret was rare. But he needed to remember that giving Avery mixed signals wasn't fair to either of them. A good woman like her deserved better than a player like him.

So instead he tried to ignore the softness of her breasts brushing against his arm, the warmth of her thigh alongside his and the way his spirit sang with the sensations that declared his body was alive.

He couldn't stop thinking about her kiss. If he took her lips now, they would be soft as butter, sweet with sugar and hungry for him. He just knew it.

Luke pulled back and held up another piece of popcorn.

The glaze over her eyes kept them from focusing, urging him to push his boundaries, but he held himself back.

Like prolonged foreplay. The best kind.

Luke gripped the blanket in his fist to keep from pushing for more. The night was dark, with barely any moon. But they weren't teenagers to be caught in a lip-lock by all the kids running by. As a matter of fact, as he glanced out at the end credits rolling up the screen, he noticed people slowing as they walked past the car.

At least no one had pressed their face to the window yet.

Finally Avery reached across him for one of the popcorn bags, the quick press of her softness against him a jolt to his senses. Then she leaned back and started to munch on her own, leaving him chilled. The cocoon of sensation they'd been lost in for the last hour and a half turned cold.

"I think you've been spotted," she mumbled.

"Meaning?" he asked, though he knew the answer already. In the periphery of his view he could see people gathering. Like the rapid building of a mob, the group grew in numbers as they murmured among themselves.

"People know you're here. You know how small towns are… They love a homegrown celebrity."

Right now, Luke felt like a celebrity for all the wrong reasons. The last thing he wanted was to be on display.

"Oh, dear."

"What?" he asked.

"I believe the mayor just joined them."

Dang it. Just like that, his vision for how this evening would go disappeared—replaced by a steady stream of people who would probably go on and on about his accident. Talk about a downer.

Tonight was about Avery, not the hometown celebrity. More than having fun or even having sex, he wanted to shake the foundations of her safe world. He couldn't do it with an audience. And having the crowd to come to him

would only put her in the public spotlight right alongside him.

He sighed, throwing the blanket aside. Playing the gentleman role, as he had two times in three days, was not
nearly as rewarding as people made it out to be.

Within minutes of Luke scooting out of the car, the real
estate between them and the next row became a revolving
door of people. Avery couldn't even see the bottom half
of the screen because of the crowd. She huddled into the
shadows of her car, shoving popcorn in her mouth like a
squirrel storing for winter, not willing to risk the exposure. She recognized more than a few patients, members
of their families, and knew her business would be a hot-
bed of gossip if she set one foot near Luke. Maybe they'd
forget the car he'd come from.

Between Luke's teasing challenge back at her office
and her desire to save face in front of Cindy, Avery hadn't
given herself time to think this decision through. She and
Luke couldn't just go out as friends. All eyes would be
searching for the slightest behavior that proved they were
more than that. She loved these people. That didn't always
mean living with them was easy.

She'd lived all her life under their scrutiny, and tried to
avoid it when she could. But it was the constant questions
and insinuations that would be thrown at her after Luke
left town that she was truly trying to avoid.

As the second set of movie credits rolled, Avery put
the leftover food back into the basket. The last thing to be
packed was the blanket, fluffy and soft. Heat rolled over
her as she remembered those few precious moments with
Luke wrapped tight against her. Would she have survived
four hours of that? Maybe not, but it would have been fun
to try.

Thirty minutes later, she couldn't help wondering if

more time under that blanket would have meant driving them both back to her house at top speed, instead of turning onto the highway that led out to Blackstone Manor. Which one did she really want?

The quivery feeling in the pit of her stomach told Avery she wasn't sure. And to her disappointment, Luke had made his position quite clear: friends, not lovers. Now he remained silent, probably exhausted from the overload of people. Her guilt over leaving him to handle himself alone weighed her down, but self-preservation was a strong instinct.

Luke leaned against his car door, staring out the window at the farmland flashing past as they left the lights of Black Hills proper.

His voice bordered on surly when he finally spoke. "Why didn't you remind me what a social event the drive-in could be?"

"Um, I've never been. Remember?"

"I just remember making out with my girlfriends," he grumbled. "Tonight wasn't what I had in mind."

Just what Avery needed. A reminder of times past and all the women Luke had had better experiences with. "It wasn't my fault. You could have stayed in the car."

"But you didn't go out of your way to help, either, did you?"

Her face flamed. "I didn't know you needed my help." After all, he was the big star. Though honestly, she had taken the coward's way out.

"You could have joined me." He turned back toward the window. "Or were you just too embarrassed to be seen with an old, broken-down celebrity?"

Uh-oh. "It wasn't that at all." She struggled to gather her thoughts while still concentrating on the road. "I just—"

"Didn't want to be seen with me?"

This was going from bad to worse. Tonight hadn't been

a dream date, but now it was turning into a nightmare. Why couldn't these things ever go right for her?

"Me staying away had nothing to do with not wanting to be seen with you, or your injuries. I work with people with mobility issues every day. What have I ever done to make you think I would be ashamed of you?"

He didn't answer, but continued to stare out the window. The silence that filled the car seemed heavy with recriminations—something Avery couldn't handle. And she couldn't leave him thinking that she was embarrassed by him in some way.

"Yes, I did choose to stay away. But you have to remember, Luke—one day you'll leave. And I'll be the one left behind, dealing with their pity." She gestured between them, wishing she could see his face. "Whether anything happens between us or not, they'll think it did." *And that I wasn't good enough to keep you here.*

The continued silence forced more words out.

"I'm sorry if that's selfish, but I don't know if I can handle that."

When he didn't respond, a glimmer of something hot sparked deep in her belly. It grew with every second he didn't speak until she recognized the anger building inside her. There he was, sulking like a spoiled boy, when she'd done nothing but protect herself, her reputation. How dare he?

Finally reaching her limit, she whipped over into a church parking lot—one of the few buildings out here in the boonies. She gave a soft growl. "I can't talk about this and drive."

"I can."

It took a moment before the flash of realization came. That's what was happening. She shoved the gearshift into Park and turned on him. "Is this about the driving? Luke, you are not broken. Not doing it right now is a protection for your body, not an indication that you are anything less than you were. You will get there. It takes time."

At first, she thought he'd continue with his silence. Instead he spoke, his voice rough with emotion.

"This just… None of it is right. I should have picked you up. I should have set up the car and made you comfortable. I should be the one protecting you, not you having to protect yourself. It's just—wrong." He shoved his fingers through his thick hair. "I feel powerless. Every day." He glanced her way in the dark. "Except when I'm with you."

She swallowed hard.

"When I'm playing with you, challenging you, kissing you, all that other stuff melts away. Until I wish you were by my side for—" His touch was firm as he pulled her close. "Why am I picking a fight when there are much more pleasurable ways to remember I'm alive?"

Whatever she'd been thinking disappeared beneath the onslaught of sensations as his lips devoured hers. Here there was no self-consciousness, no fear of being seen and judged. Only her and Luke. His body and hers. And the magic he made her feel.

His hands tilted her head to the side so his lips could cover hers fully. His tongue pressed inside, brooking no argument. Her body thrilled at his invasion. Without thought, her hands went to his biceps, pulling him closer. He sucked on her lower lip, leaving her mouth full and swollen. Then those wicked lips trailed across her jawline and down the curve to her neck.

His soft mouth contrasted with the light scrape of his teeth against her skin, sending shivers across every inch of her body. She heard herself moan as he found the pulse point at the base of her neck. His harsh breath as he devoured her. A knock at the window.

Wait—what?

Jerking her head to the side, Avery saw a stream of light

coming through the car window across the dash, then up Luke's body. She pushed him away. "Oh Lord, no."

Luke blinked. "What's wrong?" She laid her palm against his cheek and turned his head so he'd see the light.

Another knock sounded on his window.

"I can't catch a break tonight," he mumbled. With what sounded suspiciously like a chuckle, Luke straightened up and pressed the button to roll down his window. He didn't seem concerned that a sheriff's deputy stood outside, having clearly caught them in a compromising situation.

This was even more embarrassing than if they'd been caught at the drive-in. No, she had to get caught in a church parking lot. Heaven forbid!

"Everything okay, folks?" the deputy asked. Avery suspected she heard amusement in his voice.

"Oh, not by a long shot," Luke replied.

Lordy, they were going to jail if he kept that attitude up—and he was certainly in the mood to push it. "Luke, stop it." She leaned forward. "Everything's fine, sir. We're just going."

"Might want to. You be careful behind the wheel, Miss Prescott."

When he said her name, something clicked. Avery realized the dark figure outside the car was none other than Douglass Holloway—an officer she'd done some rehab with. As he walked away, Avery wondered how long it would take Deputy Holloway to relay exactly what he'd seen Avery and Luke doing at the church.

Nine

Avery slowed her jog down to a walk as the end of the wooded trail behind her house came into view. She'd hoped some exercise this Saturday morning would take her mind off last night's fiasco, but she continued to replay the officer's amusement in her mind. After twelve hours, her cheeks were permanently stained red.

She'd gotten the impression that Luke had been secretly laughing at her as she'd primly driven him home and dropped him off. Not surprising. He could laugh something like that away. He hadn't spent his entire life going on date after date where embarrassment was the main course. That was probably why she'd let the casual relationship with Mark go on as long as it had—no attraction meant no accidents, no tripping and no flying food.

And no pulse-pounding, muscle-gripping excitement, either.

Avery paused, bending to rest her hands on her knees while she breathed deep. After she'd left Luke in the drive without a word last night, she had a feeling all her excitement was over.

Her muscles now heavy with fatigue and recrimination, Avery continued down the trail until she reached the edge of the woods along the east side of her house. One of the reasons she hadn't wanted to move closer to town had been the land surrounding her family's home. The three-story house was way too big for one woman, but the thirty acres it sat on fed her need for privacy and nature—something hard to find closer to town.

She squinted as she moved from the cool shade of the woods into the bright sunlight. Walking across the side yard gave her a clear view of the drive that circled the front. To her surprise, the black Bentley that Nolen drove for the Blackstones idled in the drive. Great. Now she wasn't just embarrassed, she would have to face Luke sweaty, messy *and* embarrassed. Nice.

She diverted from the side door around to the front. Luke was navigating the stairs as she reached the porch. With a small wave and smile for Nolen, she climbed to the long veranda that ran the entire length of the front of the house. She couldn't help running her hand nervously over her damp hair.

"Whatchya doing here this morning?" she asked, a little breathless, a lot peeved. Maybe by avoiding eye contact she could keep from tripping over her own feet and tumbling off the edge of the porch.

A trip to the ER would just be icing on this week's cake.

Silence surrounded them for long moments, then she heard the thump of Luke's cane as he moved closer. Out of the corner of her eye she saw him approach, hand outstretched, until his fingers found her chin. Gentle pressure insisted she raise her gaze to his. Only then did he speak.

"I think I owe you breakfast after the way I acted last night. Would you go with me?"

Why did those amber eyes have to look so sincere?

She shook her head, trying to resist. "I don't think it's a good idea, Luke. Maybe we should just let it go."

His look darkened. "I don't want to let you go. I wasn't kidding when I said being around you makes me feel alive, cuts out all the noise."

"So this is all about you?"

She felt like a heel for saying it out loud, but she needed to know. He was already shaking his head.

"You know it isn't. I told you we needed to have fun, shake up the boundaries. Are you giving up so soon?"

"As you can tell, my track record is horrible. Last night was a disaster."

"But memorable. Right?"

"Yeah, I haven't been able to get Deputy Holloway's face off my mind all morning."

Luke laughed. "Look at it this way—you livened up his probably boring shift." His thumb rubbed along her cheekbone. "Breakfast. Please."

She shouldn't. She knew she shouldn't. She wasn't the type of woman to do casual relationships. But deep down inside, she wanted just a little more of him—even if she had to suffer humiliation to get it.

With a sigh and careful steps, she led him inside. After a quick shower and change, she almost defiantly met him back in the front parlor. He'd shown up at the last minute. She wasn't decking out in makeup and pearls. He'd have to settle for jeans and a comfortable T-shirt.

He stood in front of the mantel covered in pictures of her mother, father and herself. The reminders of her family made her both happy and sad, but she tried to hold on to the happy part.

"I'm ready."

Luke picked up a silver-framed picture of her parents

smiling at the camera, arms wrapped around each other. "Do you have any other family around here?" he asked.

"No." Avery swallowed against the lump forming in her throat. "Both my parents were only children. I was an only child. There may be some distant cousins, but no one close."

"Even after my dad died, and Mom's car accident, I've always had my brothers. We may give each other grief, but they're there, you know?"

"I've got friends," she said, hating the defensive note in her voice. Her family had meant a lot to her, but she'd known long before her mother died that they would one day be gone and she'd be alone. "I'm not isolated. I'm active in the community."

"You don't get lonely?"

"Of course. Doesn't everybody?" She shrugged. "But I'm surrounded by people all day, people I genuinely care about. That counts."

"Good."

His approval shouldn't make her glow inside. She'd shaped her life into what made *her* happy, or as close as she could get without outside interference. Though she'd love to have a family of her own, her life was full without one.

Luke didn't seem in any hurry to head out. "You've never wanted to leave? Move somewhere else? Start over?"

"There are people who need me here. I can't just abandon them." So she hadn't realized how entrenched she would become once she started on this path, but she cared too much about the people in Black Hills to leave them high and dry. She tried to shrug her doubts away. "Besides, where would I go? There's no reason for me to be somewhere else."

"I just can't imagine being content in one place. Just signing the lease on my apartment made me itchy."

And she was pretty sure he had no plans to hang around here. *Don't forget that, girl.*

She'd rather not dwell on it now. "So what was that about breakfast?"

Snagging her hand as if afraid she would change her mind, Luke led her out to the car, where Nolen patiently waited. Luke waved the butler aside and helped her into the back of the car. Nolen slid behind the wheel. They were on the road in minutes, the smooth purr of the Bentley slowly soothing her nerves.

Avery held herself stiff, back to prim and proper after her lapse the night before. Luke obviously didn't feel the same way. He leaned in close, his tempting mouth inches from her ear. "Interested in a repeat of last night?"

Would he run screaming if she said yes?

She couldn't stop the shiver that raced over her. She also couldn't stop her glance in Nolen's direction. "Shh," she warned.

Luke's laughter told her he found her reticence highly amusing. "It can't be worse than being caught by the cops."

The red flush Avery thought she had washed away in the shower returned full force—and burned until they reached the restaurant fifteen minutes later.

The Wooden Spoon had been serving Black Hills for almost half a century, and was still one of the best places to eat. Breakfast was particularly popular, and seating was at a premium despite three dining rooms full of tables and counter seating. Still, Luke swept past the hostess stand with his wicked smile firmly in place. One of the girls trailed behind them like a groupie until they reached a back booth, where she set their menus on the table with a shy smile before backing away.

"How'd you manage this?" Avery asked.

Luke was already perusing the selection, oblivious to

the magic he'd just worked. "Call-ahead seating," he said, giving her a quick wink.

Deadly, that's what that wink was to Avery. Able to get around every last barrier she built, no matter how solid. She turned to her own menu to avoid any more Lucas Blackstone charms.

"Guess you got perks like this all the time in North Carolina, huh?" she asked.

Luke shrugged. "Some."

A waitress appeared. Much older than the hostess, she handled waiting on a celebrity with a calm friendliness and efficiency that left Avery grateful.

Avery doctored her coffee with flavored vanilla creamer—her sweet morning indulgence. "Do you miss it?"

"North Carolina?"

"Yes." Avery glanced sideways at him. "You've lived there quite a while." Yet he hadn't put down any roots at all. Only what was necessary.

Luke took a sip of his own coffee, black and sweet. "The place? No. The racing? The track? My crew? You bet."

"Why?"

His look of surprise made her a little sad. Had no one ever asked about this before?

"It's thrilling, for one. I control the vehicle and use it to conquer whatever obstacles appear before me."

She could see how that would appeal to Luke.

The Blackstone brothers had spent their childhood after moving in with their grandfather James, without control over anything. Not their father's workaholic hours, which he kept in an attempt to appease his father-in-law, and not his death at the mill. Their mother had been unwilling to stand up to her father, especially after becoming dependent on him. And the constant arguing between James and Aiden Blackstone—the rebel brother who hadn't backed down over anything, including leaving home without any prospects because he couldn't live with James one minute longer.

Escape. It had become a habit for Luke. She'd watched him, had seen him work off his frustrations and anger with speed. Sometimes it had been scary, but it had worked. Most people would think Luke was the calm Blackstone brother. Oh, no. He had the same turbulent emotions; he simply handled them in a different way. Aiden raged against authority. Jacob became the authority. Luke simply drove.

"Most of all," he continued, "while I'm behind the wheel, I don't think of anything else. Nothing but the road and my next move."

The intensity, the passion in his expression rolled over her. This wasn't a guy on an ego trip. He wasn't in it for the money and the fame. Luke loved being in a car—no wonder the thought of waiting out an entire season had been immediately rejected. How tortuous was it for him to watch from the sidelines?

"It's the same with you."

Avery glanced up to find Luke's gaze tight on her face. "What?"

"It's the same when I'm with you." He reached out and ran his thumb back and forth across her bottom lip, leaving her all melty inside. "When we're together, all the buzz just stops. No more static."

Her heart almost caved in. She wanted to warn him not to say things like that, that she might get attached. But then the waitress appeared with plates loaded with fluffy omelets, stacked pancakes and crisp bacon. The smell commanded Avery's attention. Her stomach growled. "Good thing I ran this morning," she said.

He turned away from the pancakes he'd been eagerly cutting to brush back her hair, which was still damp around the edges. The feel of his skin against her cheek and ear had her breath catching in her throat. "Honey, calories are the last thing you need to worry about."

Oh Lordy, this man was dangerous—and he knew it, too. "Are you trying to butter me up?"

He swallowed his mouthful of food, then grinned. "I figured I better after last night. I'm not usually such an ass."

That much was true. Luke might speak impulsively, but he rarely lost his temper or let much push him into a bad mood. Last night had been an anomaly. Yet looking back over all Luke had been through, it wasn't surprising.

She'd been off her game, too. Dating wasn't a normal situation for her. Luke wasn't a normal guy for her.

Lifting the maple syrup, she toasted him with the bottle. "Well, if your apologies include pancakes, I'll always accept them."

To her surprise, he didn't laugh her off, but met her gaze with his own clear amber one. The darker flecks in his eyes became visible as he leaned closer, then closer still. Avery's heart thumped against her chest. Was he going to—

She quickly inhaled, afraid to pull away, but afraid not to. Then came the scent of coffee, syrup and man as Luke brushed his lips over hers. Warmth against warmth. Like a sugar rush, the thrill raced straight through her. Too quickly it was gone.

"Dammit, Avery, I'm sorry."

Reality returned, and Avery automatically glanced around to see if anyone had noticed the kiss. One nosy busybody and half the town would have her married off to him in an hour. Wouldn't that be a great gossip storm after he left town again? With her right at the center of it all, and him nowhere to be found.

Mark's brown gaze studied Luke, then flared with a dark, fiery emotion almost akin to hatred. At least, she thought it was. He quickly shuttered his expression and turned back to the man beside him, talking quietly.

Was he jealous of the kiss? She hadn't thought he would be, after all, he'd only ever initiated a few end-of-the-night brushes across her cheek. He'd never really pushed for more. Theirs was a casual, convenient relationship that benefited them both on numerous social occasions. Or so she'd thought...

Avery couldn't worry about Mark for long.

She turned to face Luke, almost afraid of what she'd see in his expression. "What?"

"You tried to explain to me last night why it would be hard for you if people assumed things." He dipped his head for an instant, reminding her of a much younger Luke. His words were hesitant. "I wasn't really in the mood to listen, but I did understand. Yet here I am, not twenty-four hours later, stepping all over that boundary once again. So... I'm sorry."

Avery realized she stood on a precipice, looking over the edge into unknown territory. Darkness loomed, scary and uncertain. The landing would definitely hurt. But wouldn't she kick herself one day if she held back now?

The past week had been a roller coaster of emotions. Making the most of their time together wasn't as easy as it should be. Too many emotions were coming to the surface. Along with physical needs that she'd allowed to lie dormant for a long time—too long. Maybe she wasn't built for casual, but she simply couldn't walk away from this chance to be with Luke. However he wanted.

"No, Luke," she said, then swallowed hard. "I'm sorry. I was only thinking about myself, and not how my actions would affect you." She thought about Mark's glare, and imagined the pitying looks she'd receive after Luke left. Somehow, she knew they wouldn't carry the same weight after having Luke's lips on hers.

"Let's just play it by ear, okay?"

Luke's brows shot up. "What? Avery Prescott without a plan or set of rules?"

"You keep it up and you're gonna owe me another breakfast…" she warned. He just laughed. And deep inside, Avery knew she'd made the right choice.

If only her decision hadn't been challenged quite so soon.

Just as they finished breakfast, a shadow dimmed their booth. Glancing up, Avery was horrified to see the deputy from the night before. Instinctively her body crowded into Luke's, as if he could shield her from the embarrassment, even as she told herself there was nothing to be embarrassed over.

The deputy grinned. "Morning, folks," he said.

Luke nodded, reaching out to shake hands. "Morning, Deputy Holloway. How are you?"

"Fine. Fine." He shook his head slightly, adopting an expression of mock concern. "I'm just glad to see you folks made it out this morning…after your late night."

A choking sound escaped Avery—one she wished she had held back. The burn had returned to her cheeks, but Luke just laughed once more.

The deputy winked at her. "Well, enjoy the rest of your day."

As he walked away, he stopped here and there to talk to several people—including a few who frequented the diner every morning to share gossip. Avery could almost see the story of their midnight encounter spreading across the room in the whispers and grins. By the time Luke had paid and they rose to leave, it seemed like all eyes were on them.

As they made their way out, the whispering seemed to follow them in a wave, until one voice rang out. "Y'all behave now."

Well, at least she wasn't paranoid.

Luke gave a salute without stopping. Even the hostesses whispered as they approached the doors, only to stop abruptly as they walked by.

"Y'all have a good morning," one said with a sly smile.

Luke just smiled back and continued to guide Avery out with the support of his hand at the small of her back. Nolen's black car was just coming up the road.

"Well, I guess it's official now," Luke said.

She cut her gaze at him, confused. "What is?"

"Us."

Her heart pounded. Maybe she wasn't as ready as she'd thought. "I'm sure it will all die down."

"I doubt it. I screwed up, so you have no choice but to date me now."

Do you want me to? "How's that?"

"You wouldn't want to make me the laughingstock of Black Hills by rejecting me, would you?"

"That's totally not how the story would go." *She'd* be the laughingstock. Probably still would be after he left. Why couldn't two adults just have some fun together without the small-town gossips automatically assuming forever after?

"Oh, Avery, you should know by now that I'm always right. That's why you should just let me have my way."

Even if his way was dangerous to her?

"Regardless," he said, "you just did your good deed for the day."

That stopped her in her tracks. "What?" Luke was talking in circles now.

"Just think how many existences you're livening up with that story. You're doing your civic duty to entertain others."

"Only a man would look at it that way."

"Honey, in a town this small, that's the God's honest truth."

* * *

Almost a week later, Luke wished more than anything that he was back in that diner with Avery. Or anywhere with Avery.

As Nolen pulled the car into the parking lot of the local playground, Luke almost had a full-body cramp. The place was covered in people.

And not just locals. Luke only recognized about one in every four faces. Deep down, stage fright set in.

How the hell had this happened?

A year ago, seeing this crowd would have had his energy and excitement skyrocketing, but not today. All he could think about was the weakness in his legs, his cane… and that Avery wasn't here with him. What if he fell? What if his legs buckled?

Locals actually knew Luke Blackstone, the person. They'd understand. These other people were here to see Luke Blackstone, racing celebrity. That was a whole different ball game, one he hadn't faced since his crash.

He'd done one press conference after his release from the hospital. After that, he'd stuck to phone interviews and private meetings. He'd prefer the world see him whole rather than broken. Just another reason to push for his return. If he never had another case of nerves, he'd die a happy man. Which made him more sympathetic to what Avery had endured for years in order to date at all.

As he stepped from the car, Christina must have read his thoughts. "I'm so sorry, Luke," she said as she rushed to his side.

"How'd this happen?" he mumbled, nodding in the direction of the crowd. "I thought this was supposed to be me with a few kids on the playground." He caught a glimpse of something out of the corner of his eye. "Is that a news crew?"

His brother appeared behind his wife.

"What the hell, Aiden?" Luke struggled to control his breathing.

Christina's big brown eyes filled with tears. "I'm so sorry, Luke."

Aiden spoke over her shoulder. "One of the board of trustees members leaked it to the university newspaper, thinking it would be great press for the fund-raising efforts." He shook his head. "It just spread from there."

And Luke hadn't heard a word. He'd stopped watching the news after his accident, afraid he'd catch a story about himself and risk seeing the footage from his crash. Even now, he could barely watch the sports stations. Though he forced himself to stay up-to-date on the racing circuit, it was hard. Harder than he'd like to admit.

Sucking in a deep breath, he forced himself into the professional persona he'd cultivated over the years. For once, the identity didn't slip on as easily as before. Like an ill-fitting coat, it pushed and pulled against him, making him uncomfortable and unusually grouchy. If only Avery were here, he'd have just a touch of the calm she usually possessed. But she'd probably hate this kind of thing. She was more a one-on-one kind of girl.

"Well, this looks interesting…"

Luke glanced over his shoulder to see those blue eyes lifting shyly to meet his and he wanted to kiss her. But he wouldn't, because despite what she might think, embarrassing her in front of large groups of people wasn't his goal. Instead, he let his voice soften with welcome. "Hey."

"Hey, yourself." She glanced around and he could see the uncertainty as it clouded her fine features. "I thought you could use a little support. Maybe."

"Definitely."

Suddenly handling himself in front of this crowd didn't seem quite so hard.

"Maybe you should work the crowd a little and give a

short interview to the news crew first," Avery suggested. "That will make it easier to move them back behind the barricades so y'all can shoot the commercial."

"Avery, that's a great idea. Thank you," Christina breathed. Aiden patted his wife's shoulder, then called a few men over to get things organized.

By the time Luke had shaken several hands and signed a bunch of autographs, he felt more in control. Avery was beside him at first, but it wasn't long before the crowd edged her away. He kept her in his peripheral vision, but he didn't really need to. It was as if his body could feel the distance between them.

Finally he stopped and found her with his gaze. Perhaps reading his thoughts, she pushed through until she once again breached the circle Aiden and several other men had formed around him to help with crowd control. After that, he kept her close, refusing to take more than a few steps without catching her hand.

How she felt about this, he wasn't sure. Somehow, he didn't care. In his selfishness, he simply knew he needed her. And in that moment, he vowed to break through the very boundaries he'd put in place. Tonight.

When he was being interviewed, she wasn't far away. He let himself talk as if talking to her, and deep inside he relaxed. This feeling was dangerous, but he was too intoxicated with her presence to care. He'd worry later—when he had no other choice but to return to the life he'd built before her.

Though he was tired after, Luke realized how right Avery had been. Now that he'd made his rounds, the crowd willingly moved back behind the barricades so they could watch without interrupting. And Luke felt much more comfortable than he had when he'd arrived. If he felt a touch of trepidation as he looked over at the half dozen kids starring in the commercial with him, he sure as hell wasn't gonna show it.

Avery walked over to the director and spoke quietly. After his nod, she came back and took his hand. "Follow me."

It didn't take him long to realize she was leading him over to the kids. He kept his persona firmly in place. "Hey, guys," he said as they approached the group.

He got a few "hi"s back, a couple of giggles and some shy smiles. If he wasn't mistaken, the kids were just as nervous as he was.

Then Avery spoke. "Kiddios, I want you to meet a friend of mine. This is Luke, as y'all know. Luke, this is Steven, Mariah…"

He tried to grab on to the names and not let them escape into thin air, but he'd simply met too many people today and his brain refused to cooperate. But he wouldn't let that stop him.

Crouching down as best he could, he brought himself to the kids' levels. They looked between five and ten or so—not that he knew a lot about telling kids' ages. But they were cute. A set of twin girls with ringlet curls. A boy in a local softball club jersey. An older girl with a bright blue cast on her arm. Two other boys, one with crutches and another with a walker.

"Luke is a friend of mine," Avery said. "And he's nervous about being in front of the camera."

Luke felt his feathers ruffle until she went on. "Y'all can help him out, right?"

As the kids started throwing out their best child-size advice, Luke realized she'd started a dialogue he could handle that was still kid-friendly, making it really easy for him to be involved. In that moment, something happened. Luke wasn't sure what, but he knew he'd never find anyone like Avery, who helped him so selflessly, looking out only for his comfort and caring about whether he succeeded or not. Yes, they'd had some fun together, but it hadn't been just him giving to her. It had been mutual.

How incredibly lucky was he to have that?

Without further thought, he grasped her hand and pulled her close. The feel of her body against his was even better than he remembered. He savored it.

Tilting his head down to hers, he murmured, "Thank you," then took her lips in a solid kiss.

Not a brush. Not a quick peck. His lips met hers without hesitation. He soaked up the feel of her, the scent and taste of her, until his body went haywire. Only then did he pull back.

His gaze met hers. He was lost in the world between them, until a sound shattered the bubble.

He looked to the side to see the audience of kids and a few grinning moms. "Ooohhhh," the kids cooed at them. Then all of them laughed. Luke couldn't help but join in. To his relief, so did Avery.

This wasn't just about sex. He wanted to do so much for Avery, big and little, just like she was doing for him. But he also wanted to take her to bed, and he had a feeling that experience would be completely different from the ones he'd had with other women.

Dangerous, but after all, he lived for the thrill.

He couldn't help but reach out and brush his thumb over the round of her cheek as she smiled, softly stating his need, his purpose. Their gazes met once more, his conveying a promise.

Tonight, she would be his.

Ten

As the crowd once more pushed her to the edge, Avery gave up fighting the flow. Weariness muted her purpose. Luke was holding his own, and she didn't want to feel like a groupie. Instead she turned in the opposite direction, finding an empty park bench to rest.

Only a few minutes passed before Christina sat down next to her. Avery could almost feel the questions before her friend asked them.

"That was some kiss," Christina started.

Avery took a deep, deep breath as her chest threatened to constrict. "Yes, it was." Part of her wanted to turn away, to not talk about this now…if ever. But avoiding it wasn't an option. That look from Luke earlier told her everything was about to change. Her body softened, anticipating that look becoming action. Even while her heart beat in fear for the future.

"Are you gonna be okay, Avery?"

Avery appreciated that her friend wasn't pushing for

details. Christina spoke from concern, not from pruri-
ent curiosity.

"I'm not sure." She searched for words. "Luke's the
most exciting thing that's ever happened to me. Has always been, from the time I was a kid."

Christina chuckled. "Yeah, the Blackstone brothers do
have a tendency to be larger than life."

"What if I can't meet that?" Avery met her friend's concerned gaze. "I've always felt a step behind when it comes
to Luke. The only place I'm in control is as his therapist."

"The woman I saw today wasn't just a therapist."

"I wanted to help."

"Because you care about him?"

"I have since we were just kids. Every day I'm with him,
it only gets worse." *Dang it.* Avery swallowed hard, choking on the words that would reveal just how deeply she'd
fallen. "One day he's gonna leave. I'll never be enough to
keep him here…and everyone knows it."

Christina's cool hand enveloped hers, squeezing in sympathy. "Oh, honey, I know exactly how that feels. And I
know that not everyone's story is going to turn out like
mine."

They were quiet for long moments. With each second
that ticked by, Avery's heart grew more uncertain. She,
more than anyone, knew how devastated Christina had
been when she'd thought Aiden would return to New York
for good. Could Avery go through that herself and have
her spirit still survive? "I'm not sure I can live through
losing someone else."

"And you shouldn't have to," Christina said quietly. "But
the alternative is never letting anyone close to you again.
I think it's a little late for that with Luke."

Very true. Avery knew it, but acting on it, opening herself up beyond this point, was still scary. Could she live
with the pain later? At least then she'd have the memories.

Could she live with the emptiness of never having those memories at all?

Christina spoke again. "Do you really want to spend your time caring if everybody thinks you weren't good enough for him later? Or would you rather focus on whether he thinks you're good enough for him right now?" She squeezed Avery's hand, flooding Avery's senses with sympathy. "He's a great guy. I promise he's not just playing with you."

Avery knew that. Though Luke was often playful, he was also genuine. She had a feeling his ambivalence up to this point had stemmed from the fact that he truly did see her as a friend. Hard as that was for her to believe.

For right now, he needed her. Wanted her. Could that be enough?

In the distance, he stood so tall, so proud. But she remembered that moment earlier when he'd needed her. Her chance to meet him more than halfway, without being model perfect or fast-lane ready. "I want him," she murmured.

"Then take him," Christina said, "and prove to him he can't live without you."

Avery doubted Luke would ever see her that way. Racing, he needed. Avery was just a bonus during the off-season. But she couldn't live that way forever. And just like that, the lightbulb went on.

Hadn't Luke been trying to teach her to live in the moment? Have fun right now, without worrying about what anyone else thought or said? And wasn't she doing just the opposite by letting gossip and giggles and other people's judgments make her decisions for her?

"Boy, am I slow." She shook her head. "I can't believe how afraid I've been all this time."

"Been there, done that," Christina agreed. "Do you want to continue that way?"

Hell, no. Avery was ready to live on her own terms. She'd known this for a while. Now she had to quit dragging her feet.

When Luke finally approached, she stood alone, more sure than she'd ever been. He met her with a tired smile.

Her nerves skittering around inside her, she drew in a deep breath. "I sent Nolen home."

She'd expected a smart remark or a sexy wink. Instead his amber gaze held hers, some of that exhaustion melting away. He traced her cheek with his thumb. The explosions under her skin were deeper this time. Instead of fighting them, she let them flow over her.

Luke's voice was low, intimate. "I guess you're stuck with me then."

"Maybe I could give you a ride," she teased.

"Your place or mine?"

Her heart picked up speed, beating hard inside her chest. "Mine?"

He nodded, his grin a mixture of relief and anticipation. "Sounds like a plan."

God, she hoped so. As he took her hand and walked to the car, none of the tension from the night of the drive-in spoiled the mood. Instead arousal built with every stroke of his fingers over the back of her hand. He continued to touch her on the ride home, but she couldn't decide if that was a good thing or not.

The closer they got to her house, the more worry set in. What if she didn't please him? It wasn't like she had a world of experience, though she wasn't a virgin. Logically, she knew how to make him feel good. But would she remember all that when the time came? Or would her body just go haywire and cause her to do something stupid?

By the time they reached her house, she was a bundle of nerves. Sure enough, she stumbled over the threshold and bumbled a few of the stairs. From behind, she felt Luke's hand grasp her own, slowing her to match his careful pace. They finished the climb to the second floor together. His touch calmed her down and ramped her nerves up at the same time. Please, don't let her mess this up.

Luke paused just inside the door to her bedroom, taking everything in with a sweeping glance. She wondered what he thought. Never having been a particularly girlie girl, there wasn't a lot of lace or pink in her room. The curtains were a floral print in soft yellows, blues and purples. She'd repainted a few years ago, covering the lavender of her childhood with a contemporary smoky blue. A darker version of the same colors graced the bed, complementing the blond wood furniture.

"Come here," Luke said, pulling her toward the bed.

This is it. How she wished she could shut off the thoughts racing through her brain. They distracted her as Luke propped his cane against the headboard and shrugged out of his jacket and button-down shirt. She allowed her gaze to soak in the muscles she'd learned so well. But there wasn't long to enjoy the view before he came toward her. Without a word he slipped off her cardigan sweater, leaving her in a silky tank top and khakis.

Guiding her to sit on the side of the bed, he eased off her slip-on shoes. She scrunched up her toes, feeling naked. Exposed. But Luke was having none of that. His strong hands enveloped one foot, his fingers digging into the arch and pushing back to stretch her calf muscles. Her moan erupted into the silence, her brain registering a level of heaven she didn't usually experience.

He glanced up, his eyes alight with sparks that made her shiver. "Feel good?"

"How could it not?"

He just grinned and moved to the other foot. When he finally made her stand again, she wondered if her feet would support her. Shaky, but she wasn't in danger of embarrassing herself. Good thing, because those wicked fingers went straight for the button of her pants. Her tummy muscles twitched at the brush of his knuckles. He didn't look up this time. Instead he concentrated until her pants lay around her ankles and her tank had sailed across the room to drape casually off the side of her cheval mirror.

Luke regained his feet with a push of his hands on the bed. At the last minute she pressed her lips together to keep herself from praising him. They weren't at therapy. The fact that she was his physical therapist was the last thing she wanted him to think about right now. Although that intent gaze trained on her bare middle was not the most comfortable thing in the world for her to focus on, either.

But he didn't rush. He soaked her in with his gaze for long moments before he picked her up and laid her on the bed.

She made a sound of protest, but he met it with a firm look. "Hush," he said. "I lift way more than your body weight at the gym every day."

He was right. And at least she hadn't tripped and tumbled into bed like she would have on her own. Curling on her side, she watched as he efficiently stripped down to a sexy pair of boxer briefs. A quick glimpse of the scars on his legs reminded her how incredible he was, how far he'd come...

Then he slid into the bed, and pulled the light comforter up against the chill in the room.

He crawled over her until she lay flat on her back with his body hovering above hers. He eased down tentatively, as if afraid his weight would be too much for her. He covered half of her body, his face buried against her neck. His erection cradled against her hip, one bent leg spreading her open without resistance. His rough thigh applied pressure to that most sensitive spot, urging her to lift her hips against him.

Perfect alignment. Automatically, her body melted, reveling in his heat and the weight that anchored her in this moment.

"What are you doing?" she whispered.

"Just relax," he murmured into her hair. "Let me soak you in."

For long moments, she couldn't let go. But then her breath changed to match his. In. Out. Slowly deepening. His warmth softened her. His mellow scent enveloped her.

Then his thumb moved along the left side of her collarbone, his forearm brushing the cup of her bra. How could such a slight touch feel better than any other man touching her...ever?

"Just relax," he said again. "Just enjoy."

But she wasn't sure how she was supposed to relax with his hands on her. He traced her collarbone out to her shoulder. Then he explored the hollow right below, and stroked down the length of her arm several times. Arousal built so quickly inside she broke out in a sheen of sweat.

He moved back up the sensitive skin on the inside of her arm before he traced the outline of her bra. That touch, so close, but not quite enough, was pure torture. She moaned, her hips twisting.

"There you go."

His voice, thick and husky, played heavily on her nerves. She dragged her eyes open, wondering if the emotion was real. His gaze followed the path of his hand, but he didn't study her with abstract interest. No, he was engrossed, just as he'd said. Utterly absorbed, his body hardened against her hip, speaking without words what she needed to know.

Her restless body urged her to move. Luke's knee kept her legs from closing, so she reached up with her free hand to test the stubble that had barely emerged along his jawline. He leaned into her touch like a cat, powerful and soft. She traveled along the side of his face to bury into his thick, sandy hair.

His heavy-lidded gaze lifted to hers, the connection complete. He rose so his mouth covered hers. His wicked hand splayed across her ribs, then meandered down to cup her hip bone.

His tongue breached her lips. His fingers tightened with lovely pressure. Avery's body drowned in sensation overload. Her hand tightened of its own accord, pulling at Luke's hair. He groaned, deep and long, as his body pushed against her, riding her through the smooth cotton of his briefs.

If she didn't have him inside her, soon, she might just explode without him—which was completely unacceptable. She twisted her head to free her mouth. Her hips lifted against his commanding thigh. "Luke," she gasped. "Luke, please."

"Just a little more, baby," he said against her skin, prompting goose bumps. "I haven't sampled all of you, yet."

That just might kill her, but at least she'd die happy.

Luke struggled to breathe deep, praying he could hold out a few more minutes. The intoxication of having Avery beneath him was a thrill not to be cut short.

Her skin brushed his fingers, soft as silk. As classy as Avery was, she'd be made of nothing less. But she wasn't passive—oh no, her hand in his hair conveyed her need without words. The sting of her pull complemented his sharp spikes of desire until he became one long pulse of need. She didn't just lie there like a pretty princess, but invited him inside with every lift of her hips and clutch of her hand.

Luke was surprised by the slight tremor in his hand as he reached for the front clasp of her bra. He'd always been wholly in control. With Avery, he felt anything but. His body demanded he ease the burning fever beneath his skin. More than that, he wanted Avery to feel the burning fever right alongside him.

He wanted it all, her all, until she'd never be complete without him again.

He didn't know why, didn't care.

Propping himself up on his elbow gave him a front-row seat to the reveal of a lifetime. His eager palms brushed the material back, revealing creamy mounds that shook with each breath she took. Awed with a kind of reverence he'd never felt before, Luke buried his face deep into the cleft between her breasts and breathed in her essence.

From his first drive, Luke had become one with his car, with that desire to eat up the ground until freedom burst over him. Now he wanted that same feeling—and he wanted Avery to share it with him.

Her rose-colored nipple felt smooth against his tongue, but quickly hardened beneath his touch. Both her hands now buried in his hair, she pulled him closer. Her body shifted and moved as if enticing him to ease the need inside her.

Yes. Oh, yes.

But it wasn't until those hands buried beneath the waistband of his briefs that he knew he'd succeeded. Unable to pull himself away from those perfect mounds, he continued to kiss her breasts as he peeled the material off. Avery's silky panties didn't fare as well. One hard pull and the barrier shredded.

It wasn't until his body was poised between her thighs that reality intruded. "Nooo," he moaned.

"What?" Eyes widening, Avery looked down between them. "Um, what's wrong?"

The last thing he wanted was for her to worry, but an

afternoon spent with kids wouldn't let him ignore the obvious. "I don't have a condom."

"Oh." She collapsed back against the pillows with a giggle.

He glared. The raging state of his body did not find this situation the least bit funny.

One look at his face sobered her right up. She pointed to the bedside table. "Top drawer."

That he hadn't expected. After all, Avery didn't date much. Wait, had she and Mark—? Luke swallowed hard. This was not going according to plan.

But the unopened box in the top drawer said if Avery had been planning for visitors, they'd never shown up. He opened it and flicked a single package between his fingers. "What are you doing with these? Huh?"

Her cheeks deepened to a darker shade of red than they'd already been. "Wishful thinking?" she murmured.

Only Avery would be embarrassed by that. "I'm glad one of us was planning ahead."

"I wouldn't thank me yet. You might want to check for an expiration date first."

Determined to pay the little hellion back for teasing him, Luke quickly sheathed himself, then buried his face into the crook of her neck. Blowing against her skin had her squealing and squirming. Before long, he couldn't resist anymore.

Long sucking kisses moved him down her body to the sensitive spot above the joint of her hip. There he slowed, brushing his lips back and forth over the soft, soft skin. The spicy scent of her arousal coated his senses. All he knew then was the need to please her.

Firm hands spread her wide, giving her no chance to hide from him. The slick, sensitive skin between her thighs reminded Luke vividly of the essence of Avery herself. So vulnerable. Yet strong.

Bending close he greeted her with a kiss. Then he opened his mouth, and proceeded to drive her crazy. Her moans and screams were music to his ears, mixing with the pounding in his blood to create a barometer measuring just how much pressure they could each take.

Finally her body pulsed one last time, her thighs tensing around his head. Instead of a scream, air trapped inside her throat, choking off the noise, ramping up the sensations. Only when her body melted into the bed and her breath released with a soft sigh did Luke rise up.

Looking across her loose limbs, sweat-slickened skin and shaking ribs, he knew he was seeing the real Avery. The woman behind the fears. The woman behind the nerves. The woman who'd got the orgasm she deserved. And he was the man who'd given it to her.

All those primitive sensations rolled around inside him, forcing him closer and closer. Lifting one of her legs, he made a place for himself between her thighs.

Her body resisted at first so he teased her with tiny strokes, then a little more. Just a little more, until she relaxed deep inside.

Like a spent battery recharging, her body regained vitality. Her hips shifted, tilting toward him, urging him deeper.

He clenched his fists in the sheet above her shoulders, desperately trying to hold out. But once his hips met hers, those primitive instincts could not be denied. Especially not while looking down at her gorgeous face.

As his body pounded into hers, their gazes met, desperately clinging to one another as if the meaning of life could be found in the other person. All too soon, their bodies betrayed them. Avery arched into him, bowing under waves of pleasure.

Her muscles tightened around him, the pressure perfect. Thrusting deep, he opened up full throttle. Heart racing, head pounding, he found the ultimate high in the arms of the woman he'd never expected to find.

In the following calm, Luke forced air into his lungs, becoming aware of his suddenly shaking arms. Easing over to the side, he settled next to Avery before he fell on her. But he couldn't stop touching her, couldn't break the connection. His palm settled easily against the slight rise where each set of ribs met. His hand moved up and down as she breathed, their heartbeats slowing. Energy dissipating into the shadows darkening the room.

What was this unnatural need, this feeling inside of Luke that screamed for him not to move too far away?

Despite the warning signals flashing in his brain, Luke had every intention of listening to his instincts. He forced himself to walk to the attached bathroom and clean up. After he'd made Avery comfortable, too, he lay next to her in the bed and pulled her against him in a reversal of their earlier positions. He smiled at her limp lack of resistance. Though he knew immediately when awareness kicked in, because her muscles grew taut one by one.

"Rest with me," he murmured.

"Clothes?" Obviously her brain wasn't on board yet, because full sentences weren't an option for her.

No way was he letting fabric rest between him and all the delicious skin tempting him to fully wake back up. "Not tonight."

"Too tired?" she whispered.

"Oh, yeah," he said, teasing a little. "I have a physical therapist who tried to kill me today."

Her giggle made him smile, even as it trailed off into even, peaceful breaths. Luke let the world fall away, until all that remained was the warmth between them and the feeling of perfection deep inside.

Eleven

Avery came to awareness by degrees, her body awakening like a closed flower to the sun, one petal at a time.

A soft light filtered between the part in the curtains—not quite full daylight. She felt the unusual warmth in her little cocoon of covers—enough to keep her sleepy. And the heavy weight of someone at her back… Had anything ever felt so heavenly? The core of her body throbbed as she remembered just who it was in bed with her.

Lucas Blackstone.

Gone were the girlish dreams from so long ago, fiercely replaced by the desires of a woman. She should feel shy, nervous about seeing him again this morning. After all, she hadn't woken up with anyone of the male species since college. And never with a specimen of Luke's caliber. Boys compared to a man.

But she feared she'd experienced far more than Luke's physical prowess last night. Touching him, savoring him, sleeping beside him… Her heart was long gone. Maybe it had been since she'd been a child. That hero worship from afar had blossomed to full maturity with time and space. But now—well, now there was no turning back.

Worried that her restless thoughts would cause her to move and wake up Luke, Avery eased out of the bed and stood for a moment in the cool air. Her naked body shivered—she wasn't sure if it was the chill or her surprise at actually being bare. But as she watched Luke reach out to find the warm spot her body had just left behind, curling toward it, she yearned to be beneath his hands once more.

But after such a long day yesterday, she imagined he'd want a hot cup of coffee this morning.

She quickly pulled on some yoga pants and an oversize T-shirt, then eased out the door before pulling it closed. He'd slept soundly all night with barely any movement. From his remarks at the center, she'd gotten the impression that wasn't common for him. She'd let him sleep… while she figured out how to act natural.

A cup of creamed coffee only served to remind her she hadn't had dinner last night. A protein bar steadied her jitters. The front bell rang as she was looking through the cabinets, wondering what she should cook for breakfast.

She hurried down the hall and into the front foyer, hoping to catch the visitor before the bell rang out again. The sound wouldn't be as loud upstairs—she knew from experience—but she wasn't sure how light of a sleeper Luke was.

With only that thought in mind, she threw the door open to find Mark standing on her doorstep. She froze. He hadn't been to her house for several months. She certainly hadn't been expecting him this morning. "Um, hi," she said with awkward hesitation, her mind still on the man sleeping in her bed upstairs. "What can I do for you?"

The classically handsome man frowned, a crease forming in his perfect brow. "You can stop talking to me like

I'm a traveling salesman, for one. We've been friends a long time, Avery. Aren't you going to at least invite me in?"

She bristled at his tone, but good manners dictated she let him in to find out what he wanted. After all, her house wasn't on the way to anywhere. He'd come here for a reason. What that was, well, she couldn't imagine.

"I'm sorry," she said, stepping back and gesturing him inside. "I haven't been up long. My wits haven't kicked in yet."

She led him into the front parlor, pausing awkwardly next to the proper antique sofa that had belonged to her father's parents. As she glanced around, she realized this entire room would easily fit in at a museum. It still had the original fabric wall coverings from when the house had been built, along with needlepoint from her great-grandmother's own hand and original furniture. She'd made it into a sort of memorial to her family. Though it wasn't comfortable for lounging, she came here often to look at the pictures on the mantel.

Just as Luke had last week, Mark paced in front of the fireplace, studying the photographs she'd framed in antique picture frames to fit the room's decor. Mark seemed to fit here—he'd been born into one of the oldest families in Black Hills outside of the founding family, the Blackstones. He'd attended the only private school in the area, same as Avery. Had gone on to a prestigious college, and had done well as far as she could tell. He'd worked his way up into executive management at the mill, though "worked up" sounded a little harder than it had actually been. He'd never actually worked on the mill floor. He'd simply held white-collar jobs there.

Mark was an intellectual kind of guy—not into sports or cars. He'd filled his own house with antiques, liked the challenge of numbers and enjoyed fine dining.

"Would you like some coffee?" she asked.

Mark turned to face her, but his gaze wandered around the room, not landing anywhere for long. "I didn't come here for pleasantries, Avery. I came to ask if you think you're making the right choices."

That forced a double take. "What?"

He shook his head, as if he were talking to a disappointing child. "Avery, I saw you with him that other day, then yesterday. Do you really think this is the best thing for you? The right thing?"

Avery felt a wave of heat roll over her as she remembered meeting Mark's gaze in the diner. For a moment, she felt ashamed, knowing she had assumed she'd be good enough for a superstar personality like Luke.

His earnest brown gaze finally met hers. "You're a small-town girl, a quiet homebody. Do you really think you can compete with his career? The attention? The freedom? The women?"

A familiar sense of inadequacy sparked deep inside Avery, spreading until her hands trembled. She knew if she took one step forward, she'd fall. If she picked up something, she'd drop it.

Instead she lowered her eyelids, wishing she could hide away from that knowing look on Mark's face. But in the darkness behind her closed lids, the sensations from the night before surfaced to flood over her. Her body moving in harmony with Luke's.

There'd been no shame last night. No clumsiness. Just two people exploring each other and giving each other pleasure. Luke may not love her, but they were friends. He wouldn't want her to be embarrassed by what they'd done.

"Mark, I appreciate your concern. But what happens between me and Luke isn't any of your business."

"We dated for a long time. Doesn't that count for anything?"

Therein lay tricky ground. "We went to community

functions together. That's not dating." But that wasn't the whole of it. "You've been my friend for a lot longer than that, Mark. That counts for a whole lot more than a few appearances. If you have something helpful to say to me, great. But I will not let you make me feel inferior, simply to make yourself feel better."

A look of almost desperation came over Mark's face, furrowing his brow and glittering in his eyes. He stepped forward, grabbing her shoulders and shaking them a little harder than she liked. "I thought we were perfect for each other, Avery. You'd be an excellent hostess, a beautiful companion. We were meant for each other."

That was so not what she'd expected. "Mark, you never acted like you felt that way." She swallowed hard, wishing she didn't have to hurt her friend on top of everything else. "I'm sorry, so sorry if you wanted something more than friendship, but I've never had romantic feelings for you."

Mark's color deepened from red to purple. "So you think a small-town girl can compete with the excitement to be had in North Carolina?"

Ouch. "There's no competition."

"There will be...the minute he steps out of Black Hills."

He wasn't telling her something she didn't already know. "That's not your concern. Or mine, either." If she worried about the future, she'd go crazy. "I'm sorry that you learned exactly what was going on like this, but I never meant to hurt you."

"So you'd rather whore it up for one of the Blackstone brothers than be the lady your parents wanted you to be?" His hands squeezed, the pressure making her wince. "You could have been my wife, one of the most prominent women in Black Hills. Why would you ruin everything for him?"

Her gasp sounded loud in the room, but she didn't have long to dwell on the shock.

"That's enough."

Luke's voice rang through the downstairs, strong and clear. Mark let go of her, turning toward the entryway. The sounds told her Luke was coming down the stairs, though she couldn't see him from her angle. But she could tell from the widening of Mark's eyes that he had a clear view of Luke's approach.

Avery looked back at the doorway just as Luke crossed the threshold, and she almost choked. It was Luke, all right. All gleaming muscles, in nothing but a pair of boxer briefs. Obviously, self-consciousness wasn't an issue for him.

From Mark's apoplexy, it was clearly an issue on his part.

As he took in all of Luke's bare skin, then turned to study Avery's loose-fitting clothes, knowledge dawned in his eyes. Uncomfortably aware of her braless state, Avery crossed her arms over her torso, only to realize the move probably made her lack of undergarments even more obvious.

Suddenly Mark twisted his lips into a smirk. "Well, well. You aren't just planning to whore it up…you already have."

"I said, that's enough," Luke said, the hard edge to his voice making Avery just a little bit scared, even though it wasn't aimed at her.

Mark's expression said the wheels were still turning in his brain. His gaze was no longer blank as he looked between her and Luke. The knowledge of the night they'd spent together added fuel to his earlier anger. He opened his mouth to speak, but Luke beat him to it.

"If you walk out right now, we'll just chalk this up to your disappointment in losing the girl." He crossed the room and placed a protective arm around Avery's shoulders. Her lashes fell for a moment as his fingers brushed over a sore spot from Mark's hold. Luke went on, "If not,

I'll see to it that Jacob hears every detail. And you can look forward to Monday being your last day at Blackstone Mills."

"You aren't my manager," Mark growled. "You can't do that."

This time it was Luke's turn to smirk. "No, but he can. And I'll make sure he does."

"Fine."

Mark stalked over to the door, and for once, Avery was glad to see him go. She didn't need people in her life who intended to tear her apart. Life had taught her that long ago.

Mark opened the door, then glanced back at where they stood in the entryway to the front parlor. Avery felt the large span of Luke's palm blanket the small of her back. Mark's gaze flicked down, then back up to her face. "Think about it," he said. The door slammed behind him.

Luke moved as if to follow, but Avery grabbed his arm.

Thankfully, Luke pulled her close. She rested her forehead against his chest, breathing in the musky scent of his skin. His hand covered the back of her head, holding her close until her trembling stopped. Then she forced herself to pull back, stand up tall and smooth down her hair—no matter how she felt inside.

"I'm sorry," she said, unable to meet his gaze…or anything else on him, for that matter. "I don't know what got into him."

"I don't, either," Luke said. "That didn't seem like jealousy. It was all aimed at you."

Avery was already shaking her head. "I didn't give him any reason to think that I—"

"I know," he assured her as he stepped closer. There was no getting around the sight of all that sexy bare skin with him two inches away.

Skin she wanted to touch. Just as she had last night.

"What we do here is between you and me. No one else. Don't let him change that, okay?"

"I won't."

As he led her back up to bed, she was determined to hold on to that promise with all her heart.

"Master Luke, there's someone at the door for you."

Luke looked up from the racing magazine he'd been reading to find Nolen in the entryway to the front parlor. "Who is it?" he asked.

For once, the butler's somber face gave way to a slight smile. "Someone I believe you will want to see."

Luke glanced across at his brothers, who were playing a game of chess near the fireplace. They both shrugged.

Guess he'd go see who the mysterious visitor was, and what he wanted, since the old guy wasn't going to say. As he walked by, Nolen's grin grew. Now Luke knew something was definitely up. Something big. Nolen's smiles were as rare as two-dollar bills.

Luke enjoyed his newfound freedom as he walked down the short hall to the foyer. He'd forced himself to give up his cane almost a week ago. Moving with care, he'd regained his equilibrium and added a bit of speed to his gait. Avery had been complimentary of his progress, though he could see the sadness beneath her smile. One step closer to freedom. One step closer to leaving…her.

Something he hadn't figured out how to handle yet.

Behind him, he could hear multiple sets of footsteps as his brothers and Nolen followed. He hoped whatever stood outside the door wasn't an embarrassment.

As he stepped out the front door onto the veranda, Luke's eyes were drawn to the shiny black hot rod in the drive. The sleek, low-slung coupe set his heart racing the way most men's would for a sexy woman. Behind him, he heard a masculine whistle of appreciation that echoed his own feelings.

Then the driver's-side door opened, and out stepped Avery. Her buttery-soft tan pants and leather jacket finally drew his gaze away from the car. The uncertain edges of her smile tugged at something in his chest he couldn't name. She closed the door and stepped around the car to meet them on the porch.

"What's all this?" he asked, his gesture encompassing the car that she couldn't have gotten anywhere around here.

She glanced at all the men in the small space, then turned all her focus back to him. She probably thought it was a safer option.

"I came to give you the good news," she said. "I've had all your X-rays and evaluation results looked over by your doctor. You passed. It's time to drive again."

Luke stared for a moment, not quite comprehending her words. They'd talked about his driving as being something he would do *in the future*, but she'd never given him a firm date. He'd known she was evaluating his progress this week, but didn't question why. He'd known he was on the right track. He'd just hoped to learn how far along it he was.

Now he knew.

The smile that burst over his face had originated deep in his gut. Pats on his back from his brothers only added to the joy.

"Very good, Master Luke," Nolen said.

But it was the beaming face before him that held his attention. Her joy reflected his. He couldn't stop himself. He drew her close and met her lips with his own, felt the spark of that touch.

By the time he pulled away, she was flushed and panting. His brothers were grinning. "You're welcome," she murmured.

She waved her hand in the car's direction. "I thought we could celebrate. And I didn't think you wanted to have your first drive in my little SUV."

"You didn't rent this car anywhere around here," Jacob remarked, echoing Luke's earlier thoughts.

Avery shrugged. "The Blackstones aren't the only people who know people."

The men gave a murmur of appreciation that had Avery's cheeks flushing even deeper. She reached in a pocket of those skintight pants and pulled out the keys with a metallic rattle. Then she held them out. "Shall we go?"

Luke grabbed her hand and started down the steps, wishing he could sprint. "See y'all later."

He was able to stay his excitement long enough to open her door, then he practically ran to the other side of the car. But after dropping into the low leather seat, Luke found himself unable to move. Beside him, Avery kept quiet.

The seat felt cool, smooth. As he squeezed his hands around the steering wheel, the familiar feel overwhelmed him. His chest tightened. One hand dropped to the stick shift in the center console. He'd learned to drive on a stick and all his personal cars had been manual transmission ever since. His memories reverberated with the hum of the engine beneath his body, the pressure of the pedals beneath his feet and the shift of the stick beneath his palm. The scent of leather filled his senses, along with the sweet scent of woman.

Avery.

Blinking his eyes, Luke cleared his vision, then turned to her. She blinked back, sitting still with her hands folded in her lap. "Sorry," he said, then realized he didn't need to apologize. Understanding shone from her blue eyes, accompanied by a sweet little smile.

"Let's go," she said.

He pushed the ignition button. A smooth purr filled the small cabin and Luke's entire body went *ahhh…*

Then he revved the engine and shifted into gear. Control was the only option. Luke kept himself to a snail's pace as they started down the drive. The ache to pick up speed sat heavy in his gut, but he knew the minute he gave in, his small exertion of will would break and he'd never get it back.

He carefully gauged every turn, every acceleration. They headed out on the highway, opposite the direction of town. The first time he hit sixty should have felt like nothing compared to his racing stints, but instead his heart pounded same as the first time he'd put tires to a track.

He was ultra-aware of his precious cargo. Avery—who'd gone out of her way to do this. Who'd given him this gift.

Acute awareness of how undermined his confidence had been by the accident shook him. The fact that he wouldn't let himself gun it. Couldn't. Because something bad might happen. And Avery sat next to him in the car.

Just when the shaking reached his hands, a warm palm covered the upper part of his forearm. He eased off the gas and looked over at Avery.

"Turn right up here," she said.

Reorienting himself to his surroundings, he realized they were about ten miles out from Blackstone Manor. The road, and the turnoff, should have been familiar to him. His late teens had practically been lived on this road.

He followed her directions down the road to the entrance beyond. "I didn't realize this place was still here," he said.

"I got the owner to open it up for you. He's kept it in good repair, but they only race here once a month now." She chuckled. "He remembers you very well, and appreciated the memorabilia you sent him a couple of years ago."

Wow. Avery had arranged for him to spend his first

time back behind the wheel since his accident at the only racetrack within fifty miles. Probably more like seventy-five. "Do you trust me to do this?"

"I'm trusting you to know your abilities…and your limits."

Would he push it too hard? He knew firsthand how addictive speed was, how desperately the fever burned in his blood for it. But as he looked into her direct gaze, her words echoed inside him.

A few minutes later, he halted the car on the lane. To his surprise, Avery unbuckled her seat belt.

"That's not safe, hon," he said.

"It's not a problem if I'm not gonna be in the car."

He sucked in his breath, simply watching her.

Her soft hand rubbed along his jawline. "I know you'd never tell me, but I have a feeling this is something you need to do by yourself. Right?"

Not by nod nor shake did he give away his answer, but she got out anyway. Waiting until she was safely behind the barricade, he eased the car into gear and took a very slow turn around the track. It had been years since he'd been on an oval track this small. He let himself and the car meld with the road. Then he took a deep breath, down into the bottom of his lungs, and hit the gas.

Forty minutes later, he wanted to cry true tears at having to stop, but knew he shouldn't press the limit of his healing limbs…or his therapist. But as he drove off the track, he knew this would stand out as one of the most important moments of his life.

Not just his career.

Twelve

As Luke hit the straightaway leading from town to Blackstone Manor, he couldn't help but sadly remember the black sports coupe Avery had rented for him. It made him miss his race car, and the beaut he normally drove every day. Instead he was driving a pickup from the Blackstone fleet.

His foot pressed harder on the gas, giving him the thrill of speed and the satisfaction of being that much closer to Avery. His woman.

After a long day walking the mill for inspections, he wanted only one type of thrill tonight—one that involved bare skin and delicious friction and hard thrusts.

It sure beat watching the door at the mill to see if Mark was going to walk through. Word must have gotten out that Luke would be there today, because the ladies in the office had said Mark decided to take personal time at the last minute. That guy had better hide. If Luke ever heard him talk to Avery, or any woman, like that again, his job wouldn't be the only thing Mark would have to worry about losing.

Maybe that straight, pretty-boy nose of his...

Luke gunned it a little harder, speeding down the road to get to the Manor, get his clothes, talk to Jacob about today and then get himself over to Avery's. Thoughts of Avery's house distracted him from his impatience. It was weird. He'd never felt at home at Blackstone Manor, or his apartment, or anywhere else. But he loved Avery's home.

Slightly smaller than the Manor, it only had three stories. She'd closed off the upper floor completely. But the light atmosphere, complemented by lots of blond wood and soothing colors, made his whole body relax. He shouldn't enjoy being there that much. Shouldn't daydream about what it would be like to live there every day, to play with Avery in the woods and eat dinner with her in the breakfast nook. To sleep beside her every night listening to the serenade of frogs and crickets outside.

He. Should. Not. Go. There.

So why did he?

Before he could answer that—or avoid answering it—he heard a pop from under the hood. He barely had time to frown before the truck pulled sharply to the left. There wasn't time to think, only react. When all was said and done, he was facing the opposite direction, hanging at a forty-five-degree angle off the side of the road. A side glance confirmed a deep water drainage ditch dug out between the road and the fields waited below him. Even worse, anything not concrete or asphalt had turned into a muddy mess after three solid days of steady rain. He could feel the incremental slips of the heavy vehicle as the top layer of soil started to give way.

Not the most stable of positions, but luckily Luke had done extensive upper body work. He was able to lift himself through the open window rather than shifting the balance by opening the door. Once he had his feet back on the asphalt, he watched the steady slide of the truck the rest of the way down the hill into about five feet of water with a bit more detachment than before. For a moment, anyway.

But then the memories rushed over him. As if his body equated this incident with the last car accident—the one he didn't walk away from—his knees went weak. Thankful there was no one to see, he let himself go down. Silence reverberated around him. His mind replayed the sounds of screaming metal, the smell of gasoline and the burning sting of smoke. But above all came the pain, like his lower body was being torn to shreds. Every laceration had been on fire, though emergency personnel had reached him before the car could erupt into actual flames.

Once the shaking stopped and the nausea subsided, Luke pulled his cell phone from the case attached to his belt. A simple call to Jacob. A few deep breaths to get himself back on his feet. He took a mental inventory of all his limbs, not finding any major issues. Some tightening in his lower back. Oh, and upper back. Hell, he was tight all over.

Great. No hiding that from Avery.

A sound in the distance had him looking in the direction of the Manor. He could see Jacob's Tahoe as it came around the bend and sped toward him. Another dark vehicle followed behind.

Only the sound of engines came in stereo. Looking in the other direction, Luke could see flashing lights and cursed. He should have kept his suspicions that this hadn't been an accident to himself. Jacob had taken the initiative and called the authorities. So now Luke would spend the night answering questions and filling out paperwork. Lovely.

Jacob pulled over to the side of the road and parked. He stopped about five feet away, arms crossed over his chest as he studied the truck. "Well, good thing you know what you're doin'."

"I agree."

A glance down the highway at the oncoming vehicles had Jacob stepping forward quickly. A single strong hug had Luke's back muscles wincing, but he wasn't gonna complain. He could feel Jacob's relief that he was okay without his twin even having to say it.

A low whistle from behind his brother separated them. Luke glanced over Jacob's shoulder to Zachary Gatlin, who must have been in the black SUV.

"Man, that takes some mad skills. How'd you manage not to roll it?" Zach asked.

Luke rubbed at the back of his neck. "Honestly, I'm not sure. All I remember is the noise, then it's a blur."

Zach nodded. "Instincts took over. Great job."

It didn't feel like a great job. It felt like a flashback from a hell he'd hoped never to endure again. He simply nodded and left it at that.

Luke had never been happier that Aiden had hired Zach. The new head of their personal security handled most of the police issues, except for the questioning. He had the truck towed and kept everyone on task. Luke only protested when an ambulance showed up and Jacob insisted Luke let them look him over.

"The only thing wrong with me is some tight muscles."

"You never know," Jacob said.

"I don't need it."

He should have known by the look on his brother's face that resistance was futile. Twenty minutes later, Avery's little SUV joined the immobile caravan parked along one lane of the highway. The rest of the scant traffic headed out this way had been diverted into the other lane. "Oh, man—you didn't."

Jacob just smirked. "You should have listened to me the first time."

Damn married men.

Avery's steps were snappy, but she didn't rush. He could almost see her taking everything in despite the fading light. Especially him. Those astute therapist eyes traveled over every inch of his body. It wasn't the kind of inspection he'd been hoping for, but then again, this evening wasn't turning out the way he'd envisioned at all.

"Are you all right?" she asked, rushing right up to him. For once, she didn't look around at their audience before touching him. Her arms widened as if to hug him, but she settled for grasping his biceps instead. "Do you hurt anywhere?"

Instead of answering, he reached around her, pulling her close. Her warmth seeped into his body, into his bones. He pressed his lips against the smooth softness of her hair. "I'm great, now that you're here."

Her body relaxed into his, but she didn't completely give in. "But you couldn't call me yourself?"

Thanks, Jacob. "Once we were done here, I was going to get another truck and head over to your house."

"Would you have told me?"

No. "I didn't want you to worry."

"Well, I did. We need to get you back to the house, to check everything out and make sure there was no damage."

"That's what I told him," Jacob said as he approached.

Luke shot daggers at his brother with his gaze. "I'm fine. The paramedics said so."

She pulled back, leaving his tired body without warmth or support. "They don't know what they should specifically be looking for based on your history," Avery said. "I'll feel better once I've checked you out." She looked over at Jacob, then past him to the police officers wrapping everything up. Everywhere but at Luke. "If you don't mind."

Luke looked at Jacob, unsure of what to do. His brother shrugged, no help whatsoever.

Right now, Luke knew just what he wanted. He'd deal with the aftermath of the wreck tomorrow. "Let's go home."

Avery stepped back even more, wrapping her arms around her middle.

"Call my cell if you need anything else," Luke said to Jacob. Then he walked toward Avery's car, using an arm around her shoulders to turn her to go with him.

Avery could sense Luke's disappointment when he came out of the bathroom and found her still in her scrubs. Men. She was rapidly learning that the old adage was true. They did constantly think about one thing.

"I thought we were going to bed early," he said hopefully.

She shook her head, secretly amused but keeping her therapist facade firmly in place. "Not yet. But if you co-operate, you might get a reward." She pointed for him to lie on the bed.

Part of her felt shocked. A month ago, she could never have imagined herself teasing about sex. But with Luke, it came naturally. And he teased her back, which made her giggle, but deep inside she stored sadness away. Because one day he would leave, and this magical time would be over.

"I want to check you out—" she started.

"Go right ahead, baby—"

"—for any damage."

His sigh echoed around her spacious bedroom. "I told you, I'm fine. Just a little tight, that's all."

This time her hands went to her hips and her attitude showed up full force. "You want some help with that, right?"

He glanced over his shoulder, his face aglow. "As in, a massage?"

Hook 'em quick. "Yes, as in a massage." She held up a warning hand. "But if you're going to be difficult..."

He settled onto the bed on his belly without another word. She needed to remember what good currency massages were. Stepping to the side of the bed, she started with his feet and worked her way up. Her palms found every knot in his normally smooth muscles, working them out. She savored his groans as much as the feel of his skin.

Only when he'd melted into a metaphorical puddle of goo did she deliver the bad news. "Well, this has set you back a bit, I'm afraid."

He lifted up on his elbows to look at her over his shoulder. "What?"

Her hands found the small areas where she could feel the changes from the last time she'd touched him. "It's minor. Some muscle damage here in your lower legs from braking so hard. Which created a chain reaction up your leg."

Her stomach quivered as she thought about him in that truck, struggling for control. Thank God he had extensive skills, or the wreck would have been devastating, what with those banks on either side of the road.

"About a week's worth of extra therapy should fix it, I think." She tried to lighten her tone. "Are you sure this wasn't a ploy to keep seeing me? A few extra massages, maybe?"

Luke rolled over onto his back, lifting himself into a sitting position against the headboard in one fluid movement. He leaned into the pillows, fully unaware that he'd laid out a smorgasbord of sexiness that she was more than ready to dive into.

"I'm not sure," he said, giving her a look that said he knew exactly where this was leading. "Is that all you have to offer me for sticking around? A few massages?"

How about my heart? But she wouldn't say that, so she countered with "Are you saying my massages aren't good enough? Maybe I'll save them for another deserving patient."

Luke reared up, grabbing her by her upper arms and dragging her down onto the bed with him. Or rather, *on* him. He was the best kind of lumpy mattress—the living, breathing kind.

"Oh no, woman. Those massages are mine." He planted a hard kiss against her lips. "All mine."

"Sounds perfect." She froze for a minute, wondering if she'd gone too far, but he didn't react to her words.

Instead he focused on her body, their bodies. Lifting her up with those glorious biceps, he helped her straddle him. Her knees naturally fell open on each side of his hips, her thin scrubs leaving nothing to the imagination. Luke's boxer briefs molded to his erection like a second skin. The position brought them into perfect alignment, and Avery's core went soft.

She pressed down, lightly grinding against him, savoring the differences between them. Luke groaned as he dug his hands into her hair. He pulled her down, teasing her mouth open. Not that she needed much coaxing. The feel of his tongue inside her mouth, like she wanted him inside her body, liquefied her. She met him stroke for stroke.

Luke's hands fisted at her sides, clenching the material from her top, which pressed her bra into her nipples. She gasped, the sensations building.

Then the world disappeared for a moment as he swept the top up over her head. Moving fast, he unclasped her bra. As cool air rushed over her, she moaned, but heat quickly followed. Luke's large hands shaped her, molded her, engendering a lovely boneless sensation that left her melting. His mouth at her breast swept away the last of her thoughts, until she could only feel.

Her thighs tensed, rubbing her most sensitive spot against him. Building the tension just where she needed it. As if he'd read her mind, Luke's hands went to her waistband and jerked with just the right amount of force. The material parted and her body went wild.

Soon she was completely naked, and riding Luke Blackstone. She didn't even have the sense to be embarrassed.

For once, Avery felt a surge of power rise. This was her show. Her time. She dipped her hips, just an inch, teasing him. He gasped, then groaned when she pulled back up. Over and over she moved, until they both broke out in a sweat.

Only when she thought she'd die without him did she sink down—one long slide until her thighs met his, and she felt stretched almost to her limit. But now Luke wanted the upper hand. His palms cupped her hips, those long fingers pressing against her flesh. His touch guided her, pleasuring them both with a hard rhythm that shook her breath in her chest. She gave herself over to his demands.

Not just her body, but her soul. No barriers. No hesitation. Her hands on his shoulders sought safety, even though there was none to be had. There never would be.

Just as she cried out, Luke stiffened. Her body tightened around his, and she dug her fingers into his skin as she exploded—oblivion quick and almost painful.

Then she lay next to him in the dark, listening to his breath even out. As he slipped into sleep, she ached for what she so desperately wanted.

But would never have.

Thirteen

Luke glanced at Jacob next to him at the bar, waiting for his fiancée to bring them drinks. KC was being helped by her brother, Zach. He wasn't officially working, but he still kept a close, protective eye on his family. Luke couldn't blame him.

"This was a great idea," Luke said, grinning as he watched his reserved older brother, Aiden, lead his wife onto the dance floor—for a fast song, no less.

He usually pictured Aiden drinking imported beer and fine dining in New York, not dancing in a honky-tonk in South Carolina. Boy, had times changed.

Jacob grinned as KC approached. "We all needed some downtime. The past few days have been intense."

"Definitely," Luke replied.

With all the suspicions and questions running through Luke's mind, he'd been hard-pressed to think about anything else. Except Avery. She consumed him on so many levels now.

Their mission for adventures had gotten derailed by his accident, then their utter physical absorption of each other. They'd spent every night wrapped up in the big bed, shutting out the world.

Luke was more than addicted…each time he visited, he was in danger of never leaving her house again.

But tonight, he wouldn't be sidetracked. If he couldn't have Avery in bed, he wanted her on the dance floor. Another adventure. After all, he couldn't recall ever seeing her dance.

He positioned her next to him on a small bit of dance floor real estate and glanced around to see what everyone else was doing. After two minutes, he had no idea why Avery didn't normally dance—she was deadly at it. She picked up the steps quickly and executed them with incredibly sexy hip action that had his mouth watering.

Luke, on the other hand, knew that he danced with more enthusiasm than skill. When he missed a step, they both laughed and kept going.

He hadn't laughed that much in a long time.

After a handful of songs, he led her back to the table for some cool drinks and bar food. Avery eyed him over her French fry.

"What?"

"You seem quite fond of surprises," she said, grinning despite her accusing tone.

"Worked, didn't it?"

Her grin turned rueful. "Guess so."

"No guessing about it." He leaned closer, invading her space until he saw the brown flecks in her eyes. "No sexy woman should be left sitting on the sidelines. You have too much to offer for that."

He watched the flush build in her cheeks. Her eyes widened, then sparkled with a look he now knew all too well.

Leaning in, he brushed her lips with his, aching for more than he could have right now.

As he pulled back, he was glad to see she didn't look around, didn't peek to see who was watching. Her entire focus was trained on him…and his on her.

"Sometimes sitting on the sidelines becomes a habit, because it's familiar," she said quietly. "It's comfortable. And we know it won't end up hurting us."

"Won't it? In the long run?"

Excuses were just that. Experience had taught him he got nowhere when he let those little half-truths direct his actions. He wanted to pull her against him and tell her it would be okay, that neither of them would hurt when this was over. But he couldn't. That was a guarantee he didn't think he'd be able to live up to. A buzz in his pocket saved him from answering.

Pulling out his cell phone, Luke saw his crew chief's number on the screen. With a gesture to Avery, he hurried for the door.

When he'd stepped into the cool night air, free from the music of the noisy bar, he answered.

"Hey, Jeff. What's up?"

They'd had regular check-ins, but Jeff hated the phone so he never called just to chat.

"Got some great news, buddy."

Anticipation added to the buzz he'd worked up from dancing. Luke walked across the parking lot to burn off his sudden burst of adrenaline. "Hit me."

"Our sponsor problem is solved."

"How come?" Luke tried to ignore the pounding of his heart in his throat.

"I was contacted tonight by someone whose interest is off the scales. You're not gonna believe this."

Probably not. "Who?"

"NC State Oil."

Hot damn. One of the biggest sponsors in his division. Luke's knees went a little weak.

"Bobby Joe is retiring," Jeff said. "Very down low right now. They want you as their new feature car."

Jeff rattled off some other details but Luke wasn't processing them. Only when the words "come back" rang in his ear did he return to earth.

"When?" he asked, his mouth dry as cotton.

"Next season, buddy. They're all set to negotiate, talk contracts."

Luke thought over Avery's careful plans, her goal of getting him back to racing—in two seasons.

Jeff was oblivious. "I'll give the head honcho your number. You can set up a meeting."

Luke barely remembered signing off. He couldn't move, standing alone in the cool night air.

A second chance.

All that he'd wanted since his accident was to return to the track, to his career. Now he could. So why wasn't he screwing up his recovery by jumping for joy?

Deep down, he knew why. Because there was more than just her disappointment keeping him from returning to the bar and breaking the news to Avery. The pain on the horizon wasn't only physical…and wasn't only his.

Almost to the building, the sound of an angry voice halted Luke's stride.

"I said I'd get you your money. I just need more time."

Luke instinctively stepped into the shadows, not far from where Mark Zabinski was speaking into his cell phone. His agitated tone indicated intense strain.

"Look—I realize I've gotten a little behind—"

His heavy sigh permeated the gloom.

"—okay, a lot. But I'll take care of it."

Another silence. Luke strained to hear beyond the pounding of his heart, surprised when Mark's voice turned whiny. "No, I can't just go to my parents for any more handouts. I told you, I can fix this." He exhaled a ragged breath.

"Forty-eight hours. Got it."

As Luke slipped back through the door into the club, he couldn't help wondering what that had been all about.

Life was too damn complicated.

Luke looked around Zach's garage at the men who'd supported him after his accident, and couldn't find the words to tell them someone had tried to kill him. Even though the evidence sat right before him, the words were hard to come by.

Luckily Zach started the conversation for him. "So do you have an idea about who's trying to hurt you yet, or do we need to do some digging?"

The shock spread in low murmurs. Luke had to face the truth he'd been avoiding. "I'm pretty sure I know who it is. I've only had problems with one person since my return."

Zach patted the truck's hood. "A certain someone who thinks you're stealing his girl?"

They all looked at Zach in surprise. Not because Zach was saying something Luke hadn't thought, but because he hadn't realized anyone else knew.

Zach smirked. "I snooped around once they towed the truck in. It's definitely been tampered with."

"Dammit." Jacob's gaze darted between Luke and the vehicle. "How long have you known this?"

"I knew the truck had been messed with right away," Luke said. He shook his head. "Mark and I had a few run-ins over Avery, but I never thought he was that vindictive." Until Mark came to Avery's house—that had been eye-opening. "Actually, I think I started suspecting him of something from the moment I stepped into the executive suite. He made me uneasy, but there was no reason to think it was anything more than that."

But there was more. "While I was outside the bar last night, I overheard a conversation between Mark and someone who wanted money from him. Badly."

Aiden asked the obvious. "What does that have to do with us congregating in Zach's garage?"

"It got me thinking." Luke paced a few steps. "The way he talked, it was obvious that he needed to raise cash, quickly. Whoever was on the other end of the line was more than unhappy. And it didn't sound like the first time."

He looked at Jacob. "One of the departments he oversees is accounting, right? He's fought to keep an outdated computer system. How many people check those paper files?"

Jacob was catching on. "That antiquated system would be the perfect tool for embezzling money," he mused. "Do you really think he'd do this? I mean, his family has money."

"Were you friends with him in high school?" Zach asked.

"We call it that now," Jacob answered, "but truthfully, we were rivals. Healthy competition for a lot of the same roles kept us motivated."

Zach glanced at Luke, who shrugged. "I had no motivation." And no guilt over never serving on student council.

Jacob threw out his former taunt. "Slacker."

"That's me," Luke said with a grin. "I just drive round and round in a circle for a living."

"It's a good thing you do," Zach said. "Otherwise, your ass would be grass. This probably wouldn't even have been too big a problem for you, except you were on a road flanked by steep ditches."

"Too bad you headed home instead of to Avery's," Jacob added.

"Nope. Probably for the best," Luke contradicted. "I drive over two narrow bridges to get to her place."

Zach winced. "Yeah, that would have been worse."

"But do we know for sure it's really sabotage?" Aiden asked.

Zach took them on a tour of Luke's truck, showing them the difference between wear and deliberate damage.

Jacob looked puzzled. "Does he really hate you enough to seriously harm you?"

"I wouldn't have thought so." Luke glanced back under the hood, remembering his last conversation with Mark. "But I did threaten his job the last time I saw him." He briefly explained what had happened.

Aiden's expression darkened. "You were fully in the right. Avery didn't deserve that."

Zachary cleared his throat. "I hate to bring this up, but it's part of my job to be suspicious." He met gazes with each man in turn. "Based on everything we've talked about here, is anyone else worried about the mischief a high-ranking employee with unlimited access to financial accounts and a possible gambling problem can get into roaming around the mill?"

Luke stiffened as a lightbulb lit up in his brain. He could see the moment it happened to Jacob and Aiden, too. So he asked for all of them, "You think he might be involved with the sabotage of the mill, too?"

Zach held up his hands. "I'm saying he might have motive for more than just vehicle tampering."

"But if the mill goes under, he'd lose his job, and the money," Luke pointed out.

"Not if he has a new source of income from a rival mill," Zach said. "They could pay him to do it, then offer him a higher position in their company once the competition is shut down."

A chorus of male curses filled the garage.

After a minute Zach said, "We don't know for sure. We need a way to find out."

"At least there's one easy place to look," Jacob said. "His accounts at the office are our best chance of finding hard evidence of embezzlement…or anything else." He shifted, obviously upset with the idea. "If it's not on the system, we're out of luck."

"Guess I'll volunteer to do some snooping," Luke said. "I'll go at night so few people will be around, but if they see me, I can just claim to be going over the accounts to acquaint myself with the business."

But first he owed Avery a long-overdue confession.

Fourteen

"It's okay, Cindy. I'll close up when I'm done."

Her office manager sent Avery a tired wave. After the long day they'd put in, she didn't have to be told to leave twice. Today had been one of those days where everything that could go wrong, had. From surly patients to computer errors to missing records, it had all hit the fan today.

Avery wished more than anything she could just close her eyes and drift away for a while. Maybe she'd enjoy the facility's whirlpool before going home. Her muscles throbbed their approval of the idea.

They ached from wanting other things, too. She'd been asleep this morning when Luke had headed out. He'd left a note that he'd see her tonight, but she'd heard nothing since.

Right now, she just wanted to relax. With the front doors locked, she shut everything else down. Grateful that she kept some clothes here, she started the tub with the water as hot as she could stand. Normally she would have put in bath salts, but she just wanted the jets tonight.

She'd just stripped down when her phone dinged. Glancing at it, she saw a text from Luke.

At the door. Brought dinner. Hungry?

She couldn't resist. Only Luke ever tempted her to be sexy, fun Avery.

In more ways than one. Hope you brought an appetite.

She grabbed an oversize towel and headed through the dark building to the front doors. She turned the key in the lock, then opened the door for Luke. He must not have noticed her state of undress until he was completely in, because he stopped abruptly. "Avery?"

Without missing a beat, she relocked the door, then headed back the way she'd come. First she let the towel droop, revealing her bare back, almost to the dimples right above her butt. After another few yards, and she let the towel fall completely, trailing behind her from the corner still clutched in her hand. She heard Luke's footsteps behind her, his sharp intake of breath, and knew he could see her pale skin in the gloom.

By the time he'd set down the food, she'd stepped into the swirling hot water of the tub. Kneeling, she let the water engulf her to the small of her back, then glanced over her shoulder at Luke. The way his gaze clung to her dampening skin was gratifying. Flattering. Desire clutched low in her body.

She heard the soft slip of clothes against skin as he undressed. Then the hiss of his breath as he stepped into the steamy water. Bubbles attacked her skin from all sides. Anticipation heated her up. Need clawed at her, forcing her to glance at him once more, the invitation clear.

He crowded in close. The heat from him and the water

shot her to supernova status. His hardness tucked against her, fitting snugly into the crease of her backside. She pressed into him.

How could he make her feel so good? A simple touch, a look, and her confidence soared. Or maybe it was just her desires overwhelming her self-consciousness. It just felt good to feel free. To not be afraid of doing something stupid.

His heavy palms against her breasts left her reeling. Her nipples tightened, needing his touch. He played with them, sending sensation shooting through her. How would she ever live without his touch?

He knew just when to tease, just when to move. His whole body rolled against hers, skin to slick skin. As if no part of him could hold back.

Her body grew hypersensitive, feeling every droplet of sweat as it beaded, every tremble of her breasts and every forceful stroke of him inside her. His thrusts shortened, his groans dragging from his lungs as he drove them both higher. Finally on the brink, she felt his mouth cover the sensitive spot where her neck met her shoulder. He sucked hard, as if to devour every ounce of her he could reach.

One final drive and they exploded together. Their cries mingled in the steamy mist coating the room. Bodies milked every last twitch of sensation before collapsing into the water. Sated. Satisfied.

If she weren't in a tub, Avery knew she'd slip right under the veil into sleep. In just a few minutes she'd get up and dry and dress. Just not yet. Not yet. But Luke was having none of it. All too soon, she was on her feet on the chilly tile floor.

As he rubbed her with a towel, she barely heard Luke's voice above the sound of the draining water. Not enough to distinguish what he was saying. "What?" she asked, struggling to open her heavy eyelids.

Her first peek told her something was wrong. For the first time ever, she'd guess that Luke Blackstone was... nervous. This time when he spoke she heard him more clearly. "I've got a new race car sponsor."

Did he say... She twisted to see his face as he moved to her back. "A sponsor? So soon?"

"Yeah. Pretty amazing, huh?" A slight grin pulled at his lips. But what worried her was his hooded look. "And it's a good one, too. A great one."

"That's wonderful." Wasn't it?

"The company is one of the biggest sponsors on the circuit right now," he said, but he still wouldn't look at her. "Their current driver is about to retire, and they want me to take his place."

"So they're willing to wait until you're fully recovered?"

His lack of words and lack of expression didn't bode well. If she hadn't been this close to him, she wouldn't have noticed the rapid beat of his pulse at the base of his throat. Nerves? Or simply the aftermath of what they'd just done together?

Avery, herself, was quickly cooling down—in a very uncomfortable way.

"Actually," he finally said, clearly and unnaturally calmly, "they want me back for next season."

"And you told them they had to wait, right?" Avery wasn't even sure why she asked. She knew from Luke's previous remarks she was fighting a losing battle.

"No. I didn't."

Without warning, he snagged a towel from the counter and wrapped it around himself, almost as if girding for battle, leaving her open, vulnerable.

Needing something to do, anything that didn't involve waiting for him to return to her, she set the tub to drain. Though he wasn't looking in her direction, her self-consciousness had already returned full force. She too rushed for a towel, stumbling a bit as she moved.

Luckily, she regained her feet and got herself covered without incident. Landing flat on her face, naked, would have been the ultimate humiliation—especially when she needed him to listen to her. She hadn't managed to get through to him before. Would she be able to now?

"Luke, that's really not what's best for you, for your body. It takes time for these things to not only heal, but for you to regain strength."

"I'm already getting around fine. No cane." He whipped around to face her. How could a man look so intimidating with only a towel on, his long blond hair sexily disheveled? "I'm back on my feet when they thought I might never be. If I continue strength training, I'll be just fine."

"Will you? I explained what happened after the accident the other night. The stress that type of incident puts on your body can be tremendous. The risks when it's happening on the track are so high. Please don't—" She choked herself off.

Begging him to stay here, not to go, would have nothing to do with risks and everything to do with herself. But personal desires couldn't have anything to do with her argument right now.

He braced his legs, as if taking a stand. Against her.

"Am I well enough to go back out on the track?"

Oh, she didn't want to do this. "Yes, but if something happens—"

"I'm well enough to do my job. That's what matters."

Stubborn man. "But a wreck on the track could do irreparable damage because you haven't built up enough resistance. You know all too well how dangerous your job can be."

His cold stare told her she'd crossed a line. "Is that really your argument or is this about something else?"

Avery jerked back as if he'd slapped her. "What?"

"Are you sure this isn't about you and me? Is it that you want me to stay, and this is the only argument you can think of to keep me here?"

Oh, she'd thought his insinuation had hurt. This was a whole other level. She fell back on her professional persona, simply dropping the towel and pulling her scrubs back over her damp, naked body. Only when she was covered and her hair was smoothed back did she ask, "Are you seriously questioning whether I'm letting my personal feelings sway my judgment?" If it was one thing she'd always prided herself on, it was that her evaluation of Luke had been first and foremost professional. Always. She could feel her own anger rise. "Would you rather I just tell you to stop being a stubborn jackass and listen to reason?"

"That's exactly what I'm asking. I mean, you've been waiting for this for an awfully long time. Maybe you can't bear to see it end. Will there be another excuse coming down the line after this one?"

"I don't want you to go." She swallowed. Keeping her emotions under control was so much harder than she'd imagined. "I'll be the first to acknowledge I've developed feelings for you...deep feelings. But I've always known you would leave, Luke. Always." Which was why she'd never verbalized those feelings.

He stood there like a mountain, arms crossed over that magnificent chest. Not giving an inch.

"But my professional opinion is just that—professional. My recommendations were backed up by your former physical therapist and your physician before we ever became involved. I would never mix that in with my—" she took a deep breath "—personal feelings for you."

She let the words hang in the air, hoping he would at least acknowledge the truth of what she was saying, but he didn't.

And that was something she couldn't live with.

"If you truly think my evaluation of you, my recommendation for your career, is based on a selfish need to keep me with you, some obsessive desire to fulfill a childhood crush—" man, was that humiliating "—then I think it's time you left."

Without waiting for his nonresponse, she swept by and stalked to her office, locking herself inside before she collapsed against the door. Silent tears trickled down her cheeks. Only after she heard him open the front doors and leave did she give in to the storm inside her.

She'd be strong later. She'd clean the tub, lock the doors and return to her empty house, just like she had every night before Luke had come back into her life. Later.

For now, she could only let the pain sweep her away from the knowledge that once again, someone would leave her behind.

Man, I am such a jackass.

Luke had always prided himself on being kind and friendly. He rarely had conflict with anyone. When he did, he'd just as soon avoid it by disappearing onto the track than provoking major fights like his brother Aiden sometimes did. Luke was a fan of letting things work themselves out.

Sure, he occasionally said things that rubbed people the wrong way. Not out of any desire to be mean, just from letting something slip that would have been better left unsaid. Just like a few nights ago with Avery. He'd known the minute he'd started talking about feelings he was gonna screw up. And sure enough, he'd dug a hole so deep he'd been stumped as to how to get himself out of it.

Now he had to figure out how to salvage the one thing that had touched him like nothing but his racing ever had. But should he? Was it fair to win her back, patch things up, then turn around and leave her behind so he could pursue his dream?

He didn't know. Pacing back and forth in his suite at Blackstone Manor had only made his leg ache, reminding him of Avery all the more. He couldn't stop thinking about his truck, either. There were too many reasons to suspect Mark had tampered with it, regardless of whether his intentions were deadly or not. Then Zach had texted him:

Found multiple log-ins from Mark's work computer to the inventory system. Only accessible by management. Possible link to sabotage.

So instead of sleeping, wrapped around Avery's warm, silky body tonight, he was poking through Mark's computer at the mill. What else was he going to do at two o'clock in the morning?

Not to mention, he had no idea if the guy might strike again. And Luke wasn't losing his life over some agenda he didn't even understand. Tonight was the best night, because the plant was shut down for maintenance that would begin in the morning.

It didn't take long. After an hour of snooping, Luke had enough evidence to confirm some of his suspicions... and awaken even more. Mark didn't know nearly enough about computers to hide what he'd been doing, or maybe he'd thought he didn't need to. The combination of a dated system and paper files had allowed him to move money without anyone noticing. The withdrawals from various company funds into a secondary account that Mark then transferred to a miscellaneous account at another bank appeared genuine enough, until someone searched for the documentation and receipts.

The deposits had grown in frequency and amount over the past few years. Since his work performance had been fine, Luke didn't think it was drugs or drinking. Gambling was still his best guess.

If Mark was unstable or desperate, he could hurt a lot of people by sabotaging the mill, even if he simply intended to destroy property. Just like the goons he'd probably hired had done to Aiden's studio.

Luke copied what he could into his online backup storage before shutting the system down. Rubbing his eyes, he blinked at the clock. Three-thirty in the morning. Maybe now he could sleep without aching for Avery by his side, her measured breath a soothing rhythm beneath the palm of his hand. First thing tomorrow, he'd meet with Jacob, Aiden and Zach.

Firing this guy outright wasn't the solution. They had to be very careful to get all the information they needed before confronting Mark.

Closing down the office, he headed for the stairwell. The accounting department was on the third floor, so Luke decided to exit via the stairs. After sitting so long, moving felt good. As he passed the door for level two, he heard a truck engine rev.

Knowing there wasn't supposed to be any activity tonight, Luke paused. The administrative offices sat over a two-story loading dock, where they shipped out the finished products.

Were they prepping some last-minute deliveries? That didn't make sense, because the whole plant closed down over maintenance weekend. Maybe it was just his heightened suspicions after everything he'd read tonight, but Luke knew he wouldn't sleep unless he checked it out.

Opening the second-floor entry, he winced as a squeal assaulted the eardrums. The sound echoed through the stairwell. He glanced toward the loading dock below. He couldn't see clearly through the iron mesh of the walkway, but there was definitely a truck. Not one of theirs, though.

He'd have to get closer.

Glancing around, Luke found a wedge to prop the door open. He scooted it closer with his foot, then forced it into place. He could always come back and close it later if this was nothing, but his niggling senses said something was up.

He took the last of the stairs to the ground floor. A turn to the left led down a long hallway to the security entrance. He could jog down there and see if anyone was home, but if no one was, he'd have wasted precious time and legwork. Right would take him down a short distance to the loading dock floor. Better to just take a cautious peek.

Thankfully the lower-level door had been oiled. He eased through with very little noise and stepped out beneath the elevated walkway. He had to lean out for a good look, because of pallets blocking his view. But then he saw the back end of a work van very clearly.

Click.

Luke froze. Anyone from the South recognized that noise—the clear sound of a gun hammer being cocked. He glanced over his shoulder to see Mark watching him with a cool gaze and pointing a pistol directly at him. And if Luke remembered correctly, Mark had taken marksmanship with Jacob in high school. They'd captained rival teams.

"Well, I didn't expect anyone to be here this late, but the fact that it's you is a nice bonus," Mark said.

The snide tone grated across Luke's senses. He turned completely as Mark stepped out of the dappled shadows beneath the walkway.

"Mark, what's going on?" he asked, attempting to keep both his voice and his body loose, casual.

"You showed up just in time," Mark said, his grin stretching a little too far.

"For what? A hunting party?"

Apparently Mark didn't find him funny. "No, you lazy

bum. It'll be a celebration, but I doubt you and your intrusive family will see it the same way I do."

"How's that?"

"A giant fireball to celebrate the ruination of the Blackstone brothers and their legacy in Black Hills."

Luke's blood ran cold. Did Mark mean to blow something up? "So you'll destroy the mill in an effort to, what? Get back at me for something?"

Mark jumped forward, the threat of the gun forcing Luke to retreat. "Not 'something,' you ignorant ass. I've spent years working a menial job, always blocked from moving up. I finally got the chance to take my rightful place in management, and you and your brothers decide it's time to ride back into town and save the day." The disgust on his face was perfectly plain. "This place should have been mine. Mine."

Luke's stomach sank. Even though he'd known Mark needed money, he'd still held on to the idea that his anger at Luke himself centered around Avery. This went far deeper than either of those issues.

He gestured for Luke to turn around. A sharp poke in the back from the gun got him moving forward. Luke tried to keep his steps slow, exaggerating his slight limp. He needed time to figure this out and find a way to get clear.

"I'm not a murderer," Mark said. "Normally I'd say that's taking things a bit too far, you know?" He herded Luke closer to the truck. "But for you, I'll make an exception."

"What makes me so special?"

He jabbed Luke hard in the back, a reward for his smart mouth. "I almost had her where I wanted her, was ready to put a ring on her finger. Then I'd have had all of Avery's money at my disposal and she'd have been none the wiser."

Luke snorted. "Avery Prescott? Are you serious?"

"What the hell's that supposed to mean?"

Luke glanced over his shoulder, just as much to see what Mark was up to as to emphasize his point. "Avery is way too smart to just hand her money over to someone because she married him. She's a good businesswoman. She'd find out about the gambling way before the wedding day."

Luke wasn't sure if the silence that greeted his statement was good or bad. He decided to push his luck.

"Thought you'd kept that pretty secret, didn't you? Why do you think I'm here tonight, Mark?" Luke's disgust hardened his voice. Maybe if he could get Mark riled up, push him off-kilter, he could get the upper hand. "I've been upstairs, going through your computer. All your files. All your emails. I know what you did."

Mark's flush deepened from red to purple. "Doesn't matter. In about fifteen minutes, I'll be the only one who knows. And all that evidence, including you, will have gone up in smoke."

Or so Mark thought. He actually thought Luke wasn't smart enough to have made copies. But Luke *was* smart enough to let him keep believing that…for now.

"And don't bother calling for help. The great advantage of doing this on maintenance weekend is the only people here are the outer guards." Mark laughed. "The local cops haven't figured me out yet and they aren't going to, either."

Maybe Luke could still do something if he could get to a radio and reach a guard, depended on how soon the bomb was set to blow. Fifteen minutes. Luke's adrenaline kicked in hard enough to summon a wave of nausea. This was not gonna be fun.

Without turning his head, he tried to look around, figure out his options. Mark didn't give him enough time. Reaching out for something nearby, he then held it up for Luke to see.

Zip ties.

"Now back up to the door. Nice and slow."

Luke moved himself up to the rear of the van. The whole time, he pumped his fists, hoping to create space once Mark tied him down. As he grabbed at Luke's hands, Luke lifted his wrists slightly against the bar, hoping Mark wouldn't notice.

Luke waited until Mark stepped away with a smirk. Then he disappeared around the front of the van. Luke heard a door open and some noise. The smell of fertilizer grew. Luke couldn't help but wonder about the size of the bomb.

Mark spoke from inside. "Amazing what you can learn to do on the internet, isn't it? Looks like I'm just making a little delivery for my parents' gardening company and oops—I had an accident."

"Why not just ask them for money?" Luke asked, curious about that since hearing Mark's side of the conversation the other night.

"You know, my older brother reminds me a lot of Jacob. He's soft. Protective. Like my parents don't have more than enough wealth to share. Like I don't deserve it—I'm the one stuck here with them, after all. But not for long. I've found someone else who will pay me very well."

Luke let him ramble while trying to work his hands free. Heaven help him, he would not leave his family, Avery, like this.

"Hasn't done you a lot of good so far, has it?" Luke prodded.

"This one last job and I'll hit the mother lode of payoffs—with a new job to boot. Now shut up and let me work."

While Mark was busy, Luke let his arms straighten once more. Then he squeezed his hands through the extra space he'd created in the ties. Not as much space as he'd like, but luckily he'd started to sweat from nerves and heat. Five minutes and he'd managed to wring his big hands back out.

Luke looked for a weapon, but footsteps told him he'd run out of time. Mark stepped around the corner. "Time to leave—"

"Yep." Luke swung the heavy half door of the van in Mark's direction, catching his face with a weighty *thunk*.

He didn't stop to check the bomb—he simply grabbed the gun and ran. Adrenaline kept his body from resisting, though Luke had a vague thought he'd be hurting tomorrow.

If there was one.

He reached the door to the hallway, only to find Mark had locked or jammed it somehow. He had to detour to the next door down the line. Damn—why was this room so long? Through that one and back down the hall. This one wasn't a straight shot, so Luke had to guess which turns to take.

He'd maneuvered his way back to the main hall before he heard a voice behind him. "Where are you going, Luke? You'll never make it out in time."

Luke wasn't giving up, but a sudden hard rumble erupted from the middle of the building and Luke knew his time was up. He wasn't going to reach a radio or phone or even a door. He saw the entrance to a room and threw himself into the doorway just as the building seemed to explode around him.

Fifteen

Avery stood in the hallway just outside the emergency room, though she wasn't quite sure how. She didn't remember driving, didn't remember coming inside. Heck, she didn't remember much past Jacob's quick explanation that Luke had been in an explosion at the plant and was being med-flighted to a hospital over an hour away.

She remembered a few choice words from a special newsbreak on the radio—namely *bomb* and *explosion* and *serious injuries*—before she'd turned it off. Not knowing was better than letting vague info whip her into sheer panic.

Common sense told her she shouldn't even be here. After the way Luke had spoken to her the last time they'd been together, it was clear he didn't have a very high opinion of her. Unfortunately, that didn't mute the love that had grown in her heart. Her need to know he was okay overrode all the arguments to stay away that her brain could come up with.

So here she stood. She hadn't been allowed behind the

big metal doors to where the family had already gone. After all, she wasn't family, just the woman Luke had been sleeping with for a few weeks. She didn't know if anyone knew she was here. Christina wasn't answering her phone. But she'd wait as long as she had to, until someone came through those doors who could give her news.

It took another forty-five minutes before a familiar face appeared. Christina paused at the nurse's station before looking in her direction. Then she rushed over. Her arms around Avery were the first warmth Avery had felt since she'd received that phone call.

"I'm so sorry," Christina said. "We were speaking with the doctor then Luke woke up and I just didn't think about them not letting you come back to the family waiting area."

"He's awake?" she asked, focusing on the important part.

Christina nodded, her eyes welling with tears. "He has a concussion where some debris hit his head, but he's very lucky. No broken bones, only a few stitches. No internal damage."

"What happened?"

"He was at the mill when a bomb went off."

Avery quickly reached out to the wall, because she knew she was going down. Her knees hit the floor with a painful sting, but at least they stopped her descent.

"Oh, Avery, I'm sorry," Christina said, kneeling down, too. "I thought Jacob had told you."

Avery only managed to shake her head. "Not much," she murmured. Images of broken bones, surgeries and traction had raced through her brain while she'd waited. "He didn't give any details. Just that Luke had been hurt."

"Men." Christina helped her to her feet, then led her down the hallway with an arm around her waist, though Avery couldn't really tell who was supporting who. All too soon they breached the forbidden doors that Avery had stared at for so long. "I'm so sorry he left you guessing, Avery. I guess he was freaked out by it all, too."

"I bet."

"From what we can tell," Christina said as they walked, "he was at the accounting office doing some work during the night. As he left, he heard a truck on the loading dock, which wasn't supposed to be there during mandatory shutdown. He found the makings for a bomb in there—"

Oh, lord.

"Mark is involved somehow, too."

"Mark?"

Christina nodded. "The police are with them now."

"Mark made it out, too?" she asked as they came into a waiting room filled with Blackstones, including KC with little Carter, Nolen and Mary.

"Yes," Jacob said, reaching out to pull her close for a quick hug. "I'm so sorry. All I could think about was Luke."

"I understand."

"I was there while the police spoke with him," Jacob said. "Looks like Mark drove one of his parents' work vans into the mill loading dock, intending to blow it up with a bomb made from fertilizer. Luke found evidence of embezzlement on Mark's computer." Jacob shook his head. "Mark tied Luke to the truck and was gonna leave him there."

"Why?" Avery gasped.

Jacob took on a very uncomfortable look. The women glanced at each other. "Jacob, hon, you can tell us," Christina said.

KC appeared at his side. She looked at Avery in sympathy. "I'm sorry, Avery, but from Luke's account, it seems Mark was trying to marry you for money. He resented Luke's interference."

She rubbed up and down Jacob's back with her palm. "Mark called the Blackstones the golden sons. Said that they came back and took over everything he wanted. Said he'd ruin the whole town rather than let them take it."

Avery squeezed her eyes shut, unable to process it all. "What about the mill?"

"Zach is there now, assessing the damage," Jacob said. "But it's confined to the admin building, so fingers are crossed that it's minimal."

"Thank goodness," Christina said, echoing all their thoughts.

A doctor came into the room and called for their attention. Everyone turned. "Luke has asked to see his family, and I've granted permission, but only immediate family for now, please. He's not in serious danger, but I'd like to keep him overnight to observe him. The rest of you will get your chance soon enough."

Murmurs of relief spread through the room. There were hugs before the men gathered near the door. Aiden spoke quietly with Christina, who came and took Avery's hand, leading her down the hallway with the men. Avery's heart pounded. After all, she wasn't family.

"Christina, maybe I should go back," she whispered.

The other woman squeezed her hand. "Don't be silly."

Maybe Christina didn't know what had happened the last time she and Luke had seen each other. "Christina, really, this is a bad idea."

The men paused outside a door. Aiden turned to look at her. "No, Avery, it isn't. Luke needs you here, just as much as he needs us."

Only he didn't.

There was no time to explain as everyone moved inside. The beep of monitors made Avery wince. She'd been around many patients before who were hospital-bound in serious condition or in a coma. But this, this was different. This was Luke. Thoughts of him hurting and near death were almost her undoing.

He lay still on the bed, bandages around his head and one arm. Avery studied his body, looking for signs that would tell her about the damage, but couldn't find them. Her gaze traveling back up, and she found his amber eyes open and trained directly on her. Then his unhampered hand lifted, reaching out to her.

Despite what had happened between them, Avery couldn't stop herself from moving forward. She parted the crowd, resting with her hand in his, fingers laid lightly against his wrist so she could feel that life-giving pulse for herself. Even so, she couldn't lift her eyes to his. Then he might see the utter devastation she'd been through over the past few hours. She blinked away the wash of tears. But she couldn't let go of that hand.

Not yet.

"Good to see ya, brother," Aiden said. Jacob murmured the same.

Luke let his bandaged head drop against the pillows with a wince. "Glad I'm still here to be seen."

Christina's tears were much freer than Avery's. She skirted around Jacob to give Luke a hug. "The doctor says everything will be okay?"

"Yep. There was absolutely no reason for them to medflight me here. An ambulance would have been perfectly acceptable."

Jacob smirked. "Especially since Luke hates flying."

"Well, it did wake me up hella quick."

"I bet."

Avery could see Luke's hard swallow before he asked, "The mill?"

"Zach is there to evaluate the fire, last I spoke to him. If everything's sound, the plant floor and outbuildings will be saved with only smoke damage. The admin building wasn't so lucky. It will have to be rebuilt."

"I got electronic copies of the emails. Zach has the log-in info. Make sure the police check his home computer."

Aiden straightened, his height imposing. "Then we'll nail Mark's ass to the wall."

"He made it out?" Luke asked.

His heartbeat sped up beneath her fingertips.

Jacob nodded. "From what the police chief said, he had a spot all picked out to shelter in when the bomb went off, so he could claim it was an accident. Didn't work out so well for him."

Luke glanced around, then zeroed back in on his twin. "Why?"

Jacob looked to Aiden for confirmation before he said, "Part of the concrete wall came down on his legs."

Avery gasped, shocked, but found little sympathy in her heart. Mark had made his choice; he got what he deserved.

Christina laid her hand on Aiden's arm. "I think that's enough business for now, right, guys?"

Aiden covered her hand with his own. "She's right. I'm glad you're gonna be okay, Luke."

"Me, too," Jacob added. "This is one hospital too many, in my opinion."

"Mine, too," Luke agreed.

The others turned to the door, but Luke refused to let go of her hand.

Avery studied their clasped hands, unsure of what to do or say to avoid tears she wouldn't be able to stop.

"Thank you for coming," Luke said.

"I couldn't not come," Avery conceded.

Because it was the truth. No matter how Luke felt about her now, she wouldn't have been able to stay away, knowing he'd been hurt. She wanted to ask about his legs, his previous injuries, but she daren't open that can of worms.

"I appreciate that, Avery. Especially after the way I treated you the last time we were together." He squeezed her hand. "I've been trying to find a way to apologize, to let you know I didn't believe those things I said, but I didn't know how. So I took the coward's way out and stayed away."

"If you didn't believe them, why did you say them?"

"Because I was angry. And, I think, because it gave me an excuse to dismiss your concerns without having to evaluate their merit." He kissed the back of her hand, drawing her tears closer to the surface. "I wanted you to support me, to agree with me wholeheartedly. When you didn't, I lashed out. I'm sorry."

Avery wished the apology meant more. Luke had almost died. She didn't want him to be sorry. She wanted him to say he loved her, that he would stay for her. But she couldn't ask him for that, wouldn't.

"Does it really matter?" she asked. The *yes* bloomed on his face, but he'd just been through a terrible experience. Two in a year. He was thinking about now. She was thinking about the future. She squeezed his hand. "I just don't think I can do this, Luke."

Now that she knew he would be okay, she had to find the strength to end this. "I love you, more than I ever thought I could, but my life is here. My home, my job, these people." Her throat closed, choking her for a moment. To her chagrin, a tear marched a single line down her face. "Your dreams are elsewhere. And I don't want to be the one who holds you back."

Luke lay against the pillow, exhaustion graying his face. She was a horrible person to do this now. But she simply couldn't support him through recovery, then watch him walk away from her.

"I'm so sorry, Avery. The other day I made a mistake."

"I did, too," she said with a sad smile. "But I can't say I'll ever be sorry."

She made it to the door, but she couldn't force herself

to open it. Maybe deep down, a part of her still wished he would say he loved her. That she was worth not walking away from. But she knew that wasn't the answer in the long run, either. So she took a deep breath and put her hand on the doorknob.

"It really was fun, wasn't it?" she asked.

He nodded, his face grim.

She let herself out the door, down the hall and out to the parking lot. Her car provided the solitude she needed. She cried all the way back to her house. Only when wrapped tightly inside bedsheets that still smelled like Luke did she close her eyes, and let herself wish it was all a dream.

Luke finally spotted that unique combination of blonds in Avery's gorgeous hair at the far side of the ice rink at Rockefeller Center. He'd been searching for an hour in the crowds of New York City holiday visitors. The doorman at Aiden and Christina's New York apartment had been extremely helpful, since he'd recognized Luke and had helped Avery plan her route before she'd left today.

When Luke had finally returned home for the woman he couldn't live without, it had never occurred to him that he wouldn't just waltz into Avery's clinic and sweep her off her feet. What an arrogant dumbass he was.

Now he was hot on her trail, rueful and jealous. He'd have loved to have traveled with her, but he'd never told her that… He'd never told her a lot of things.

How could she reciprocate when he'd offered her nothing in the first place? Not even a phone call since he'd left Black Hills. So she'd set out to find adventure on her own.

He'd resorted to begging his brother for info. The connection between Luke and both his brothers had strengthened in the past month. Though he and Jacob had always been close, they were now never out of touch for more than a day. He and Aiden texted a lot, and called more often than they ever had.

Luke had missed them while he was in North Carolina, more than he'd thought he would. He'd gone home to share his news, and was grateful that Christina had helped him find his little homebody in New York City for the holidays. Now he only had to convince Avery to accept his humble Christmas gift.

She stood twenty feet from him, wrapped in a thick suede jacket and wearing black gloves. But that gorgeous hair was loose to the cold breeze in his favorite style. Not a hair band in sight.

As he angled toward her, he caught a glimpse of her face. Her gaze jumped around as she took in the people skating below her, then it moved up the giant Christmas tree and across holiday decorations. She seemed interested, happy, but not engaged in her surroundings.

An observer, not a participant.

Like she'd always been, from the first time he'd known her. Little Avery that watched everything from the sidelines. Never jumping in with both feet. Never forcing people to notice her. Never owning the excitement and life that were hers to enjoy.

Except for a short time…with him. He wanted to see that Avery again.

She'd turned in the other direction, so he navigated the crowd until he found a spot next to her and leaned against the rail. "Happy holidays, Avery."

Startled, she turned to him. He got to glimpse a few seconds of welcome, of excitement, before that beautiful face shut down, hiding her emotions behind a polite mask.

"Luke. I didn't expect to see you here."

"I didn't expect to see you here, either," he said. "I thought I'd find you in Black Hills, at the clinic."

A slight frown wrinkled her careful expression. "Why would you expect to see me anywhere?"

Because I can't imagine going through one more step of my life without you. Hmm…maybe a bit much. He should start slower.

"Because I couldn't imagine sharing my big news with anyone but you."

She nodded slowly. "The big meeting was this week?"

"It was." Luke had met with his racing sponsor. Avery's sad eyes told him she expected him to expound on the incredible deal he'd accepted. But… "After all the wining and dining he'd done, I don't think it went quite how he'd planned."

Avery took a slow breath in, exhaling a white puff of air after a moment too long. "What do you mean?"

"I told him I'd love to represent their company…in two seasons. Not one."

Avery might have the calm bearing of a sphinx, but he could tell he'd startled her. Still, she wasn't jumping through his hoops very fast.

"What did he think about that?"

"Well, he was a little shocked." To say the least. "But I had a few offers of my own up my sleeve."

He slipped a little closer, his heart speeding up just from being near her. "I offered to shoot a comeback movie chronicling my journey back to racing, at my own expense, for them to use for promotional purposes. I'd already talked to Bobby Joe, who agreed to stay on for an additional year."

Luke could read the shock in those beautiful blue eyes, but he wasn't through yet. "All for a stake for each of them in my new racing venture."

"You see—" Luke grinned, so at peace with his decision that it seemed unreal "—I've arranged to purchase that old racetrack outside of town. I'm creating a racing experience that allows people to experience driving a race car at a professional facility, along with professional and amateur training. Jeff is going to help me."

She shook her head. "Luke, you can't give up your dream—"

"That is, when I'm not racing myself."

The mask dropped, giving him a glimpse of the sheer misery she felt, but she remained silent.

"I managed to convince them I was worth the wait. And that they should develop the whole me, not just the racing me. So I win, they win and the town wins."

"Wow. That's awesome," she said. Her breath shook a little. He could tell she truly was excited for him, not just saying the words, even though her eyes quickly darkened again.

"I figure it will be something I love, that I can do from home in my off-season. And it'll help bring more jobs and revenue to the town," he said. "And it's all because of you."

Those beautiful blues widened. "Me?"

"Yep. You and that hour back on the old track. I never would have thought of doing this if you hadn't planned something so special for me, Avery." To his surprise, his throat tried to close.

"I just— I knew that would be special for you."

Of course she had. Because she understood what he needed, even when he was being stubborn and stupid.

She glanced out over the skaters. "Your family will be thrilled that you'll be around more often."

Luke nodded, not quite trusting his voice. When he finally had his emotions under control, he said, "I hope you will be, too."

A look of sheer panic bloomed on her face and she started to shake her head, but Luke was having none of that.

"As you already know, I can be persistent when I want something really bad. And right now, I'm after something that I want more than anything I've had in my life."

Her voice was barely above a whisper. "What's that?"

"You."

She wasn't giving an inch. "What if I can't do this?"

"Then I'll be the saddest, loneliest man Black Hills has ever known."

Right there in front of God and country, he got down on his knee. Avery blushed, trying to pull him up, but he wasn't budging until she said yes.

"Avery, I love you." Reaching into his coat pocket, he pulled out something a little less traditional than an engagement ring. Instead, he'd had a custom key made, engraved with their names and the year. A key to something far more important than a car—no, this was a symbol for the commitment he had a hard time putting into words. But he had to try. "I've spent my entire life running, not realizing I was looking for a home. I found it—in you. Will you be there with me, every day, as I build a new life? Knowing I'm leaving the key to my heart with you, safe and sound?"

Seeing her excitement light her up was the greatest gift he'd ever been given. But her next words gave him pause.

"On one condition."

"What's that?"

"That you continue to drag me into all kinds of adventures. You know, someone told me once fun's the only thing that makes life worth living." She grinned big this time, letting the love he'd felt from her all along shine in her gaze. "After all, who better to show me how to have fun than Renegade Blackstone?"

Oh, yeah. "It's a deal."

* * * * *

MILLS & BOON®

Desire™

PASSIONATE AND DRAMATIC LOVE STORIES

A sneak peek at next month's titles...

In stores from 14th July 2016:

- **For Baby's Sake** – Janice Maynard *and*
  The CEO Daddy Next Door – Karen Booth

- **An Heir for the Billionaire** – Kat Cantrell *and*
  Waking Up with the Boss – Sheri WhiteFeather

- **Pregnant by the Maverick Millionaire** – Joss Wood *and*
  Contract Wedding, Expectant Bride – Yvonne Lindsay

Available at WHSmith, Tesco, Asda, Eason, Amazon and Apple

Just can't wait?
Buy our books online a month before they hit the shops!
visit www.millsandboon.co.uk

These books are also available in eBook format!

MILLS & BOON®

Why not subscribe?
Never miss a title and save money too!

Here is what's available to you if you join the exclusive **Mills & Boon® Book Club** today:

* *Titles up to a month ahead of the shops*
* *Amazing discounts*
* *Free P&P*
* *Earn Bonus Book points that can be redeemed against other titles and gifts*
* *Choose from monthly or pre-paid plans*

Still want more?
Well, if you join today we'll even give you
50% OFF your first parcel!

So visit **www.millsandboon.co.uk/subscriptions**
or call **Customer Relations on 0844 844 1351***
to be a part of this exclusive Book Club!

*This call will cost you 7 pence per minute plus your phone company's price per minute access charge.